GW01398032

# Savory Triumph

## Luna Grey

Published by Luna Grey, 2024.

SAVORY TRIUMPH

**First edition. October 20, 2024.**

Copyright © 2024 Luna Grey.

ISBN: 979-8227932778

Written by Luna Grey.

# Chapter 1: Behind the Spotlight

The aroma of fresh herbs and roasted garlic enveloped me like a warm embrace, pulling me deeper into the sanctuary I had created in my tiny apartment kitchen. I loved how the sun filtered through the window, casting golden rays that danced across my countertop, illuminating a sea of vibrant ingredients waiting to be transformed. Today, I was working on a saffron risotto, its creamy texture and rich flavor a delicate balancing act that reflected my own existence. As the rice simmered gently, I lost myself in the rhythm of stirring, the soothing sound of wooden spoon against pot providing a soundtrack to my thoughts. Each stir felt like a heartbeat, a reminder that I was alive and in control of this moment.

Kayla burst through the door without knocking, her laughter like a chime, pulling me from my culinary reverie. "You know, if you spent as much time studying as you do cooking, you'd probably be at the top of your class," she teased, plopping down on one of the mismatched stools at my breakfast bar. Her fiery red hair flared out like an explosion, her personality mirroring the chaotic energy that trailed behind her.

"Maybe I should just drop out and start a cooking show," I quipped back, lifting a spoonful of risotto to her lips, which she accepted with exaggerated enthusiasm. "Taste this. I think I've finally perfected it."

"Ugh, it's like a warm hug wrapped in a Parmesan blanket. You should charge people for this," she declared, rolling her eyes dramatically as she savored the bite. "You could be the next big thing, Julia the Culinary Star!"

I couldn't help but chuckle at her enthusiasm. "And how do you suggest I break into the cooking world? Appear on a reality show where I have to battle celebrity chefs while wearing a football jersey?"

"Now that's a sight I'd pay to see." She winked, crossing her arms on the counter. "But seriously, you know you have a gift. You need to stop hiding behind the quarterback mask. It's exhausting just thinking about it."

Her words hit a little too close to home, and I busied myself with the risotto, stirring with a bit more force than necessary. The truth was, I was trapped beneath the weight of expectations—those from my father, my coaches, and even the team. It felt easier to be the star athlete everyone expected than to venture into the unknown territory of pursuing my passion. "I'm just a guy trying to get through college," I said finally, allowing a hint of vulnerability to creep into my voice.

"College is about finding yourself, not fitting into a mold," she urged, her tone turning earnest. "You can't keep pretending you're someone you're not. You have dreams, Julia. Don't bury them."

"Maybe I like the burying part," I retorted lightly, though my heart didn't fully agree. There was something comforting about remaining under the radar, invisible behind a series of accolades. Being a football star came with its own set of perks, but each one felt like a gilded cage, a constant reminder that I was tethered to a life that didn't quite fit.

Kayla leaned forward, her brow furrowed in determination. "You know, I was talking to Hannah from the design department. She mentioned there's a showcase coming up for student creations. You could enter one of your dishes. Show them you're more than just the quarterback."

The idea lingered in the air, tempting yet terrifying. What would people think? The thought of trading in my helmet for an apron made me want to both laugh and cry. "Hannah is sweet, but she doesn't understand the kind of pressure I'm under. I can't just switch gears like that," I said, resisting the pull of her suggestion.

"Why not?" Kayla pressed, her blue eyes sparkling with mischief. "You're a creative genius trapped in a jock's body. You don't have to live up to anyone's expectations except your own."

Her words were like little firecrackers, igniting something deep within me. Maybe she was right. Maybe it was time to step out of the shadows and show everyone the real me. I had never imagined myself on a stage—what a spectacle that would be. But there was something alluring about it, the idea of sharing my passion with others, of letting them see the Julia I hid away.

Before I could second-guess myself, I plopped down on the stool next to her, a grin spreading across my face. "Okay, fine! I'll think about it. But if I do this, you're going to help me with the presentation. I can't just throw a plate out there and hope for the best."

Kayla laughed, a melodic sound that filled the kitchen. "Deal! Just think about it. You might surprise yourself."

The risotto continued to bubble away, and I found comfort in the warmth radiating from the pot. There was something undeniably invigorating about the idea of stepping outside my comfort zone, like tasting the first bite of a dish I had never tried before. Maybe, just maybe, I was ready to create my own path, to blend the flavors of my dreams with the reality of my life.

As the sun dipped lower in the sky, casting long shadows that danced across the walls, I felt the stirrings of hope mingling with the intoxicating scent of garlic and saffron. It was an unusual sensation, one that whispered of possibilities yet to unfold, urging me to embrace the messiness of life. And in that moment, with Kayla beside me and the promise of new adventures simmering in the air, I dared to imagine a world where I could truly belong—both as a quarterback and as a creator.

The chatter in the cafeteria swirled around me like a hurricane of adolescent angst, but my thoughts drifted elsewhere. I stirred my coffee absentmindedly, the steam curling up like the hopes I tucked away in a drawer marked "future." Kayla slid into the seat across from me, her vibrant red hair bouncing as she plopped down, her eyes alight with mischief.

"Earth to Julia! What's got you so deep in thought? Planning your escape to culinary stardom?" she teased, a smirk playing on her lips.

I chuckled, grateful for her attempt to pull me from my reverie. "You know, maybe I should start a secret cooking blog. 'The Kitchen Quarterback.' It could be my escape plan."

She raised an eyebrow, her laughter infectious. "As if the world needs another blog about avocado toast and smoothie bowls. What would your first post even be? 'How to Grill a Steak Like a Football?'"

"Perfect! I can throw in some tips about tackling leftovers, too," I shot back, leaning into our banter. Our playful exchanges often provided a necessary respite from my internal struggles.

The room buzzed with conversation, but it was a murmur, a white noise backdrop to my spiraling thoughts. Everyone seemed to move with purpose, while I felt suspended, like a star athlete trapped in the role of a supporting actor in my own life. It was exhausting, donning the mask of the perfect quarterback—everyone's hero and yet a stranger to himself.

"I don't get why you keep pretending to be this football god when you could easily be the next culinary genius," Kayla pressed, her tone shifting from playful to earnest. "You have a talent, Julia. People would kill to see you step into the limelight for that instead."

Her words hung in the air, heavy and laden with expectation. "It's not that simple. What if I fail? What if they see me as just another jock trying to make a splash in an arena he knows nothing about?"

"Or what if you soar?" she countered, leaning forward, her emerald eyes sparkling with a fervor that was hard to ignore. "You owe it to yourself to try."

My heart raced at the prospect, but the weight of the football scholarship and the looming specter of family expectations pulled me back. My father's voice echoed in my head: "Calderons are winners, Julia. You're not just playing for yourself."

Kayla noticed my hesitation. "What about that cooking class you were talking about? You've already got the skills. Just think of it as practice, not a grand reveal."

I hesitated, the thought of it sending both a thrill and a chill down my spine. Could I take that step? A world where I could lose myself in flavors and textures instead of touchdowns and tackles felt almost like a fantasy.

"Alright," I finally said, the resolve in my voice surprising even me. "I'll sign up for that class. Just one, though."

Her triumphant smile was a beacon of encouragement. "Now you're talking! Just imagine: 'Chef Calderon' has a nice ring to it."

We continued to banter, the earlier shadows receding as I found comfort in the familiar territory of our friendship. Yet, beneath the laughter, an unshakable sense of impending change loomed, like a storm cloud on the horizon.

The next morning, I found myself in the culinary lab, an eclectic mix of novices and seasoned cooks. My heart raced with anticipation and anxiety as I took my place behind a gleaming countertop, surrounded by sizzling pans and fragrant herbs. It felt liberating, standing there, apron donned, an artist ready to sculpt masterpieces instead of yards on a field.

"Welcome to Cooking 101! I'm Chef Margot, and I'm here to unlock your culinary potential," the instructor announced, her presence commanding yet inviting. "Today, we'll be exploring the art of the perfect risotto. It requires patience and a little love—like relationships!"

The class erupted into laughter, and I felt a strange sense of belonging. For the first time in ages, I was among people who didn't know me as the quarterback. They were just fellow food enthusiasts, each with their own dreams and aspirations. As I stirred the arborio rice, the creamy texture emerging under my careful touch, I could feel a shift within me.

"Julia, right?" A voice broke my concentration, and I turned to see a girl with tousled blonde hair and an infectious grin. "Are you really a quarterback? What are you doing here?"

"Just trying to discover my inner chef," I replied, my confidence buoyed by the spirit of the class. "What about you?"

"I'm Mia. Honestly? I'm here because I burned my last dinner attempt to a crisp. Thought it was time to learn from the pros," she admitted with a chuckle.

Her lightheartedness was refreshing, a stark contrast to the pressures that loomed over my usual life. We chatted as we cooked, laughter and camaraderie flowing easily, but I couldn't shake the feeling that this moment was too perfect, like a bubble waiting to burst.

As we plated our risotto, the scent wafting up made my stomach rumble. I glanced at Mia, a thought brewing. "What if we teamed up for a dish for the final exam? Two quarterbacks—one in the kitchen and one on the field!"

"Only if we can use lots of butter," she grinned, her eyes sparkling. "And maybe some herbs—gotta impress the judges!"

Just then, a sharp noise shattered the laughter—a loud crash from the storage area. We all turned, the lighthearted energy replaced by tension. Chef Margot rushed toward the sound, her demeanor shifting into something fierce.

"Stay here!" she barked, her voice cutting through the murmur of confusion. "I'll check it out."

As the door swung shut behind her, the weight of uncertainty settled over us. The cheerful atmosphere vanished, replaced by a palpable tension. Whispers erupted among the students, and I exchanged a worried glance with Mia.

What was happening? And more importantly, was I still going to have a chance to discover my passion before everything unraveled? The clock ticked away ominously, each second stretching into a moment of uncertainty that felt thick enough to slice through.

Then, a piercing scream echoed from the storage room, freezing the blood in my veins. In that instant, I realized I might not just be fighting for my own identity anymore but for something much larger—a battle that would soon demand all of us to choose between the safety of the familiar and the daring call of the unknown.

# Chapter 2: The Tough Girl

The gym smelled of sweat and determination, a pungent cocktail that mingled with the faint scent of liniment, clinging to the air like an uninvited guest. The rhythmic thud of fists meeting leather filled the space, each impact echoing the battle cries of countless souls who had come before me. It was in this sacred arena that I first met Kayla Hart, a force of nature wrapped in a tight tank top that seemed almost too small for her ferocious spirit. She moved with the grace of a dancer and the precision of a predator, her cropped hair a daring proclamation against the conventions of femininity. She embodied strength, and I found myself utterly captivated.

I leaned against the wall, absorbing the spectacle unfolding before me. Kayla's gloves flew through the air with a confidence I had only ever dreamt of. Her opponents fell back, shaken, not just by her blows but by the sheer audacity of her presence. It was as if she had carved out a space in the world that belonged only to her, a space where weakness was merely an afterthought. Each punch she threw resonated with the kind of defiance that seemed to drown out the disapproval of the outside world. I watched, wide-eyed, as she wiped the sweat from her brow, a victorious grin spreading across her face like the sunrise breaking through a stormy sky.

"Hey!" She caught my gaze and waved me over, her voice a melodic challenge that resonated over the din of the gym. "You look like you could use a lesson in standing up for yourself. What's your excuse for lurking like a shadow?"

My heart raced as I crossed the distance between us, the air crackling with the electricity of her bravado. "I'm just... observing," I stammered, feeling out of place in my oversized hoodie and worn-out sneakers. "I'm not exactly cut out for this."

Kayla raised an eyebrow, her expression a mix of amusement and challenge. "Not cut out for it? Honey, everyone starts somewhere.

8

The only difference between you and me is that I chose to stop being scared."

Her words wrapped around me, both invigorating and terrifying. What was it about her? The way she carried herself, as if every step was a statement, made me both envious and eager to know her. It was hard to believe someone could exist in such vivid color while I felt perpetually painted in shades of gray.

As the afternoon wore on, I found myself joining Kayla in the ring. She started me with the basics: stance, balance, and the all-important jab. The first time I threw a punch, I felt ridiculous, my arm flailing awkwardly. Kayla laughed, a sound that danced through the air, contagious and warm. "You look like you're swatting a fly! Come on, put some spirit into it! Imagine you're hitting something that annoys you."

"Like my boss?" I quipped, earning another chuckle from her.

"Exactly! Give him a good smack for all those times he stared at your paperwork like it was written in ancient Greek."

With every lesson, I felt a small piece of myself begin to unravel and reshape. Kayla's encouragement cut through my self-doubt like a knife through butter. "You've got more in you than you realize," she said, her eyes locking onto mine with a fierceness that made my heart race. "You just need to find it."

After our sparring sessions, we would collapse onto the floor, our bodies glistening with sweat and laughter. Those moments, however fleeting, turned into shared confessions as we caught our breath. "You know," I started one evening, my voice barely above a whisper, "I've always wanted to be brave. To feel like I could take on the world."

"Then why don't you?" she challenged, her brows furrowing slightly. "Being brave isn't about not being scared. It's about doing it anyway."

Her words lodged in my mind, a spark igniting within me. I had spent too long hiding, wrapped in layers of insecurities and what-ifs. Being around Kayla felt like being lit from within, a contrast to the shadows I had inhabited for so long. The stories we shared began to weave together, creating a tapestry of camaraderie and mutual understanding.

But the deeper we delved into each other's lives, the more I saw the cracks in her armor. Beneath her tough exterior lay a girl who fought fiercely not just against others, but against her own fears. There were moments when I caught the fleeting shadow of sadness crossing her face, an almost imperceptible flicker that hinted at past wounds. It made me want to peel back the layers and understand the struggles she faced—the ones that mirrored my own.

One afternoon, as the sun dipped below the horizon and bathed the gym in a warm, golden light, I broached the subject. "You're not just a fighter, are you?" I asked, my voice steady despite the vulnerability of the question. "What are you fighting for?"

She paused, her expression shifting from playful to contemplative, the grin fading momentarily. "I guess... I'm fighting for the girl I was supposed to be. The one everyone thought I should be."

The honesty in her words hung in the air, heavy yet liberating. "I never wanted to be the pretty one," she continued, her voice barely above a whisper. "I wanted to be the strong one. But it's hard when the world keeps telling you otherwise."

Her admission struck a chord deep within me. Here was this girl, seemingly invincible, struggling with her own doubts. It was a reminder that strength came in many forms, often intertwined with our vulnerabilities.

As the days turned into weeks, our bond deepened. We became each other's safe haven, two girls navigating the tempestuous waters of life and identity. Each punch, each shared laugh, brought us closer, weaving our hearts together in an intricate dance of friendship that felt both exhilarating and terrifying. In a world that often felt harsh and unforgiving, Kayla and I were finding solace in each other, even as we battled our inner demons.

And with every shared secret and laugh, I found myself drawn to her—not just for her strength, but for her courage to confront the parts of herself she was still learning to embrace.

The evenings at the gym became our sanctuary, a place where sweat and laughter melded into an unbreakable bond. Each session ended with us sprawled on the wooden floor, our bodies spent and our hearts brimming with camaraderie. As we recovered, I often caught Kayla glancing at her phone, a flicker of tension darting across her face. I wondered what ghosts haunted her outside of our shared fortress. But before I could voice my curiosity, she would shake it off, her laughter ringing out like a battle cry.

"Okay, next round," she'd say, rising to her feet with the exuberance of a child ready to play, oblivious to the exhaustion that clung to us both. "Let's see if you can throw a punch without looking like you're trying to swat a wasp."

One evening, the glow of the setting sun spilled through the gym windows, casting long shadows on the floor, and I decided to confront the growing tension that lingered between us. "You know," I began cautiously, wiping the sweat from my brow, "it's not just me who needs to be brave here. You have your own battles, don't you?"

Kayla paused, her hand hovering over her water bottle. For a moment, her vibrant energy dimmed, replaced by a vulnerability I rarely saw. "We all have our battles," she replied, her tone softer. "Some of us just choose to fight in public."

I studied her, wanting to reach through the gap she kept so carefully guarded. "I mean it, Kayla. You're not invincible, no matter how much you pretend to be."

She sighed, rolling her eyes but with a hint of a smile tugging at the corner of her lips. "You sound like a therapist. How about we trade? You tell me your secrets, and I'll tell you mine."

I laughed, the sound mingling with the fading echoes of the gym. "I'm not sure my secrets are as interesting as yours. I mostly just daydream about winning the lottery and moving to a tropical island."

"Is that all?" she shot back, her playful banter easing the weight in the air. "What happened to wanting to be brave? Winning the lottery doesn't sound like a battle."

I felt a rush of warmth at her insistence on keeping the conversation light, even as I considered her offer. Maybe it was time to peel back my own layers. "Fine," I said, half-tempted, "how about I share something embarrassing?"

"Now you have my attention," she replied, leaning closer, her eyes glinting with mischief.

I took a deep breath, gathering my thoughts. "When I was in high school, I had this huge crush on the captain of the soccer team. One day, I finally worked up the courage to talk to him and tripped over my own feet while trying to impress him. I ended up sprawled on the grass while he just stood there, staring at me like I was a bizarre species of insect."

Kayla erupted into laughter, her eyes bright with amusement. "Oh, that's classic! Did you ever recover from the humiliation?"

"Not really," I admitted, chuckling at the memory. "I spent the next few weeks avoiding him like he had a contagious disease."

"Good choice," she quipped, wiping a tear from her eye. "Avoidance is a solid strategy for high school heartbreak."

Just as the laughter faded, her phone buzzed, and the shift in her demeanor was palpable. She glanced at the screen, her smile faltering as shadows danced in her eyes. "Sorry," she murmured, her tone now heavy. "I need to take this."

I watched her walk away, the buoyancy of our exchange evaporating like dew in the morning sun. I could see her body tense as she stepped out of earshot, and I wondered what call could dampen the spark she carried so effortlessly. While she spoke, I busied myself by kicking the heavy bag with more ferocity than I intended, letting the rhythm of the punches drown out my growing concern.

When she returned, the lightness between us had shifted, a fragile tension replacing our earlier levity. "Everything okay?" I asked, sensing the change in her energy.

"Yeah, just... family stuff." She waved her hand dismissively, but her eyes told another story. "Nothing I can't handle."

The honesty in her gaze called to me, urging me to dig deeper, but the moment felt delicate, as if the wrong word might shatter the fragile trust we'd built. Instead, I offered her a half-hearted smile. "You know I'm here for you, right?"

Her expression softened, and she nodded, the corners of her mouth twitching back into a smile. "I appreciate that. Really. But enough about me; let's see if you can land a solid hook without sending me flying across the room."

The playful banter resumed, but I couldn't shake the sense that something was amiss. As we sparred, I kept my gaze on her, searching for cracks in her bravado, but she fought fiercely, her focus unwavering. Each jab she threw felt less like a physical exchange and more like a dance we both needed to perform—a rhythm that allowed us to ignore the unspoken worries lurking beneath the surface.

Weeks passed in a blur of punches, laughter, and shared moments of vulnerability. The gym became our second home, the ring our confessional. Yet, no matter how close we grew, I could sense a barrier lingering, an invisible wall she erected to keep certain parts of herself hidden. One evening, as the last rays of sunlight filtered through the windows, I decided it was time to push a little harder.

"You know, we could be fighting alongside each other instead of against," I suggested as we sprawled on the floor, the coolness of the wood beneath us soothing our tired bodies. "You don't have to carry everything alone."

Kayla rolled onto her side, propping her head up with her arm. "And risk being seen as weak? I can't do that. You saw how people reacted when I started boxing. I'd rather be the tough girl than the girl who needs help."

"That's the thing, though," I countered, leaning closer. "Everyone needs help sometimes. It doesn't make you weak; it makes you human. And honestly, I like you better when you let your guard down."

She studied me, her gaze piercing. "Do you really think that? You're not just saying that because we're in the moment?"

"I mean it. You're more than the tough girl; you're someone who fights for others too. I see how you look out for everyone, how you inspire them."

Her expression shifted, a mix of surprise and something more profound flickering in her eyes. "I've never thought of it that way. But what if I let my guard down and it all falls apart?"

"Then we'll pick up the pieces together," I replied, feeling the weight of my words settle in the space between us. "I'll be here, even if it means we have to drag each other through the mess."

She hesitated, a fleeting moment of vulnerability passing across her face before her defenses returned, but this time, I saw a glimmer of consideration in her eyes. It was a start, a tiny crack in the armor she wore so fiercely. And for the first time, I felt a shift—not just in our friendship, but in the understanding that beneath her tough exterior was a heart yearning to be seen and accepted.

In that moment, the weight of unspoken words hung heavy in the air, filling the space with a promise of what was to come. The journey ahead would not be easy, but we would face it together, one punch at a time.

Our friendship deepened with each passing day, intertwining like vines climbing a trellis, robust and defiant. We were two disparate souls finding refuge in each other's imperfections, each sparring match a blend of competition and camaraderie. The rhythm of our laughter echoed through the gym, drawing curious glances from others, but I found solace in our shared moments. Kayla's fierce spirit and quick wit were intoxicating, igniting a flame of courage within me that I had long thought extinguished.

One Friday evening, as the autumn air turned crisp, we decided to extend our ritual to a cozy diner just a few blocks away from the gym. The moment we stepped inside, the rich aroma of coffee and freshly baked pies enveloped us, and I felt an overwhelming urge to share the warmth of our newfound bond with the world. I chose a booth in the corner, where the flickering candlelight bathed us in a soft glow. "Perfect for our post-fight debrief," I said, grinning.

Kayla rolled her eyes, a playful smirk dancing on her lips. "You make it sound like we're about to solve world hunger or something. All I'm interested in is the pie."

"Don't underestimate the power of pie. It can solve most problems," I shot back, scanning the menu. "Especially when paired with a hefty side of fries."

As we ordered, the conversation flowed effortlessly, veering from our recent boxing exploits to our childhood dreams. The diner buzzed with the chatter of families and friends, the sounds blending into a comforting hum that felt like home. Yet, beneath the laughter and banter, I sensed the familiar tension in Kayla's demeanor, as if she were fighting a battle far deeper than the ones we engaged in at the gym.

"Okay, spill," I said, setting down my fork as the pie arrived, a slice of heaven topped with a dollop of whipped cream. "What's going on with you? You keep looking at your phone like it's about to explode."

She hesitated, her gaze shifting to the window where the last light of day was retreating. "It's just... family stuff," she repeated, but this time her voice held a tremor, a crack that let me glimpse the uncertainty within.

"Family stuff or family drama?" I probed gently, knowing how precarious those words could be. "You know you can tell me anything, right?"

Kayla picked at the crust of her pie, her expression pensive. "It's just... my dad wants me to quit boxing. He doesn't think it's feminine or something. He wants me to focus on school, maybe get into some 'nice' college. You know how that goes."

I felt my heart sink, the weight of her words hanging between us like a storm cloud. "But you love boxing. It's who you are. You can't just give it up because someone else thinks you should."

"I know," she sighed, her frustration palpable. "But I also know that the pressure from my family isn't going anywhere. They've never been supportive of my choices, especially when it comes to anything that doesn't fit their idea of what a girl should be."

Her confession struck a chord within me, resonating with my own struggles against familial expectations. "You deserve to pursue your passion, Kayla. Don't let anyone box you in. Life is too short to live for someone else's approval."

She met my gaze, a flicker of gratitude mingling with uncertainty. "You make it sound easy, but it's not. When you've been fighting for approval your whole life, it's hard to let go."

I reached across the table, my hand covering hers. "You're tougher than you think. You've already shown that in the ring. Now it's time to fight for yourself outside of it."

Just as she opened her mouth to respond, a figure loomed at our booth—a tall man with a buzz cut and a leather jacket that screamed trouble. He stood there, a predatory glint in his eyes that made my stomach drop. "Kayla Hart?" he asked, his voice low and gravelly.

She tensed, her entire demeanor shifting in an instant. "Who's asking?" she replied, the tough girl I had come to admire reappearing as she squared her shoulders.

"I'm here on behalf of the Elysium Boxing Club," he said, his expression unreadable. "They want you to join. You've got potential, and they're willing to offer you a spot on their team."

Kayla's brow furrowed, confusion etched across her face. "I'm already training at the gym. What's Elysium got that they don't?"

"The best coaches, state-of-the-art facilities, and a chance to go pro," he said, his gaze unwavering. "You could make a name for yourself. All you have to do is sign with us."

I glanced at Kayla, searching for signs of excitement or fear, but her expression remained stoic, a carefully constructed mask that betrayed nothing. "I'm not interested," she replied flatly, her voice cutting through the thick tension like a knife.

He leaned closer, an unsettling grin spreading across his face. "You should think twice about that. Opportunities like this don't come around often, and they could really change your life."

"Or they could ruin it," she shot back, fire igniting in her eyes. "I'm not interested in jumping into some corporate boxing machine."

The man's smile faltered, his demeanor darkening. "You think you can afford to turn down this chance? You don't want to be a nobody forever, do you?"

I felt a surge of protectiveness rise within me. "She's not a nobody," I snapped, surprising myself with the strength of my voice. "She's more than your stereotype of a fighter."

His gaze flicked to me, annoyance simmering just below the surface. "You should mind your business, sweetheart. This isn't about you."

"Maybe it should be," I countered, refusing to back down. The air crackled between us, tension electrifying the moment, and I sensed Kayla's gratitude beneath the layer of unease.

With a sharp exhale, Kayla stood up, her eyes blazing with determination. "I'm not going anywhere with you. You can tell your 'club' to take a hike. I'm not looking for shortcuts."

The man narrowed his eyes, his demeanor shifting from persuasive to menacing. "You have no idea what you're walking away from, Hart. But mark my words—this is not the last you'll hear from us."

With that, he turned on his heel and strode away, leaving behind an air thick with unspoken threats. I looked at Kayla, my heart racing. "Are you okay?"

"I will be," she replied, though her voice trembled slightly. "I just can't believe he showed up like that."

"Is Elysium a big deal?" I asked, trying to keep my tone steady, though the knot in my stomach tightened.

"Yeah, they are," she admitted, her voice dropping to a whisper. "They've got connections, and if they wanted to, they could make things really difficult for me—maybe even my family."

The weight of her words hung in the air, and my heart sank further. "But you can't let them intimidate you. You've fought too hard for this."

"Maybe I don't have a choice," she murmured, the spark of defiance dimming in her eyes.

The weight of our conversation felt heavy, the remnants of the encounter casting a shadow over the evening. As we finished our pie in silence, the diner buzzed with life around us, oblivious to the storm that had just rolled in.

Suddenly, Kayla's phone buzzed again, and this time, the blood drained from her face. She glanced at the screen, her eyes widening in disbelief. "No... no, no, no," she whispered, her breath hitching.

"What is it?" I leaned closer, my heart racing with concern.

"It's my dad," she said, her voice barely above a whisper. "He's been in an accident. I have to go."

In that moment, the world around us faded, and all that remained was the urgency in her eyes and the weight of unspoken fears hanging heavily in the air. The diner, the pie, even the lingering echoes of laughter felt like a distant memory. As Kayla stood to leave, her face set with determination, I couldn't shake the feeling that this was just the beginning of something darker—a fight far greater than either of us had anticipated. And in that uncertainty, I felt the ground shift beneath us, pulling us both into a chasm of unknowns, where courage and heartache would be tested in ways we couldn't yet fathom.

# Chapter 3: Secrets Unveiled

Laughter bubbled like the warm dough I was mixing, each chuckle rich with the sweetness of friendship. Kayla lounged on the edge of my bed, her head thrown back as she recounted some legendary mishap from our freshman year. I glanced at her, a glimmer of nostalgia softening my expression, and then returned to my task. The soft thud of my mixing spoon against the bowl was a comforting rhythm, punctuating the delightful chaos of our lives.

The cozy dorm room bore witness to our shared moments. Posters of long-gone pop stars clung stubbornly to the walls, while the faint scent of lavender from a candle flickered on my cluttered desk. Stacks of books, half-read and teetering, formed precarious towers that threatened to tumble at any moment, much like our sanity during midterms. I could almost hear the whispers of our late-night debates and pillow fights echoing in the corners. It was our sanctuary, a place where dreams flourished between the ever-present anxieties of adulthood looming just around the corner.

As I melted butter, the rich, nutty aroma curled around me, mingling with the vanilla and brown sugar I'd added. It was a symphony of scents, one that brought with it the promise of warmth and sweetness, much like the friendship I had with Kayla. She caught my eye, the light catching the flecks of gold in her hair, and I couldn't help but smile back. In that moment, everything felt perfect. Until my phone buzzed insistently on the countertop, shattering the serene atmosphere like a jarring note in a melody.

I picked it up, curiosity and annoyance intertwining, and found a text from Ryan, a name that stirred both adrenaline and exasperation in my chest. "Heard you're cooking up something new. Don't forget to keep the kitchen away from the field." His words, dripping with sarcasm, were like ice-cold water splashed on my sun-kissed afternoon. They sliced through my moment of bliss, reminding me that for every ounce of joy, there seemed to be an equal measure of judgment, especially from someone like Ryan.

"Ugh, him again," Kayla muttered, her playful expression morphing into one of righteous indignation. "You should just ignore him. He doesn't know the first thing about good food."

"Maybe not," I replied, attempting to maintain a lighthearted demeanor, but my heart sank. "But he knows a lot about winning—and how to twist the knife." I could feel my resolve crumbling under the weight of his words. My passion for baking, a place where I felt safe and capable, suddenly felt like a liability. I was supposed to be a star athlete, not the girl with a penchant for cookies.

Kayla moved closer, her brow furrowed in concern. "What's really bothering you? This isn't just about the text, is it?"

The question hung in the air, heavy and expectant. For the first time, I hesitated to answer, fear constricting around my heart. I had built walls around my insecurities, fortified them with laughter and bravado. Yet, looking into her warm, understanding eyes, I felt those defenses crumbling, brick by brick.

"Sometimes, I worry that I'm not enough," I confessed, my voice trembling slightly. "I mean, I love soccer, but it feels like everyone expects me to be this perfect athlete, the one who lives and breathes the game. And when I bake, it feels like... I don't know, like I'm just giving them more ammunition to laugh at me."

Kayla's expression softened, a mixture of empathy and fierce determination. "Are they laughing at you? Or are they just scared because you're good at something they can't touch?"

I chewed on my lip, the taste of doubt mingling with the sweet scent of my cookies. "Maybe both. It's just hard to balance everything. I want to excel in soccer, but when I bake, it's like I'm a different person. It feels so... freeing. But then I remember that I'm also the girl on the field, and I wonder if I'm letting everyone down."

"Listen," Kayla said, leaning forward as if sharing a great secret. "Those cookies? They're a part of you, just like soccer. You can be both. You're not defined by one thing. So what if Ryan thinks he can push your buttons? You have something he doesn't—a heart, and a soul that shines when you create. That's way more important than any trophy."

Her words wrapped around me, warm and reassuring like a soft blanket on a cold night. The truth in them seeped into my bones, illuminating the corners of my self-doubt. I wanted to believe her, to embrace the fullness of my identity, but the fear of judgment lingered like an unwelcome shadow.

"Do you really think so?" I asked, my voice barely above a whisper.

"I know so," she replied fiercely. "Now, can we please focus on these cookies? I can already tell they're going to be legendary. And besides, we can use them to fuel our plans to crush Ryan in the next match."

The shift in the air was palpable as I chuckled, a sense of lightness returning. I returned to mixing, and with each fold of the dough, I felt a little more like myself again. "If we can survive my baking and his sarcasm, we can conquer anything," I joked, and for the first time that afternoon, I felt a spark of hope flicker to life.

As I scooped the dough onto the baking sheet, I marveled at how my passion for baking could feel so intertwined with my love for soccer. Each chocolate chip nestled into the dough was like a step toward reconciling the two parts of me that had felt so at odds. Maybe Ryan's words would sting less if I focused on the joy that came from both the field and the kitchen.

With a renewed sense of purpose, I slid the tray into the oven, a transformative heat swirling within. I turned to Kayla, who was flipping through my recipe book, her laughter lighting up the room. "So what's next? Do we make a strategy for how to serve these cookies to Ryan, or do we save them as a secret weapon for after the game?"

I grinned, feeling a newfound strength bubbling up within me. "Why not both?"

As we plotted our strategy over the enticing aroma of melting chocolate and golden cookies, the tension between my worlds felt less daunting. In this vibrant chaos of friendship and baking, I found a glimmer of clarity. I was ready to embrace every part of me, confident that the right mix of courage and cookies could withstand even the most cutting remarks.

A light flickered in the corner of the kitchen, casting playful shadows that danced along the walls as I stirred the dough, the metallic clang of a spoon against the bowl providing a steady beat to my thoughts. Kayla leaned against the counter, a playful smirk on her face, her fingers drumming lightly against the cool granite. The tension from Ryan's text still clung to the air like smoke, but with Kayla beside me, it felt manageable, like an itch I could scratch away with some good-natured banter.

"Okay, so here's the plan," Kayla announced, her eyes sparkling with mischief. "We bake these cookies to perfection, and then we present them as our secret weapon at practice. I can already picture Ryan's face when he realizes the 'cookie girl' is actually an undefeated cookie assassin."

I couldn't help but laugh, the tension easing a little more. "A cookie assassin? Really? You do realize that my skills are more suited for a bakery than a battlefield, right?"

"Don't sell yourself short! You know how to wield a whisk like a pro. Plus, I'd argue that your cookies could tackle any rival—and then make them feel guilty about it afterward." She winked, her laughter infectious, and soon I was caught up in the lightness of the moment.

The oven chimed, signaling the cookies were ready to be pulled out, and as I opened the door, a wave of warmth enveloped me, rich with the scent of melting chocolate and caramelized sugar. My heart swelled with pride as I gingerly placed the golden-brown cookies on the cooling rack. Each one felt like a victory in itself, a testament to my passion that Ryan's words could not diminish.

"See? This is what I'm talking about! You just created magic," Kayla exclaimed, peering over my shoulder. "You need to take a picture of these for Instagram. Let the world know that the 'cookie girl' isn't just a title—she's a force to be reckoned with!"

"Okay, but let's make sure the world knows that these are high-performance cookies," I joked, holding up my phone for a quick snap.

"Only if we can include a warning label for Ryan: 'Beware! May contain traces of sass and sugar-induced confidence.'"

I snorted, trying to keep a straight face while snapping pictures. "I like it. But do you think it'll go over well with the team?"

"Absolutely. Ryan won't know what hit him. Or, rather, what deliciously sweet thing has just entered his life," she said, feigning a dramatic swoon.

We fell into a rhythm, teasing and laughing, and for a brief moment, it felt like nothing could disturb the balance we had created. But just as the warmth of the cookies spread through the room, a shadow flitted across my mind. With a determined breath, I steered our conversation back to the more serious matter at hand. "You know, Kayla, I really do love soccer. It's just... there's always this pressure to be perfect, to never slip up, and I hate that I can't just enjoy it without feeling like I'm letting everyone down."

Kayla paused, her expression shifting from playful to contemplative. "That's the thing about expectations—they can be suffocating. But if anyone can rise above them, it's you. Just remember that no one expects you to be perfect. They just want you to be yourself, on and off the field."

"Easier said than done," I muttered, feeling the weight of her words settle heavily around my shoulders. "I keep thinking that if I mess up even once, it will confirm all the doubts Ryan and others have about me. Like, the cookie girl can't possibly be an athlete, right?"

"Okay, but let's think about it this way: what if Ryan isn't the end of the world? What if you took that pressure and flipped it around? What if you used it to fuel your game?"

I watched her closely, intrigued by the idea. "So, you're saying I should bake with a side of rebellion?"

"Exactly! Instead of hiding behind the fear of judgment, let your passion ignite your confidence. Bake those cookies and serve them with pride—just like you serve the ball on the field. Show Ryan that you can own both worlds."

Her fierce conviction stirred something within me, a flicker of defiance that ignited my spirit. "Alright, you've convinced me. It's time to bake my way to victory, both on the field and in the kitchen."

As we laughed and plotted our next moves, the day unfolded into a delightful blur of flour dust and laughter. Soon, the cooling rack was filled with golden cookies, each a testament to the evening's spirit. We packed them up, preparing to bring a little sweetness to the next day's practice.

The next afternoon, the sun hung low in the sky, casting a golden hue over the soccer field as I approached, a plate of cookies cradled in my arms. I could hear the familiar sounds of laughter and shouts, the echo of shoes pounding on grass, a melody that always made my heart race. Ryan stood in the center, his characteristic swagger on display as he demonstrated a particularly impressive drill.

"Look who decided to join us," he called out, an eyebrow arched in mock surprise. "You bring cookies? Is that your secret weapon? Or are you just trying to bribe us to let you win?"

His taunts dripped with sarcasm, but instead of shrinking under his scrutiny, I felt the warmth of Kayla's encouragement echoing in my mind. With a quick inhale, I stepped forward, the plate held high like a trophy. "Actually, Ryan, these are for the whole team. But if you want to take one, I'd advise you to check for the special ingredient."

He looked intrigued, leaning forward with a mix of curiosity and skepticism. "Oh? And what's that?"

"Confidence. Made from scratch. Guaranteed to give you a sugar rush and maybe even some humility."

Kayla stood beside me, stifling her laughter, while the rest of the team began to crowd around, curiosity piqued by the sudden shift in my demeanor. "I think she's challenging you," one of my teammates quipped, a grin spreading across her face.

"I can handle a challenge," Ryan smirked, extending a hand to grab a cookie. "But I'm not promising to share."

"Wouldn't dream of it," I replied, my heart racing with a mix of adrenaline and laughter.

As he took a bite, his expression changed from cocky to contemplative. "Hey, these are actually really good," he admitted, the surprise in his voice not lost on anyone. "Not that I expected anything less from the 'cookie girl.'"

"Just remember that the 'cookie girl' can also score goals," I shot back, the playful banter flying between us.

The laughter of the team echoed across the field, and for the first time in a long while, I felt like I belonged—like I had carved out my own space in this world where soccer and sweetness collided. With each passing moment, the walls I had built around myself began to dissolve, and I realized that perhaps I could be both. I could revel in the joy of baking while fiercely pursuing my passion for soccer.

As Ryan's teasing melted into camaraderie, I caught Kayla's eye and winked. This was just the beginning, and I was ready to embrace every delicious moment.

The sun began to dip below the horizon, painting the sky in hues of orange and pink as laughter echoed across the soccer field. I stood there, my heart racing, reveling in the camaraderie that enveloped me like a warm blanket. Ryan, mid-bite of my chocolate chip creation, was an unexpected ally at that moment. The other players milled around, their casual banter a comforting backdrop to the tension that had, until recently, felt all-consuming.

"Not too shabby, cookie girl. If only your soccer skills matched your baking," Ryan called out, a teasing lilt in his voice. But instead of feeling the sting of his usual sarcasm, I found myself laughing alongside him. "Watch out, I might start charging for these," I shot back, my confidence buoyed by the playful exchange.

"Wouldn't dream of robbing you of your sweet treats, but just so you know, I don't do paychecks." He grinned, a playful glint in his eye, and something about the challenge in his tone made me want to rise to it.

With each cookie devoured, the team grew more animated, the earlier tension dissipating like morning mist. It felt good to be included, to have my baking serve as a bridge rather than a barrier. "Okay, who knew cookies could spark this much joy?" Kayla chimed in, a gleam of mischief dancing in her eyes.

"Maybe we should use them as a strategy in the next game," another teammate suggested. "A cookie distraction! They'll never see it coming."

"Forget the game plan; I'm all about cookie diplomacy," I quipped, grinning at Kayla, who was nodding sagely as if considering the tactical merits of dessert.

Just then, Ryan leaned closer, a playful smirk tugging at his lips. "You know, if you keep this up, I might have to start taking you seriously as a competitor. I can't have my rivals baking me into submission."

"Wouldn't that be a shame?" I replied, arching an eyebrow. "Having to contend with the cookie queen on and off the field? That might just throw your whole game off."

We exchanged a playful stare, and for a brief moment, the tension that had previously existed felt like a distant memory. As the practice continued, my laughter mingled with the sound of sneakers pounding the grass, the rhythm of friendship and competition weaving together into something beautiful. The team played on, and each cheer felt like a small victory, a testament to the fact that I belonged.

But just as I began to relish this newfound confidence, the wind shifted. The late afternoon breeze carried an unsettling chill, a whisper of something ominous lurking at the edges of my bliss. I caught Ryan's gaze again, and for a split second, I wondered if he could sense it too.

"Hey, cookie girl," he called out, shifting from playful to serious, the light in his eyes dimming slightly. "You're still coming to the party at Jake's this weekend, right?"

The question hung in the air, heavy with implications. My mind raced. Parties were not my scene; they were loud, chaotic, and full of expectations I often felt ill-equipped to handle. Yet, something about the way Ryan asked made me pause. "Yeah, I guess I'll be there. Just... bringing cookies, of course."

"Good," he replied, his expression shifting back to the teasing mask I was becoming accustomed to. "Just be prepared for the onslaught of terrible dance moves. You've been warned."

"Please, as if I'd let you overshadow my cookie prowess with your questionable moves," I shot back, feeling a thrill of defiance.

As the sun slipped lower, casting long shadows across the field, practice wrapped up, and the team began to disperse. I turned to

Kayla, who had been observing the playful exchange with an approving smile. "You're really holding your own out there," she said, her voice brimming with excitement.

"Thanks! It felt good, you know? Almost like I can be both—the cookie girl and the soccer player."

"That's the spirit! Just wait until you see how the team rallies around you at the party. It's going to be epic," she added, a mischievous grin spreading across her face.

We walked back to the dorm together, our laughter blending into the evening air. The warm glow of streetlights flickered on as the night wrapped itself around us, a blanket of stars twinkling above.

But as I entered the dorm, a familiar sense of unease crept back. The thought of the party tugged at my mind, unraveling the threads of confidence I had woven during practice. What if I didn't fit in? What if the old feelings of inadequacy returned, shadowing my newfound confidence?

As I opened the door to my room, the silence inside felt oppressive. My phone buzzed again, a notification from Ryan lighting up the screen. "Can't wait for the party! I'll save a dance for you. Just don't embarrass me."

A smile tugged at my lips, but the warmth of his words did little to chase away the chill of apprehension settling in my stomach. I tossed my phone onto the bed, my heart racing as I contemplated the weekend ahead.

"What if you just go and enjoy it?" I murmured to myself, trying to muster the courage I had felt earlier. I turned to Kayla, who was rifling through her own belongings, blissfully unaware of the storm brewing in my head.

"Hey, Kayla? What if... what if I'm not ready for this party?" I asked, the vulnerability creeping into my voice.

She turned, her expression shifting from playful to concerned. "What do you mean? You've been so confident lately. What's changed?"

"Honestly? I just... I don't want to go back to feeling small and out of place. What if they see me as just the cookie girl again? I don't want that to overshadow everything else."

Her brows knitted together in thought. "You've come so far. Remember, you're not defined by anyone else's perception. You're a great athlete and an incredible baker. You've got this. Just be yourself."

"Easier said than done," I mumbled, biting my lip as I watched her.

"Trust me. Just go and be you. And if anyone tries to box you in, just hit them with a cookie!"

We laughed, but my heart still felt heavy. As I prepared for bed that night, my mind churned with uncertainty. I wanted to believe Kayla's words, but the specter of doubt loomed larger than ever.

That evening, as I lay awake, the darkness around me seemed to whisper fears I had tried to bury. What if I couldn't measure up to my own expectations? What if Ryan turned the party into a showcase for all his friends, reminding me just how easily I could slip back into that shell of doubt?

As I stared at the ceiling, the phone buzzed again, pulling me from my thoughts. This time, it was a message from an unknown number. "Heard you're baking up some competition. Hope you're ready to be put in your place at the party. See you there."

My heart raced, the implications of the message sending a chill down my spine. Who could it be? Did someone know about my insecurities? I sat up, my breath quickening, uncertainty clawing at the edges of my confidence. Suddenly, the party didn't seem like the celebratory affair I had envisioned; it felt like a minefield.

The shadows in my room shifted ominously as I realized this was about more than just cookies or soccer. Someone was clearly out to undermine me, to chip away at the fragile self-assurance I had just begun to build.

I grabbed my phone, staring at the message in disbelief, the glow illuminating my worried expression. The words echoed ominously in my mind. My heart pounded as the realization hit me—this was just the beginning. The game was on, and I wasn't sure if I was ready to play.

# Chapter 4: The Rivalry

The evening air clung to my skin like a familiar shawl, warm yet laced with the crisp bite of autumn, the kind that reminded me that change was afoot. The sun dipped low on the horizon, painting the sky in shades of gold and crimson, a perfect backdrop for the chaos that was about to unfold on the field. Practice was in full swing, the sound of cleats pounding against the turf echoing like a heartbeat, a rhythm I had grown accustomed to in the weeks since I had joined the team. Yet tonight, unease danced in my chest, a shadow lurking just out of sight.

Ryan, with his easy charm and effortless talent, was the reigning star of the team. He was the type to stride onto the field and have everyone's attention within seconds, tossing a football with a flick of his wrist that made it seem almost effortless. His confidence radiated like the sunset, warming some while casting long shadows on others. I could feel his eyes on me now, like two twin suns, evaluating, dissecting. Beneath the façade of camaraderie, there was an unspoken rivalry brewing, one that had me glancing over my shoulder far too often.

"Hey, are you going to actually catch one today?" Ryan called out, his voice slicing through the laughter and shouts around me. His tone was teasing, but the glint in his eye suggested something deeper, a challenge wrapped in a jibe. It was a public jab, and the laughter of our teammates hung in the air, heavy and suffocating.

I adjusted my stance, the tension in my shoulders betraying my bravado. "You know, if you spent less time showing off and more time focusing on your own game, you might just realize I'm not the one who needs catching practice." I flashed a smile that I hoped was more defiance than insecurity, but even I could hear the tremor in my voice.

"Is that right?" He stepped closer, his demeanor shifting from playful to something more serious. "I've heard whispers, you know. You have a secret."

A secret. The word echoed in my mind, a siren song that threatened to pull me under. My heart raced at the thought of my hidden passion for cooking and design, a world far removed from the sweat and grass stains of football. Kayla, my steadfast ally, urged me to embrace this side of myself, to let the vibrant colors of my true self splash across the canvas of my life. She would often catch me daydreaming during lunch, sketching out ideas for the next culinary masterpiece or the layout of a dream kitchen in the margins of my notebooks. "Why not share it with the world?" she'd say, her voice brimming with enthusiasm. But the very thought of revealing that side of me to my teammates felt akin to stepping into a raging river, uncertain of where I might end up.

I shifted my weight, gripping the football with a resolve that belied my inner turmoil. "You know, Ryan, some of us are good at more than one thing. Just because you can't imagine being anything other than the 'big man on campus' doesn't mean the rest of us are locked into that stereotype." I aimed the ball at a nearby target, the thud of leather against the ground resonating with the thump of my heart.

"Touché," he replied, a flicker of surprise crossing his face before he recovered. "But do you think you can really juggle both worlds? One wrong step, and your whole balance could come crashing down." His gaze lingered a moment too long, the weight of unspoken words hanging between us like a curtain drawn too tight.

The team continued their drills, oblivious to the undercurrent swirling around us, but I felt it like a thunderstorm brewing. I could almost hear Kayla's voice in my ear, urging me to rise above, to stand tall against the storm, yet the fear of rejection gnawed at my confidence. I didn't want to lose this slice of belonging, even if it meant suppressing the essence of who I was.

As practice wore on, I lost myself in the rhythm of the game, the camaraderie wrapping around me like a comforting blanket. Yet, in the back of my mind, the nagging tension remained. Ryan's probing words echoed in my thoughts, relentless in their insistence.

After practice, while the sun dipped below the horizon, painting the world in dusky shades of violet and navy, I found myself lingering at the edge of the field, away from the laughter and banter of my teammates. My breath fogged the cool air as I wrestled with my conflicting desires. Kayla found me there, her presence a balm to my frayed nerves.

"Hey, you okay?" she asked, her brows knitting together in concern. Her golden hair, a wild cascade of curls, bounced as she approached, a halo of sunlight even in the twilight.

"I'm fine," I replied too quickly, the lie tumbling out before I could catch it. "Just...thinking."

"About Ryan?" She leaned against the goalpost, arms crossed, her stance relaxed yet attentive, as if she were the calm in my brewing storm.

"Is it that obvious?" I huffed, the corner of my mouth twitching into a reluctant smile.

"Only to someone who knows you well," she said, her expression softening. "You've got to stop worrying about what he thinks. You're so much more than this. You have a gift, and it's time to show it off."

"But what if they don't understand? What if I lose everything I've built here?" The words spilled out, raw and unfiltered, a torrent of fears that had been bottled up for far too long.

Kayla stepped closer, her eyes sparkling with determination. "Then maybe it's time to build something new. You're not defined by the football field alone. You have a world waiting for you beyond those lines."

Her unwavering belief in me was like a beacon, illuminating the dark corners of my doubt. I felt the weight of her words settle into my bones, a kind of hope I hadn't dared to entertain before. The rivalry, the challenges, the whispers of secrets—perhaps they were not the end of me but the beginning of a new journey, one where I could stand unapologetically as both a football player and a dreamer, ready to carve my own path.

As the last light of day faded, a newfound resolve began to take root within me. The world was larger than I had imagined, filled with endless possibilities. And for the first time, I felt ready to face whatever came next, whether it was on the field or in the kitchen, with my head held high and my heart open wide.

The following week unfurled like a tangled ball of yarn, each day bringing with it a new knot of anxiety and expectation. Football practices morphed into a landscape fraught with tension, where the camaraderie I had once relished felt overshadowed by Ryan's relentless pursuit of my hidden truth. The autumn breeze, which had once danced playfully through the leaves, now felt like a harbinger of uncertainty. I couldn't shake the feeling that my secret simmered just beneath the surface, waiting for the opportune moment to erupt, much like a pot left unattended on the stove.

"Don't let him get to you," Kayla advised as we huddled together in the corner of the cafeteria, the smell of overcooked broccoli wafting through the air. She had a knack for turning the mundane into something delightful with her infectious enthusiasm, even if the cafeteria food was doing its best to thwart that ambition. "You've got to own who you are. Just think about the joy that cooking brings you."

I picked at my food, feeling the weight of her words, the sincerity behind them. "Joy? Sure, when I'm in my kitchen, but here? This is my battlefield, Kayla. The stakes are higher than a soufflé gone wrong." I laughed half-heartedly, hoping to mask the real turmoil roiling within me. The bright orange of my mac and cheese seemed to mock my predicament, reminding me that I was still playing a part that didn't entirely fit.

"Okay, but what's the worst that could happen?" she pressed, her blue eyes sparkling with determination. "Let's say Ryan exposes your secret. So what? Will the world end? Will the sky fall?"

"Maybe not, but I can't imagine the team would be thrilled to know I've been cooking gourmet meals while they've been tackling each other on the field," I countered, crossing my arms in defiance. "What if they think I'm some kind of fraud? I'm not a true athlete if I have dreams that don't involve being on the field."

Kayla tilted her head, considering my words. "And who defines what a true athlete is? The one who can run the fastest or the one who has passion? You love football, but you love cooking just as much. Why can't you be both?"

"Because being both means risking losing everything." The vulnerability crept into my voice, and I hated how exposed I felt. "I've finally carved out a place here, and it's terrifying to think I might lose it."

"Then don't lose it," she said with the simplicity that only true friends possess. "Hold on to both. You're amazing, and anyone who can't see that isn't worth your time."

Her conviction hung in the air, a thread of hope weaving through my tangled thoughts. I felt the stirrings of resolve, yet beneath it lay an undercurrent of dread. As the days slipped by, the tension between Ryan and me escalated, morphing from playful banter to sharp, barbed exchanges that left me reeling. Each practice turned into a chess match, where every pass and tackle felt calculated, a move in the larger game of uncovering my secret.

One particularly crisp afternoon, as leaves crunched underfoot and the scent of freshly mown grass filled the air, I stood at the edge of the field, the autumn sun casting a warm glow around the chaos of practice. Ryan strode over, his expression unreadable, a storm cloud lurking just behind his blue eyes.

"Let's see if you've really got what it takes today," he said, an edge to his voice that made my stomach flip. "How about a little wager?"

"What are we betting on this time? Your ego versus my dignity?" I shot back, a hint of humor masking my anxiety.

His lips curled into a smirk, the challenge igniting a familiar fire between us. "If I win, you tell everyone about your little culinary dreams. If you win, I'll take you out for a home-cooked meal. My treat."

"Wow, Ryan. That sounds like a punishment," I replied, feigning indifference while my heart raced at the implications of the wager. The thought of revealing my passion made my stomach twist, yet the idea of cooking for him, of sharing that part of myself, ignited a flicker of excitement.

"Think you can handle it?" He raised an eyebrow, confidence radiating off him in waves.

"Oh, I can handle it, just like I can handle that horrendous haircut," I said, gesturing toward his short, tousled hair. "But if I win, you'll have to wear a chef's hat to practice for a whole week. And I get to choose the recipes."

Ryan laughed, the sound surprisingly warm. "You've got yourself a deal."

As the practice began, every pass, every sprint felt magnified. The air was electric, the stakes higher than they had ever been. I was a whirlpool of nerves and determination, the taste of victory dancing tantalizingly on my tongue. My teammates buzzed around us, unaware of the bet brewing just beneath the surface.

With each play, the tension escalated, and the dynamic shifted. Ryan's competitive spirit pushed me to dig deeper, to reach beyond my own limits. We moved together like a well-oiled machine, each play intertwining our fates in a way I hadn't anticipated. It was exhilarating and terrifying all at once.

Then, in a moment that felt almost surreal, the ball soared through the air, gliding like a bird against the brilliant blue sky. I leaped, catching it with precision, adrenaline surging through me. As I landed, the cheers of my teammates erupted around me, the rush of victory filling my lungs like sweet nectar.

"Not bad for a wannabe chef," Ryan quipped, a genuine smile breaking through his usual bravado. "But let's see if you can keep that up."

We continued to push each other, a furious exchange of energy that culminated in a final, triumphant play. I could hardly believe it when the whistle blew, signaling the end of practice, and with it, the end of our competition. The exhilaration surged through me, but as I glanced at Ryan, a thought flickered—was this the moment I would finally confront my truth?

The echo of laughter and shouts faded as I stood facing him, heart hammering in my chest. The realization that the wager loomed over us like a cloud began to settle in. I could no longer hide. The walls I had built around my dreams felt more like a prison than a refuge, and I needed to break free.

"Ryan," I started, but he cut me off, his expression shifting from playful to serious.

"Let's grab that meal soon. I owe you," he said, his voice softening, revealing a glimpse of something deeper. "And maybe I'll even wear that chef's hat if you promise it'll be worth it."

"Sure," I managed, though the weight of my secret hung heavy in the air between us. I wondered if he could sense the storm swirling inside me, a tempest of fear and excitement as I contemplated revealing who I truly was. The moment hung between us, thick with anticipation, yet I could feel the very ground shifting beneath my feet.

As we walked off the field, I felt the strange mix of anticipation and dread, knowing the truth would surface soon. The rivalry had morphed into something far more complicated, and I was ready to embrace the chaos that came with it.

The days blurred into one another, each marked by the familiar cadence of practice and the weight of unspoken truths. Autumn's chill crept in like an unwelcome guest, wrapping around the edges of my resolve. Each evening, after leaving the field, I found myself caught in a loop of reflection, pondering the boundaries of my identity. The conversation with Ryan lingered, twisting and turning in my mind, and as the sun dipped behind the horizon, it illuminated my uncertainty in shades of dusky orange and deep purple.

One Thursday evening, the air crackled with energy, thick with the promise of a storm. The sky hung low, dark clouds swirling ominously, a mirror to my tumultuous thoughts. I watched as the team gathered for practice, the camaraderie palpable but tinged with an undercurrent of competition. Ryan stood at the center, his confident demeanor an unshakeable force. The very sight of him made my stomach twist, a mixture of admiration and frustration swirling together in a potent cocktail of feelings I couldn't quite untangle.

"Ready for the big dinner?" he asked as I approached, his eyes glinting mischievously, the weight of our bet hanging heavily in the air.

"More like ready to see you wear that ridiculous hat," I shot back, the sharpness in my tone a weak shield against my rising anxiety. "What kind of chef do you want to be? The 'invisible' kind?"

"Oh, come on," he chuckled, shaking his head, that casual charm of his disarming my tension. "Just admit it. You're a little excited for me to be in the kitchen."

"Excited is a stretch," I retorted, trying to maintain my bravado while imagining him stumbling through my recipes. "Let's just say it'll be an experience. I hope you can handle the heat."

He laughed, the sound rolling over me like summer rain. "I'm not scared of a little heat. Bring it on!"

But as practice commenced, I couldn't shake the sense that this was merely the calm before a storm. The drills felt more intense, our movements sharp and aggressive, and I couldn't help but glance at Ryan, whose competitive edge seemed more pronounced. He was relentless, pushing everyone, including me, to their limits. I could feel the weight of his gaze, a reminder that he was watching, waiting, and perhaps strategizing for the moment when he would lay my secret bare.

As the practice dragged on, my focus wavered. With each tackle, my mind drifted to the prospect of revealing my passion for cooking. Would it be a simple acknowledgment of my identity or an unveiling of everything I had kept hidden? The thought churned in my stomach like a poorly executed soufflé. I had prepared myself for this moment—had even practiced how I would articulate my truth—but every time I opened my mouth, the words fell short, swallowed by fear and doubt.

"Hey!" Ryan's voice cut through my thoughts, startling me back to reality. "You good? Or are you too busy dreaming of the kitchen?"

I shot him a look, half annoyed and half amused. "Not everyone dreams of meatloaf and macaroni, you know."

"Seems like a solid dream to me," he quipped, his smirk teasing the corners of my mouth. "But I guess we can't all be so easily impressed by culinary masterpieces."

With the evening practice coming to a close, we gathered for the final huddle. The air buzzed with anticipation, the team reveling in the energy of our combined efforts. As the captain started to rally us for the next game, my heart raced. This was the moment. The wager loomed, and I could no longer hide behind my uncertainty.

"Ryan!" I blurted out, cutting through the chatter, my voice stronger than I felt. "I think we should do our dinner soon. I mean, we made a bet, right?"

His eyes narrowed slightly, interest piqued. "What are you saying? You want to lose to me sooner rather than later?"

I rolled my eyes, the playful banter flowing easily between us, but my heart was pounding. "No, I just mean, I'm ready. Let's do this."

The team erupted in laughter, their playful nudges and teasing shouts filling the air, but the underlying tension between us remained. Ryan studied me for a moment, as if weighing the gravity of my words, and then he grinned, an unexpected warmth softening his features. "Okay, I'm game. How about tomorrow night?"

"Fine. Just be prepared," I replied, matching his grin but feeling the weight of the impending conversation settle around my shoulders.

As the sun set, casting long shadows across the field, I couldn't shake the growing anxiety that bubbled beneath my calm exterior. Tomorrow would be the reckoning, the moment of truth where I would have to face the fears that had haunted me for so long.

The next evening arrived with an electric anticipation. The kitchen was my sanctuary, filled with the scents of simmering spices and the gentle clinking of utensils. It was a world where I felt confident, and yet, a gnawing apprehension bubbled within me as I prepared for Ryan's arrival. I chose a simple yet delicious menu: lemon herb chicken, roasted vegetables, and a decadent chocolate mousse for dessert.

When the doorbell rang, I took a deep breath, wiping my hands on the apron I wore like armor. I swung the door open to find Ryan standing there, a chef's hat perched comically atop his head and a bottle of wine clutched in one hand.

"Ready for the real challenge?" he declared, his grin infectious, and for a moment, the tension ebbed away, replaced by laughter as I gestured for him to come in.

"Don't get too cocky," I warned, gesturing for him to set the wine down on the counter. "You might be in over your head."

"Please, I'm not afraid of a little cooking." He shrugged off my sarcasm, looking around with curiosity. "This is nice. Cozy."

"Thanks. It's where I feel most like myself." I paused, the admission slipping from my lips before I could stop it. "I've put a lot of time into it."

"Then let's make a masterpiece," he said, stepping closer, the playful banter falling away. The air thickened as we moved together through the kitchen, navigating the recipes, our laughter punctuating the silence.

As we chopped, sautéed, and stirred, I could feel the walls beginning to crumble, but as the conversation deepened, so did the tension. I caught myself hesitating, the words choking me. Here, in this vibrant sanctuary, was the perfect opportunity to share my truth, yet my heart raced with the thought of exposing myself to judgment.

"What about you? What's your hidden talent?" Ryan asked, his hands busy kneading dough, completely unaware of the storm brewing inside me. "Besides football, of course."

I swallowed hard, fighting the impulse to retreat into safer topics. "Well, if you must know, I've always had a thing for cooking," I admitted, my voice barely above a whisper. "It's where I feel... alive."

Ryan paused, his hands stilling for just a moment, surprise flickering across his face. "You cook? Like, really cook? Why didn't you tell me?"

"I guess I didn't want it to change how you see me," I replied, the words spilling out like confetti. "You know, 'just a football player' or something. I thought if I told you, you'd think I was just... different."

He stepped closer, a playful seriousness in his eyes. "Different how? Are you saying you're not just a football player?"

I laughed, but it was a nervous sound. "Yes! No! I mean, I'm more than just a football player. But it feels like I'm supposed to fit into this mold, and the thought of being anything else is terrifying."

Ryan's expression softened, and the laughter faded from his eyes. "You don't have to be what everyone expects. You're allowed to be yourself, and if they can't handle it, that's on them."

Just as the warmth of his words began to ease the tension coiling inside me, the doorbell rang again, jarring me from the moment. I exchanged a glance with Ryan, uncertainty flooding my mind. "I'll get it," I said, moving towards the door with a sense of foreboding.

But when I opened it, the sight that greeted me sent a chill racing down my spine. Standing there was Kayla, her face pale and frantic. "You need to come with me, now," she said, urgency threading through her voice.

"What? Why?" I stammered, glancing back at Ryan, who was now watching with concern etched on his features.

"It's about your secret," Kayla insisted, her eyes wide with panic. "It's worse than I thought. You need to see this."

As the reality of her words crashed over me, I felt the ground shift beneath my feet, my heart racing as the implications settled like heavy stones in my gut. The dinner, the truth I had been so ready to share, slipped away as uncertainty and fear gripped me in a vice. I glanced back at Ryan, who stood frozen, the warmth of our connection extinguished, and suddenly, the question lingered like a dark cloud: Would I ever be able to be my true self, or was the past about to swallow me whole?

# Chapter 5: Shadows of Doubt

The gym buzzed with electricity, the kind that made your heart pound against your ribcage like a wild animal desperate to escape. Bright lights blazed down on the polished hardwood floor, illuminating the sweat-slicked bodies of my teammates as we prepared to face off against the Westfield Hawks, our fiercest rivals. The air was thick with the smell of liniment and popcorn, the crowd outside howling like a tempest ready to crash through the doors. My heart, however, thrummed to a different beat. It was not the excitement of competition that had my pulse racing but an unsettling tide of anxiety that coursed through me, washing away any thrill I might have felt.

Just moments before, I had opened my locker to find a folded slip of paper tucked inside, its edges crumpled as if it had been tossed aside in haste. With a sinking feeling, I unfurled it, bracing myself for the blow. There it was, a cruel collage of images—an unflattering photo of me in a floral apron, an ill-timed snapshot of a charred casserole I'd mistakenly baked for my mother's birthday, and a meme that boldly declared my taste in fashion as "tragically lost." Laughter bubbled up around me from the nearby lockers, bright and mocking. The bright chatter of my teammates felt distant, and I could only focus on the way the slip of paper felt like a cold, clammy hand squeezing around my throat.

"Hey, Ash!" Kayla's voice broke through the fog of humiliation. She strolled over, her confidence practically radiating off her in waves, oblivious to my moment of crisis. "Are you ready for tonight? The Hawks won't know what hit them!"

I forced a smile, one that felt more like a grimace. "Yeah, totally ready," I replied, though my mind was still swirling with the implications of that stupid note. I could see the determination in Kayla's eyes, a fiery ambition that often made me feel as though

I was dragging my feet through mud. She was everything I admired—brave, unapologetically herself, and fiercely competitive. As she continued to prattle on about plays and strategies, I couldn't help but wonder if I would ever measure up.

"Are you okay?" She tilted her head, her expression shifting from excitement to concern as she caught my pained expression. "You look like you've just seen a ghost."

"I'm fine," I lied, tucking the slip back into my locker as if doing so would make it disappear entirely. "Just thinking about the game."

"Thinking about the game or thinking about some dumb note?" Kayla challenged, a knowing smirk playing on her lips.

A wave of heat flooded my cheeks. "How did you—"

"Please, Ash. You wear your heart on your sleeve." She leaned against the locker next to mine, her arms crossed, daring me to open up. "You know it doesn't matter what anyone else thinks, right? You're a damn good player. And who cares about burnt casseroles? I once made a meatloaf that looked like a crime scene. And you should see my attempt at a dress for the Winter Dance."

The tension in my shoulders eased a fraction. Her earnestness was like a balm, and I felt the urge to spill everything, to lay bare the worries and insecurities that twisted my stomach into knots. But then, the doubt crept back, a cold whisper in the back of my mind. What if she didn't understand?

"I just..." My voice faltered, and I looked down, examining the fraying threads of my shoelaces as if they held the answers I desperately sought. "I guess I want to be more like you. More confident. Less afraid."

"Why on earth would you want to be like me?" she replied, laughter dancing in her eyes. "I mean, have you seen my hair today? I look like I lost a fight with a tornado."

"Still, you pull it off," I admitted, unable to stifle a chuckle. "I just wish I didn't feel so... exposed sometimes."

Before she could respond, the gym doors swung open, and the raucous crowd burst into the space, like a wave crashing onto the shore. The noise enveloped us, an all-consuming roar that filled every corner. I could feel the energy shift, excitement radiating through the room as our coach rallied the team. Kayla flashed me a wink before heading to the court, her confidence infectious, yet I lingered for a moment longer, my thoughts tangled in the threads of my self-doubt.

The game started, and I fell into the rhythm of the court, the cacophony of cheers blending with the pounding of my heart. Each pass, each shot, was a dance, the adrenaline pushing me forward. But even amidst the chaos, I felt that slip of paper weighing heavily in my pocket, a constant reminder of the shadows that loomed at the edges of my joy.

As the first quarter ticked away, I found myself in a flow, the ball feeling almost like an extension of my own body. Yet, with every triumph—each point we scored—I was painfully aware of the lurking shadows of doubt and ridicule. With every cheer that erupted from the stands, I could almost hear the mocking laughter from that slip, weaving through the cheers like a ghostly thread.

"Get it together, Ash!" I chided myself as I sank a three-pointer, the net swishing triumphantly. But the sense of victory was fleeting, fading like the echoes of laughter I wished would vanish into thin air. The game surged on, each moment a battle against not just the Hawks but against the relentless tide of my insecurities. The weight of expectations hung like a shroud, and I couldn't shake the feeling that all eyes were on me, judging, dissecting every move.

The fourth quarter loomed closer, tension mounting as we held a precarious lead. I felt my mind unraveling, spiraling back to that slip of paper, to the faces of my teammates—would they still cheer for me if they knew? Would they see me as less than worthy if they caught a glimpse of the awkward, fumbling parts of me I worked so hard to hide? The questions raced through my mind like wildfire, threatening to consume me whole.

In that moment, I caught Kayla's eye across the court. She flashed me a grin, a knowing, steadying force amidst the chaos. For a fleeting second, I allowed myself to believe that maybe, just maybe, I was more than the sum of my fears. Perhaps I could be strong enough to face not just the Hawks but the shadows that lurked in the corners of my mind.

With a deep breath, I steeled myself for the next play, the fear and doubt giving way to something resembling hope.

The final buzzer blared like a siren, echoing through the gym and snapping me back to reality. We'd won—a hard-fought victory against the Hawks that left the crowd roaring with exuberance. But as the cheers washed over me, they felt hollow, an echo of the laughter that had haunted me all night. I stumbled off the court, my legs heavy, adrenaline crashing against the walls of my chest as I fought to catch my breath.

"Did you see that three-pointer?" Kayla shouted, her eyes sparkling with exhilaration. "You were on fire, Ash!"

"Yeah, I guess," I replied, forcing a smile that didn't quite reach my eyes. I wanted to be swept up in the post-game euphoria, to bask in the glory of our victory. Instead, I felt a storm brewing just beneath the surface, a swirl of insecurities and self-doubt that I couldn't quite shake off.

We ambled toward the locker room, the atmosphere thick with celebration. Teammates slapped high-fives and exchanged playful jabs, their laughter cascading around us. But with every chuckle, I felt myself drifting further away, an outsider in my own moment of triumph. I hurriedly shoved my gear into my bag, the slip of paper still tucked away, a persistent reminder of everything I wished to leave behind.

"Hey," Kayla said, her voice low and steady as she approached me. "You okay? You seem a little... distant."

I waved a hand, brushing her concern aside. "Just tired, I guess. Big game and all that."

"Sure, but you don't have to pretend with me," she replied, her brow furrowing with genuine worry. "You know I'm here for you, right? You're one of us."

The sincerity in her voice struck a chord, pulling me back into the moment. I turned to face her fully, taking a deep breath, trying to gather the scattered fragments of my thoughts. "I appreciate that, really. I just... It's hard sometimes, you know? Feeling like I have to be someone I'm not."

Her expression softened, and for a moment, I could see the echoes of my own struggles reflected in her eyes. "You're not alone in that. Everyone's trying to fit into this box that society made, and it's suffocating. Just be you, Ash. That's enough."

Her words wrapped around me like a warm blanket, comforting yet heavy with the weight of their truth. I wanted to believe her, wanted to cast off the insecurities that threatened to suffocate me. But as we made our way to the locker room, the tension in my chest grew tighter, coiling like a spring ready to snap.

Once inside, I flung open my locker and fished out the slip of paper, determined to confront the mockery that had taunted me through the game. "Look, Kayla," I said, holding it out for her to see. "This is what I'm talking about. It feels like I'm constantly being judged, and I can't shake it."

Her eyes widened as she scanned the contents. "This is ridiculous. Who even did this? It's just mean."

"I have no idea," I replied, feeling a mix of anger and embarrassment swell within me. "But it doesn't matter. It just... it makes me feel like I'll never fit in. Like I'm just a joke."

"Listen," Kayla said firmly, stepping closer. "People can be cruel, especially when they're insecure themselves. But you can't let this nonsense define you. You're not just a basketball player; you're so much more than that. And anyone who can't see that doesn't deserve your energy."

A flicker of hope ignited within me, though the shadows of doubt still loomed large. "How do I stop caring, though? I wish I could just shake it off like you do."

Kayla chuckled lightly, tilting her head. "Oh, please, I don't shake anything off! I have my moments, too, where I feel like I'm under a microscope. It's just that I've learned to channel it into something productive. When I feel small, I make myself big."

"Make myself big?" I echoed, tilting my head in confusion.

"Yeah! It's like when I want to crawl under a rock, I instead put on my brightest lipstick and strut out like I own the place," she said, her voice buoyant. "You should try it! Confidence is the best accessory."

"I don't think the world is ready for me to strut," I joked, an uncertain smile breaking through.

"Hey, it's about time we change that!" She grinned back, and for a moment, I felt a flicker of that vibrant energy I had during the game. The weight of my insecurities lifted slightly, if only for a heartbeat.

As we left the locker room, the atmosphere shifted, the post-game buzz intertwining with my own swirling emotions. The crowd had started to disperse, but lingering whispers of victory floated around us like confetti. I felt buoyed by Kayla's unwavering support, yet beneath it all lurked that persistent shadow, reminding me of the slip of paper and the judgments it represented.

"Let's go celebrate!" Kayla suggested, her voice bubbling with enthusiasm. "How about some ice cream? You know, sweet treats for sweet victories!"

"Are you suggesting that calories don't count when you win?" I laughed, already warming to the idea.

"Exactly! Winning means indulging. It's practically a rule," she declared with an exaggerated flourish, and I couldn't help but join in her laughter.

As we stepped into the cool night air, the stars twinkled above us, like a million tiny affirmations glittering in the darkness. But even as Kayla and I made our way to the ice cream parlor, a nagging feeling curled in my gut, refusing to let go.

"Hey, Ash," Kayla said, breaking the comfortable silence as we walked. "I know this might sound odd, but do you ever feel like there's something more out there for you? Something you haven't yet explored?"

The question hung between us, heavy with possibilities. I opened my mouth to respond, but found my thoughts racing. What was I searching for? A feeling of belonging, perhaps, or maybe an identity that felt like home.

"Sometimes," I finally admitted, glancing sideways at her. "But I don't know what that 'more' is."

"I think that's part of the adventure," she replied, her gaze focused ahead, as if envisioning the unknown. "Sometimes you have to dive into the chaos, embrace the uncertainty. You might just discover parts of yourself you never knew existed."

I contemplated her words, each one a pebble dropping into the pond of my thoughts, rippling outward. The more I thought about it, the more appealing the idea became. Perhaps I could embrace the chaos, confront those lurking shadows instead of hiding from them.

As we entered the brightly lit ice cream shop, the sweet scent of waffle cones and freshly made sundaes enveloped us, momentarily distracting me from my worries. I was ready to choose my flavor, to indulge in something that felt deliciously indulgent. But even with the jovial atmosphere around us, I couldn't shake the feeling that my journey was only just beginning. The slip of paper still nestled in my pocket felt like an uninvited guest, but maybe it was time to turn the tables.

With a renewed sense of purpose, I stepped to the counter, determined to savor this moment and perhaps, in the chaos of ice cream and laughter, find a glimpse of the "more" that awaited me.

The ice cream shop buzzed with the comforting chaos of laughter and chatter, the air thick with the sweet, heady aroma of freshly baked waffle cones. As I approached the counter, the sight of dozens of vibrant flavors lined up like jewels in a treasure chest momentarily distracted me from the weight of my worries. Kayla hopped in place beside me, her excitement palpable as she pointed to the "create your own sundae" sign with childlike glee.

"Look at this! Chocolate fudge, sprinkles, whipped cream... it's practically begging to be turned into a masterpiece!" She flashed me her best sales pitch smile, and I couldn't help but chuckle.

"Are we really going to call it a masterpiece if it's just a mound of sugar?" I teased, feeling lighter than I had just moments ago.

"Absolutely! It's a culinary creation worthy of Michelin stars," she declared, dramatically sweeping her arm toward the array of toppings as if unveiling an art exhibit. I felt my laughter bubble up, a welcome relief against the backdrop of my earlier tension.

After we ordered—Kayla's towering sundae of fudge, whipped cream, and every imaginable topping, while I opted for a more modest scoop of cookies and cream—we snagged a booth by the window. The night outside was alive with the glow of streetlights and the murmur of passing cars, a comforting backdrop to our delightful sugar binge.

"So, tell me," Kayla said, settling in with her sundae, which now looked like a precarious mountain of sugar that could collapse at any moment, "what's next for you? Besides basking in the glory of your athletic prowess, of course."

I took a tentative bite of my ice cream, savoring the creamy texture. "Honestly? I don't know. Part of me is ready to dive into something new, but the other half is scared to death. What if I fall flat on my face?"

"Wouldn't be the first time, right?" she quipped, her eyes dancing with mischief. "You should see me trying to bake! I once attempted a soufflé that could have doubled as a doorstop."

Her laughter was infectious, easing the remnants of my anxiety. "Okay, fair point. But what if this time it's different? What if I take that leap and end up in a free fall?"

"Then you get up, dust yourself off, and try again," she replied, leaning forward earnestly, her sundae wobbling dangerously. "But you know what? I have a feeling you won't fall. You've got this inner strength that you don't even see. It's time to let it shine."

I pondered her words, a flicker of hope igniting in the depths of my uncertainty. "I guess it wouldn't hurt to try. Maybe I'll sign up for that cooking class I've been eyeing. Who knows? I might discover a hidden talent for soufflés."

"Now you're talking! A cooking class sounds like a perfect idea. Just think of all the delicious disasters you could create."

"Delicious disasters—now that's a title I could own." I couldn't help but laugh at the thought of my culinary escapades, both thrilling and mortifying. "But seriously, I think I need to put myself out there, even if it terrifies me."

Kayla leaned back, arms crossed, a satisfied smirk on her face. "That's the spirit! The world needs more Ashes, even if they come with a side of burnt casseroles."

Just then, the shop door swung open, and a gust of cool air swept through, causing a few papers on the counter to flutter like startled birds. My heart sank when I recognized the silhouette stepping in. It was Jenna, the girl who had gleefully mocked me with that slip of paper. I quickly turned my face away, hoping she wouldn't notice me.

"Look who it is! The queen of the court!" Jenna called, her voice dripping with sarcasm as she approached with a gaggle of her friends in tow. My stomach knotted, and I could feel my cheeks flush. "How's it feel to be the star of the show? Oh wait, wasn't that just a game of pretend?"

"Can you take a hint?" Kayla shot back, her tone as icy as the scoop of ice cream in front of her. "Why don't you go back to your little realm of negativity?"

"Charming as always, Kayla. Just remember, everyone's watching." Jenna tossed her hair over her shoulder, as if she were draping a cape, and I felt the weight of her words settle over me like a thick fog. "And we all know Ash here has a reputation for being... well, let's say, less than graceful."

The other girls giggled, and I could feel my heart racing, panic clawing at my insides. I wanted to curl up into a ball and disappear, to vanish into the background where I wouldn't have to face the scorn. But instead, Kayla stood up, her hands on her hips, unfazed.

"You're pathetic, Jenna," Kayla shot back, her voice steady. "It's no wonder you need a crowd to feel good about yourself. Look at us—we're celebrating a victory. Why don't you join us instead of sulking in your own misery?"

"I think I'd rather pass. I can smell the desperation from here," Jenna retorted, her smirk faltering slightly at Kayla's boldness.

My heart raced in my chest, torn between the urge to sink into my ice cream and the desire to stand up for myself. But before I could gather my thoughts, Kayla pressed on. "You know what? You're right, Jenna. You're right to say that everyone is watching. Why don't you take a good look in the mirror? You might discover that the real joke is on you."

The words hung in the air, a tense standoff between two opposing forces. I could feel the weight of the moment pressing down on me, and a flicker of admiration for Kayla washed over me.

She was fierce and unapologetic, traits I desperately wished I could emulate.

"Let's go, girls," Jenna said, her tone clipped as she waved her hand dismissively. "This ice cream shop is clearly in need of a palate cleanser after whatever this is."

As Jenna and her entourage strutted away, I felt a wave of relief crash over me, mixed with a tinge of exhilaration. "Wow," I breathed, staring at Kayla in disbelief. "That was... amazing."

"Just doing my part to stand up for my friends," she said nonchalantly, but I could see the spark of triumph in her eyes. "Besides, you shouldn't let someone like her define your worth. You're better than that."

"Maybe I am," I murmured, my confidence slowly building. For the first time, I felt a flicker of resilience igniting within me.

"Now, let's celebrate!" Kayla said, shoveling a massive spoonful of sundae into her mouth, and I couldn't help but laugh.

We spent the next few minutes indulging in our ice creams, the moment of tension fading into sweet, creamy bliss. I savored each bite, the flavors dancing on my tongue and drowning out the whispers of doubt still lurking at the edges of my mind.

"Hey, Ash," Kayla said, wiping a smear of whipped cream from her cheek, her expression growing serious. "Promise me you'll think about that cooking class. I can't wait to see what you create."

"I promise," I said, a smile breaking across my face. "I'll give it a shot."

As we wrapped up our ice cream adventure, the bright shop lights flickered, momentarily plunging us into semi-darkness before they blared back to life. The moment sent a ripple of unease through me, a feeling I couldn't quite shake off.

"Everything okay?" Kayla asked, sensing my shift in mood.

"Yeah, just... a weird feeling," I said, glancing toward the door. It opened again, and a cold draft swept through, carrying with it the faintest sound of laughter.

"Maybe it's just the ice cream talking," Kayla teased. "Or maybe you're finally embracing your inner culinary genius."

As we stepped outside, the night air was crisp and cool, and the stars glittered overhead. But as we walked down the street, I couldn't shake that sense of unease, that something was brewing just beneath the surface. The laughter echoed again, taunting me, mingling with whispers that felt all too familiar.

"Okay, so what's next?" Kayla asked, her eyes sparkling with excitement.

"Maybe we should head to the park? It's nice out," I suggested, hoping to shake off the creeping feeling.

As we turned the corner, I glanced back one last time at the ice cream shop. And there, standing just outside, was Jenna, her gaze fixed on us with a smirk that sent chills down my spine.

In that moment, the laughter faded, leaving an unsettling silence in its wake. The feeling in my gut twisted, and I could sense that this was far from over. With every step we took, the shadows seemed to stretch and lengthen behind us, whispering secrets I wasn't ready to confront.

I felt the weight of her stare on my back, a shadow that lingered long after we left, as though the game had just begun.

# Chapter 6: Confessions

The café exuded a gentle warmth, the kind that wrapped around me like a favorite blanket, coaxing out the secrets I usually tucked away under layers of bravado. The air was rich with the scent of freshly ground coffee, mingled with hints of vanilla and caramel wafting from the pastries nestled behind the glass display. Outside, the world thrummed with energy, but here, nestled in our dimly lit corner, it felt as though time stood still. The chatter of other patrons blurred into a comforting hum, allowing me to focus solely on the depths of my emotions spilling forth in a way I had never anticipated.

Kayla sat across from me, her presence a beacon of calm amidst my stormy thoughts. Her hair fell in soft waves, framing her face with an effortless elegance that seemed to mock my carefully curated exterior. With every sip of her steaming chai latte, I found myself captivated not only by the way she savored the moment but also by the steady gaze of her green eyes. They were alive with understanding and a hint of mischief, urging me to dig deeper into the murky waters of my vulnerability.

"I don't know what I'm so afraid of," I confessed, the words tasting foreign on my tongue. "It's like standing on the edge of a cliff, looking down into a vast unknown. What if I fall? What if I don't land gracefully?" The rush of anxiety that had settled in my chest felt as heavy as a stone, threatening to drag me under.

Kayla leaned forward, her fingers curling around her cup, the steam rising between us like an invisible thread of connection. "Falling is part of life. You might stumble, sure, but there's also the possibility of soaring," she replied, her voice smooth as silk, each word woven with a sincerity that pierced through my doubts. "Have you thought about what soaring could look like for you?"

In that moment, I felt the weight of her encouragement, urging me to take the leap. But my heart still echoed with the fear of being seen, of my secrets spilling into the world like ink from a burst pen. "What if they find out about my designs? About my dreams?" I said, barely above a whisper, the thought of being outed as a budding fashion designer curling around my mind like a vine, strangling my confidence.

Kayla raised an eyebrow, the hint of a smile playing on her lips. "What's wrong with wanting to create beautiful things? Fashion is art, and art is meant to be shared, not hidden away like some guilty pleasure. Besides," she added, leaning back with an air of playful defiance, "you're too fabulous to be stuck in the shadows. What's the point of having dreams if you don't let the world see them?"

Her words ignited a spark within me, though it was quickly tempered by the embers of anxiety that still smoldered. I had spent so many nights holed up in my room, sketching designs under the dim light of a desk lamp, pouring my heart into fabric swatches and color palettes that only ever saw the inside of my drawer. What if I dared to let someone in? What if I dared to show the world?

"What about you, Kayla?" I ventured, eager to shift the focus. "What dreams do you keep tucked away?" My gaze fell on her, searching for signs of her own hidden desires. She was a kaleidoscope of contradictions—both the life of the party and a quiet observer. There was a depth to her I yearned to understand.

Kayla chuckled softly, her laughter a melody that danced in the air between us. "Me? I don't hide much. I'm more of a 'take it or leave it' kind of girl," she replied with a smirk, but her eyes flickered with something deeper. "But I suppose I do keep my love for photography on the down-low. It's hard to find the time between classes and work, but capturing moments through a lens? That's where I feel most alive."

The way she spoke about photography ignited a light within her, a passion that shimmered in her eyes. I imagined her behind a camera, capturing fleeting moments—the joy in a child's laughter, the serenity of dawn breaking over a sleepy town, the raw emotion of life unfolding. It was a beautiful revelation that added another layer to her vibrant personality.

"Why don't you share it?" I prodded, feeling the excitement bubbling between us. "Let people see your work! You could have an exhibit, or even just post your photos online." I was suddenly filled with the fervor of my own dreams, urging her to step out of her comfort zone just as I was trying to do.

Her expression shifted slightly, a flicker of uncertainty clouding her features. "I don't know. What if they don't see the beauty in it? What if I'm not as good as I think?" The vulnerability in her voice struck a chord within me, echoing my own fears about my designs.

"Then they're fools," I replied, the words spilling forth with more conviction than I felt. "But what matters is that you see the beauty in it. You create for yourself first, and if others connect with it, that's just icing on the cake." The metaphor rolled off my tongue, and I couldn't help but chuckle at the absurdity of it all. "And trust me, if you're as good as you say, then you'll have people lining up to see what you create."

Her smile returned, brighter this time, like the sun peeking through clouds. "You really think so?" The hope in her eyes was intoxicating, stirring something deep within me, a reminder that perhaps we were both just two souls navigating the murky waters of our aspirations.

"Absolutely," I said, feeling a rush of determination. "We owe it to ourselves to chase after what sets our souls on fire, don't you think?" The words hung in the air, a promise not just to her but to myself. In that moment, the fear of being outed faded, replaced by a shared courage. If I could help Kayla embrace her dreams, perhaps I could do the same for myself.

As I watched Kayla's eyes shimmer with the shared thrill of vulnerability, I felt something shift between us. The café, once a backdrop to my swirling anxieties, now transformed into a cocoon, wrapping us in a shared understanding. The moment hung heavy with unspoken possibilities, each heartbeat amplifying the connection that crackled like static electricity in the air.

"So, what's the first design you'll showcase to the world?" Kayla asked, leaning forward, her elbows resting on the table. The eagerness in her voice made my heart leap, as if I'd just been handed a spotlight on a grand stage.

I chuckled, suddenly filled with a rush of ideas. "Well, I've been toying with this concept of a dress that changes color with the mood of the wearer. Think of it as a mood ring, but fabulous!" I waved my hands animatedly, picturing the fabric shifting from a deep, sultry red to a cool, serene blue with the flick of a wrist. "Imagine walking into a room, and everyone's just... drawn to you. Like moths to a flame, but with far more glitter."

"Now that's an idea!" she exclaimed, her enthusiasm infectious. "You could even add a little sparkle—like tiny lights embedded in the fabric. That way, if you're feeling especially fabulous, you could just glow. Maybe even flash a little for emphasis!"

I laughed, the vision of a dance floor illuminated by my color-shifting creation igniting my imagination. "Oh, just imagine! I'd be like a disco ball on legs!"

"Exactly! You'd be the star of the party." Kayla's laughter rang out, light and airy, drawing the attention of a couple at the next table who shot us bemused glances. I took a deep breath, feeling the tension of the earlier conversation ease slightly. The weight of my fears still lingered, but in this moment, my dreams sparkled just a bit brighter.

"So, you think I should really go for it?" I asked, my tone shifting slightly serious. "What if it flops? What if no one gets it?"

Kayla tilted her head, her gaze steady and reassuring. "You can't let fear dictate your path. If you believe in your designs, that passion will resonate with others. And even if one dress doesn't land, it's just one step on a much bigger journey. Besides, what if it's a hit? You could be starting a whole new trend!"

I met her eyes, her unwavering confidence offering me a lifeline I desperately needed. "You make it sound so easy." I let out a wistful sigh, the weight of reality pressing down. "But what if it costs me my future? My parents expect me to pursue a career in something 'stable'—like finance or law. They wouldn't understand this... this dream."

The brief flicker of hurt crossed Kayla's face before she quickly masked it with determination. "You know, I once had a friend who pursued law only to become a florist. Turns out, her passion for flowers outweighed the pressure of expectations. She's never been happier."

"Isn't that a bit cliché?" I teased, trying to lighten the mood, but her expression held steady.

"Clichés exist because they're often true." Her voice softened, and I could see the resolve in her eyes. "You deserve to chase what lights you up. Your happiness is the priority, not what others think you should do."

As I mulled over her words, the barista wandered over, sliding a couple of warm pastries onto our table. "On the house, for the inspiration," he said with a wink, his curly hair bouncing as he walked away.

I raised an eyebrow, half amused and half intrigued. "Inspiration, huh? I should keep you around more often," I said, nudging Kayla with my elbow.

"Just wait until I bring my photography. Free food and art? I might just start a revolution," she quipped back, her laughter mixing with the soft clinking of cutlery around us.

In that fleeting moment, the café transformed into our little universe—a space where dreams felt tangible, even if just for a heartbeat. But the weight of reality still loomed over me, reminding me that the risk of being outed felt like a thundercloud on the horizon, threatening to cast a shadow over my newfound optimism.

"I want to create something beautiful," I finally admitted, my voice barely above a whisper. "But what if my truth gets tangled up in all this? What if people can't separate my designs from who I really am?"

Kayla's expression softened, a knowing look passing between us that felt almost intimate. "That's the thing, though. Your truth is a part of your designs. It's what makes them authentic. If you hide who you are, you'll never be able to fully embrace your art."

I shook my head, the enormity of her words washing over me. "That's a lot to put on one little dress."

"It's not just a dress," she replied, her tone gentle yet firm. "It's a declaration of who you are. And trust me, it's a lot better than hiding in the shadows, wishing you had taken the leap."

Her words sank in like stones thrown into still water, sending ripples of hope mingling with my fears. I thought of all those nights sketching, pouring my heart into every line, every swirl of fabric. Those designs were an extension of me, an unfiltered glimpse into my soul.

"What if I were to take that leap?" I pondered aloud, excitement mingling with trepidation. "What if I dared to show the world who I am?"

Kayla leaned back, her eyes sparkling with encouragement. "Then you'd be a step closer to becoming who you're meant to be. And hey, I'll be right there, cheering you on—maybe even helping with a few photos for your portfolio."

I chuckled, the warmth of her support wrapping around me like a soft embrace. "You'd better bring your A-game, then. I have high expectations for my photographer."

"Only the best for you, my fabulous friend."

As laughter spilled from our lips, I felt the weight of my fears begin to lift, replaced by the intoxicating promise of possibility. With Kayla by my side, I dared to imagine a future where I could not only design beautiful things but also live authentically. The café around us buzzed with life, but in our little corner, a quiet revolution was brewing—one filled with dreams, laughter, and the courage to embrace who we truly were.

The moment felt charged, alive with unspoken possibilities. As laughter danced between us, the café transformed into our private haven, where we could dream freely, unshackled by the weight of the world. My heart raced at the thought of unveiling my true self, of stepping into a realm where my designs could not only exist but flourish. Yet, beneath the surface, the anxiety still simmered, a reminder that this was merely the beginning.

"What about your next steps?" Kayla asked, her tone light yet probing, as she adjusted her mug, the steam curling upward like wisps of my own burgeoning aspirations. "Have you thought about a launch or maybe showcasing your work at the upcoming student art fair?"

I took a sip of my coffee, the warmth spreading through me but failing to fully thaw the ice of uncertainty clinging to my thoughts. "The fair is coming up, and I could definitely showcase something, but what if no one likes it?" The fear slithered back, wrapping around my confidence like a cold fog.

Kayla's eyes narrowed in playful reproach. "You mean 'what if they're all dazzled by your brilliance and beg to wear your creations on the red carpet?'"

I snorted, unable to help the smile that broke across my face. "Oh sure, I can just see it now: 'Step aside, runway models; here comes the undiscovered genius, wearing a dress made from fabric that changes color when she blushes!'"

"Exactly!" she shot back, her laughter ringing out, effortlessly lighting up the dim corner of the café. "And if anyone dares to say anything negative, you'll just flick the switch and turn the fabric to a bright, fiery red. Instant revenge."

"Talk about a fashion statement!" I grinned, and for a moment, we were two dreamers, weaving a tapestry of laughter and ideas, one thread at a time.

But as the banter faded, reality crept back in, quiet and insistent. I leaned back, glancing around the café, suddenly feeling exposed. "You know, my mom has been asking me about my future plans again. She really wants me to consider an internship at some law firm over the summer."

Kayla's expression softened, a frown creasing her brow. "What do you want?"

The question hung in the air, heavy and foreboding. "I want to design," I replied finally, the truth tasting bittersweet. "But I also don't want to disappoint her. It's just—"

"Just what?" she pressed, leaning closer as if the intensity of her gaze could draw out my buried fears.

"It's just that I'm terrified," I admitted, my voice barely above a whisper. "What if I pursue this, and it all crumbles? What if I end up broke and living with my parents at thirty?" The thought made my stomach turn.

Kayla reached across the table, her fingers brushing against mine, grounding me. "So what? So what if you end up back home? It doesn't mean you're a failure. It means you took a chance. Besides, I'd probably be there too, eating your mom's cookies while you're working on your next big design."

Her lightheartedness cracked the heavy shell of my anxiety, but a flicker of doubt remained. "What if my parents can't see that? What if they can't accept that I want something different?"

"Then it's their loss," she said firmly, her voice steady like a well-crafted garment, structured and resolute. "But you have to show them who you are first. You have to let them see your passion, even if it scares them."

A silence settled between us, charged with unacknowledged truths. I let out a long breath, contemplating her words, the reality of what she was suggesting settling like a stone in my stomach. I had been keeping my designs hidden, a secret life folded neatly within the confines of my bedroom. What if I stepped out into the light, only to find the world unwelcoming?

"Hey," Kayla interrupted my spiraling thoughts, her voice suddenly soft. "Let's start small. What if we have a little showcase right here at the café? Invite some friends, some faculty members? Nothing big—just a few pieces, a little light, and a whole lot of fun. You could put on a mini runway show right here!"

"Are you serious?" I asked, my heart quickening at the prospect. "In a café? With just... us?"

"Why not? Think of it as a testing ground! We can set up a little area, get some chairs, maybe even use your sketches as decor. It'll be intimate and low pressure. Plus, we can bake some cupcakes!"

"Cupcakes will totally sell the concept," I teased, my spirits lifting.

"Of course! Who can resist a cupcake while watching fabulous designs?" she said, her eyes sparkling. "It'll be like a mix of high fashion and a bake sale. Who could say no?"

Her enthusiasm was infectious, and for the first time that day, my stomach flipped with excitement rather than dread. "Okay, let's do it. Let's host a little showcase. It might be the push I need."

"Yes!" she exclaimed, pumping her fist into the air like she had just won the championship of optimism. "I'll start designing the invitations! We can have everyone RSVP, and I'll even make a fabulous playlist."

The air felt lighter, filled with the kind of energy that ignited the spark of hope. But as the laughter bubbled back into the room, a sudden hush fell across the café, the clinking of cups and low chatter abruptly silenced.

I turned to see what had caused the stir, my stomach dropping as a tall figure stepped through the door. It was Julia, the captain of the soccer team and the embodiment of my worst fears, striding in with an air of confidence that seemed almost palpable. He caught sight of us and his eyes narrowed, a smirk forming on his lips as he approached.

"Fancy seeing you here, taking a break from... whatever it is you do," he said, his tone dripping with sarcasm, the gleam in his eyes suggesting he'd just found a new toy to poke at.

The laughter evaporated, replaced by a thick tension that hung in the air like a dark cloud. Kayla stiffened beside me, her previous excitement quickly fading. I could feel the walls of the café closing in, my heart racing with the realization that my fears had just walked through the door.

"What are you talking about, Julia?" I managed, my voice steady but my insides twisting.

His smirk widened as he leaned casually against the wall. "I just thought it was amusing to see you two together, plotting whatever little dreams you have. I mean, it's cute."

With that, the world felt like it tilted on its axis, the weight of his words crashing down around us. I glanced at Kayla, whose expression mirrored my own—uncertainty mixed with a glimmer of defiance. But as the tension thickened, I realized this was the moment of truth. Would I let fear dictate my response, or would I stand tall against the wave crashing over me?

"Just so you know, Julia, we're planning something that will blow you out of the water," I said, surprising even myself with the strength in my voice.

"Oh really? I'd love to see that," he replied, amusement dancing in his eyes.

The tension crackled between us, and as I prepared to fight back against his mockery, the air around us buzzed with potential, both terrifying and exhilarating. In that charged moment, everything felt possible—and everything felt like it was about to change.

# Chapter 7: The Turning Point

The night shimmered with promise as Kayla and I stepped into the gallery, the air thick with anticipation and the unmistakable scent of fresh fabric mingling with a hint of perfume. Soft lighting cascaded down from the ceiling, illuminating the myriad colors of textiles displayed like gems waiting to be uncovered. Each corner of the room burst with vibrancy, a riot of patterns and textures that seemed to dance under the glow, a vivid contrast to the monochrome existence I often found myself tethered to.

"Look at that!" Kayla exclaimed, tugging at my arm and pointing toward a dress that cascaded to the floor in waves of silk, the fabric swirling like liquid sunset. I turned my gaze, the excitement bubbling within her infectious. "Can you believe someone actually created that?"

I couldn't help but smile at her enthusiasm. "It's breathtaking," I admitted, though my heart thudded uneasily in my chest. Just a week ago, I wouldn't have dared to step foot in a place like this. My world had always revolved around the structured lines of a football field, the whistle piercing through the chatter of spectators, and the predictable cadence of the game. Now, here I was, surrounded by the pulse of creativity, feeling the thrill of potential weave its way through my veins.

As we navigated through the crowd, a soft murmur of conversation filled the air, punctuated by laughter and the occasional clink of glasses. The attendees, a mix of fashionistas and curious onlookers, floated around in their sleek outfits, each person a testament to their unique style. Kayla, dressed in a fitted black jumpsuit that hugged her curves perfectly, seemed to blend seamlessly into this new world. Meanwhile, I had opted for a casual ensemble—an oversized sweater and a pair of jeans—but somehow felt both out of place and entirely myself at the same time.

"Do you ever think about doing something like this?" Kayla asked as we paused in front of a display of bold, avant-garde pieces that seemed to defy gravity. "I mean, not necessarily designing, but just... embracing it?" Her eyes sparkled with mischief, and I knew she was hoping to pull me further into this realm of possibility.

"I don't know," I replied, my voice barely above a whisper as a part of me yearned to leap into the unknown. "I love fashion, but the fear of being exposed... It's overwhelming." I glanced away, a familiar shadow creeping in. Ryan's presence loomed in my mind like a storm cloud, threatening to rain on this newfound excitement. He was a constant reminder that the world I longed to explore could quickly turn into a battlefield of judgment and rejection.

Kayla tilted her head, studying me with a seriousness that surprised me. "You've spent so long being someone you're not. What's the worst that could happen if you just... let go for one night?" Her challenge hung in the air, and I could feel the weight of it, pressing down on my shoulders. Could I really allow myself to let go, if only for an evening?

"Okay, let's do it," I said suddenly, surprising even myself. "Let's find something that screams, 'This is who I am!'"

Kayla grinned, her excitement palpable. "Yes! Let's find your fashion spirit animal!" With that, we plunged deeper into the exhibit, diving into the sea of clothing racks and displays. Each piece told a story, the vibrant colors and intricate designs whispering of dreams and inspirations, and I felt the pulse of creativity resonate in my chest.

As we rummaged through the clothes, I could feel the skepticism fade. The audacious pieces beckoned me, urging me to shed my insecurities. I picked up a striking top, its intricate beadwork catching the light, and held it against me. "What do you think?" I asked, turning to Kayla.

Her eyes widened, and she clapped her hands together. "Oh my God, yes! You need that!"

With renewed energy, I moved through the racks, losing myself in the fabric, the texture, the stories woven into every seam. Kayla's laughter echoed around me as she tried on oversized hats, each more ridiculous than the last, while I slipped into a pair of high-waisted pants that hugged me in all the right places.

"Look at us!" I said, admiring our reflections in the long mirror. "Who knew we could do this?"

"Who knew you could do this?" she corrected playfully, tossing her hair back with a flourish. "You're shining, girl. Just remember, if Ryan shows up, we'll just pretend we're high-fashion spies on a mission."

The thought made me chuckle, and for a moment, the specter of Ryan faded into the background. But then, a chill swept through me as I remembered the threats that lay just outside this sanctuary of creativity. My phone buzzed in my pocket, a stark reminder of my reality.

"Let's get a drink," I said suddenly, needing a distraction from the unease that bubbled beneath the surface.

Kayla nodded eagerly, leading me to a small bar tucked away in a corner. We ordered two sparkling cocktails, the drinks adorned with colorful garnishes that practically screamed celebration. As we clinked our glasses together, I allowed myself to bask in the moment, the glimmer of hope flickering in my chest.

"Cheers to stepping out of our comfort zones!" Kayla declared, her eyes gleaming with mischief.

"Cheers," I echoed, the sound of the glasses ringing out like a bell of liberation.

As we sipped our drinks, the atmosphere enveloped us, and I could almost forget the darkness lurking outside. Yet, just as I began to feel truly free, I spotted him. Ryan, standing in the doorway, the very picture of arrogance wrapped in a tailored suit. His gaze swept over the crowd until it landed on me, and the air around us crackled with tension.

A rush of anxiety flooded my senses, a jolt that threatened to shatter the delicate bubble of courage I had begun to weave. The brightness of the evening dimmed, and I felt the weight of his stare bearing down on me, a reminder that my world was not as safe as I wished it to be.

The moment stretched out like a rubber band, the noise of the crowd fading into a dull hum as Ryan's presence crashed over me. He stood there, arms crossed, exuding an air of authority that made my stomach twist. I could feel my heart racing, each beat a reminder of the conflict brewing beneath the surface.

Kayla, ever perceptive, followed my gaze. "Oh, no," she muttered, setting down her drink with a determined clink. "What's he doing here?"

"Probably hunting for a reason to ruin my evening," I whispered, half-joking but fully aware of the reality. My gaze darted around the gallery, scanning for an escape route. The bold colors of the evening blurred in my periphery, overshadowed by the dark silhouette of Ryan.

"Just keep your cool. He can't control the night," Kayla said, her voice steadying. "Remember what we said? Fashion spies on a mission." She flashed a grin, a defiant spark igniting my own resolve, however fragile it felt.

With a deep breath, I turned to face him, lifting my chin. The atmosphere was thick with unspoken challenges, but I had come too far to let him snuff out this flicker of freedom I'd begun to kindle. Ryan approached, his smile polished yet predatory, as if he were sizing up prey rather than engaging with a person.

"Well, well, if it isn't my favorite quarterback," he said, a hint of mockery threading through his words. "You look... different."

"Different in a good way, I hope?" I shot back, the bravado surprising even me. "Or is that just your way of saying I've finally stepped out of the locker room?"

He leaned in slightly, his gaze flickering to the garments surrounding us, taking in the cacophony of creativity with a cynical arch of his brow. "So, this is where you've been hiding? Among the fabrics and frills? Not bad."

I opened my mouth to retort, but Kayla interjected, stepping between us with the confidence of a seasoned diplomat. "Ryan, darling, your time here is fascinating, but we're kind of busy transforming into high-fashion spies."

He chuckled, clearly unfazed by her intrusion. "Right. Fashion spies. How cute."

The mockery in his tone was like a slap, and I felt my courage waver. Did he think he could undermine me in my newfound space? The fire in my belly ignited once more, fueled by the boldness that had gotten me here in the first place. "Cute's just a color on the spectrum of fabulous," I countered, my voice steadying. "What are you doing here, Ryan? Did you run out of football games to ruin?"

His expression shifted, just for a heartbeat, the confidence cracking like glass under pressure. "I came to see the designs, but clearly I should have come sooner to witness the transformation of my favorite football star."

"Transformation?" Kayla echoed, her tone dripping with skepticism. "You mean his journey into something meaningful? Sounds terrifying for you, Ryan. Can you handle it?"

Ryan's lips curled into a smirk, but the tension in the air thickened like smoke. "Oh, I can handle a lot, Kayla. Just hope he can handle the truth."

A sharp silence ensued, the surrounding chatter fading into a muted backdrop. I could feel my heart pounding, uncertainty and defiance warring within me. "The truth is that I'm done living for others. I'm here to embrace what I want, and if that means I'm different, then so be it."

Kayla nodded, her eyes sparkling with support. "Right! So why don't you just skedaddle back to whatever sad corner of the earth you crawled out of?"

Ryan's expression faltered, surprise flaring across his face. For a moment, he looked almost human, stripped of the facade he wore like armor. But just as quickly, it vanished, replaced by a practiced charm that could soothe the most jaded hearts. "You really think this little foray into fashion will change anything? You're still the same player, trying to run away from the field."

The words hung in the air like a noose, tightening around my throat. My palms itched, the instinct to flee swirling within me. But I couldn't allow him to control this moment. "What's wrong, Ryan? Afraid I might actually enjoy myself?"

His eyes narrowed, a flicker of something—anger, concern—crossing his face. "Just remember, every time you step out there, it's a reflection of who you are. Don't lose sight of that."

I scoffed, waving a hand dismissively. "This isn't about forgetting who I am; it's about discovering who I can be beyond your shadow."

He opened his mouth to respond, but the cacophony of laughter and chatter erupted around us, momentarily drowning out the tension. A designer on the stage gestured dramatically, the audience leaning in to catch the latest creation being unveiled, a dress that shimmered like the night sky.

"Excuse me, I have to see this," I declared, grabbing Kayla's arm and moving past Ryan. "Let's go."

As we weaved through the crowd, Kayla leaned closer, her whisper barely audible above the excitement. "You were brilliant! Seriously, he had that 'I'm losing control' look on his face."

"Good," I replied, my pulse still racing, but a smile tugged at my lips. "I want him to see I'm more than just a player. I'm a person."

The designer's creations unfolded before us, vibrant colors and wild shapes taking the stage, each piece a statement of rebellion against conformity. It was exhilarating, a whirlwind of fabric and creativity that threatened to sweep me off my feet. I felt the heat of the spotlight, an electric thrill coursing through me, but the lingering shadow of Ryan still loomed in the corners of my mind.

"Look at that!" Kayla pointed, her voice a mix of awe and excitement. "It's like something out of a dream!"

I watched as a model glided down the runway, the gown flowing behind her like water, shimmering in the light. The designer had truly captured something magical, a sense of freedom and boldness that resonated deep within me. I felt a tugging sensation in my chest, a yearning to explore this creativity that was burgeoning inside me, daring me to break free of the chains that bound me to my past.

As the show continued, I surrendered myself to the experience, each design drawing me further into the world I longed to inhabit. But just as I began to lose myself completely, a familiar figure slipped into my line of sight. Ryan had maneuvered through the crowd, his presence looming like a storm cloud.

I hesitated, the exhilaration of the moment faltering. Was he here to sabotage my joy, or was it just my paranoia that painted him as a villain? Either way, I knew I wouldn't allow him to dampen this light that had begun to flicker within me.

"Stay close," I murmured to Kayla, my voice laced with determination.

"Always," she replied, her gaze steady, a silent promise that we'd face whatever came next together.

With a newfound sense of purpose, I straightened my shoulders and turned to face the runway, reminding myself that I was more than the sum of my past. I was ready to step into the light, even if it meant confronting the shadows lurking just beyond the glitz and glamour.

The tension in the air thickened as Ryan drew closer, his gaze locking onto mine with an intensity that sent a shiver down my spine. The vibrant energy of the fashion show surged around us, but in that moment, it felt as if the world had narrowed to just the two of us. I refused to let him steal my thunder, but with each step he took toward me, my resolve wavered.

"Still think you can play dress-up and pretend this is your new reality?" Ryan's voice dripped with condescension, like honey turned bitter. "You know you're just delaying the inevitable, right? The game is waiting for you."

"Why do you always have to bring up the game? Can't you just let me enjoy this for once?" My voice was steadier than I felt, and I hated how I still felt the urge to defend myself to him.

His expression morphed into something almost contemplative, as if I were a puzzle he couldn't quite solve. "Because, for you, it's never just a game. It's your whole life. You can't simply toss it aside."

Kayla stepped in front of me, her stance defiant. "You know what? You're wrong. She's not tossing anything aside. She's finally stepping into something new. Maybe you should try it sometime."

Ryan raised an eyebrow, clearly unfazed. "Is that how you see it, Kayla? A bold new adventure? What happens when she realizes this isn't the fairy tale she dreams of?"

I felt a rush of anger wash over me. The remnants of the old me, the one who played by Ryan's rules, were clawing their way back into my thoughts. "This is not about you. I'm not your puppet, and I'm tired of dancing to your tune. I'm here to explore who I can be, not who you think I should be."

"Good luck with that," he shot back, his tone edged with mockery. "But remember, you're always going to be tied to the field."

Before I could respond, the spotlight on the runway shifted, illuminating a breathtaking model clad in a floor-length gown that billowed like the sails of a ship caught in a storm. The gown shimmered with every movement, catching the light in a dazzling display that left the crowd breathless.

"Wow," Kayla breathed, her gaze glued to the model. "See? That could be you one day."

I turned my focus back to the runway, the fleeting magic of the moment momentarily distracting me from Ryan. The fabric seemed to pulse with life, an embodiment of freedom and strength. Just as I began to feel a sense of connection to that vision, Ryan's voice cut through once more.

"Pretty gown," he said, rolling his eyes. "Too bad it won't protect you from reality."

"Why do you care so much?" I snapped, anger flaring within me. "Do you want to see me fail?"

Ryan leaned closer, lowering his voice as if sharing a secret. "I just don't want to see you hurt. You think this world is glamorous, but it can chew you up and spit you out before you even know what hit you."

"Like you have any room to give advice about getting chewed up." I shot back, irritation flaring. "Isn't that your entire MO? To bulldoze everyone and pretend you're the good guy?"

The look in his eyes shifted, a flash of something softer peeking through the bravado. But just as quickly, it was gone, replaced by that familiar veneer of arrogance. "Maybe you need someone who understands the stakes. This is serious, and you're playing dress-up like it's a game."

"Enough!" Kayla exclaimed, stepping between us again. "This isn't your show, Ryan. Just let her be."

The words hung in the air, a clear boundary drawn in the sand. Ryan opened his mouth, but no sound emerged. Instead, he stood there, a silhouette against the vibrant backdrop of the fashion world, caught between two worlds—the one he controlled and the one I was desperately trying to seize.

With a last frustrated glance, he pivoted on his heel and walked away, his presence still palpable, like a storm cloud threatening rain. As I turned back to the runway, I could feel a weight lift from my shoulders, the air clearing just enough for me to breathe again.

"I can't believe you stood up to him," Kayla said, admiration shining in her eyes. "That was epic! Who knew you had that fire in you?"

"I didn't until just now," I admitted, feeling a surge of exhilaration. "Maybe it's this whole experience, or maybe I just hit my limit."

"Maybe it's both," she said, nudging me gently. "Let's find something truly fabulous to celebrate this moment."

As the next model strutted down the runway, showcasing a daring ensemble that seemed to shimmer with a life of its own, I felt my heart race again, this time with excitement. The designs flowed and twisted, each piece telling its own story, each story a thread woven into a tapestry of aspirations and dreams.

The audience erupted into applause, and for the first time, I allowed myself to fully immerse in the moment. This was it—the beginning of something new. My mind swirled with visions of fabrics, colors, and ideas that I wanted to explore. Maybe I could create my own path, one that diverged from the rigid expectations I had carried for so long.

"Ready for a little more adventure?" Kayla asked, her eyes sparkling with mischief.

"Always," I replied, my spirit igniting with possibilities.

We ventured further into the heart of the gallery, browsing through an array of clothing racks that seemed to whisper secrets of their own. I picked up a bold jacket adorned with vibrant embroidery, each stitch a little reminder that I could break free from the mold.

"Look at this!" I exclaimed, holding it up against my frame. "It's practically begging to be worn."

"You should totally try it on!" Kayla urged, her enthusiasm infectious.

I laughed and darted into a nearby fitting room, excitement thrumming in my veins. As I slipped the jacket on, the transformation felt electric. I couldn't help but admire myself in the mirror, the bold colors contrasting beautifully against my skin, awakening a side of me I had forgotten existed.

"Do I look like a fashion goddess?" I called out, twirling dramatically.

"You look like you're ready to conquer the world!" Kayla cheered from the outside.

Just as I stepped out to show her, a figure appeared at the end of the hallway—Ryan again, but this time he wasn't alone. Beside him was a striking woman in a sleek red dress, her confidence radiating like sunlight. She glanced at me, then back at Ryan, her smile wide and knowing.

"Who's this?" she asked, her voice smooth and laced with curiosity.

"Just someone playing dress-up," Ryan replied, his tone dismissive yet layered with something else, something I couldn't quite place.

The words stung, a sharp reminder of how he viewed my attempts at self-discovery. My heart raced, caught between the thrill of newfound identity and the familiar anxiety that came with his judgment.

Kayla stepped forward, her posture fierce and protective. "Actually, she's redefining herself, Ryan. Maybe you should take a note."

The tension crackled in the air, and I could feel every eye in the gallery turning toward us. The stakes were rising, the stakes of this encounter rising higher than I had anticipated.

"Hey, I'm not the enemy here," Ryan replied, but the frustration in his voice was palpable.

"What do you want?" I blurted, my frustration boiling over. "Why do you keep coming back?"

Ryan's gaze locked onto mine, and for a moment, it felt like the chaos around us faded into the background. "Because I care," he said, the admission hanging heavy in the air.

Before I could process his words, the striking woman beside him laughed lightly, a sound that sliced through the tension like glass shattering. "Caring's great, but actions speak louder, don't they?"

And then, without warning, she stepped forward, looking straight at me with an intensity that made my stomach twist. "You might want to rethink where you're putting your trust."

Her words hung in the air like a dark cloud, each syllable brimming with an unspoken threat, a warning that sent a chill down my spine. The crowd buzzed around us, excitement and drama swirling together in a dizzying whirl. I stood frozen, the weight of uncertainty crushing down as I struggled to comprehend her meaning.

"Wait, what do you mean?" I asked, my voice barely a whisper.

But before she could respond, an unexpected sound pierced the tension—a phone ringing loudly, slicing through the crowd. It was mine, vibrating insistently in my pocket, a jarring reminder of the reality waiting outside this fleeting world of creativity.

I fumbled to pull it out, glancing at the screen. The caller ID sent a jolt of fear straight through me. It was a number I recognized all too well, one that sent my heart plummeting to the pit of my stomach.

As I answered, the room around me blurred, Ryan's gaze still boring into me, and the woman's smile now felt like a knife at my back.

"Hello?" I said, my voice steady despite the turmoil rising within me.

"Is this you?" The voice on the other end was urgent, slicing through the fabric of the night. "We need to talk. It's important."

The atmosphere shifted, the laughter and applause

# Chapter 8: Breaking the Mold

The morning of the culinary festival dawned bright and crisp, the sun spilling golden light across the sprawling campus like warm honey drizzled over pancakes. I stood in front of the mirror, adJuliag my apron for the third time, a vibrant shade of crimson that somehow felt both empowering and suffocating. The fabric was soft and worn, evidence of countless hours spent in my tiny kitchen, where the chaos of spices and the dance of pots had become my solace. Today, however, I was stepping into a different arena—one with eyes watching, ready to judge every sprinkle of salt and flick of the wrist.

"Breathe," Kayla said, her voice laced with that familiar mix of encouragement and playful sarcasm that I had grown to rely on. She was perched on the edge of my bed, flipping through the pages of a glossy cooking magazine, her long dark hair cascading around her shoulders like a waterfall. "You're not entering a culinary war; it's a demonstration. They're here to learn, not to critique your life choices."

"Right, because nothing screams 'expert' like overcooked pasta and an inability to slice an onion without shedding a few tears," I replied, my stomach swirling with a concoction of nerves and excitement.

Kayla rolled her eyes, a gesture so theatrical it could have earned her a spot in a comedy troupe. "Please, you can out-cook anyone in this room. Besides, who even wants to slice an onion properly? It's all about the flavors, not the finesse. Now, let's go over your menu again."

I took a deep breath, pulling the scent of my favorite spices into my lungs as if to infuse them with confidence. "I've decided on a lemon herb chicken with roasted vegetables and a creamy garlic sauce. And for dessert, chocolate lava cakes." Each dish echoed the essence of my culinary journey: bold flavors, comfort, and just a hint of daring.

"Perfect! Just remember, cooking is like flirting. You've got to be confident, but a little playful, too," she winked, and I couldn't help but laugh.

With her laughter still echoing in my mind, I grabbed my knife kit and apron, bracing myself for the impending storm of attention that awaited. The university's courtyard was a sea of colorful tents, fragrant with the mingled aromas of herbs, grilled meats, and sweet pastries. As I stepped into the bustling atmosphere, my heart raced like a wild stallion, each thud reverberating in my ears. I surveyed the space: students, faculty, and families gathered around the booths, their faces lit with anticipation. I felt like a deer caught in the headlights, my pulse quickening as I approached the designated cooking station.

A small crowd began to gather, their expressions a mix of curiosity and encouragement. I set up my workspace, carefully arranging my ingredients as though they were soldiers in a culinary battalion. There was a sense of community here, a shared love for food that turned strangers into friends. As I laid out fresh herbs and colorful vegetables, a voice broke through my concentration.

"Hey there, Chef! Ready to show us what you've got?" It was Ryan, the charismatic senior who seemed to glide through life with effortless charm. His playful smile was infectious, a spark that lit up the gathering crowd.

"Ready as I'll ever be," I managed, forcing a smile that felt a little too tight. The tension in my chest was a persistent reminder of my insecurities. But with each glance at the eager faces, something began to shift within me. Maybe this wasn't just about cooking; it was about connection.

I launched into the demonstration, my voice gaining strength with each explanation of the steps I was taking. "Cooking is about balance, much like life. You need a little acidity to brighten the flavors, a touch of sweetness to keep things interesting," I said, tossing lemon zest into the bowl with a flourish, my confidence growing like the rising dough I had once struggled with.

The crowd leaned in, nodding, some taking notes while others recorded snippets on their phones. As I stirred the fragrant chicken in the pan, the scent wafted through the air, mingling with the chatter and laughter surrounding us. For a moment, I forgot my worries, lost in the rhythm of cooking, the sizzling sounds and aromatic notes becoming my comfort zone.

"Why did you choose to make chicken?" someone called out from the back, their voice bright and curious.

"Because chicken is versatile! It's like the trusty friend who can adapt to any situation," I replied, the metaphor rolling off my tongue like butter. "But honestly, it's my go-to dish when I want to impress someone without freaking out."

Laughter erupted from the crowd, a wave of sound that washed over me, encouraging me to lean into my vulnerability. I glanced up to catch Ryan's eye; he was grinning, obviously enjoying the banter as much as I was. His presence was a grounding force, reminding me that I wasn't alone up here.

As I continued to slice, sauté, and serve, a sense of ease began to settle in. I could feel the adrenaline morphing into a thrilling exhilaration, turning this daunting task into something far more enjoyable. The audience responded to my playful anecdotes, sharing their own cooking disasters and triumphs, each story weaving us together in a tapestry of laughter and camaraderie.

Then, in a moment that felt both thrilling and surreal, I dared to share a personal story, one that had long been tucked away like a forgotten spice jar in the back of my mind. "You know, cooking wasn't always my passion. I grew up thinking I could only be good at one thing—getting A's in class and being the 'smart one.' But the moment I tried to cook my first meal, a charred disaster of a pizza, something clicked. I realized I could create something out of nothing. And that feeling, my friends, is the magic of cooking."

A hush fell over the crowd, the weight of shared experience hanging in the air. I could see the understanding in their eyes, a collective nod to the importance of embracing our imperfections and the lessons learned from them. This was more than a cooking demonstration; it was a celebration of resilience and growth.

In that instant, the fear of judgment melted away like butter on a hot skillet. I was not just a cook; I was a storyteller, a creator of moments, and today, I was daring to break the mold that had held me captive for so long.

The week slipped away like a finely crafted soufflé, light and airy yet precariously balanced, leaving me dizzy with the thrill of the upcoming culinary festival. My hands shook slightly as I read the invitation for the third time, absorbing the words: "We would be honored to have you demonstrate your culinary skills." My skills. It was a subtle compliment, but my inner critic, a relentless beast, quickly pounced. Who was I to think my skills were worthy of demonstration? I was just a home cook, not a professional chef. What if I burned the garlic? What if the audience turned up their noses at my signature dish?

Kayla, ever the cheerleader, had decided to make it her mission to quell my doubts. "You know, you're not just a home cook. You're practically a food magician!" she proclaimed, her eyes sparkling with a mix of mischief and encouragement. "Besides, if they boo you, I'll throw tomatoes at them. It'll be a hit!" Her laughter was contagious, a balm for my nerves, yet I couldn't shake the feeling that I was a fish out of water.

As the festival drew closer, the excitement grew, each day punctuated by my preparation. I spent countless evenings honing my technique, whipping up my grandmother's beloved pasta dish.

There was something inherently comforting in her recipe, a melody of flavors that danced on the tongue, and I longed to share it with the world. However, with each practice, my self-doubt morphed into a shadowy figure, whispering that I would never live up to the expectations of those who might taste it. I visualized the crowd, a sea of critical faces ready to dissect my every move, and my stomach knotted in response.

"Just think of it as an intimate dinner party," Kayla suggested one evening as we stood shoulder to shoulder in my cramped kitchen, the scent of simmering tomatoes filling the air. "You're just serving a few friends, right?"

"A few hundred friends," I muttered, stirring the sauce with less enthusiasm than usual.

Kayla rolled her eyes, clearly not buying my attempt at humor. "You're going to do great. And if all else fails, remember—food is love. As long as you put your heart into it, no one can ever truly hate your dish."

Her words hung in the air, warm and inviting, wrapping around my anxiety like a cozy blanket. Perhaps she was right. If I could embrace the spirit of love in my cooking, maybe the audience would feel it, too. I could already picture their expressions, the way their eyes might light up as they tasted the first bite. The thought sent a flutter through my stomach, an exhilarating cocktail of hope and fear.

The day of the festival dawned bright and clear, the sun spilling golden rays over the university's sprawling grounds. A vibrant atmosphere buzzed with anticipation, students and faculty mingling amidst colorful stalls filled with culinary delights from around the globe. My heart raced as I approached the cooking station, a modest setup adorned with a sign bearing my name. It felt surreal, yet oddly exhilarating.

"Breathe," I whispered to myself, feeling a warm hand on my back.

Kayla appeared at my side, her presence a steady anchor in the whirlwind of excitement around me. "Look at this place! It's like a food lover's paradise!" she exclaimed, her eyes wide with wonder. "And you, my friend, are the star of the show. Don't you dare forget that."

The moment I stepped up to the stage, a hush fell over the crowd, an ocean of eager faces looking up at me. I could feel the weight of their gazes, but I steadied myself, recalling Kayla's words. I squared my shoulders, put on my brightest smile, and began to speak. "Thank you all for being here today! I'm thrilled to share one of my favorite dishes with you."

As I demonstrated the intricate dance of flavors—how to sauté garlic just until golden, the art of rolling out pasta—my initial nerves transformed into an electric thrill. The kitchen was my sanctuary, and as I poured my heart into each step, I noticed the crowd leaning closer, captivated. A few even nodded in appreciation as I seasoned my sauce, and that small validation sparked a flame of confidence within me.

But then, as if on cue from the universe's playbook of drama, disaster struck. A mischievous breeze, seemingly summoned by fate itself, whisked my carefully arranged herbs off the counter and into the air. "Oh no!" I exclaimed, watching helplessly as they twirled around like confetti, landing scattered about my feet.

Laughter erupted from the crowd, and I couldn't help but chuckle at the absurdity of it all. "Well, I suppose that's one way to add a little 'herb-flavored flair' to the performance!" I quipped, playing along with their amusement. The laughter grew, warm and infectious, and I realized this was not just a demonstration—it was a shared experience.

As I continued cooking, the audience became a part of my process, responding to my every move. I engaged with them, asking for their input on ingredients, tossing in playful banter. With each interaction, the fear of judgment faded, replaced by a genuine connection. They were no longer strangers but rather a community, united by a shared love for food.

By the time I plated the pasta, the air was thick with the rich aroma of garlic and tomatoes, and the crowd was buzzing with anticipation. As I served the first plate to a volunteer from the audience, the moment felt monumental. Would they taste the love I'd infused into the dish? Would they feel the warmth of my grandmother's kitchen in each bite?

"Here goes nothing," I murmured, biting my lip as the volunteer took a tentative forkful. The world slowed as I held my breath, my heart drumming like a celebratory drumroll.

The audience watched, wide-eyed, as the volunteer savored the first bite. A slow smile spread across their face, and with it came a chorus of gasps and murmurs of delight. "This is incredible!" they exclaimed, prompting a round of applause that reverberated through the festival.

In that moment, a wave of joy washed over me, erasing all traces of self-doubt. I had stepped out of my comfort zone and embraced vulnerability, and the result was nothing short of magical. The rest of the demonstration flew by in a blur of laughter, shared stories, and delighted faces, each one affirming my place in this vibrant world of culinary creativity.

As I wrapped up, the applause echoed in my ears like a sweet melody. I had broken the mold, not only of who I thought I should be but of what cooking meant to me. It was about connection, joy, and the simple pleasure of sharing something made with love.

With the culinary festival behind me, a giddy sense of triumph bubbled beneath my skin, filling me with a new kind of energy.

The applause still echoed in my ears like a comforting soundtrack, a reminder that perhaps I could carve out a place for myself in this expansive world of flavors and creativity. Each evening that followed, I found myself in the kitchen, not out of obligation, but for the sheer joy of it. The ingredients transformed from mere components into my allies, their vibrant colors and textures dancing before me like a well-rehearsed troupe.

Kayla became my most frequent companion during these culinary escapades, often sneaking bites and offering unsolicited but always entertaining commentary. "If you keep cooking like this, you'll have a line out the door of eager diners," she teased one evening, her eyes sparkling with mischief as she snagged a piece of freshly baked focaccia. "I might even need to get a bouncer to keep the crowds at bay."

"Maybe I'll hire you as my PR manager," I retorted, wiping my hands on a flour-dusted apron and rolling my eyes. "But if we're being honest, I'm still worried about keeping a single person coming back."

"Are you kidding? You're a culinary Picasso!" she declared dramatically, throwing her arms wide as if unveiling an abstract masterpiece. "You paint with flavors, and that's more than most chefs can say. Just don't burn anything, okay? We can't have you giving people charred offerings as your grand finale."

With her playful encouragement, my confidence continued to swell. Yet, underneath the thrill of my newfound culinary identity, an unsettling thought lurked in the back of my mind. What if this was merely a fleeting moment of clarity, soon to be overshadowed by self-doubt once more?

As if the universe was tuned into my thoughts, the next surprise hit hard. It arrived in the form of a text from my mother, her words crisp and filled with urgency. "I'm coming to visit this weekend. We need to talk." My heart sank, the thrill of my triumph replaced by a tight knot in my stomach. I could only guess what the conversation would entail.

Kayla, always perceptive to my moods, caught the change in my demeanor. "What's up?" she asked, arching an eyebrow.

"My mother is coming for a visit," I said, trying to keep my voice light, but failing miserably.

"Ah, the one who thinks you should be an accountant instead of a chef?"

I nodded, a wave of tension pooling in my shoulders. "Exactly. I can already hear her now, lecturing me about practicality and security. You know, all those heartwarming topics."

"Look, I know she means well, but you've got to stand your ground. This is your passion. You've shown it to the world, and you can't let anyone dim that spark."

Her words resonated with me, but the thought of my mother's disappointed expression haunted my mind. Could I truly defend my newfound identity as a cook when I still felt like a fraud at times?

The weekend arrived with the grace of a runaway freight train. My mother swept into my apartment, an aura of authority trailing behind her. "Darling! It's so good to see you!" she exclaimed, her embrace both warm and suffocating.

As we settled in the living room, the conversation started harmlessly enough—discussions about the weather, lighthearted anecdotes from her week. But as the minutes passed, the air thickened with anticipation, the kind that foreshadows a thunderstorm.

"Now, about your cooking," she began, her tone shifting from cheerful to serious in an instant. "I've been thinking about your future, and while I admire your dedication, it's time we had a talk about practicality."

I felt my heart sink as her words loomed over me like an unyielding storm cloud. "Mom, I—"

"Let me finish, dear. I'm worried that this cooking obsession is a phase, and you need to focus on a career that can sustain you. You have so much potential!"

Each word was like a jab to my confidence, twisting and turning until I felt utterly defeated. "But Mom, I love cooking. It's not just a phase; it's who I am!"

"Who you are?" she echoed, raising an eyebrow. "It's not practical. You need a steady job, something that will provide stability. This 'cooking' is charming, but what about your future?"

The tension in the room became almost palpable. I felt a fire igniting within me, fueled by a blend of frustration and desperation. "What if my future is about cooking? What if I want to open my own restaurant or teach others how to cook?"

She blinked, her expression softening slightly, but her resolve remained. "That's lovely, but you must consider the reality of it. There are risks, and do you really want to bet your life on something so uncertain?"

Before I could respond, Kayla burst into the room, her exuberance illuminating the heavy atmosphere. "Hey! Sorry to interrupt, but I thought I heard someone talking about dreams! I brought cookies!"

My mother turned to Kayla, a forced smile replacing her earlier concern. "Hello! I didn't realize we had guests. I'm just trying to help my son see the bigger picture."

Kayla's gaze flickered between us, sensing the tension. "Oh, I love cookies! Can I get in on that bigger picture?"

I shot her a grateful look, appreciating her ability to diffuse the situation. Kayla handed my mother a cookie, her smile genuine. "These are to celebrate a recent achievement! Did you know your son just gave a cooking demonstration at the culinary festival?"

"What? A cooking demonstration?" My mother's tone turned inquisitive, her previous skepticism momentarily forgotten.

Kayla launched into a vibrant retelling of the event, embellishing the details with dramatic flair. I watched as my mother's expression shifted from skepticism to genuine interest, a flicker of pride sparking in her eyes. For a brief moment, I thought I might just break through the wall of practicality that had built between us.

"So, you're really passionate about this?" my mother finally asked, her voice softer, almost vulnerable.

"Yes," I said, my voice steady. "I want to make this my life."

She regarded me closely, weighing her response, but just as I felt the tide turning, my phone buzzed violently on the table, pulling all eyes to it. The screen lit up with a message from an unknown number, its urgency cutting through the moment like a knife. "We need to talk about your demonstration. You've caught someone's attention."

My stomach dropped, a chill running through me. Who could this be? What did they want? As I glanced back at Kayla, her expression mirrored my own confusion, while my mother's brows furrowed in concern. The warm moment I'd felt just seconds ago dissolved, replaced by a jarring sense of uncertainty that loomed over us like a shadow, heavy and foreboding.

# Chapter 9: A Recipe for Change

The crowd swelled with anticipation, a living entity of gasps and whispers, the collective heartbeat of the culinary festival reverberating through the air like an electric pulse. The vibrant colors of the market stalls blurred into a kaleidoscope of sights, each more alluring than the last. Tables were draped in cheerful checkered cloths, and pots of herbs basked in the sun, their fragrances competing for attention. My heart thrummed wildly in my chest, but beneath the initial anxiety was a flicker of excitement, stoking the flames of my creativity.

I stood behind the makeshift kitchen, my sanctuary amid the chaos. The stainless steel surfaces gleamed under the bright lights, a testament to the countless hours spent honing my craft. Each knife, pot, and pan was an extension of my will, tools in the hands of an artist ready to paint a masterpiece. As I took a deep breath, the sweet scent of basil mingled with the sharpness of garlic, invigorating my senses and urging me to create.

Kayla, my rock in this whirlwind, stood at the forefront of the audience. With her tousled hair and mischievous grin, she was the embodiment of encouragement. She mouthed the words "You've got this!" and I felt a surge of warmth wash over me. If anyone understood the complexity of my journey, it was her. Together, we had navigated the narrow alleys of self-doubt and emerged into the wide expanse of possibility, like the sun breaking through a stormy sky.

I grabbed my chef's knife and began to slice through the vegetables, the blade gliding through the tender zucchini and crisp bell peppers with satisfying precision. Each cut was a dance, a rhythm that seemed to quiet the chaos around me. My hands moved automatically, guided by muscle memory, but I was alive in the moment, each slice an expression of who I was becoming—a creator who poured love into every dish, transcending the confines of my past.

The audience leaned in, their eyes bright with curiosity as the aroma of the sautéed vegetables began to rise. I tossed in a pinch of salt, letting it rain like a gentle summer shower over my creation, enhancing the flavors that bloomed beneath the heat. The energy around me shifted; murmurs of appreciation rippled through the crowd, a symphony of approval that filled my chest with hope. I was not just cooking; I was storytelling, my emotions woven into every ingredient, transforming mere sustenance into an experience.

As the vegetables sizzled and the spices danced in the air, I glanced around the festival. Families with children, couples whispering sweet nothings, and food enthusiasts eagerly snapping photos—all part of the tapestry of life I had longed to embrace. But just as I was reveling in this newfound freedom, my heart dropped as a familiar figure pushed through the throng, slicing through the crowd like a knife through butter.

Mason, my past personified, emerged from the sea of spectators, his presence a dark cloud in my otherwise sunny day. His slick hair, expertly styled as always, framed a face I recognized but wished to forget. It had been years since our paths had crossed, and yet here he was, a specter haunting the culinary world I was trying to claim as my own. The tight knot in my stomach tightened further, a reminder of the insecurities I had battled for so long.

"Didn't expect to see you here," he called out, his tone light, yet I could hear the underlying mockery.

The air around me felt thick, heavy with tension as if the very atmosphere understood the weight of our history. I focused on the pan, the vegetables bubbling and popping, desperate to drown out his voice. "Well, surprise," I shot back, my tone sharper than I intended. The crowd's gaze flicked between us, eager for the drama unfolding in real time.

"Looks like you've traded in your soccer cleats for a chef's hat," he smirked, leaning against the booth like he owned the place, his confidence both infuriating and unnerving.

I clenched my jaw, determined not to let him steal my moment. "And you've traded in your dignity for a front-row seat to watch me thrive," I retorted, heat flooding my cheeks.

A ripple of laughter swept through the crowd, but Mason's expression faltered. For a fleeting moment, it felt as if I had regained some control. Yet the reality of his presence loomed large, a reminder that the past was never truly behind us. The line between courage and vulnerability blurred, and I stood precariously on that edge.

I forced my focus back to the task at hand, the vibrant colors of my dish inviting me to lose myself once more in the art of cooking. The sautéed vegetables beckoned, their charred edges whispering promises of flavor, and I could feel the audience leaning closer, anticipation crackling in the air like the first spark of a flame.

"Maybe I'll give your little dish a taste," Mason continued, his casual bravado grating on my nerves. "You know, just to see if you really have what it takes."

I paused, the spatula hovering above the pan, and glanced at him. The challenge hung between us, a gauntlet thrown down in front of the eager crowd. "I think you'll find I've always had 'what it takes,'" I shot back, my voice steady, the truth of it ringing clear.

Kayla's nod from the front row was like a lighthouse, guiding me through the fog of uncertainty. I turned my back to Mason, letting the heat of the stove fuel my determination. I was more than just the sum of my past mistakes; I was here, alive, and ready to seize my future. The laughter, the cheers, the joy of creation enveloped me like a warm embrace, reminding me that I was not defined by anyone but myself.

With renewed focus, I added a splash of lemon juice, its zesty brightness cutting through the savory richness of the dish. The citrus lifted my spirits, each drop a promise of renewal. And in that moment, as the flavors melded together, I felt the shackles of my past loosening their grip. The crowd's anticipation surged like a wave, washing away my fear, leaving only the thrill of the moment—the thrill of possibility.

The sizzling of the vegetables served as my heartbeat, punctuating the silence that had enveloped us after Mason's taunt. I turned back to my pan, focusing on the rich medley of colors and smells, letting the aroma of roasted garlic and fresh herbs transport me from this moment of confrontation. The cacophony of the festival faded slightly, and I concentrated on the next steps, determined to drown out the noise of my past.

"Do you even remember how to cook, or are you just winging it?" Mason's voice cut through again, a mocking sweetness clinging to each word, but I held my ground, refusing to let him shake my confidence.

I threw a glance over my shoulder, shooting him a smirk that felt half-formed but full of defiance. "Cooking is just like soccer—it's all about knowing when to pass and when to take a shot." I grabbed a handful of fresh basil, tearing the leaves with a flourish that sent their fragrant oils into the air. "And right now? I'm shooting for the stars."

Laughter erupted from the crowd, and I felt buoyed by their response. For a fleeting moment, Mason's presence seemed to shrink, overshadowed by the warmth of the audience. I scooped the colorful mixture into a large serving bowl, my heart swelling with pride as I created a vibrant salad, topped with a drizzle of tangy vinaigrette. Each component spoke of my journey, of my willingness to evolve from the person who once measured success solely in gold medals and trophies.

"Not bad, not bad," Mason quipped, crossing his arms as he surveyed my dish like a critic sizing up a work of art. "But I hope you realize that no amount of culinary flair will change the fact that you're still that scared kid who hid behind a soccer ball."

"Funny, I thought I was more of a scared kid who discovered cooking," I shot back, a playful smirk tugging at my lips. "But hey, you do you, right? Still stuck in that old playbook?"

The crowd erupted in laughter again, and a flicker of uncertainty crossed Mason's face. He quickly masked it, shrugging as though my words hadn't landed. Yet I saw it—his discomfort, the way his bravado cracked just a bit under the spotlight. It was empowering, like taking the ball down the field, feeling the adrenaline rush as I outmaneuvered him.

"Look, I'm here to support the community," he said, feigning nonchalance, but I could hear the edge of irritation in his voice. "And you know, it's all about honesty, right? Wouldn't want to mislead anyone about your... new career choice."

"Oh, you mean my passion?" I replied, tossing my hair over my shoulder, letting my voice dance with confidence. "You wouldn't know about that, would you? Being passionate about something other than yourself?"

The audience roared again, and the laughter felt like a warm hug around my shoulders. I took a deep breath, drawing strength from their support. This moment was mine, and I wasn't about to let it slip away. I turned back to my dish, finishing with a flourish as I garnished the salad with a sprinkle of feta cheese, the creamy white contrasting beautifully with the vibrant greens and reds.

"Ladies and gentlemen!" I announced, raising my voice above the chatter. "Behold, my summer garden salad, bursting with flavors and colors that celebrate the beauty of this festival—and of life itself!"

The applause rang out like a thunderclap, drowning out Mason's attempt to retort. I grinned, soaking in the energy as I served samples to the eager hands reaching out for a taste. My heart soared as I watched their eyes widen with delight, each bite a small victory, a testament to my journey from the sidelines of my own life to the center stage of creation.

"Wow, this is amazing!" a woman exclaimed, her eyes sparkling with genuine appreciation. "I never thought of adding lemon like this!"

"Thank you!" I beamed, feeling the warmth of her praise seep into my bones. "It's all about balancing the flavors—like life, really. You need a little zing to make it memorable."

Mason stepped forward, his expression shifting as the crowd reacted to the dish. "Maybe there's hope for you yet," he said, this time lacking his usual bite, as if he was reconsidering his stance.

I raised an eyebrow, intrigued by the shift in his tone. "Coming from you, that's practically a compliment," I replied, genuine surprise creeping into my voice. "Are we having a breakthrough here? A moment of personal growth?"

"Don't push it," he shot back, but there was an undercurrent of something softer, a hint of respect maybe, or perhaps mere resignation.

I couldn't help but chuckle. "Just kidding. But you know what? I'm glad you came. It's not every day you get to see someone you thought you left behind."

"Yeah, well, maybe I wanted to check out the competition," he muttered, looking anywhere but at me.

"Oh please," I laughed, my heart lighter. "You think I'm competition? You've got a PhD in pretentiousness. I'm just here to cook."

The laughter from the crowd punctuated my words, enveloping me in a cocoon of camaraderie that warmed my spirit. For a moment, I felt as if I were floating above the ground, untethered from my fears and past mistakes. The reality of my passion and the joy of sharing it with others filled the void that Mason's presence had momentarily threatened to create.

Suddenly, a voice broke through my reverie. "Can I get a picture with you?" A young girl, maybe ten, with wide eyes and a messy braid approached me, her face lit with enthusiasm.

"Of course!" I replied, kneeling to her level, all thoughts of Mason evaporating. The girl grinned as we posed together, and I felt a rush of warmth, the kind that comes from knowing you might inspire someone else.

As I stood up, I caught a glimpse of Mason watching from a distance, arms crossed, his expression unreadable. Yet in his eyes, I could see a flicker of something—maybe admiration, maybe envy, but either way, it was a welcome change. With each passing moment, I felt the foundations of my old self beginning to crumble, replaced by something far more powerful.

Here I was, a creator not merely surviving but thriving. With every dish I crafted, I was rewriting the narrative of who I could be, defying not only the expectations of others but my own limitations. And as I turned back to my cooking station, with the aroma of fresh ingredients swirling around me like a fragrant halo, I knew I was no longer just a soccer player trying to find my way. I was an artist, unafraid to embrace the palette of my life, eager to paint my future with bold strokes and vibrant colors.

The vibrant festival atmosphere buzzed around me as I plated my summer garden salad, a crescendo of colors and flavors melding into something beautiful and bold. With each sample I handed out, I felt the audience's energy shift, like a tidal wave of support crashing over me. Laughter echoed, mingling with the clinking of glasses and the chatter of families enjoying their day. This was my world now—messy, lively, and unfiltered. Yet, Mason lingered at the edge of my vision, a persistent shadow in my bright moment.

"Looks like you've got a fan club," he remarked, his tone laced with sarcasm as he nodded towards the girl who had just taken her picture with me. "Just don't let it go to your head, alright? You're still competing in a culinary race against real chefs."

"Real chefs?" I repeated, my voice deliberately airy, masking the irritation that bubbled beneath. "You mean like those guys over there?" I gestured toward a pair of culinary students battling it out in a neighboring booth, one nearly tripping over his own apron while attempting to impress a judge. "That's a sight I wouldn't want to compete with. I might actually start feeling bad for them."

Mason rolled his eyes, but I caught a hint of a smile on his lips. "Keep it light. That's the spirit, I guess." There was a pause, and for a moment, the world around us faded away. Perhaps I could change the narrative between us, even if it was only a flicker of understanding.

"Isn't that what life is about? Finding humor in the chaos?" I asked, surprising even myself with the question. My voice softened as I continued. "You should try it sometime. You might like it."

His facade slipped just a bit, revealing the tension beneath. "Sure, but I find life's a bit more complicated than just a punchline."

Before I could respond, a commotion erupted nearby, pulling our attention away from the uncomfortable dialogue. A young chef in an extravagant chef's coat, decorated with colorful badges of culinary achievements, was waving his arms wildly, drawing a crowd. "I need a volunteer!" he shouted, eyes darting through the sea of onlookers. "We're going to spice things up a bit!"

"Oh no," Mason muttered, leaning back slightly as if anticipating the chaos that was about to unfold.

"What do you think? Should we get involved?" I smirked, unable to resist the temptation of diving into the unpredictable energy that swirled around us.

Before he could answer, the chef caught sight of me, grinning like a child on Christmas morning. "You! Yes, you with the salad!" He beckoned me forward, and the crowd parted like the Red Sea, eyes glinting with curiosity.

"Oh no, not you too," Mason groaned, though there was a glimmer of amusement in his voice.

Ignoring Mason's protest, I stepped forward, my heart racing with excitement. "What's the challenge?" I asked, curiosity piqued.

"We're going to create a mystery dish!" the young chef announced. "Everyone here has a favorite flavor combination—something that defines them. I need you to take those flavors and create something magical in just ten minutes!"

The crowd erupted into cheers, and I felt the adrenaline course through me. Ten minutes? I had never been one to shy away from a challenge. "Alright, I'm in!" I called out, meeting the eager eyes of the audience. I turned back to Mason, who wore a mixture of disbelief and reluctant admiration. "You in or just going to spectate?"

He hesitated, glancing between the crowd and me. "You really think you can handle this?"

"Absolutely," I said, my confidence swelling. "But I'd like a partner. How about it?"

He scoffed, but I could see the spark of intrigue flickering in his eyes. "Fine. Just don't drag me down with your last-minute chaos."

"Last-minute chaos is my specialty!" I grinned, and together we approached the makeshift cooking station that had been hastily set up under the festival's vibrant canopy.

With the clock ticking, I rummaged through the ingredients laid out before us, a hodgepodge of fresh produce and spices, a treasure trove of culinary possibility. "Alright, what's your flavor?" I asked Mason, feeling the thrill of collaboration ignite a familiar fire in my belly.

"Um, I guess I like... truffle oil?" he replied, his brow furrowing as if he had just been asked to identify a rare species.

"Truffle oil? Fancy choice! What else?" I pressed, tossing a handful of cherry tomatoes into a bowl.

"Maybe garlic? And... something unexpected?"

"Unexpected? You mean like you showing up today?" I teased, and he shot me a look that was part annoyance, part amusement.

"Okay, okay. How about some jalapeños for a kick?"

"Now we're talking!" I exclaimed, already envisioning a dish that could tantalize taste buds and make a statement. "Let's get to work!"

As we dove into the task, the audience watched intently, their energy palpable. I felt a renewed sense of purpose, my past insecurities melting away in the heat of the moment. Mason and I moved in sync, a surprisingly effective duo as we chopped, sautéed, and mixed.

With every passing second, I felt the bonds of our old rivalry dissolve, replaced by the thrill of teamwork. "You know," I said between chopping, "this isn't half bad. Who knew you had a culinary side?"

"Don't get used to it," he shot back, a smirk on his face. "This is strictly business. Besides, I'm just here to make sure you don't burn anything."

"Sure, buddy, keep telling yourself that," I laughed, the sound light and carefree, wrapping around us like a cozy blanket.

As we added the final touches, the aroma of our creation wafted through the air, rich and inviting. I glanced at the clock. "We have just a few moments left. What should we call this masterpiece?"

"Let's call it 'The Unexpected Turn,'" he said, and the title rolled off his tongue with surprising flair.

"Perfect!" I grinned, feeling the adrenaline surge as the timer began its final countdown. "Okay, let's plate this beauty."

Just as we finished arranging our dish, an ominous rumble echoed overhead. The sky, previously a cheerful blue, darkened, clouds swirling ominously. Gasps rippled through the crowd, and I felt a chill run down my spine.

"What's happening?" Mason asked, glancing around, his bravado faltering.

Before I could respond, the first drops of rain began to fall, then turned into a torrential downpour. The audience gasped, scrambling for cover, while the festival atmosphere shifted from joyful excitement to chaotic urgency.

"Great timing, nature," I muttered, my heart racing as the rain drummed down on the makeshift roof.

"Do we still serve it?" Mason yelled over the din, eyes wide with surprise.

"Why not?" I grinned, feeling the rush of adrenaline mixed with exhilaration. "Let's show them how to embrace the storm!"

With that, we lifted our creation, dodging raindrops, and presented 'The Unexpected Turn' to the remaining brave souls huddled under the canopy. The crowd's laughter rang out against the pounding rain, a strange sense of camaraderie blossoming amid the chaos.

But just as we began to serve our dish, a loud crack of thunder echoed through the air, shaking the ground beneath us. Instinctively, I reached for Mason's arm, the electricity in the air igniting something new, a spark of connection amidst the wild unpredictability.

And then, from behind the crowd, a figure emerged, drenched but unmistakable. My breath caught in my throat as I recognized the familiar face that haunted my thoughts. The world around me blurred, the laughter fading into a distant echo. I felt as if time had slowed, my heart pounding in rhythm with the storm, and as I locked eyes with the approaching figure, everything I thought I knew about this day shifted irrevocably.

# Chapter 10: Unwelcome Revelations

The sun glinted off the polished bleachers, casting a blinding reflection that danced around the field, competing with the cacophony of cheers and the rhythmic thud of footballs spiraling through the air. I tightened my ponytail, the strands of hair pulled back like a soldier preparing for battle. Just yesterday, I had stood in the soft glow of the culinary festival, surrounded by the fragrant aroma of garlic and rosemary, mixing my ingredients with unbridled joy. Today, I was back among the warriors of the gridiron, but the echoes of Ryan's mocking words clung to me like an unwanted shadow, heavy and suffocating.

As I jogged to join my teammates, their shouts of encouragement felt like a balm against my bruised spirit, but the moment I caught sight of Ryan, that smirk carved into his face, the salve melted away. He lounged against the fence, arms crossed, a king surveying his court. "Did you see Calderon cooking?" he called out, his voice dripping with condescension. "What a joke."

A collective chuckle rippled through the crowd, the kind that hung in the air like an insidious fog, settling into the crevices of my confidence. I tried to shake it off, focus on the play calling and the sharp cadence of the coach's voice, but each word felt like an avalanche, burying my spirit deeper beneath a mountain of doubt. Ryan's words haunted me, twisting in my mind, reshaping my culinary triumph into a cruel parody. The images of the festival faded, replaced by a relentless replay of my blunders. I had fought hard to carve a space for myself in the kitchen, to be more than just the girl with the perfect seasoning; I wanted to be taken seriously, to belong.

But in this world, football had always been my sanctuary, the place where I felt strong and alive. I needed to channel that strength now, to shake off the doubts that snaked through my mind. With a deep breath, I focused on the ball, feeling the weight of it in my hands. I needed to throw with precision, to run with the kind of ferocity that would drown out the whispers, the doubts, the mocking laughter. As the whistle blew, I felt the familiar rush, the exhilaration of movement, and for a moment, I was untouchable.

Yet, Ryan's voice crept back into my thoughts, taunting and relentless. "You're just a kitchen princess trying to play with the boys," he had said, and I couldn't shake the image of his mocking face. Even in the middle of a practice drill, I could almost hear his laughter echoing off the bleachers. My teammates were shouting for me, their encouragement clashing with the cacophony of Ryan's taunts, and I stumbled slightly, the ball slipping from my grasp.

"Get your head in the game, Calderon!" The coach's bark cut through the haze, and I nodded, shaking off the distraction. This was my battleground; I wouldn't let Ryan win. I regained my composure and focused, the adrenaline pulsing through my veins. Each pass, each run, built a wall against Ryan's words. But I could still feel that knife-edge of his smirk, and the taste of defeat lingered on my tongue like burnt sugar.

The afternoon dragged on, the sun dipping lower, casting long shadows across the field. Each practice felt like an uphill climb, a relentless push against a tide of negativity. Finally, as the whistle blew for a break, I found a moment to breathe. I pulled away from the group, seeking a quiet corner by the water cooler, my mind a swirl of emotions.

"Hey, Calderon, you good?" Jake, one of my teammates, leaned against the cooler, his expression concerned but light. Jake always had a knack for knowing when I was off-kilter.

I forced a smile, brushing a stray hair from my forehead. "Yeah, just... you know how it is. Trying to juggle everything."

He chuckled, shaking his head. "You cook, you play, you do it all. Just don't let Ryan get to you. He's a jerk, and he knows it."

I appreciated his sentiment, but it felt like trying to plug a hole in a sinking ship. "It's just hard. I thought I could share my passion for cooking and not be mocked for it. I mean, what's wrong with wanting to be good at something outside of football?"

Jake shrugged, leaning back, crossing his arms. "Nothing at all. You're a beast on the field, and you whip up magic in the kitchen. Ryan just doesn't know how to handle someone who can be both. Keep your head high. He's just scared of a little competition."

I nodded, feeling a flicker of warmth at his words, but the doubt still simmered beneath the surface. I wanted to believe it, to let that flicker ignite into a flame. "Maybe. But it feels like every time I step out of my comfort zone, he's there to remind me I don't belong."

Jake scoffed, clearly not willing to let Ryan take the last word. "Forget him. What's he got? A loud mouth and a flabby gut. He can't even hold a candle to your nachos."

We both laughed at that, the tension easing slightly as I imagined Ryan fumbling with a plate of my nachos, only to have them topple onto his shoes. "You have a point," I admitted, a smile breaking through my earlier frustration. "But I want to prove that I can be more than just a football player. I want to show them I can shine in the kitchen too."

As I said the words, a spark ignited within me. I didn't want to be just a player; I wanted to be a force to be reckoned with in both worlds. The sting of Ryan's words felt a little lighter, the weight of his smirk loosening its grip on my heart. Maybe, just maybe, I could carve out my space, blend my passions seamlessly, and shove Ryan's taunts back into the shadow where they belonged.

With renewed determination, I stepped back onto the field, ready to face the practice, ready to let the rhythm of the game wash over me like a wave of clarity. My heart raced with the thrill of the challenge. I wouldn't let Ryan dictate my narrative; I would be the author of my story, weaving in layers of resilience and creativity. Each play was a step toward reclaiming my confidence, and as I caught the ball and made my way down the field, I could almost hear the soft, approving murmur of spices swirling together, echoing the rhythm of my heartbeat.

The following day unfurled like a ruffled napkin, creased and unyielding, as I navigated the school hallways, the air thick with the scent of stale lunches and adolescent chatter. My stomach churned with a mixture of anticipation and dread, each echo of laughter sending tendrils of anxiety snaking through my veins. The culinary festival was still a vibrant memory, an enchanting swirl of flavors and colors, yet Ryan's derisive commentary had dampened its brilliance. The remnants of confidence I had built felt like fragile glass, threatened to shatter with the slightest push.

As I moved through the throng of students, I heard whispers like the rustling of leaves, fragments of conversations swirling around me, each more biting than the last. "Calderon thinks she's a chef now," one voice sneered, and I felt a flush of heat creep up my neck. I couldn't tell if they were mocking me or simply echoing Ryan's sentiment. Either way, the sting felt real and immediate, twisting my stomach into knots that even a well-cooked pasta couldn't unravel.

By the time I reached my locker, the metallic clang of it opening resonated like the final note of a symphony, both hollow and unresolved. I fished out my textbooks, my fingers brushing against the well-worn spine of a cookbook tucked in the corner. It was a silent reminder of my passion, the dishes I could create with a flick of my wrist and the right blend of spices. But it felt like a distant echo now, overshadowed by Ryan's laughter and the weight of expectations pressing down on me.

"Hey, you!" The exuberant voice broke through my reverie, pulling me from my thoughts. I turned to find Mia bounding toward me, her curly hair bouncing like a vibrant spring. She was a whirlwind of energy, bright and infectious, always radiating positivity. "Did you hear about the pep rally? You should totally showcase some of your recipes!"

A flicker of hope ignited in my chest, yet it was quickly tempered by doubt. "You think I should? After what Ryan said?" My voice barely rose above a whisper, the thought of putting myself out there again felt as daunting as running a marathon.

"Who cares what Ryan thinks? You've got this amazing talent! You need to flaunt it." Her enthusiasm was a warm blanket, wrapping around my shoulders, but I still felt exposed, like a novice cook tossing ingredients into a pot without knowing how it would turn out. "Besides," she added with a smirk, "he probably can't even boil water without burning it. Just imagine his face if you blow everyone away with your cooking!"

I couldn't help but chuckle at the mental image, the thought of Ryan fumbling with a spatula while I effortlessly whipped up a culinary masterpiece. "Alright, maybe I'll think about it," I said, a hint of resolve creeping back into my voice. "But only if you help me set up. I can't do this alone."

"Deal!" Mia clapped her hands, practically vibrating with excitement. "We'll create a display that'll knock their socks off. Just you wait."

The day passed in a haze of classes and whispered jabs. I tried to stay focused on the teachers, but my thoughts kept drifting back to the pep rally. With each passing period, I could feel the tide of my uncertainty begin to shift, building momentum. The prospect of showcasing my cooking felt like a blossoming flower, vibrant and full of potential, yet still vulnerable to the harsh winds of judgment.

As the final bell rang, a wave of exhilaration washed over me, mingling with my trepidation. I met Mia by the parking lot, and together we headed to my house, armed with a plan that felt both thrilling and terrifying. The air was tinged with the sweet scent of autumn, leaves crunching beneath our feet, a reminder that change was inevitable, and perhaps, just perhaps, I could embrace it.

Once inside my cozy kitchen, the comforting aroma of familiar spices enveloped me like an old friend. It was a sanctuary, a place where I could be myself, unburdened by the expectations of others. "Alright, what are we making?" Mia asked, her eyes sparkling with enthusiasm as she rummaged through my pantry.

I surveyed my ingredients, the vibrant colors of fresh vegetables and the rich, inviting hues of spices. "How about we start with a killer salsa and some guacamole?" I suggested, already envisioning the vibrant spread that would showcase my skills without overwhelming me.

Mia nodded, and we dove into the rhythm of chopping, mixing, and blending, the sounds of our culinary symphony creating a backdrop of laughter and chatter. "You know," Mia said between chopping onions, "Ryan's just mad because he can't handle someone being good at multiple things. He probably spends his evenings binge-watching reality cooking shows, hoping to learn how to make toast."

I laughed, the tension from earlier easing like steam escaping from a boiling pot. "And yet he thinks he's a culinary critic." The banter flowed effortlessly, an antidote to the poison of Ryan's taunts. Each slice of onion brought with it the catharsis of taking control, of reclaiming my narrative.

The salsa came together beautifully, the tangy tomatoes mingling with zesty lime and fresh cilantro, while the guacamole was a creamy masterpiece, rich and indulgent. As we plated our creations, I could feel the electric charge of anticipation surging through me. This wasn't just food; it was my heart and soul laid bare, an invitation for others to see me beyond the football field.

Just as I was about to lose myself in the moment, the door swung open, and my brother Alex ambled in, his presence a mix of chaos and charm. "What's that smell?" he exclaimed, plopping onto a barstool with a wide grin. "You're cooking again? You should be on one of those cooking shows!"

I rolled my eyes, a smile creeping across my lips. "Thanks, but I think I'll stick to high school pep rallies for now."

"Seriously, you need to take Ryan down a peg. Maybe poison his food."

I laughed, shaking my head. "As tempting as that sounds, I'm trying to rise above. Cooking is about joy, not revenge."

He raised an eyebrow, leaning back with mock seriousness. "Right. Just don't let him ruin your moment. You're a rock star in the kitchen. Own it!"

As we set the table for a feast, I felt a surge of excitement blend with the nervous energy thrumming beneath my skin. This was my chance to embrace my culinary identity, to transform the whispers of doubt into a chorus of support. The air crackled with potential, each dish a testament to my resilience, a symbol of the journey I was carving for myself.

The evening unfolded with laughter, each bite of salsa eliciting exclamations of delight, and with every passing moment, I felt the layers of tension beginning to peel away. I was a chef, a player, and above all, I was me, ready to step into the light. As we cleared the table, my heart swelled with determination, the taste of success mingling with the aroma of freshly chopped herbs, a promise of what was yet to come.

The following days unfolded with the frenetic energy of a rapidly spinning top, each moment tinged with a sense of urgency that propelled me toward the pep rally. The hallways buzzed with anticipation, a carnival of vibrant banners and enthusiastic chatter as students prepared for the event. My heart raced alongside the rhythm of school spirit, but beneath the excitement lay a persistent undercurrent of anxiety. I could still feel the echoes of Ryan's laughter swirling in the back of my mind, like a stubborn melody that refused to fade.

Mia and I had been brainstorming our display, plotting a culinary takeover that would highlight not just my cooking skills but also my determination to rise above Ryan's barbs. With the clock ticking down, we arrived early to set up our station, my heart thrumming with a mix of excitement and dread. I could already envision the crowd's reaction to my creations: the bright salsa glistening under the gymnasium lights and the creamy guacamole waiting to be devoured.

As we arranged the platters, I glanced at Mia, who was adJuliag the colorful streamers we had draped around our station. "You think this is enough?" I asked, a hint of doubt creeping into my voice as I surveyed our handiwork.

She grinned, adJuliag her headband. "More than enough. This place will smell so good, Ryan won't be able to resist making a fool of himself trying to critique your food." The laughter that bubbled up between us felt like the perfect antidote to the nerves tightening my stomach.

As the crowd began to gather, the energy shifted, and I felt a mix of apprehension and exhilaration. The students milled about, some darting glances at our table, their curiosity piqued by the vibrant colors and enticing scents. It wasn't just a display; it was a statement—a declaration that I belonged in both worlds, kitchen and field alike.

When the pep rally officially began, the gymnasium erupted with cheers and spirited shouts, a symphony of voices reverberating against the walls. Our principal took the stage, rallying the crowd with anecdotes about the football team and their recent victories. I stood at our table, my heart pounding, eager for the moment when I could share my culinary creations with everyone.

But just as the excitement reached a fever pitch, Ryan made his grand entrance, striding in like he owned the place, flanked by his posse. His swagger radiated confidence, the kind that made my stomach twist into knots. "What's this? A cooking station at a pep rally? I thought we were here to celebrate real talent," he called out, his voice cutting through the noise.

I felt the temperature in the room drop, the playful buzz evaporating like mist in the morning sun. My heart raced, each beat echoing louder than the last. "Who invited the culinary critic?" Mia whispered beside me, her eyes narrowing at Ryan.

"Just breathe," I murmured back, determined not to let him shake me. I could feel my courage waver, but I wasn't about to back down.

Ryan sauntered over, his confidence palpable, and the laughter that followed him rippled through the crowd like a wave. "What do you think you're doing, Calderon? Cooking up another disaster?" He leaned against our table, inspecting the salsa with exaggerated skepticism. "Is this even edible, or just a clever way to distract from the game?"

I straightened my spine, refusing to let his mockery penetrate my resolve. "Why don't you try it and find out?" I challenged, my voice steady despite the fluttering in my stomach.

His eyebrows shot up, and for a fleeting moment, I could see the surprise in his eyes. "Oh, I wouldn't want to ruin my taste buds," he replied, smirking. "But I'd love to watch you flop."

The crowd shifted, curiosity piquing as they watched the exchange unfold. It felt like standing on the edge of a precipice, the air thick with tension, and all eyes were on us. I could feel my pulse quicken, the weight of their expectations pressing down like a heavy blanket. "What are you so afraid of, Ryan? That I might actually be good?"

He chuckled, the sound rich with disdain. "Good? Please. You're a joke trying to be taken seriously."

The laughter from the crowd stung, each chuckle a dagger aimed at my insecurities. I glanced at Mia, her fierce gaze igniting something inside me. This was my moment. I had worked hard for this, and Ryan's derision wouldn't dictate my worth.

"Fine, let's make this interesting," I said, my voice cutting through the tension like a knife. "How about a taste test? You and I will both prepare something, and the crowd will decide who's the real chef here."

Ryan's eyes gleamed with mischief, and for a moment, I feared he would laugh it off. Instead, he leaned in closer, a challenging grin plastered on his face. "You're on, Calderon. But don't cry when you lose."

The crowd erupted into cheers, the excitement growing as students eagerly encouraged us to proceed. It felt like stepping onto the field for the championship game, every nerve in my body firing in anticipation. "Alright, then. Let's do this," I said, my voice steady despite the storm brewing inside me.

As we gathered our ingredients, I felt the adrenaline coursing through my veins, sharpening my focus. I was no longer just a football player or a wannabe chef; I was a force to be reckoned with, ready to prove myself. I quickly sketched out a plan in my mind, merging flavors and techniques I knew would impress, channeling the essence of the culinary festival into a dish that would leave no room for doubt.

The time flew by as I moved through the steps of preparation, my hands dancing over the cutting board, the vibrant colors of fresh vegetables coming together in a symphony of flavor. I glanced up to see Ryan assembling his dish with the kind of smug confidence that made my blood boil. His concoction was nothing but a hodgepodge of ingredients, all show and no substance.

"Are you planning to serve that or is it just for decoration?" I shot back, the words spilling out before I could think.

He shot me a glare, his brows knitting together. "Just wait. You'll see who the real chef is."

With a smirk, I returned to my task, determined to showcase my skills. The clock ticked down, and the anticipation in the room felt electric, the murmurs of the crowd rising to a crescendo. Finally, the moment arrived, and as we plated our dishes, the tension in the air was palpable.

"Ladies and gentlemen, it's time for the ultimate showdown!" Mia announced, her enthusiasm infectious. "Taste both dishes and vote for your favorite!"

The crowd surged forward, eyes wide with curiosity and excitement. I set my plate before the judges, a vibrant salsa verde atop perfectly seasoned fish tacos, garnished with fresh cilantro and lime. Ryan presented his dish, a chaotic assortment that resembled a last-minute attempt to clean out a fridge. The students erupted in laughter, the contrast stark between the two plates.

Just as the first bites were taken, the gym doors swung open, and a figure entered—one I hadn't expected to see. My heart dropped, the joy of the moment crashing down like a wave upon a rocky shore. Ryan glanced over, a look of surprise morphing into a sly grin. "Looks like we have an audience," he muttered, the corners of his mouth twitching.

I turned, my stomach plummeting as I recognized the newcomer. It was my father, standing at the entrance, eyes scanning the crowd before landing on me. Confusion etched across his face, and in that moment, the world felt like it had shifted beneath my feet. My heart raced, uncertainty flooding my mind as I confronted the reality of his presence at the pep rally.

I tried to muster a smile, to project confidence, but the thrill of the competition faded into the background as the weight of my father's gaze bore down on me. Would he see me as a joke, just as Ryan did? Would this moment shatter the fragile confidence I had built?

The cheers of the crowd faded into a dull roar, and as my father stepped further into the gym, I could feel the stakes rise, the tension tightening like a noose around my neck. The fate of my culinary ambitions now hung in the balance, poised on the edge of a knife, ready to tip in either direction.

# Chapter 11: Allies and Adversaries

The vibrant tapestry of autumn unfolded around us as Kayla and I jogged along the winding path. Leaves, ablaze with hues of gold and crimson, danced in the gentle breeze, creating a canopy that rustled like a thousand whispers. My lungs filled with the crisp, earthy scent of fallen foliage, each breath a grounding reminder that the world continued to spin, indifferent to the heartache that lurked in the corners of my mind. Kayla's rhythmic footfalls kept pace with mine, a steady heartbeat that reassured me amidst the disarray.

"He doesn't define you," she said, her voice as warm as the sunlight filtering through the branches. I glanced sideways, her face glowing with determination, her eyes sparkling with the kind of confidence I so desperately craved. "You're more than his words. You have dreams, passions that light you up. Don't let him dim that fire."

A smile tugged at my lips, the corners turning upward at her fierce loyalty. "You make it sound so easy. Just brush it off and move on, right? If only it were that simple." I kicked a stray pebble, watching it skitter away as if it, too, wanted to escape the weight of negativity.

Kayla matched my stride, her expression thoughtful. "It's not easy, but you're tougher than you realize. Remember when we used to climb the cliffs by the lake? You were terrified at first, but you faced that fear head-on. This is just another cliff to scale. And I'm here, every step of the way."

The memory flooded my mind—us perched at the edge, adrenaline pulsing through our veins as we dared each other to leap into the cool, inviting water below. That leap had been exhilarating, a brief moment of doubt swallowed by the thrill of the plunge. If only facing Ryan's cruelty could feel the same. The ache in my chest tightened, the words he had flung like daggers replaying in my head. I shook my head, trying to dispel the dark cloud hovering above.

"What if I can't face him? What if he keeps coming at me?" The vulnerability slipped from my lips before I could rein it in. I hated sounding weak, yet the fear pooled in my stomach like a rock.

"Then you'll face him together with me," Kayla asserted, her chin tilting defiantly. "You're not alone in this. We'll come up with a plan. Besides, have you seen how awful he is at basketball? I'm pretty sure he couldn't hit water if he fell out of a boat."

A laugh bubbled up, breaking the tension. Kayla's ability to lighten the mood was nothing short of miraculous. "Okay, I guess that's true. Maybe he should stick to the insults instead of the hoops."

"Exactly!" She nudged me playfully with her shoulder, and I felt a surge of warmth in my chest. It was moments like these—when laughter was the bridge over the troubled waters of my mind—that I cherished most. The world around us faded, the vibrancy of the leaves and the chill in the air replaced by the pulse of our friendship.

As we approached the park, the vibrant community center nestled at its edge loomed into view. It had always been a hub of life and activity, a place where laughter echoed and friendships flourished. But today, a tension rippled through the air like a pre-storm silence, leaving a bitter taste in my mouth. The benches, usually filled with families and children playing tag, were mostly empty, the distant sounds of laughter muted by an unsettling hush.

"Let's hit the swings," I suggested, needing a moment of childlike freedom to counteract the heaviness of my thoughts. We drifted towards the playground, the familiar creak of the swing set inviting me back to simpler times.

As I settled onto the swing, my feet brushing the ground, Kayla mirrored my actions, and we began to sway gently. The rhythmic motion grounded me, the sky above sprawling into a brilliant blue canvas, streaked with wisps of white clouds. "You know," I began, the words spilling out, "I thought things would get easier once I graduated high school. I dreamed about starting fresh, leaving behind all the drama." I kicked my feet, pushing higher, trying to launch my worries into the sky.

Kayla kept pace beside me, her brow furrowing in contemplation. "Yeah, but the world doesn't work like that. Sometimes, you carry pieces of your past with you, whether you like it or not. The real challenge is deciding what to do with those pieces."

I halted, feet brushing against the soft earth, and turned to face her, my heart racing with a sudden clarity. "So, what do I do with the piece that's Ryan? Do I confront him? Stand my ground?" The prospect sent a shiver down my spine. "I can't just let him walk all over me."

"You're not one to back down," she said, her voice firm. "Face him with your truth. You don't owe him an apology for being who you are. He's the one in the wrong."

I nodded slowly, each beat of my heart resonating with the steeliness in her words. Maybe I didn't have to cower. Perhaps I could stand tall, eyes blazing with the conviction that had always been buried beneath layers of self-doubt. I could confront him, but what if that confrontation only escalated things?

In that moment of uncertainty, the air shifted. A figure loomed at the edge of the playground, casting a long shadow that darkened my resolve. Ryan leaned against a tree, arms crossed, the smirk on his face as familiar as the burning anger it ignited in me. He radiated the kind of arrogance that made me want to scream, yet I felt the knot of fear tightening.

"Looks like our little planning session just got a little more interesting," Kayla murmured, her eyes narrowing with determination.

"Yeah," I whispered, the thrill of challenge rushing through me like wildfire. Perhaps it was time to transform that fear into something powerful. The weight of his gaze felt like a leaden blanket, but this time, I wouldn't let it suffocate me. I took a deep breath, a resolve hardening within me. Whatever was about to unfold, I would face it head-on.

With Kayla beside me, I stepped forward, ready to reclaim my narrative, my strength, and my identity.

The air shimmered with unspoken tension as I approached Ryan, who stood lazily against the gnarled trunk of the oak tree, arms crossed and a smirk playing at the corners of his lips. It was infuriating, that sense of entitlement he wore like a badge, but beneath my anger, a flicker of something else sparked—fear. I glanced back at Kayla, who remained steadfast beside me, her eyes locked on Ryan with the intensity of a lioness protecting her cubs.

"Hey there, princess," Ryan called, his voice dripping with mockery. "I see you've brought your bodyguard. What's next? A playdate at the local park?"

I took a deep breath, grounding myself in Kayla's unwavering presence. "Nice to see you, Ryan. I didn't realize this was your personal stage."

"Everything's a stage for some, sweetheart," he shot back, his arrogance wrapped tightly around him like a comfort blanket. "What are you going to do? Whine to your friend about how the big bad wolf is being mean?"

Kayla stepped forward, her confidence almost tangible, like heat radiating off the asphalt. "Actually, we were just discussing how some wolves get a little too comfortable in their dens, thinking they can huff and puff without consequence."

A flicker of surprise crossed Ryan's face, momentarily disrupting his swagger. "Oh, look at you, all brave and clever. How cute." He pushed off the tree, taking a step closer, his eyes narrowing with the predatory gleam of someone who enjoyed the chase. "You really think you can take me on?"

"Why not?" I replied, my heart pounding with each word that broke free of my mouth. "I'm tired of being afraid of your pathetic attempts to intimidate me. This isn't high school drama; it's just pathetic. You might want to grow up."

"Pathetic?" He laughed, but there was an edge to it. "You think you can just walk around here and pretend like you matter? Trust me, I'm the least of your worries."

"Then what is it?" I shot back, the warmth of anger fueling my courage. "Is it that hard to face someone who won't back down? Or are you too busy trying to convince yourself that your words actually have weight?"

Ryan's expression twisted, and for a moment, he looked almost human, the mask of arrogance slipping to reveal something darker. "You really want to dance with me? Fine, but remember this: not everyone has your best interests at heart."

Before I could reply, he turned and walked away, a gust of air following his retreat as if he'd stolen the vibrancy of the moment. I stood frozen, the adrenaline still coursing through my veins, the thrill of confrontation battling with the leftover sting of his words.

"Did you just see that?" Kayla exclaimed, eyes wide with astonishment. "That was... epic!"

I could hardly believe it myself, but the moment felt surreal, like an out-of-body experience where I had watched myself stand up to the very person who had haunted my high school life. "I can't believe I said all that," I confessed, still catching my breath. "It felt... good, but also terrifying."

"Good and terrifying are often best friends," she said, a proud grin lighting up her face. "And trust me, you did not back down. I think he was actually taken aback."

"I hope so," I replied, still slightly trembling. "Maybe I can start a trend of standing up to bullies. I might need to take notes from you on how to be that confident."

Kayla nudged me with her shoulder. "You already have it in you. Just keep reminding yourself: you're not what he says you are. And you know what? We should celebrate this. We deserve a treat after this little showdown."

"Oh, I'm always in for food," I said, feeling my mood lighten as we began to walk away from the playground. "Let's head to that little café down the street, the one with the giant cinnamon rolls."

"I could inhale one of those," she agreed, her eyes sparkling with delight. "But first, we need to bask in the glory of your heroic moment."

We strolled toward the café, laughter spilling from our lips, the weight of earlier encounters dissipating with each step. The aroma of coffee and baked goods wafted through the air, wrapping around us like a warm hug. As we entered, the familiar hum of conversation welcomed us, the cozy atmosphere inviting.

The café was a sanctuary of warmth and laughter, with mismatched chairs and a wall lined with bookshelves overflowing with novels and board games. It was one of those places where time seemed to pause, the world outside blurring into a distant memory. I made my way to the counter, the glass case filled with sugary treasures tempting me like a siren's call.

"Cinnamon roll, please," I said, my mouth watering at the sight of the pillowy dough topped with a thick layer of cream cheese frosting. Kayla ordered a slice of carrot cake, her eyes gleaming with anticipation.

We settled into a small table by the window, sunlight streaming in and casting a golden glow across the rustic wooden surface. As we waited for our treats, I felt a rush of gratitude for this moment, this friend who had become my anchor amidst the storm.

"Here's to you, my fearless warrior," Kayla said, raising her mug of steaming hot chocolate. "May you continue to conquer the world one confrontation at a time."

"Cheers to that," I replied, clinking my mug against hers. We both took a sip, the rich chocolate warming me from the inside out, a comfort that felt almost like a protective shield against the uncertainties ahead.

"Okay, spill," Kayla said, leaning in with an exaggerated seriousness. "What's your plan for Ryan? You can't just let him off the hook that easily."

The cinnamon roll arrived, its scent intoxicating, and I took a moment to savor the sweetness before answering. "Honestly, I'm not sure. Part of me wants to keep standing up to him, but another part is afraid of what happens next. If I push too hard, will he retaliate? He's not exactly known for playing fair."

"Let him retaliate," she said, eyes fierce. "What can he do? Call you names? You're stronger than that, and every time you stand up for yourself, you take away his power. It's like deflating a balloon."

"An angry balloon, no less," I quipped, eliciting a laugh from Kayla.

"Exactly! And who doesn't love a good balloon deflation?" She took a big bite of her cake, her eyes closing momentarily as she savored the flavor. "You need to focus on the things you love. Find your fire again."

I pondered her words, the warmth of the café surrounding us like a cozy blanket. "You're right. I need to immerse myself in the things that make me happy, the things that remind me of who I am. I want to paint more, explore new ideas, and maybe even write some poetry. Who knows?"

"That's the spirit! Find the things that fuel you and let them drown out the noise," Kayla encouraged, her enthusiasm infectious.

As we continued to chat and laugh, I felt the weight of the world slowly lifting, replaced by a flickering hope that perhaps I could navigate the turbulent waters of my life with newfound strength. Maybe facing my fears wasn't just about standing up to Ryan but also about rediscovering the joy in the things I loved.

With that thought swirling in my mind, I leaned back in my chair, a genuine smile spreading across my face. The café, the vibrant conversations, the sweet scent of cinnamon rolls—all of it felt like a promise that I was beginning to reclaim my narrative, one delicious bite at a time.

The café buzzed with life, and for a moment, the world outside faded into a backdrop of muted colors, leaving only the warmth of friendship and the comforting scent of baked goods. Kayla's laughter wrapped around me like a soft blanket, shielding me from the anxiety that had gripped me earlier. Each bite of my cinnamon roll melted in my mouth, sweet and rich, reminiscent of the carefree days of our childhood when sugar was a cure-all for life's troubles.

"Okay, so what's the next step in your grand plan?" Kayla asked, leaning forward, her eyes glimmering with mischief. "Are we going to start a club? 'Confronting Your High School Bullies 101'? I'll be your first recruit."

I chuckled, picturing a ragtag group of misfits armed with self-help books and bravado. "I can see it now. We'll make matching t-shirts and everything."

"Definitely. We'll add 'Keep Calm and Kick Ryan's Ass' on the back," she declared, her voice dripping with faux seriousness.

I couldn't help but smile. The thought of taking a stand with Kayla by my side gave me a sense of power. "You know, it's not just about Ryan. There are other battles I need to confront—like figuring out what I really want to do after high school. Sometimes I feel like I'm just coasting."

"Coasting?" she exclaimed, her eyebrows shooting up. "You're not a boat, you're a fierce speedboat cutting through the waves! You have talent, ambition. I mean, have you seen the way you paint? Your work could hang in a gallery! You should be out there making your mark."

Her faith in me sparked a light that had long been dimmed by self-doubt. "You really think so?"

"I know so," she insisted, a hand resting on mine. "You've always had that spark. It's just hiding behind a fog of doubt."

I took a deep breath, contemplating her words. Perhaps I could turn the fear of failure into a canvas, paint my insecurities in bold colors, and showcase them rather than hide them. "You might be onto something. Maybe I'll take a leap—enter a local art show or something."

"Now you're talking!" Kayla's enthusiasm radiated across the table. "And just imagine Ryan's face when he sees your work displayed for everyone to admire. Priceless!"

"Too priceless," I mused, a playful grin creeping onto my face. "But what if no one likes it?"

"Who cares? You're doing this for you, not for a popularity contest. This is your time to shine. And if anyone dares to say anything negative, I'll bring my trusty air horn and blast them off the stage."

I laughed, picturing the absurdity of it all. "I can just see the headlines now: 'Local Artist Silenced by Overzealous Friend with Air Horn.'"

"Right? It'll be a scandal!"

Just then, a flash of movement outside the café caught my eye, and my heart sank. There stood Ryan, leaning casually against a lamppost, his phone held up as if he were taking a picture. My stomach twisted into knots as the laughter between Kayla and me faded into silence, replaced by a heavy blanket of dread.

"Why is he here?" I murmured, my voice barely above a whisper.

"Is he stalking you now?" Kayla's eyes narrowed. "We need to go outside and confront him. Maybe we can scare him away with our brilliance."

"Scare him away or start a photo war?" I replied, my heart racing.

We peered through the window, watching as Ryan laughed at something on his phone, his attention elsewhere. "What's he doing?" I wondered aloud. "Is he really taking pictures of me?"

Kayla scoffed, the fire of indignation igniting within her. "Let's give him a show then. Get ready."

I swallowed hard, a surge of adrenaline rushing through me. "Are we really going to confront him again?"

"Why not? You just stood your ground like a champ. Let's keep the momentum going."

We stepped out of the café, the crisp autumn air filling my lungs as I squared my shoulders. Ryan's laughter faded as he caught sight of us, his smirk widening into a grin that sent shivers down my spine.

"Look who decided to grace us with her presence," he called out, feigning surprise. "Didn't expect to see you here, busy plotting your next masterpiece or something."

I fought the urge to shrink under his gaze, instead holding my ground. "Nice to see you too, Ryan. I'm actually taking suggestions for my next piece, and I was thinking of painting a portrait of an overgrown toddler."

The air crackled between us, a silent challenge lacing the atmosphere. Kayla snickered beside me, a hint of amusement shining in her eyes.

Ryan stepped forward, his confidence still palpable. "You're really going to play this game? You think you're so clever? You're just digging your own grave."

My heart thudded in my chest as I glanced at Kayla, who nodded in encouragement. "You know, that sounds like a threat. You might want to check yourself before you say something you'll regret."

"Regret? Ha! What do you know about regret?" he shot back, the facade of coolness slipping for a brief moment. "You're just a wannabe artist trying to pretend you're something special."

At that moment, I felt an unexpected wave of calm wash over me, like the eye of a storm. "You think I'm pretending? I've spent years honing my craft while you've spent years coasting on your reputation. But what happens when that reputation fizzles? What do you have left?"

Ryan's face darkened, and for a fleeting moment, I thought I saw a flicker of vulnerability behind his bravado. "You don't know anything about me," he spat, but there was a tremor in his voice, a crack in the armor he so proudly wore.

"Maybe I don't," I admitted, stepping closer, the distance between us narrowing. "But I do know that bullying is a weak person's game. And if you keep playing, you'll find yourself standing alone."

He hesitated, the defiance in his eyes wavering. Just as I thought I'd struck a nerve, the sound of a car screeching to a halt interrupted us. A sleek black vehicle came to an abrupt stop nearby, and the passenger door swung open. Out stepped a tall figure—someone I recognized instantly, and my heart dropped.

"Ryan!" the newcomer shouted, striding towards us with an intensity that sent an unsettling chill through the air. "What are you doing?"

The tension in the air thickened, and I exchanged a bewildered glance with Kayla. This was no ordinary confrontation. The very air crackled with the promise of chaos as the figure approached, their intentions unclear, and suddenly, the ground beneath me felt precarious, as if I were teetering on the edge of something monumental.

"Who's your friend?" Kayla murmured, her eyes darting between me and the newcomer, who was now only a few paces away.

"Someone you don't want to mess with," Ryan shot back, a flicker of anxiety passing across his face.

Just as the stranger reached us, I took a step back, instinctively sensing that whatever was about to unfold could change everything. And in that moment, the world around me faded, the air thick with uncertainty as I braced myself for what came next, my heart racing with the realization that I was standing on the precipice of something I never saw coming.

# Chapter 12: Threads of Connection

The gentle hum of the sewing machine filled the air, a rhythmic backdrop to our late-night sessions, as Kayla and I settled into a routine that felt both exhilarating and terrifying. Sunlight had long surrendered to twilight, casting a warm glow across my studio, the dim light bouncing off spools of thread and half-finished designs. The walls, adorned with sketches of dresses and suits, now bore witness to a new chapter—a fusion of fabric and fists that sparked an idea. The air smelled faintly of fabric softener mixed with the sweet aroma of the cookies I'd baked earlier, a small peace offering for our creative marathon.

Kayla, her dark hair pulled into a messy bun, leaned over the drafting table, her brow furrowed in concentration. "What if we did a theme based on strength?" she proposed, her voice laced with the confidence of someone who knew how to throw a punch both in the ring and in life. "Like, the elegance of movement—showing how beauty and strength can coexist."

I couldn't help but smile. It was a perfect reflection of who she was, both a fighter and a beacon of grace. The way she spoke about boxing brought it to life for me; it wasn't just about physical prowess, it was an art form, much like fashion. I found myself nodding, excitement bubbling inside me. "We could have the models wear outfits that reflect the sport. Think boxing shorts made from shimmering fabric, and blazers that flow with each step. We could even incorporate some boxing motifs into the designs."

Her eyes lit up, a spark igniting as she jotted down ideas. I could see her mind racing, envisioning the catwalk transformed into a battleground of color and form. As the ideas flowed, so did the moments between us—those shared looks that lingered just a beat too long, electrifying and complicated, hinting at an undercurrent of something deeper.

I shook my head, almost laughing at my own naivete. Why was I entertaining the idea that there could be more than friendship between us? I reminded myself that we were in this together for the cause, the youth who needed hope and guidance. I pushed my feelings aside, burying them beneath sketches and fabrics, but the way her laughter intertwined with mine made it increasingly difficult to ignore.

The planning phase turned into a whirlwind of excitement. We enlisted the help of local businesses, each eager to support a cause that resonated with the community. Posters splashed with vibrant colors began to populate the campus, each showcasing the date of our event and the dual purpose it served—style and strength, empowerment and unity. I reveled in the process, using my creativity to capture the essence of what we wanted to convey, while Kayla lent her physical prowess to the promotional efforts, rallying friends and teammates alike.

As we spent those late evenings sketching and planning, I couldn't help but admire Kayla's spirit. She was relentless, a true force of nature, and watching her pursue her passion with such fervor made me question my own motivations. I was drawn not just to her ideas, but to the fire in her soul that illuminated every dark corner of my own insecurities. It made me yearn for something more than just friendship—something more than the sweet camaraderie we shared over takeout containers and coffee-stained sketches.

Yet, as the days melted into each other, I wrestled with the fear that threatened to suffocate my burgeoning feelings. I found myself wondering if she sensed the tension, if she could feel the way my heart raced whenever her shoulder brushed against mine or how I felt the world blur when she laughed.

One night, as we spread out the designs across the table, I caught her gaze lingering on one of my more daring pieces—a gown with flowing fabric that would dance around the model like a breeze.

"This is incredible," she said, her voice softening, almost reverent. "It's beautiful. It's you."

My heart skipped a beat, and I felt a flush creep up my neck. "Thanks," I replied, trying to keep my tone light. "I just wanted to create something that could inspire others."

Kayla's expression shifted, a flicker of something unspoken passing between us. "You inspire me," she said, and the weight of her words hung in the air, a palpable charge. I dared to look up, to meet her gaze, and for a moment, I was lost in the depth of her eyes, the warmth they radiated.

But then reality intruded, slicing through the moment like a sharp blade. I thought of the potential backlash, the judgment we might face from those who failed to understand our vision. My heart sank at the thought of losing her to misconceptions, to the whispers of a campus that often judged without understanding.

Yet, just as I prepared to pull away, Kayla reached out, her fingers brushing against mine, grounding me in the moment. "You know," she said, her voice low, almost conspiratorial, "this is more than just a fashion show. It's a statement. We're telling people that it's okay to be both strong and beautiful."

Her words wrapped around me, a comforting embrace, and in that moment, I realized I wanted to stand beside her, to fight for our vision together. This wasn't just a collaboration; it was the beginning of something larger, a shared mission to empower those who felt unheard.

With a new sense of purpose igniting my spirit, I knew I had to overcome my fears. We would show them how beautiful it could be when strength and grace intertwined. Together, we would craft an unforgettable experience, one that would echo in the hearts of those who attended, and maybe, just maybe, we could weave our own connection into the fabric of something remarkable.

The weeks flew by in a flurry of fabric swatches and late-night brainstorming sessions, and I could hardly keep up with the surge of excitement building around our charity event. Our small town was buzzing, its streets painted with the vibrant colors of anticipation and curiosity. Posters hung in every window, announcing the date and encouraging people to support a cause that felt deeply personal to both of us. I reveled in the idea that we were crafting something meaningful together, a message wrapped in sequins and strength.

Kayla and I met almost daily, each session brimming with laughter, debate, and the occasional playful argument about which design truly captured the essence of our vision. I marveled at her ability to juggle her responsibilities as a student and a budding athlete, all while keeping our collaboration at the forefront. She was like a whirlwind—full of energy, laughter, and unexpected insights. It was contagious, and I often found myself laughing long after she had left, the echoes of her spirit lingering like the scent of my favorite perfume.

One evening, as we settled into my studio surrounded by crumpled sketches and fabric remnants, she leaned back in her chair and sighed dramatically. "So, if you could design an outfit for anyone in the world, who would it be?"

I raised an eyebrow, intrigued by the question. "Oh, that's easy. I'd create something fabulous for you. You've got that fierce attitude; you need a wardrobe that matches."

Kayla chuckled, her laugh bright and airy. "Flattery will get you nowhere, but I appreciate the vote of confidence." She leaned in closer, her eyes glinting with mischief. "But really, let's say it's for a celebrity. Who would it be?"

I pondered for a moment, the possibilities swirling in my mind. "Maybe someone like Zendaya. She has such a unique style; it's bold yet effortlessly chic."

"Now that's a challenge," Kayla grinned. "I can picture it—an outfit that allows her to box her way into a gala, maybe with a sequined skirt that flows while she throws punches. Imagine the headlines!"

"Right? 'Zendaya Knocks Out the Competition in Couture!'" I laughed, and for a moment, our conversation spiraled into a playful frenzy of imagining celebrity collaborations, each one more outrageous than the last. The laughter was a balm, an escape from the underlying tension of my feelings that bubbled just beneath the surface.

As the event approached, the air was electric with anticipation. The day before our big night, we found ourselves in the final throes of preparation. My studio, usually an oasis of organization, had devolved into a creative battlefield, with sketches and fabrics sprawled across every surface. Kayla stood in front of the mirror, adJuliag the boxing gloves I had bedazzled just for her, the glimmer of rhinestones catching the soft light.

"You know," she said, turning to face me, her expression serious yet playful, "if this whole fashion thing doesn't work out, you could always become a bedazzler for aspiring boxers."

I rolled my eyes, feigning indignation. "Hey! Bedazzling is an art form. I'm sure I'd have a line of clients begging for my services."

"True, but I'm not sure how well the 'fierce yet fashionable' approach would go over in the ring." Her laughter was infectious, filling the room with warmth and camaraderie. It was moments like these that made me forget my worries, even if just for a heartbeat.

As I made my way through the chaotic preparations, I felt the weight of my feelings for her pressing down. My heart raced with every interaction, each one a delicate dance between friendship and something unspoken. I wasn't sure how to navigate the complexity of it all, especially with the charity event looming over us like a double-edged sword, a blend of excitement and anxiety.

The day of the event dawned bright and clear, the sun illuminating the world as if it were in on our secret. The venue, a charming old theater, had been transformed with splashes of color and life. Models practiced their walks in the backstage area, while volunteers buzzed around, adJuliag decorations and ensuring everything was perfect. I stood in the middle of the chaos, feeling both exhilarated and overwhelmed.

"Are you ready for this?" Kayla appeared beside me, her energy infectious, her presence grounding. She was clad in one of my designs, a fitted top paired with sleek shorts, her boxing gloves resting on her hips. She looked like a goddess ready for battle.

"More than ready. I just hope the models remember their cues," I admitted, biting my lip as I surveyed the bustling backstage.

"Oh, they'll be fine," she reassured me, nudging my shoulder with hers. "Besides, if anyone stumbles, just call it part of the show. We're merging elegance with strength, remember? It's all about embracing the unexpected."

I chuckled, her confidence washing over me like a wave. "Right, just like when I tripped during that fashion show in my freshman year. It was all part of the grand performance!"

We shared a laugh, but as the clock ticked down, the reality of the situation crept in. The atmosphere crackled with anticipation, and I caught sight of a few familiar faces among the crowd. My heart raced as I spotted a group of students who had previously dismissed my designs, their skeptical gazes making my stomach churn.

"Hey, don't let them get to you," Kayla said, reading my expression with an uncanny knack. "Remember, we're here for a bigger purpose."

I nodded, inhaling deeply, trying to drown out the doubts. "You're right. We're making a statement."

Just then, the music began to play, a pulse that reverberated through the room, drawing everyone's attention. Models began to emerge, their strides confident, the outfits I had poured my heart into gliding seamlessly across the stage. I watched, breathless, as each design told a story of strength and beauty, a testament to everything we had worked for.

And then came Kayla's moment. As she stepped onto the stage, the atmosphere shifted, the energy crackling like static. She held herself with such poise, every movement precise yet fluid, her boxing gloves gleaming in the spotlight. The audience erupted into applause, and I found myself breathless, completely captivated by her presence.

Just as she began to demonstrate a few boxing moves, I noticed a figure standing at the back of the crowd—Jake, her ex, arms crossed, an expression that was difficult to read. The smile on Kayla's face faltered for a brief second, a shadow passing over her radiant spirit. My heart raced, an unsettling feeling coiling in my stomach. What was he doing here?

But before I could dwell on it, Kayla's focus snapped back to the crowd, her confidence unyielding. She resumed her demonstration, showcasing a blend of strength and grace that was nothing short of mesmerizing. In that moment, the world outside faded away, leaving only the two of us, intertwined in a performance that felt destined to unfold.

The atmosphere in the theater was electric, each heartbeat synchronized with the rhythm of the music that pulsed through the air. Kayla's performance captivated the crowd, her movements fluid and fierce as she demonstrated punches and footwork with the grace of a dancer and the power of a boxer. I could hardly tear my eyes away from her, the way she commanded the stage with every strike and jab made my heart swell. The applause was thunderous, a testament to her skill and the undeniable connection we shared, a thread woven between us in that moment.

As she finished her demonstration, the energy in the room shifted; it was as if the audience had collectively caught their breath.

Kayla stood there, radiating confidence, sweat glistening on her forehead, and for a brief second, the world around us faded into oblivion. I wanted to rush to her side, to revel in her triumph, but my feet felt glued to the ground. Instead, I smiled, cheering along with the crowd, hoping she could sense my pride from where I stood.

But then, just as the last of the applause faded, I noticed Jake's presence growing more pronounced at the back of the crowd. His arms were still crossed, and his expression was unreadable, shifting between intrigue and something more sinister. A knot tightened in my stomach as I saw Kayla glance his way, her bright smile faltering momentarily. I knew that look, the flicker of uncertainty that brushed her features.

"Not now," I muttered under my breath, willing her to shake off whatever doubt lingered at the edge of her thoughts. She was the star of the show, and nothing should detract from that.

But just as she began to step down from the stage, he moved toward her, weaving through the audience with an unsettling confidence that made my blood run cold. My heart raced, fueled by a protective instinct I hadn't known I possessed. I started to make my way through the throng of attendees, dodging well-wishers and excited chatter, desperate to reach her before he could say anything.

"Kayla!" I called, my voice rising above the chatter, but it was drowned out by the murmurs of the crowd.

"Hey, you did great!" I heard her say to someone nearby, forcing a smile that didn't quite reach her eyes. My breath hitched as Jake reached her, an insufferable grin plastered across his face, and I felt the familiar heat of jealousy simmering in my chest.

I finally pushed my way through the last barrier of people and approached them just in time to hear him say, "I didn't think you'd actually go through with this, Kayla. I mean, fashion and boxing? Sounds like a mid-life crisis waiting to happen." His tone dripped with condescension, and I could see her stiffen at his words.

"Or it sounds like a great way to inspire young people," she replied, her voice steady but lacking its usual vibrancy. "You wouldn't understand, would you?"

I stepped forward, the protective fire igniting within me. "What's he doing here?" I interrupted, directing my question at Kayla but glaring at Jake. "Didn't you get the memo? This is about empowerment, not your latest attempt to undermine her."

Jake raised an eyebrow, amusement flickering in his eyes. "Oh, look at you, the little fashionista coming to the rescue. How adorable."

"Don't you have better things to do?" I shot back, the words spilling from my lips before I could stop them. I could feel the weight of the moment thickening, a palpable tension hanging in the air.

Kayla shifted her weight, looking between us with concern. "Guys, can we just—"

"No, I want to hear what he has to say," I cut her off, feeling a surge of defiance. "Please, enlighten us with your wisdom on how you can be both a boxing champion and a total jerk."

"Fine," Jake shrugged, the smirk never leaving his face. "Just know that whatever little dream you think you're building here is a fantasy. You're not going to change the world with a fashion show. It's all fluff."

Before I could respond, Kayla stepped forward, her demeanor shifting from discomfort to determination. "You know what, Jake? I'm done with your negativity. I'm doing this for the kids, and you're not going to ruin it for me. You might want to look in the mirror and figure out why you're so bitter."

Her words hung in the air, and for a brief moment, I felt a swell of pride. There she was, the fierce fighter I adored, standing her ground against the very person who had once tried to diminish her spirit.

But Jake wasn't finished. "Cute speech, but I can't help but wonder if you'll really be able to pull this off without falling apart," he said, his voice dripping with sarcasm. "Let's be real; the last time you were this excited about something, it blew up in your face."

The crowd around us hushed, and I could see Kayla's expression harden, a flash of hurt crossing her features before she masked it with a steely resolve. "I've got this, Jake. And if you're not here to support me, then you should probably leave."

With that, she turned away, her jaw set, but I felt the tension radiating off her like heat waves. I wanted to reach out, to comfort her, to tell her that she was incredible and that she didn't need to prove anything to anyone, especially not to someone like him. But before I could speak, Jake stepped forward again, blocking her path. "You really think this is going to go well? What happens when you stumble? When you fail?"

It was like a dagger aimed straight at her heart. I could see the cracks forming in her facade, and I took a step closer, ready to intervene, but before I could utter a word, she held up a hand, silencing us both.

"Do you honestly think your opinion matters to me?" she said, her voice steady despite the storm brewing beneath the surface. "I'm doing this because I believe in it. And I believe in me. So you can either support that or keep talking to the wall because I don't need you in my life."

The defiance in her words made the crowd buzz with murmurs of approval, and I couldn't help but smile. She was a force to be reckoned with, standing tall against the weight of his doubt. But just as the applause began to swell again, I noticed Jake's expression shift, a calculating glint flashing in his eyes.

"Fine, Kayla," he said, his tone almost smooth, "but you might want to think twice about what you're getting into. Sometimes the past has a way of creeping back in, and it doesn't always play nice."

A hush fell over the crowd, and I felt my heart race, the air thick with anticipation. Kayla blinked, uncertainty creeping into her gaze, and I wanted to reach out, to hold her, to shield her from whatever darkness lurked behind Jake's words. But before I could step forward, he turned and melted into the crowd, leaving behind a charged silence.

I took a deep breath, the weight of his warning hanging heavy in the air, the moment suspended like a pendulum. I turned to Kayla, wanting to convey my support, to assure her that she was stronger than anything Jake could throw at her, but her gaze was distant, staring into the crowd as if searching for something she couldn't name.

"Hey," I said softly, reaching for her arm, but she pulled away, her eyes wide with emotion.

"I... I need a moment," she whispered, her voice trembling slightly.

"Kayla, wait—"

But she was already moving, weaving through the crowd, her shoulders squared, determination and fear warring within her. I felt a gnawing anxiety settle in my chest. What had he said that had shaken her so deeply?

And just as I prepared to follow, a loud crash reverberated through the theater, the sound of glass shattering mingling with startled gasps. The audience turned, and I felt the blood drain from my face as I realized the source: the display case showcasing the most exquisite pieces of my collection lay in ruins.

Panic surged through me. The night had begun with such promise, and now it felt like everything was unraveling. I scanned the crowd for Kayla, but she was lost in the thrumming chaos, her expression a mixture of determination and dread, leaving me with a haunting feeling that this night was far from over.

# Chapter 13: A Game of Hearts

The lights hung low, casting a warm glow that danced like fireflies across the crowd, illuminating faces filled with eager expectation. I took a moment to soak it all in—the scent of fresh flowers mingling with the crispness of the autumn air drifting through the open windows. Laughter bubbled like champagne, intertwining with the soft strains of music that floated through the hall. Each note wrapped around me, wrapping me in a cocoon of joy and a hint of anxiety, as I awaited the spectacle about to unfold.

Kayla stood at the edge of the stage, her silhouette framed by the sparkling drapes that hung like cascading waterfalls. As the spotlight caught her, it transformed her from a friend into something ethereal, as if she were carved from starlight and ambition. Her outfit, a flowing gown in rich burgundy, hugged her figure in all the right places, accentuating her curves while allowing the fabric to flutter elegantly with each movement. The delicate lace that adorned the sleeves whispered secrets of grace, each flutter revealing just enough skin to tease the imagination without crossing into the realm of vulgarity.

As she stepped forward, her heels clicked confidently against the polished wooden stage, each sound resonating through my chest. I felt like an imposter in this world of glamour, yet at the same time, a proud cheerleader for the woman who had transformed my quiet life into something bursting with color and possibility. There was something almost magical in her presence; she seemed to draw everyone's eyes, and even the most jaded guests leaned forward, captivated.

"Look at her," I murmured to my friend Ben, who stood beside me with a knowing smile. "She's like a shooting star."

"She's definitely on fire," he replied, chuckling softly, his gaze glued to Kayla. "But you know that, right? You can't just stand there with that look of awe. She's going to need you out there, not just a spectator."

I rolled my eyes, though I couldn't suppress the grin creeping across my face. "You make it sound like I'm the one who's supposed to sweep her off her feet."

"Why not? She's the one with the magic, and you're the one who's always cheering her on." Ben nudged my side playfully, the warmth of his friendship comforting against the whirlwind of my thoughts. "I mean, she definitely lights up a room. Have you told her how you feel?"

The weight of his question hung between us, and for a moment, the atmosphere around us dulled, muffled by the internal chaos swirling in my mind. Did I really want to dive into that particular abyss? The thought of confessing my feelings felt like standing on the precipice of a great cliff, the plunge downwards promising both liberation and a perilous landing.

But there was no denying the flicker of something deeper in my chest as I watched Kayla. Every time our eyes met, my heart tripped over itself, stumbling into a dizzying state of joy and fear. Yet to voice those feelings, to risk the friendship we had so carefully built, felt like courting disaster.

"Just keep your eyes open," Ben said, bringing me back to the moment as he leaned forward, his gaze riveted on the stage. "She's about to dazzle."

And indeed, she did. As Kayla reached the center of the stage, she paused, taking a breath that seemed to ground her in the moment. The audience erupted into applause, a wave of sound that crashed over us, lifting her into the air as if she were floating on a cloud of encouragement. Her face shone with a mix of surprise and delight, and the way her lips curled into a smile ignited a spark within me, a deep yearning to be the reason behind that light.

The show continued, each model striding onto the stage, showcasing extravagant designs that spilled over with layers of creativity and color. But my focus remained steadfastly anchored to Kayla, who became the beating heart of the event. Every time she returned to the stage, the world around me faded into a haze. I felt both exhilarated and terrified, like a child clinging to the edge of a cliff, eager to leap into the unknown.

When the final model exited, leaving behind a flurry of applause and cheers, the moment finally came for Kayla to take her bow. She turned, eyes sparkling with the thrill of the evening, and my breath hitched as she scanned the crowd. Then, just as her gaze flickered over me, it lingered, and the world around us fell away. In that instant, it was just the two of us—a connection electric enough to spark flames.

Kayla rushed off the stage, her smile widening as she drew closer. "Did you see that?" she exclaimed, eyes alight with excitement. "I can't believe I did it!"

"You were phenomenal," I said, unable to hide my admiration. "You lit up the entire room."

Her laughter rang out, pure and genuine. "I felt like I was flying. It was terrifying but exhilarating! Thank you for being here. It means the world to me."

With that simple phrase, my heart did a little flip, and in that moment, the cacophony of applause faded, leaving only the rhythm of our shared joy. It was in the way she stood before me, flush with the thrill of her success, that I realized I was indeed a part of her world, just as she was of mine.

"Of course," I replied, the gravity of the moment shifting beneath my feet. "But if you think this is it, you're wrong. We have a celebration to plan!"

"Now that sounds like a challenge," she teased, eyes sparkling with mischief. "What do you have in mind?"

As we stepped away from the fading applause, I felt the air shift, thickening with unspoken possibilities and the promise of something more—something that could change everything.

The lights dimmed, and a hush fell over the crowd, thickening the air with a mix of expectation and curiosity. Kayla, clad in a striking ensemble that danced between avant-garde and classic elegance, commanded attention as she strode confidently across the stage. Her fiery red dress, adorned with intricate lacework, flowed behind her like a cape, whispering tales of boldness and defiance. Each step was deliberate, calculated, as if she were weaving a spell over the audience. A single spotlight illuminated her, casting a golden halo around her figure, making her appear almost ethereal.

I leaned forward in my seat, the plush fabric of the chair soft against my back, but my focus was entirely on her. Her hair cascaded down her shoulders in effortless waves, framing her face with an alluring glow. Every glance she received was accompanied by a whisper of awe, a testament to her magnetic presence. It was more than just the clothes; it was the way she carried herself, a confident blend of grace and fierceness that made her utterly captivating. In that moment, I realized how deeply I admired her spirit—a spirit that could light up even the darkest corners of a room.

As she reached the end of the runway, the applause erupted, thunderous and invigorating, enveloping her like a warm embrace. I couldn't help but clap along, my hands moving instinctively to match the rhythm of the cheers. My heart swelled with pride, a contradiction of emotions swirling within me. I was overwhelmed by a mix of love and envy; her dreams were unfurling before her, while I found myself tethered to the sidelines, the security of the familiar wrapping around me like a comforting blanket.

Moments later, the show unfolded in a whirlwind of colors, fabrics, and styles, each model showcasing unique designs. Yet, amidst the sea of creativity, I found my thoughts drifting back to

Kayla. She was a force of nature, but beneath the surface, I sensed the quiet anxieties that often accompanied her audacity. I imagined the sleepless nights she spent worrying if she was good enough, if her dreams were too big. With every garment that glided down the runway, I longed to reassure her that she was destined for greatness.

The event was more than just a fashion show; it was a celebration of resilience and ambition, punctuated by moments of unexpected camaraderie. At one point, I caught a glimpse of Michael, Kayla's business partner, in the crowd. He was impeccably dressed, his tailored suit a striking contrast to his playful demeanor. As he caught my eye, he flashed a grin that was both charming and mischievous. The energy between us had shifted recently; an unspoken understanding had grown, igniting a spark that danced tantalizingly between us.

"Hey! Save some applause for the rest of us!" he teased, his voice cutting through the buzz of the audience as he leaned toward me, his words laced with playful sarcasm.

I raised an eyebrow, unable to suppress a smile. "What can I say? She's my favorite model," I shot back, the banter flowing easily between us like a well-rehearsed duet.

"Careful," he replied, his eyes twinkling with mischief. "You might give the other models a complex."

"Let them try to keep up," I laughed, reveling in the lightness of our exchange. The camaraderie felt familiar yet exhilarating, a reminder of how much I cherished our shared moments, even amidst the swirling chaos of ambition.

As the final model took her turn, the atmosphere shifted, an electric charge buzzing through the air. Kayla returned to the stage for a final bow, her face glowing with triumph. She took a deep breath, the weight of her journey reflected in the proud set of her shoulders. I could see her heart racing, a visceral reaction that mirrored the exhilaration in the room. The applause crescendoed, enveloping her as she soaked in the moment, her joy infectious.

I couldn't help but feel a pang of longing. Would she allow me to be part of this world she was carving out for herself? I envisioned our future intertwined, navigating through the highs and lows of success, side by side. But doubt gnawed at me; would I be enough?

After the show, the crowd began to disperse, laughter and chatter filling the air like confetti. I spotted Kayla, surrounded by a throng of admirers, her laughter ringing out, bright and genuine. She radiated happiness, a glowing sun amidst the fading twilight. It was a sight that made my heart swell and my throat tighten. I pushed through the crowd, buoyed by an impulse I couldn't quite understand.

"Hey!" I called out, making my way toward her, my heart racing with a mixture of hope and fear. She turned, her eyes sparkling like the stars, and I caught a glimpse of something deeper, something profound beneath her vibrant exterior.

"Did you see that?" she exclaimed, her excitement palpable. "It was everything I dreamed it would be!"

"More than everything," I replied, my voice steady despite the fluttering in my chest. "You were phenomenal, Kayla. Truly. It felt like you were made for this."

Her smile faltered for a brief second, and in that flicker, I saw the vulnerability beneath her bravado. "Thanks. It was... overwhelming," she admitted, her voice dropping to a more intimate tone. "I just hope it's enough to get us noticed."

In that moment, I reached out, my hand brushing against hers, grounding us both amidst the chaos. "You are enough. You always have been. This is just the beginning."

Her eyes searched mine, and for a fleeting moment, the world around us blurred. It was just us, the noise fading into a gentle hum. "Do you really believe that?" she asked, her voice barely above a whisper, a quiet plea for affirmation.

"I do," I assured her, my grip tightening slightly. "And I'll be here, cheering you on, every step of the way."

Her gaze softened, and I felt the weight of unspoken promises hanging between us. Just as the moment deepened, Michael reappeared, the playful spark in his eye returning. "There you are! I was beginning to think you'd abandoned us for the glamorous life of a runway model," he joked, his lightheartedness cutting through the intensity.

As he joined us, the magic of the moment shifted, dissolving into laughter and banter. I watched Kayla's spirit return, the vibrant energy flowing back into her demeanor. But beneath the laughter, a current of tension remained, a silent acknowledgment that our paths were evolving, perhaps in ways we had yet to fully comprehend.

And as the evening wore on, the laughter continued to echo, yet I couldn't shake the feeling that our lives were about to intertwine in unexpected ways. The night was alive with promise, but I sensed the shadows lurking just beyond the glow, ready to pounce when we least expected it.

The energy in the room swirled around us, a living entity filled with murmurs of excitement and glimmers of hope. As the last model made her way off the stage, Kayla returned to the center, her smile a dazzling beacon that illuminated the space. The audience's applause rose to a fever pitch, and I could see her soaking in the moment, a blend of exhilaration and disbelief crossing her features. My heart surged with pride, knowing how hard she had fought to reach this point, yet tinged with the fear that came from standing on the sidelines.

"Did you catch my good side?" Kayla shouted playfully, striking a pose as the cheers intensified. The crowd loved her, and I couldn't help but join in the laughter, buoyed by her infectious spirit. But beneath the humor lay a question that nagged at me. Was this truly the pinnacle for her, or merely the first step into a world fraught with challenges?

The mingling began soon after, the atmosphere thick with the aroma of hors d'oeuvres and the sound of clinking glasses. As I maneuvered through the throng of guests, I caught snippets of conversations—praises for Kayla's collection, speculation about upcoming fashion weeks, and the inevitable whispers of envy from those who felt overshadowed. The juxtaposition of excitement and tension was almost palpable. I felt a rush of urgency to reach her, to tell her that she was not just a part of the event but a star of her own making.

"Congratulations, superstar!" I exclaimed, finally reaching Kayla, who was still basking in the afterglow of the show. Her cheeks flushed with a mixture of delight and disbelief.

"Thank you! I can't believe it's over. It feels like I've been waiting for this moment forever, and now..." Her voice trailed off, and I noticed the fleeting shadow of uncertainty clouding her eyes.

"It's just the beginning," I reassured her, my voice steady. "You've set the bar high, but I know you'll exceed it. This is just the tip of the iceberg."

She chuckled, a sound that seemed to momentarily push away her doubts. "If I'm the iceberg, does that make you the shipwrecked sailor? I mean, you've been hanging around for a while now."

"More like the faithful first mate," I shot back, matching her wry humor. "Steering the ship while you chart the course. Just promise me you won't leave me stranded on some deserted island of couture."

"Only if you promise to bring the sunscreen," she teased, her smile returning with renewed vigor. But as she laughed, I sensed a flicker of something deeper—perhaps fear or uncertainty about what lay ahead. It was a reminder that beneath her radiant exterior was a woman still grappling with the weight of her dreams.

As the evening progressed, Michael reappeared, effortlessly charming everyone around him. He flitted from one conversation to the next, his infectious laughter breaking through the backdrop of the event like a trumpet solo. When he approached Kayla, his expression shifted into one of genuine admiration.

"You were incredible," he said, his voice warm with sincerity. "I think you just turned this event into something extraordinary."

"Thank you!" Kayla beamed, the glow on her face unmistakable. "I couldn't have done it without your support."

"Of course, but let's not forget who's the real star here." He gestured toward her, his tone light yet underscored by an intensity I recognized from my own emotions. "You're the one who made it happen."

Watching them, I felt an odd mix of pride and jealousy. Michael had always been her partner in this venture, but a part of me wondered if he saw her as something more than just a business associate. Perhaps I was projecting my insecurities, but it gnawed at me nonetheless. Kayla deserved all the success in the world, yet I didn't want to feel sidelined.

"Hey, why don't we celebrate?" Michael suggested, his eyes gleaming with excitement. "Let's grab a drink and toast to this magnificent night. Kayla, you're buying the first round!"

"Only if you're buying the second!" she countered, laughter spilling from her lips like sparkling champagne.

As we navigated toward the bar, I fell slightly behind, observing the dynamic between them. Their banter was electric, each teasing remark and shared glance weaving an intricate tapestry of friendship and something deeper. I felt like an outsider looking in, grappling with an insatiable desire to be part of their world while wrestling with the fear of losing my place beside Kayla.

The bar was bustling, and as we ordered our drinks, I stole glances at the crowd. The mingling guests, a mix of supporters and skeptics, fueled my unease. Suddenly, amidst the jovial atmosphere, a commotion caught my attention. A figure, clad in a dark overcoat, stood at the edge of the venue, their presence radiating an unsettling energy. The laughter around me faded as I watched the mysterious individual, a sense of foreboding washing over me.

"Everything okay?" Kayla asked, her brow furrowing as she noticed my distraction.

"Just... someone over there. I don't know. They look out of place," I replied, my instincts prickling. The figure seemed to be observing us, their gaze sharp and penetrating. It sent chills down my spine, and I couldn't shake the feeling that they were somehow connected to the night's celebration in ways we hadn't yet uncovered.

"Probably just someone who stumbled in for the free drinks," Michael remarked, but I couldn't dismiss the unsettling sensation that clung to me. The figure's eyes bore into us, and as they stepped forward, I realized we were about to face something far more than just a mere distraction.

"Kayla," I began, urgency creeping into my voice, "I think—"

Before I could finish, the figure moved closer, revealing a familiar face cloaked in shadows. My heart plummeted. It was someone from Kayla's past, someone I thought was long gone. The atmosphere shifted dramatically, the air thick with tension as time seemed to stand still.

"Looks like the night is just getting started," Michael quipped, his jovial demeanor faltering as he caught sight of the newcomer. I felt the weight of the moment, a palpable fear coursing through me, and I knew that this was only the beginning of a night filled with unforeseen challenges.

"Isn't it, Kayla?" the figure sneered, their voice low and smooth, sending a ripple of unease through the crowd. The revelry around us faded, leaving a deafening silence as we all awaited her response, the air heavy with impending conflict.

# Chapter 14: Cracks in the Armor

The vibrant fabric of the night draped over the gala like a warm embrace, the kind that wrapped you in an effervescent glow, whispering promises of laughter and connection. Glinting chandeliers cast sparkling rainbows across the polished floor, where elegantly dressed guests twirled and swayed, their laughter mingling with the sweet notes of a string quartet tucked away in a cozy corner. Each note seemed to dance, weaving its way into the very fabric of the event, a symphony of celebration that swirled around me as I showcased my latest collection.

I stood there, heart racing, amidst a sea of color and texture that I had poured my soul into—each piece a reflection of my journey, stitched with threads of hope and dreams. The satin dresses caught the light just right, and the intricately designed jackets promised stories of confidence and charm. As I gazed at my creations, pride swelled in my chest, a testament to countless late nights filled with sketches, fabric swatches, and a fair share of self-doubt. But tonight, in this moment, I felt like a queen on a throne, ready to conquer the world, or at least my corner of it.

That serene bubble burst when Ryan entered the room, the very embodiment of chaos, striding in with the self-assuredness of a man who had never been told no. He commanded attention the way a storm commands the sea—uninvited and utterly relentless. With his tousled hair and a grin that could charm even the most stoic, he was a jock wrapped in the guise of effortless cool. I had seen him on the field, where he seemed to float, but here, in a realm I had built from the ground up, he was an intruder armed with disdain.

"Looks like the jock's trying to play dress-up," he sneered, his voice dripping with mockery as it slithered through the jubilant atmosphere, silencing the laughter and conversation around me like the sudden fall of a curtain. The weight of his gaze felt like a dark cloud blocking the sun, casting shadows over the vibrant hues of my creations.

Kayla, my steadfast friend and fierce defender, stepped forward as if she could shield me from the barrage of his disdain. "Ryan, back off," she snapped, her tone fierce, a fierce warrior protecting her realm. But even with her rallying cry, the air grew thick with tension, coiling around us like a serpent ready to strike.

In that electrifying moment, I could feel the decision pressing down on my shoulders, a heavy mantle of choice. Should I stand my ground, allow my voice to rise above the cacophony of his ridicule, or should I retreat into the comforting shadow of silence, letting his words seep into the fabric of my confidence? The room felt smaller, the laughter fading, leaving only the pulsing beat of my heart that thrummed in time with the hushed whispers.

I inhaled deeply, trying to capture the essence of the night—the taste of sweet champagne, the lingering scent of fresh blooms—and fortified my resolve. My creations deserved to be celebrated, not ridiculed. "I'll have you know, Ryan, that this is a showcase of passion and artistry, not a playground for your tired jokes," I replied, injecting a playful sharpness into my words. The crowd began to turn its gaze toward us, the once-sparkling atmosphere now crackling with intrigue.

His eyes narrowed, surprise flickering across his face before he masked it with that arrogant smirk. "Artistry? Please, they look like something my little sister would wear to a school play," he shot back, his voice dripping with condescension.

Laughter erupted from a group nearby, igniting the embers of humiliation burning in my chest. But beneath the sting of his words lay a flicker of determination. This was my moment, not just to defend my work, but to reclaim the narrative of my passion from his mocking grasp. "Perhaps your sister has better taste than you," I quipped, a smile creeping onto my lips, surprising even myself. "At least she appreciates creativity instead of hiding behind arrogance."

For a heartbeat, the crowd gasped in shock, the air thick with anticipation. Then, a ripple of laughter broke out, and it felt like the walls around me began to lift. Ryan's face paled, and in that moment, I reveled in the power of defiance. "I guess I'll have to let you know when I start taking fashion advice from someone who thinks 'sweats and sneakers' is a style," I added, folding my arms defiantly, feeling a surge of adrenaline coursing through me.

"Cute comeback," he scoffed, but I could see the uncertainty in his eyes now, the facade of confidence cracking like fragile glass.

With every quip, I felt the strength of the room behind me, a community of dreamers who understood the artistry behind fabric and thread. As the laughter continued, it reminded me that the world was full of voices, and mine deserved to be heard just as loudly.

The lights glimmered around us, reflecting the joy of the moment, and I could feel the warmth of my creativity flooding back, drowning out the remnants of Ryan's derision. "Thank you for your critique, but I think I'll stick to my vision," I declared, channeling the elegance of the evening as I straightened my posture. I refused to allow his taunts to overshadow the hard work I had poured into these designs.

A small cheer erupted from a few supporters in the crowd, and I glanced around, catching glimpses of understanding and camaraderie. Kayla shot me a look of pride and encouragement, her smile radiant. Perhaps this night wasn't just about the clothes but about forging connections and celebrating the tenacity of dreams, no matter how insistent the naysayers might be.

As Ryan's glare bore into me, I sensed a shift, a change in the dynamic. The laughter had restored a semblance of balance, and for the first time that evening, I felt buoyed by the community surrounding me. In that moment, I resolved to embrace my passion with unwavering confidence, to let the vibrant tapestry of my dreams shine as brightly as the sequins adorning my designs. The night was far from over, and I was ready to reclaim it.

The laughter reverberated around me, a warm embrace that filled the gaps Ryan's derision had tried to carve. Yet, even as I basked in the glow of unexpected support, a flicker of uncertainty danced in the corners of my mind. I had faced critics before, but there was something different about Ryan. His presence loomed like a dark cloud, casting shadows over the vibrant evening. I could feel my heart beat in time with the soft music, each note coaxing me back into the moment, urging me to reclaim my power.

As the crowd began to part, whispers of my retort to Ryan hung in the air, like a fragrant bloom spreading its scent through a garden. I caught snippets of conversations: "Did you hear that?" and "I never thought she'd stand up to him." Each word was a petal unfolding, a testament to the strength that was building within me. I had woven my designs not just from fabric but from the threads of my spirit, and if Ryan thought he could unravel that with mere words, he had another thing coming.

Kayla remained by my side, her eyes bright with mischief as she leaned in closer. "That was brilliant! You're like a fashion gladiator taking on the lions of judgment." Her enthusiasm was infectious, and I felt a smile creep across my face, lighting up the shadows that had dared to linger.

"Maybe I should charge him admission," I quipped, scanning the crowd to gauge the reaction to our verbal sparring. But my levity was cut short when I spotted Ryan, his expression shifting from amusement to irritation, the tightness in his jaw hinting at a deeper frustration. My heart raced. Was he going to retaliate?

Just then, a figure stepped forward from the crowd—a striking woman in a sapphire gown that shimmered like the night sky, her confidence radiating as fiercely as her beauty. "What's this? The jock's temper tantrum over a little creativity?" Her voice, smooth as silk, sliced through the tension, her smile brightening the atmosphere. It was Amanda, a well-known designer and one of the judges for the evening's showcase. I felt a swell of gratitude toward her; her presence was like sunlight breaking through clouds, illuminating the path forward.

"Nice to see you, Amanda," Ryan replied, attempting to play it cool, though I could sense his discomfort bubbling beneath the surface. "Just sharing my thoughts on... fashion choices."

"Your thoughts?" she teased, tilting her head. "You do realize this isn't a football field, right? It's a celebration of artistry."

His eyes narrowed at her playful rebuke, but I could see the crowd's interest piquing, everyone hanging on the banter like moths to a flame. "Listen," he retorted, desperation creeping into his voice, "not everyone has to love the same thing. Some people appreciate the classic look."

"Classic?" Amanda interjected, her eyebrows arching. "More like tired. Creativity is meant to challenge, to push boundaries." She turned to me, a knowing smile dancing on her lips. "Keep pushing those boundaries. It's what makes you an artist."

Her words enveloped me in warmth, a cloak of encouragement that fortified my resolve. I felt like a flame igniting in the cool night air, a blaze ready to spread. "Thank you, Amanda," I replied, my voice steady and full of gratitude.

As I glanced back at Ryan, his bravado was crumbling, and a hint of embarrassment crept into his demeanor. It was satisfying, a sweet taste of victory laced with the thrill of unexpected camaraderie. Yet, beneath my triumph, a pang of sympathy tugged at my heartstrings. What had made him so bitter? Perhaps it was the fear of being overshadowed or the pressure to always perform. Even as I wrestled with that feeling, I couldn't help but feel that a small part of him longed for acceptance.

"Ryan," I began, surprising myself with the softness in my tone, "it's okay to not like what I create, but art is subjective. It's meant to stir something, to elicit a reaction, even if it's uncomfortable."

He blinked, momentarily taken aback, as if my words had punctured his bravado. "I—" he started, but then hesitated, his mouth twitching into an uncertain frown.

"Honestly, if everyone agreed, we'd be stuck in a boring loop of the same thing over and over," I continued, my heart racing with the thrill of this new dialogue. "You might find something beautiful in unexpected places, even if it's not what you think you like."

Ryan's expression shifted; the hardness around his eyes softened, and for a moment, I glimpsed a flicker of vulnerability. "Maybe," he muttered, his voice barely audible, yet the sincerity behind it was palpable.

The tension in the room began to dissolve like morning mist under the sun. Laughter bubbled back up, and the conversations resumed, weaving a lively tapestry around us. Kayla shot me a grin, a mixture of pride and disbelief. "Did you just do that? Is Ryan actually contemplating not being a jerk?"

"I think he's considering it," I laughed, feeling buoyed by the magic of the night.

As the evening progressed, I found myself drawn back into the heart of the gala. People began approaching me, sharing compliments and asking about my designs, their faces lighting up with genuine interest. Each conversation added layers of warmth, building connections that transcended Ryan's earlier jibes.

Amanda stayed nearby, engaging in conversation with other guests, her laughter a melodic backdrop to my newfound confidence. With every moment that passed, I felt the shadows of self-doubt receding. I was an artist in my element, no longer afraid to let my creations speak for themselves.

But as I immersed myself in the revelry, I could still feel Ryan's presence lurking in the background. Occasionally, I would catch him watching from a distance, his expression shifting like the tides, sometimes contemplative, sometimes irritated. There was a strange mix of satisfaction and curiosity within me. What was going on behind that wall of bravado?

I couldn't ignore the nagging feeling that this night was just the beginning of something unexpected, a prelude to a deeper story that remained unwritten. As the music played on, I felt the rhythm of possibility thrumming through me, intertwining with the laughter and shared moments. Each interaction felt like a brushstroke on the canvas of the evening, vibrant and full of potential, beckoning me to step further into the unknown.

As the night surged on, the air crackled with renewed energy, each laugh and cheer swirling around me like a vibrant whirlwind. I was still riding the high of Amanda's support, the sting of Ryan's words dulled by my defiance. The string quartet resumed its enchanting melody, notes spiraling into the corners of the room, coaxing guests to dance and revel in the moment. I moved among them, a bright thread weaving through the tapestry of the evening, feeling the warmth of camaraderie wrap around me like a beloved shawl.

"Have you ever considered a career in public speaking?" Kayla teased as she sidled up beside me, her dark hair glinting in the warm light. "Because that was nothing short of theatrical brilliance." Her eyes sparkled with mischief, and I couldn't help but smile at her enthusiasm.

"Maybe I should just add 'Fashion Diplomat' to my resume," I replied, giving her a playful nudge. It was hard not to feel buoyant. With every compliment and inquiry about my designs, my confidence blossomed, unfurling like the petals of a flower basking in the sun. Each guest who approached me became a brushstroke on my canvas, and I savored the vibrant exchanges, feeling more and more like the designer I aspired to be.

But amidst the laughter and the clinking of glasses, Ryan remained a shadow, lurking at the edge of my vision, a specter from my past. Occasionally, I would glance over to find him caught in conversation with others, but his expression was a tapestry of irritation and contemplation. The way he clenched his jaw suggested he was wrestling with something beyond mere annoyance. Perhaps he was realizing that my designs had stirred something deeper within him—a recognition of his own insecurities.

"Are you going to let him stay there, brooding like a dark cloud?" Kayla asked, her voice laced with concern. "It's ruining the mood. Let's go dance!"

"Dance?" I echoed, a playful smirk forming on my lips. "And give him the satisfaction of watching me enjoy myself? Not a chance." The idea of indulging in joy while he sulked sent a spark of rebellion through me.

"Alright, Ms. Fashionista, what do you suggest we do? This is your show, after all," she quipped, glancing back at Ryan.

"Let's not give him the spotlight," I said, feeling a flicker of mischief ignite. "I know just the thing." I caught sight of a nearby table draped in a sea of decorative lights, sparkling like stars scattered across the night sky. "Watch and learn."

With a grin, I led Kayla toward the makeshift stage that had been set up for impromptu performances. "Hey, everyone!" I called out, my voice cutting through the hum of conversation. "Can I get your attention for a moment?" The crowd turned, their curious gazes drawn toward us.

"Is she going to perform a fashion show?" someone whispered, laughter rippling through the audience. I felt my heart race with excitement as I gestured for them to gather around.

"Tonight, we're not just showcasing clothing; we're showcasing spirit!" I proclaimed, my eyes sparkling as I surveyed the gathering crowd. "So, who wants to join me for a little catwalk?"

"Catwalk? Are you serious?" Kayla laughed, eyes wide. "You want us to strut like we're on a runway?"

"Exactly! It's time we take ownership of this night," I said, scanning the faces in the crowd. "Who's in?"

One by one, guests began to rise, laughter spilling out as they clambered onto the stage, encouraged by my enthusiasm. A chorus of voices chimed in, eager to join the fun. Even Amanda moved to the front, her confidence infectious as she struck a pose that drew cheers from the crowd. I reveled in the moment, a radiant sun drawing everyone into my orbit, deflecting any darkness Ryan had cast.

As the impromptu parade commenced, I felt exhilarated. The tension with Ryan melted away with every cheer and clapping hand. Guests twirled and strutted, their personalities shining as brightly as the gowns they wore. Laughter filled the room, and it was as if we had created our own universe, a bubble where creativity thrived unencumbered by judgment.

Just as I was beginning to lose myself in the joy of the moment, I glanced toward Ryan, expecting him to be glowering in the corner. Instead, he stood at the edge of the crowd, arms crossed, a bemused expression on his face. The tension in his posture suggested a battle within, as if he were trying to reconcile his cynicism with the infectious energy surrounding him.

"See?" Kayla nudged me with her elbow, her laughter bubbling like champagne. "You've made him curious. Maybe he wants to join in!"

"Yeah, right," I said, but the spark of mischief ignited once more. "Let's see if he can strut it like he thinks he can." I motioned to the crowd. "Hey, Ryan! Come join us! Show us how a jock does it!"

A ripple of laughter danced through the crowd, and for a moment, Ryan hesitated, caught off guard. The crowd was egging him on, and his brows furrowed, disbelief evident on his face.

"Me?" he replied, incredulous. "You can't be serious."

"Come on!" I encouraged, unable to resist the challenge. "We're just having fun! Or are you afraid you'll fall off the imaginary runway?"

"Not afraid, just not interested in parading around like some kind of clown," he shot back, yet there was a flicker of intrigue in his eyes.

"Fine, I'll do the catwalk alone then!" I declared dramatically, pretending to swoon as I sashayed away. "But the audience will surely lose interest without a handsome jock to spice things up!"

And then, against all odds, something remarkable happened. Ryan took a step forward, a slow, deliberate motion that seemed to draw every gaze in the room. He squared his shoulders, an air of defiance brimming in his stance, and the crowd fell silent, anticipation hanging thick in the air.

Was he really going to do it?

"Alright, but if I do this," he said, his voice barely above a whisper but strong enough to carry, "you all have to promise to go easy on me." A smirk broke through his earlier irritation, and the crowd erupted into cheers.

With a deep breath, Ryan walked toward the makeshift stage, and I felt a jolt of excitement run through me. He began to move, his gait surprisingly confident, but there was something endearing about the way he hesitated between steps, as if he were wading into unfamiliar territory.

"Look at him!" Kayla exclaimed, clutching my arm. "He's actually doing it!"

The crowd cheered louder, the energy shifting in an exhilarating wave. Ryan gave a tentative spin, arms raised in mock grandeur, and for a moment, the tension dissolved, replaced by pure delight. Laughter rang out, and it felt as if he were finally shedding the weight of expectations.

But just as he was beginning to embrace the absurdity, a sharp sound sliced through the laughter—a crash followed by an ominous silence that swept through the crowd. I turned, heart racing, to see that one of the decorative pillars had toppled over, sending glittering lights scattering like stars across the floor.

Before I could process what was happening, Ryan was caught off balance, stumbling backward as his foot caught on the fabric of his own outfit, tipping dangerously close to the edge of the stage. Time slowed, the laughter and cheers fading into a hushed gasp as the room held its breath.

"Ryan!" I shouted, my heart pounding. In a split second, he teetered, grasping for something—anything—to steady himself, and I felt a surge of instinct, the desire to reach out and catch him before he fell into the chaos.

But the moment hung suspended, and as he leaned too far back, the tension snapped like a taut string, propelling him into the air. My breath caught as I lunged forward, but would I reach him in time? The world around us faded, leaving only the thrilling uncertainty of what would happen next.

# Chapter 15: The Choice

The air was thick with tension, a palpable energy that crackled like static electricity just before a storm. The chatter of the crowd had died down, replaced by an expectant silence, each face turned towards us, their expressions a mixture of shock and intrigue. My heart raced, a wild creature thrashing against the confines of my chest as I stood toe-to-toe with Ryan. His stature loomed over me, broad shoulders casting a shadow that felt almost oppressive, but I wasn't going to let him intimidate me any longer.

"I'm more than just a quarterback," I proclaimed, my voice steady, imbued with a conviction I hadn't known I possessed until that moment. I glanced around, catching the eyes of my friends, my teammates, and even some classmates who had quietly watched the spectacle unfold. The glimmers of surprise and admiration sparked something within me—a rush of adrenaline that propelled my words forward. "I love cooking and design. I refuse to be ashamed."

The roar of support that followed my declaration was like the sweet sound of rain after a long drought, washing over my fears and insecurities. Laughter erupted from the back of the crowd, and I caught a glimpse of Kayla's beaming smile, a fierce pride shining through her eyes. Her unwavering support buoyed my spirits, as if I had just been handed a lifeline amidst the turbulence of high school drama. Yet, even amidst the excitement, a chill swept through me at the sight of Ryan's twisted smirk, a sinister grin that made my stomach churn.

"Cooking? Design? How quaint," he replied, his tone dripping with sarcasm. The crowd shifted uneasily, some whispering amongst themselves as if the very air had become charged with a sense of impending conflict. "What's next? You going to host a bake sale for the football team?"

The jibe landed with a heavy thud, the laughter around us evaporating like mist in the morning sun. I felt a flush rise to my cheeks, anger simmering just beneath the surface. I could practically hear the gears turning in his mind as he sought to undermine my moment, eager to prove that I was just a joke, a novelty in a world that thrived on strength and athleticism.

"Better than relying on gimmicks to get attention, don't you think?" I shot back, my words sharper than I intended, but fueled by a desire to stand my ground. "Maybe you should try expanding your horizons beyond the football field."

The words hung in the air, heavy with implications. The crowd gasped, a collective intake of breath that only amplified the tension. Ryan's smirk faltered for a brief moment, surprise flashing in his eyes, but it quickly morphed back into that cocky grin, as if he had just cracked the code to a riddle he thought only he could solve.

"Touché," he said, a hint of admiration lacing his voice. "But we all know what really matters, don't we? Popularity, winning games. That's what makes you relevant."

I took a step closer, closing the distance between us. "And what if I don't want to be relevant by your standards? What if I want to create a world where I'm valued for more than just my athletic ability?"

In that moment, I could feel the crowd leaning in, their collective breaths held, captivated by the spectacle. Ryan's expression faltered, just for a second, as if he was beginning to realize that the narrative he crafted about me was unraveling at the seams.

"Isn't that just a fancy way of saying you're afraid to compete?" he challenged, eyes narrowing as he took a half-step back, trying to reclaim his dominance. "Face it, you're in a world where winners write the history."

"Maybe," I said, my voice firm, "but winners don't get to define who I am. I'll write my own story."

And just like that, the atmosphere shifted. I could sense a ripple of murmurs in the crowd, a subtle shift as more students began to side with me. It felt like the tide was turning, and for the first time, I dared to hope that I could be more than just a quarterback. I could be a chef, a designer—an artist in my own right, unconfined by stereotypes.

Just then, a voice broke through the tension. It was Emily, my friend from the art club, standing on the edge of the crowd, her eyes fierce and unwavering. "You go, girl!" she shouted, her encouragement echoing against the concrete walls of the gym. The ripple of support surged, igniting an electric atmosphere that surged through the space, lifting my spirits.

Ryan's eyes darted towards her, his bravado wavering, and for a split second, I saw the uncertainty that lurked behind his confident facade. The silence was deafening, the crowd hanging onto our exchange like it was the climax of a play.

"Maybe you should ask yourself what you really want, Ryan," I challenged, my voice steady and clear. "Do you want to win, or do you want to be remembered?"

His smirk faltered once more, but this time it was accompanied by a flicker of something almost human. Anger? Fear? I couldn't quite place it, but I felt emboldened. The noise of the crowd faded into the background, and in that moment, it was just the two of us—two players in a game far larger than the one we were currently embroiled in.

"I want to win, and I'll do whatever it takes to make that happen," he retorted, his bravado slipping back into place like a mask. But the edge of desperation in his tone didn't escape me.

"And what about the cost?" I countered, feeling a surge of strength within me. "How many people do you plan to step on to reach the top?"

The air thickened, and as the crowd buzzed with anticipation, I realized that this moment was no longer just about Ryan and me. It was about everyone who had ever felt silenced, everyone who had hidden their passions for fear of ridicule. This was a choice, a pivotal moment that could shift the dynamics of our high school, and perhaps, even beyond.

Ryan shifted uncomfortably, his bravado cracking ever so slightly. I could see him weighing his next words, perhaps realizing that his usual tactics were failing him. He opened his mouth, likely to hurl another insult, but the words never came. Instead, he glared at me, his expression a mixture of resentment and begrudging respect, before he turned on his heel and stormed away, leaving the crowd buzzing with energy and the promise of change.

As I watched him retreat, my heart raced—not with fear, but with exhilaration. I had taken a stand, and the world before me felt brighter, bursting with possibility. I was ready to embrace who I was and fight for a narrative that was unapologetically mine.

The atmosphere shifted, the air crackling with the energy of unspoken thoughts and emotions. Ryan's retreat had left a void, but it was one that crackled with potential. I turned to my friends, their faces reflecting a mix of disbelief and excitement. The buzz of conversation resumed, hushed whispers weaving through the crowd like a secret language.

"What just happened?" Kayla breathed, her eyes wide. "Did you really just stand up to him? I mean, wow!"

"It felt like the right moment," I replied, a nervous laugh escaping my lips. "I guess I finally decided to stop letting him define me."

"More than just a quarterback, huh?" she teased, a twinkle of mischief in her eye. "I'm proud of you, but let's be real—you're going to need more than just a passion for cooking to deal with Ryan's ego."

"True," I said, taking a deep breath as I surveyed the room. The crowd had begun to disperse, but the adrenaline still surged through me, leaving a giddy sensation tingling in my fingertips. "But maybe I just opened a door for others. If I can stand my ground, maybe others will too."

"Definitely," she replied, a sly grin spreading across her face. "And who knows? Maybe we'll start a trend where the football players can, I don't know, actually express their feelings or something."

"Revolutionary, isn't it?" I quipped back, grinning as I thought about the shift that could be brewing beneath the surface of our high school hierarchy.

As we made our way out of the gym, I felt the weight of eyes on me—some were curious, others judgmental, and a few offered genuine admiration. It was exhilarating and terrifying, the mingling of emotions swirling around me like confetti in a breeze. I leaned against the cool metal of the doorframe and took a deep breath, letting the crisp air fill my lungs.

"What's next for you, oh fearless one?" Kayla asked, nudging me gently. "Are you going to become the next Top Chef?"

I laughed, picturing myself in a kitchen filled with chaotic energy, pots bubbling over while I balanced a soufflé in one hand and an awkward smile in the other. "More like a design challenge on reality TV. I can see it now: 'Watch the quarterback try to make a decent pillow!'"

Her laughter rang out, bright and infectious, and for a moment, the fears that had clung to me melted away. I was reminded of the small joys that life offered—the camaraderie of friends, the thrill of new beginnings, and the satisfaction of embracing one's true self.

But as we walked toward the parking lot, the shadow of Ryan's twisted smirk lingered in my mind, nagging at me like an itch that couldn't be scratched. I couldn't shake the feeling that this confrontation was merely the first act of a far more complex play.

"Hey, do you want to grab something to eat?" I asked Kayla as we neared her car, a gleam of hope in my voice. "I need to celebrate this little victory."

"Only if you promise to share the secrets of your cooking prowess," she shot back, winking. "I want to know how you'll transform basic nachos into a culinary masterpiece."

"Oh, prepare to be dazzled," I laughed, the idea of crafting something delicious lighting a spark of excitement in me. But as we climbed into her car, a sudden thought struck me like a thunderbolt.

"What if Ryan tries to get back at me?" I asked, my voice wavering as anxiety crept in. "What if he uses the team to make my life miserable?"

Kayla's expression turned serious. "Well, he can try, but he can't take away your voice. You've already shown that you won't back down. Besides, the football team isn't just his kingdom; it's a collective effort. There are other guys who might appreciate your talent. Maybe they'll even see you as an asset."

I nodded, knowing she had a point, but uncertainty still wrapped around me like a shroud. "I guess I just need to keep pushing forward. Focus on what I love."

"Yes! And maybe throw a few more zingers Ryan's way while you're at it. That should keep him on his toes," she suggested, laughter creeping back into her voice.

The rest of the evening passed in a blur of lighthearted banter and delicious food, each bite reinforcing the idea that life could be both simple and joyful. I lost myself in the rhythm of our conversations, and the nagging worries about Ryan seemed to fade into the background, eclipsed by the warmth of friendship and camaraderie.

As we returned home, however, the tension coiled tighter within me, and I found it impossible to shake the sense that the confrontation with Ryan was far from finished. That night, I lay in bed staring at the ceiling, thoughts swirling like autumn leaves caught in a gust of wind. I began to plan my next steps, crafting a roadmap that led not only to success in my passions but also a path through the turbulent landscape of high school politics.

With dawn breaking the following morning, I awoke to a world drenched in golden light, its promise of a new day mingling with the residue of yesterday's confrontation. My phone buzzed, pulling me from my musings. A message from Emily flashed on the screen, and I couldn't help but smile at the excitement bubbling in her words.

"Let's meet up before school! I have a brilliant idea for our art project!"

Eager to immerse myself in something creative, I quickly dressed, the sunlight streaming through the window igniting a fire within me. Maybe a fresh start would help me gain clarity, not only about my passion for design but also about how to tackle the complexities of my new reality at school.

As I walked towards Emily's house, I felt a renewed sense of purpose. The cool breeze tousled my hair, filling my lungs with fresh air, invigorating my spirit. Each step was a reminder that I was forging my path, ready to embrace the unknown with all its challenges and opportunities.

Upon reaching her house, I found Emily sitting on the porch, her sketchbook spread wide open, colorful pencils scattered around her like confetti. "You're going to love this!" she said, her eyes sparkling with enthusiasm. "I've been thinking we should create a mural for the art show, something that showcases individuality and strength. A celebration of who we are!"

My heart raced at the thought. "That sounds incredible! A way to express everything I'm feeling right now."

"Exactly!" she exclaimed, her hands moving animatedly as she spoke. "Let's gather a group—bring in other artists, maybe even some of the athletes who appreciate art but are too scared to show it. We can make it a collaborative piece!"

"Brilliant!" I agreed, the idea blooming in my mind like a spring flower, each petal unfolding into a possibility. "It could be the perfect counter to the stigma Ryan and others have created. A chance to redefine who we are!"

Emily's excitement was infectious, and as we brainstormed ideas, the colors of our dreams began to swirl together. This was more than just art; it was a movement, an anthem of our collective resilience against the shadows that loomed. With each stroke of imagination, I felt the weight of yesterday lift, replaced by the exhilaration of what was to come.

The thought of standing shoulder to shoulder with my classmates, challenging the narrow definitions of who we could be, filled me with an eagerness I hadn't felt in a long time. Maybe this mural would become a beacon of hope, a testament to our ability to break free from the confines of expectation and create a world that was truly ours.

And as the sun climbed higher, illuminating the path before us, I realized that every choice I made from this point onward would be a brushstroke on the canvas of my life, each moment a vibrant splash of color that reflected not just who I had been, but who I was determined to become.

As the crowd murmured in disbelief, I felt a mixture of exhilaration and trepidation course through me. It was a small victory, but in the presence of Ryan, whose arrogance seemed to cloak him like a thick fog, it felt monumental. Kayla stepped closer, her gaze a potent mix of admiration and concern, as if she could sense the storm brewing beneath my calm exterior. "You don't need to explain yourself to anyone," she whispered, her voice a soothing balm against the rising tide of tension.

But Ryan, ever the master of theatrics, scoffed. "You think this is some sort of victory? You're nothing but a wannabe. You'll always be in my shadow, even if you're waving around your spatula." His words dripped with contempt, but the laughter that followed from the back of the crowd pierced through the moment, sharpening my resolve. It was a reminder that even in the face of ridicule, there was strength to be found in solidarity.

"Maybe I don't want to be in your shadow," I shot back, feeling the heat of adrenaline spike in my veins. "Maybe I want to stand in the light of my own dreams, whether that's on a field or in a kitchen." The clarity of my vision was like a gust of fresh air, sweeping away the cobwebs of self-doubt that had clung to me for too long. The laughter in the crowd shifted, a subtle change in tone, as they began to lean into my words rather than against them.

Ryan's facade cracked ever so slightly, and for a brief moment, I thought I saw something akin to fear flicker in his eyes. But he quickly regained his composure, straightening his posture and shifting the narrative. "Cute. But everyone knows a real quarterback isn't just a pretty face. What are you going to do? Host a cooking show after you fail?" He aimed for laughter again, but the jeers sounded forced, as if the crowd was tiring of the script he had written for this scene.

Kayla stepped in, her voice cutting through the tension like a hot knife through butter. "You know, Ryan, success doesn't look the same for everyone. Maybe you should take notes." The crowd erupted in applause, and I felt a swell of gratitude toward her. In that moment, she was my shield, deflecting the barbs he aimed at me.

"Success, huh? Is that what you call it? Hosting dinner parties for your little friends?" Ryan sneered, but his words fell flat against the backdrop of genuine support. The laughter from the crowd morphed into cheers, rallying around the idea of authenticity and passion over the hollow promises of conformity.

I took a breath, feeling emboldened. "You may call it dinner parties, but I call it creativity. I create spaces and experiences where people feel at home. That's more valuable than any trophy." The words hung in the air, and I could see Ryan's anger boiling beneath the surface, the veins in his neck taut, a stark contrast to the casual facade he often wore.

The energy shifted again, a palpable tension crackling between us like static electricity. "And what about your little design dreams?" he countered, his tone shifting to a mocking sing-song. "You think anyone cares about those? People want a winner, not a home decorator."

"Newsflash, Ryan," I shot back, an unexpected smile breaking through. "It's possible to be both. Why don't you try it sometime?" A ripple of laughter swept through the crowd, this time directed at him, and it felt good, exhilarating even, to see the tables turn.

But just as I thought the tide had fully shifted, Ryan's smirk returned, this time more dangerous. "You think this is just about you, don't you? You think the spotlight is yours to keep?" His voice dripped with a sudden menace, and a chill crawled up my spine. "Let me remind you, this isn't a fairytale. You may get some applause today, but it can all change in an instant. Just wait until tomorrow's game."

A wave of unease washed over the crowd, the excitement flickering like a candle in the wind. My heart raced as I grappled with the implications of his words. Tomorrow's game wasn't just a game; it was the championship. If I faltered, if I stumbled, everything I had just fought for could be reduced to ash.

Before I could respond, the sudden blare of an air horn echoed through the crowd, jarring everyone back to reality. The game announcer's voice rang out, breaking the tension. "Attention, everyone! We're starting the halftime festivities. Please make your way to the field for the grand reveal!"

As the crowd began to disperse, I felt Kayla tugging at my arm. "Let's get out of here," she urged, her eyes wide with concern. "You don't need this drama right now." But I couldn't move. Something held me rooted to the spot, a feeling that this wasn't over, that Ryan wasn't finished with his games.

"I can't just walk away," I insisted, my voice steadying. "He doesn't get to dictate my narrative." Just as I spoke, I caught sight of Ryan in the distance, whispering with a couple of his friends, his eyes darting toward me with an intensity that sent shivers down my spine.

"What is he planning?" I muttered under my breath, the question lodged in my throat like a stubborn piece of food.

Kayla leaned closer, her expression serious. "We should find out. It's not just about the game anymore, is it? He's playing a deeper game, and we need to be ready for whatever he throws at you next."

The air felt charged, thick with unspoken words and hidden threats. I nodded, determination settling in my bones. As we moved through the crowd, I couldn't shake the feeling that tomorrow would be a crossroads—not just for me, but for everyone involved. Would I rise to the occasion or fall under the weight of expectation?

The ground beneath us vibrated with anticipation as we stepped onto the field. I scanned the crowd, hoping to catch a glimpse of familiar faces, anyone who might lend support in this unexpected battle. Just then, my phone buzzed in my pocket, breaking my concentration. Pulling it out, I saw a message flash across the screen, sending my heart plummeting into my stomach.

"Meet me by the old bleachers. I have something important to tell you. — R."

The urgency of the message pierced through the din of the festivities, wrapping around my thoughts like a noose. I exchanged a look with Kayla, and without another word, we slipped away from the crowd, navigating toward the shadows of the bleachers where secrets often hid, waiting to ensnare the unsuspecting.

But as we approached, a sense of foreboding enveloped me. I couldn't shake the feeling that whatever awaited us was about to change everything.

# Chapter 16: Tides of Change

The bustling campus had transformed into a canvas of excitement and uncertainty, the echoes of the charity event still ringing in the air. I felt a surge of pride as I walked through the quad, sunlight filtering through the branches of ancient oaks, casting dappled shadows on the ground. My peers exchanged knowing glances, smiles of recognition illuminating their faces like the sun breaking through clouds. Gone was the singular identity of Julia the athlete; I was now a multi-faceted person, each layer revealing something different—Julia the artist, the chef, a man willing to shatter the rigid expectations that had long been prescribed to me.

Yet, for all the applause and appreciation, there was a shadow lurking in the corners of my newfound fame, one that followed me relentlessly. Ryan, with his crooked smile and sharp tongue, had never been one to take a slight without retaliation. His last encounter with me still echoed in my mind like the tolling of a bell—every vibration a reminder of the threat he posed. I could feel the tension in my muscles, a coiled spring ready to snap at the slightest provocation. As I navigated the campus, I found myself glancing over my shoulder more than once, half-expecting him to emerge from behind a tree or a corner, his presence suffocating like a thick fog.

The cafeteria, usually a bustling hub of laughter and chatter, felt different. I entered, the familiar smells of fried food and fresh coffee wrapping around me like a warm blanket, yet I couldn't shake the chill that ran down my spine. I spotted Mia at our usual table, her hair a wild halo of curls that danced around her face. She waved me over, her grin contagious, pulling me into her orbit. "You did it, Julia! You were incredible at the event. I still can't believe you made that chocolate torte. Did you slip something magical into it?"

I laughed, the sound surprising me with its buoyancy. "Only a little bit of love and a lot of sugar. No magic, I promise." I took a seat across from her, grateful for the distraction she provided. Mia had always been a bright spot in my life, her enthusiasm a stark contrast to the dark clouds I feared Ryan would unleash.

"Well, whatever you did, it worked," she said, leaning in closer, her eyes sparkling with mischief. "I overheard some people talking about you joining the culinary club. You know that's practically unheard of for someone in your... shall we say, athletic circle?"

I shrugged, trying to play it cool even as my heart raced. "I figured it was time to explore something different. I've spent enough time being defined by my position on the field." The weight of those words felt heavier than I anticipated. What if I was stepping too far outside the lines? What if this journey of self-exploration was merely a prelude to my undoing?

Mia leaned back, crossing her arms with a skeptical look. "And what about Ryan? You think he's just going to sit back and watch you reinvent yourself? Come on, you know him better than that. He'll find a way to turn this into a spectacle."

Her words were like ice water splashed in my face. I had hoped to avoid the conversation about Ryan, the suffocating dread creeping back into my chest. "I can handle him. I mean, I have to, right? I can't let him dictate my life."

"That's the spirit! But you know what they say—don't poke the bear unless you're prepared for the claws." Her tone was light, but the undercurrent of concern was unmistakable.

I wanted to dismiss her worries with a wave of my hand, but the truth was, Mia's words lingered. What if I was just a kid playing at being brave? I could already picture Ryan's sneer, the way he'd use my newfound passions as fodder for his cruel games. Just thinking about it twisted my stomach into knots, a tight spiral of anxiety that refused to loosen.

Our conversation flowed into lighter topics—the upcoming football game, a rumor about a mysterious new professor, and Mia's own ambitions for a study abroad program in Italy. Each laugh and shared secret wove a small tapestry of normalcy around me, helping to fend off the encroaching shadows of doubt. Yet, even as I laughed, the gnawing feeling persisted.

Later that afternoon, as I made my way to the art building for my painting class, I noticed the subtle shift in the atmosphere. Students milled about, but there was an electric hum in the air, an unspoken tension that seemed to pulse like a heartbeat. I brushed it off, attributing it to my own anxieties, but as I stepped into the studio, a sense of foreboding washed over me.

The room was alive with color—vibrant strokes of paint splattered on canvases, the scent of turpentine mingling with the warmth of the sun streaming through the tall windows. I took a moment to breathe it all in, grounding myself in the familiar chaos of creativity. Just as I picked up my brush, the door swung open, and in walked Ryan. The collective silence that fell over the room was palpable, a thick veil of uncertainty that wrapped around us all.

"Well, well, if it isn't the Renaissance man himself," he drawled, his voice dripping with mockery. I could feel the heat rise in my cheeks, a surge of adrenaline fueling my response. "What's next, Julia? Sculpture? Ballet? Maybe you'll finally find your true calling."

His laughter sliced through the air, and I gripped my brush tighter, fighting the urge to let my anger explode. "Nice to see you too, Ryan. I didn't know you were taking up stand-up comedy. Should we expect an open mic night next?"

Murmurs rippled through the class, the tension thickening as eyes darted between us. This was it—the moment I had dreaded. But as I stood there, the vibrant colors of the paint swirling before me, something inside shifted. I could be the artist and the athlete, the man with layers, refusing to let anyone, especially Ryan, define who I was. I straightened my posture, prepared to stand my ground, even if it meant facing the claws of the bear.

The energy in the room crackled, a tangible force that seemed to draw everyone's attention toward Ryan. He leaned against the door frame, a smirk plastered across his face, the very embodiment of everything I had fought against. My heart raced, but I pushed aside the instinct to retreat. Instead, I planted my feet firmly on the ground, as if anchoring myself to the vibrant world of paint and canvas surrounding me.

"Is that really the best you've got?" I shot back, the words spilling out before I could think them through. "I'd expect something more original from you, Ryan. You've got a reputation to uphold, after all."

The class erupted into a chorus of gasps and muffled laughter, the kind of laughter that bubbles up when people are trying not to encourage a fight but can't help themselves. For a brief moment, the tension in the air shifted, and I could almost see the gears turning in Ryan's head. His smile faltered, just for a moment, as if my jab had struck a nerve. But he quickly recovered, his confidence radiating like the sun through the studio windows.

"You think you can just waltz in here and play Picasso?" he challenged, stepping further into the room, his body language radiating aggression. "You're still just a jock, pretending to be something you're not. I mean, what's next? A poetry slam? You might want to leave that to the real artists."

With every syllable, his words dripped with disdain, a sharp blade meant to cut deep. But instead of flinching, I felt a flicker of determination ignite within me. "Maybe I'll do that," I retorted, rolling my shoulders back, "and you can just watch from the sidelines, wishing you could step out of your one-dimensional role as the school bully."

He laughed, a hollow sound that echoed through the studio, and I could see the gears in his mind churning, strategizing his next move. "Good luck with that. I'll be sure to bring popcorn for the show. I can't wait to see how long your little act lasts."

As the words left his mouth, I felt a strange wave of calm wash over me. It was as if I had crossed an invisible threshold, stepping into a space where I no longer felt the need to apologize for who I was. I picked up my brush, my mind buzzing with a rush of colors that mirrored my emotions. "You know, Ryan, there's a whole world outside of your little bubble. You should try stepping into it someday. You might find that it's a lot bigger than you thought."

His eyes narrowed, and the tension in the room thickened. Yet, as I turned back to my canvas, the familiar scents of paint and linseed oil enveloped me like a comforting embrace. Each stroke of my brush felt powerful, as if I were rewriting my own narrative right there in front of everyone.

The class resumed, the awkward silence replaced by the sound of brushes against canvas and the occasional quiet chuckle. Ryan lingered, hovering near the door like a storm cloud unwilling to let the sun shine through. I tried to focus, but I could feel his eyes boring into my back, a constant reminder of the challenge I was facing. It was unsettling yet oddly motivating, the way he seemed to fuel my determination.

"Hey, if you need help with that canvas, I can always give you a few tips," Mia piped up, her voice a cheerful antidote to the lingering tension. She nudged my side gently, her smile infectious as she flitted around the studio, engaging with other students. "Or maybe we should take a field trip to an art gallery? Nothing like some inspiration to chase away the bullies."

"Art gallery?" I quirked an eyebrow, pretending to consider it seriously. "Isn't that where they keep all those old, dusty paintings that make you question your life choices?"

She rolled her eyes, an exaggerated gesture that drew laughter from a few nearby students. "Oh please, that's what you think? You're just afraid of discovering your hidden talent for abstract expressionism. Just think—an entire series inspired by your battles with Ryan."

I chuckled, picturing a series of chaotic swirls and jagged lines, capturing the essence of my ongoing duel with Ryan. "I can see it now. 'The Jock vs. The Art: A Turbulent Love Story.'"

"Exactly! You can even do a performance piece where you fight a canvas with paintbrushes." She feigned a dramatic gasp, eyes wide with mock horror. "The canvas can be your greatest rival!"

The laughter that followed felt liberating, a momentary reprieve from the weight that had settled on my shoulders since Ryan had entered the room. I was grateful for Mia's lightheartedness; it had the uncanny ability to dissolve tension. Yet, just as the air seemed to lighten, Ryan took a step forward, eyes glinting with mischief.

"Speaking of rivalries, I hope you're ready for the next football game, Julia," he called out, voice dripping with sarcasm. "I hear our team is counting on you to actually show up. Wouldn't want to disappoint your fans."

His words hung in the air, a gauntlet thrown down that I could not ignore. I could feel the heat rising in my cheeks, a mixture of embarrassment and anger. "I'll be there, and I'll give it my all," I shot back, refusing to show any weakness. "What about you, Ryan? Are you planning to sit on the sidelines, cheering for the guy who finally took you down a peg?"

The room erupted again, laughter cascading around us as I realized the absurdity of the moment. Here we were, engaged in a battle of wits and words, and for the first time, I felt like I might actually be winning.

Ryan's expression shifted from mockery to irritation, and I could sense the change in the atmosphere. It was a small victory, but it was mine, and the weight of it buoyed me. As the class continued,

I lost myself in the rhythm of paint and laughter, painting over the remnants of Ryan's hostility with vibrant strokes of color and joy.

But that moment of triumph was fleeting, and the familiar knot of anxiety crept back into my stomach as I caught Ryan's eye in the mirror's reflection across the room. His expression had hardened, a promise of retribution lurking behind his gaze. The joy of the moment dimmed, and I felt the impending storm brewing just beneath the surface.

Still, as I stood in the midst of my classmates, laughter bubbling around me, I clung to the glimmer of hope that this time I could navigate the chaos. With each stroke of my brush, I reminded myself that I was no longer merely a victim of circumstance. I was Julia the artist, and I was ready to paint my own future—whatever colors that might entail.

The studio buzzed with energy, and I painted with fervor, each stroke an expression of defiance against Ryan's taunts. I mixed vibrant hues on my palette, channeling my frustration into a canvas that had quickly transformed into an extension of my thoughts. The cacophony of brushes scraping against surfaces blended into a rhythm, a soundtrack to my internal battle. As I layered the paint, I could almost visualize my fears dissipating into swirls of color, reclaiming my space with every bold movement.

Mia hovered nearby, her own canvas a riot of colors that seemed to mirror my own state of mind. "You know," she said, tilting her head to observe my work, "if you keep this up, you'll be able to hang that in the gallery. They love 'em raw and emotional. The whole tortured artist thing is practically a trend."

I chuckled, wiping a smudge of paint from my cheek. "Tortured, huh? Maybe I should consider adding a little more angst to it. Perhaps a splash of dark crimson for the impending doom that Ryan represents?"

"Definitely," she replied, rolling her eyes in that exaggerated way only friends can pull off. "Throw in some shadows for dramatic flair. You'll have critics fawning over the depth of your personal struggles."

Just then, a shadow fell across my canvas, and I looked up to find Ryan standing at the edge of the room, arms crossed, a scowl etched on his face. The laughter around us dimmed, the vibrancy of our moment snuffed out like a candle in a gust of wind.

"Nice work, Julia," he drawled, feigning admiration. "Looks like you've finally found a way to express yourself beyond tossing a ball. Who knew you had it in you?"

"Ah, Ryan, always the poet," I replied, injecting a note of sarcasm. "I didn't know you had such an eye for talent. How does it feel to be outclassed? Must sting a little."

His expression twisted, and the laughter of my classmates faded into an uneasy silence. "Don't get too cocky," he shot back, stepping further into the room, the tension palpable. "This isn't over. You think you can just strut around, pretending to be someone you're not? I've seen better art from a toddler with finger paints."

"Cute comeback," I said, my voice steady despite the storm brewing within. "But I don't need to prove anything to you. I'm not competing in your little world anymore."

He leaned in closer, the smile slipping off his face, replaced by a cold, hard glare. "That's rich coming from someone who's been on the sidelines of the real game. Just wait. I'll make sure everyone remembers why you belong there."

I felt a tremor in the air, an unspoken promise of chaos lying just beneath the surface. My heart raced, but I forced myself to remain composed. "You know, Ryan, if you're that threatened by my art, maybe you should take a class. It might help you channel your insecurities."

The class collectively inhaled, a chorus of tension that swelled around us. For a heartbeat, it seemed like time stood still, the world narrowed down to just the three of us—Ryan, Mia, and me. But just as I thought he would retaliate, a flicker of uncertainty crossed his features, and he stepped back, recalibrating.

"Whatever," he huffed, running a hand through his hair, frustration radiating off him like heat from a flame. "You'll regret this. You think this is all fun and games? Just wait until you're back on that field."

With that, he spun on his heel and strode toward the door, his footsteps echoing like a thunderstorm retreating into the distance. I exhaled, feeling the tension in the room release with his departure.

"Wow," Mia said, breaking the silence that followed. "That was intense. You handled that like a pro. I'm impressed."

"Thanks," I replied, trying to shake off the unease that clung to me like a second skin. "I just—"

But before I could finish my thought, the sound of glass shattering from the hallway interrupted us, followed by a cacophony of shouts. My heart leapt into my throat, and without thinking, I dropped my brush and raced toward the noise, adrenaline propelling me forward.

The corridor was a whirlwind of confusion and chaos. Students were darting back and forth, their faces a mix of shock and fear. I pushed through the crowd, dread twisting in my stomach, my mind racing with possibilities of what had happened.

"Julia!" Mia called, her voice barely rising above the din. "What's going on?"

"I don't know!" I shouted back, scanning the area. Then I spotted Ryan standing at the end of the hall, his expression twisted in anger. He was facing a group of students, his fists clenched at his sides, the remnants of shattered glass scattered around his feet.

"What the hell happened?" I demanded, striding toward him.

He shot me a dark look, his eyes blazing with a fury that made my skin crawl. "You think this is a game? You want to play artist? Fine. Let's see how you handle some real-world consequences."

Before I could process his words, one of his friends stepped forward, brandishing a broken bottle. "You think you can just mess with him?" the guy sneered. "You're in over your head, pretty boy."

My heart raced as I recognized the situation spiraling dangerously out of control. "This isn't the answer!" I yelled, desperate to defuse the escalating tension. "We can talk about this!"

"Talk?" Ryan laughed, a harsh, brittle sound. "You think I want to talk? I want to show you what happens when you cross me. This isn't just art, Julia. This is survival. And in this game, only one of us is coming out on top."

The atmosphere shifted, and I could feel the weight of his threat looming in the air. My pulse quickened, and I took a step back, feeling the crowd shift restlessly behind me. In that moment, I realized the stakes had escalated far beyond my artistic expression. This was a direct challenge, and it echoed through the hall like a bomb ticking down to zero.

As I tried to find my footing in this chaotic showdown, Ryan's friend advanced, the broken bottle glinting ominously in the overhead lights. Fear coiled in my stomach, but something deeper surged within me—a fierce determination to stand my ground, no matter what the cost.

"Enough!" I shouted, my voice ringing out with an authority I didn't fully feel. "If you want to settle this, let's do it the right way. No weapons, no chaos. Just us."

Ryan paused, his brow furrowed as he considered my offer. The tension hung in the air, thick enough to cut, and for a heartbeat, the world around us held its breath, waiting to see how this would unfold.

# Chapter 17: Complications of the Heart

The kitchen glowed under the warm light of the hanging pendant, illuminating the small yet inviting space where Kayla and I often found ourselves lost in the rhythm of cooking. The aroma of sautéing garlic danced through the air, mingling with the crisp scent of fresh herbs from the small window herb garden she had nurtured with surprising dedication. As I stirred the bubbling sauce, I couldn't help but steal glances at her, focused and determined, a soft brow furrowed in concentration. She moved gracefully around the kitchen, her laughter bubbling like the pasta boiling on the stove, and in that moment, it felt like the universe had conspired to create this perfect sanctuary for us.

"Do you think we're actually making something edible?" I teased, stirring a little too vigorously, splattering a few drops of tomato sauce onto the counter.

Kayla chuckled, the sound light and melodic, a symphony against the backdrop of our culinary efforts. "If we survive this, I'll consider it a success. But I should warn you, my specialty is burning toast."

"Burning toast? Well, that's a skill worth mastering." I raised an eyebrow playfully, leaning against the counter as I watched her. "Do you have any other hidden talents I should be aware of?"

She turned to face me, a cheeky grin spreading across her face. "Only if you're prepared for the grand reveal. My hidden talents might include interpretive dance and a dubious ability to quote movie lines at inappropriate moments."

I laughed, the warmth of her presence enveloping me like a cozy blanket on a chilly evening. Our friendship, once a safe haven, now felt like a fragile glass teetering on the edge of a shelf, threatening to shatter with the slightest push. In the comfortable silence that followed our banter, the tension simmered just beneath the surface, a palpable thing that I could almost reach out and touch.

As our fingers brushed over the spice jar, a spark of electricity jolted through me, leaving my heart racing. The moment felt suspended in time, every sound muffled, as if the world outside had faded into a distant echo. I searched her eyes for a flicker of recognition, a sign that she felt it too, but the light in her gaze was playful, unaware of the storm brewing within me. I opened my mouth to speak, to shatter the silence that had grown too heavy, but the words caught in my throat.

"Salt or pepper?" she asked, her brow slightly arched, oblivious to the whirlwind of emotions swirling around us.

"Um, salt. Definitely salt," I managed, forcing my mind to clear. "Unless you prefer a little pepper to spice things up?"

"Who knew you were such a culinary wizard?" she shot back, laughter spilling from her lips again, and I felt the warmth of her humor wash over the cold edges of my uncertainty.

"Culinary wizard by necessity, I assure you," I replied, grateful for the reprieve. "I've survived too many dinners with my mother to let any meal pass without a bit of drama."

"Oh, drama in the kitchen! That sounds like a cooking show waiting to happen. We could call it 'Whisk and Whine.'" She tossed her head back, the laughter spilling out like a sparkling fountain, and I joined in, the sound echoing off the walls, filling the space with life.

But as the laughter faded, so did the momentary distraction. My heart thudded heavily against my chest, a reminder of the fragile line we were tiptoeing. I wanted to reach out, to bridge the growing chasm of fear and longing that had taken root in my heart, but every time I contemplated taking that step, doubt clawed at my resolve. What if I misread the signs? What if I risked everything for a fleeting moment of closeness that could shatter our friendship entirely?

"Have you ever thought about why we're such good friends?" she asked, her voice low and contemplative, pulling me from my spiraling thoughts.

I blinked, caught off guard by the sudden weight of her question. "I guess it's just... natural? You get me in a way that no one else does. I can be myself around you."

She nodded slowly, her eyes searching mine, and for a heartbeat, I believed we were standing on the precipice of something monumental. The space between us hummed with unspoken words, each heartbeat echoing the possibility of more.

"Yeah, it's like we just... click," she murmured, glancing down at the simmering sauce. "But sometimes I wonder if it's just comfort or something deeper."

The air thickened with her words, a charged silence descending like a soft blanket over us. I could feel the flicker of hope igniting within me, battling the fears that had haunted my thoughts for weeks. "What if it's both?" I ventured, my heart pounding in my ears. "What if we're at the edge of something incredible?"

She turned, eyes widening slightly, and for a moment, the world around us faded away. The sound of the boiling pasta, the sizzle of garlic, the warmth of the kitchen—all fell into a hushed background as I stared into her bright eyes, willing her to understand.

Before she could respond, the timer rang, a harsh reminder of reality. The moment shattered like fragile glass, and I hurried to drain the pasta, my hands trembling slightly. The tension shifted, the connection simmering just below the surface, and I cursed the timing of it all. Why did life have to throw in distractions at the most critical junctures?

As we plated the food, the air crackled with possibilities, each shared smile and lingering glance heavy with what could be. I caught her looking at me again, a flicker of something unspoken in her gaze. The evening stretched on, filled with laughter and stolen moments, yet the question lingered like an unfinished symphony, a melody waiting for resolution.

In that cozy kitchen, surrounded by the scents of herbs and warmth, the complications of my heart tangled deeper. Would I dare to take that leap?

The clatter of plates and the soft melody of jazz floated through the kitchen, mingling with the scent of freshly cooked pasta and the promise of something unspoken lingering in the air. As I settled into the evening, I couldn't shake the tension that had woven itself into the fabric of our friendship, a tapestry of laughter and warmth now threaded with the undeniable spark of desire. I caught Kayla's eye, and the moment stretched, filled with a weight that seemed to hum just below the surface.

"Here's a question for you," I said, attempting to keep the mood light, my voice tinged with feigned nonchalance. "If you could have dinner with any fictional character, who would it be? And why?"

Kayla leaned back against the counter, her chin resting thoughtfully on her hand, eyes sparkling with mischief. "I'd say Mr. Darcy, because who wouldn't want a brooding gentleman with a penchant for romantic misunderstandings? What about you? Are you going to pick someone equally cliché?"

"Maybe I'd go for someone unexpected. How about Dobby from Harry Potter? Imagine the conversation! House-elves have such rich life stories," I replied, unable to contain a smirk.

"Oh, come on! A sock-loving elf? You can't be serious!" She rolled her eyes playfully, a teasing smile lighting up her face. "Where's the romance in that? We need a little more spice in our lives."

"Spice? Well, you're the one who added an entire jar of cayenne to our sauce. I'm still recovering from the heat." I gestured dramatically, clutching my throat as if I were gasping for air.

"Consider it culinary adventure! I thought we were spicing things up, both in the kitchen and, you know, life," she shot back, her voice playful yet laced with an undertone I couldn't quite decipher.

As the banter continued, I felt a strange pull between us, a thread weaving our playful exchanges into something deeper. I wondered if she sensed it, too—the delicate balance we were navigating, dancing on the edge of friendship and something more. I wanted to reach out, to wrap my fingers around that connection, but each time I thought about taking that leap, the fear of falling loomed larger.

After dinner, we settled into the living room, the soft glow of fairy lights casting a warm ambiance that wrapped around us like a comforting shawl. Kayla curled up on the couch, her legs tucked under her, the remnants of our dinner plates forgotten on the coffee table. I sank into the opposite end, stealing a glance at her. She was flipping through a book, her brow furrowed in concentration, the way she always looked when she was absorbed in a story.

"What's so riveting?" I asked, hoping to peel back the layers of her thoughts, to discover what lay behind that focused expression.

She looked up, her cheeks slightly flushed, and grinned. "Just a rom-com, the kind where everything goes hilariously wrong before it miraculously comes together. You know, the kind of unrealistic nonsense that gives you hope?"

"I thought you were a realist?" I raised an eyebrow, intrigued by the glimpse of vulnerability that flickered in her gaze.

"I am, mostly. But there's something about those stories that makes me giddy. Life can be messy, and sometimes I just want to escape into a world where everything turns out alright." She shrugged, a hint of wistfulness threading through her words.

I could relate to that longing, that desire to escape into a world where love was uncomplicated and friendships didn't tread precariously over the cliff of the unknown. "So, if your life were a rom-com, what would your big moment be? You know, the one where everything changes?"

Kayla paused, her eyes thoughtful as she considered my question. "I guess it would involve a grand gesture, something unexpected. Like a surprise confession at the top of a Ferris wheel or a dance in the rain. But knowing my luck, I'd probably slip and fall flat on my face."

I chuckled, the sound ringing through the air. "Well, I think you'd land on your feet, just like you always do. But wouldn't it be fun to see that happen? To experience that kind of excitement?"

"Excitement? Sure, but you'd have to promise to catch me if I fall," she said, her tone playful yet layered with something deeper, something that tugged at my heartstrings.

"I promise," I replied, my heart thundering in my chest as the words slipped from my lips, holding a weight I hadn't anticipated.

The room seemed to shift, the air thickening with an unspoken understanding, a glimmer of possibility flickering between us. I wanted to reach across the space that separated us, to bridge the gap of uncertainty, but a surge of fear clutched at my heart. What if I ruined everything?

Suddenly, the doorbell rang, slicing through the charged atmosphere. I jolted upright, grateful for the interruption as Kayla jumped up, a mix of surprise and relief dancing across her face. "I'll get it," she called over her shoulder, her voice cutting through my spiraling thoughts.

I took a deep breath, the sudden chaos of the moment clearing my mind. When Kayla opened the door, the bright porch light spilled into the room, illuminating the figure standing there. It was her neighbor, Ethan, his hair tousled as if he'd just sprinted over, a clipboard clutched tightly under his arm.

"Hey, Kayla! Sorry to interrupt, but I wanted to drop off these notes about the community event next week," he said, his voice casual but bright, eyes glancing between us with an inquisitive edge.

"Of course! Come in," she replied, her demeanor shifting to accommodate the unexpected visitor. The moment I had been holding onto slipped through my fingers like grains of sand, each one a reminder of what could have been.

Ethan stepped inside, the warmth of the room mingling with the cool evening air that trailed behind him. "I didn't realize you were entertaining. Hope I'm not intruding," he said, shooting me a friendly smile.

"Not at all," I replied, forcing the words through a smile that felt a little too tight. "Just a casual dinner. You caught us in the middle of a cooking debacle, actually."

"Cooking? What did you make? Or is it still a mystery?" He laughed, leaning against the doorframe with a relaxed confidence that felt like a jarring contrast to my racing heart.

Kayla chuckled, stepping further into the room. "More like a culinary adventure. We survived, somehow."

The conversation flowed, light and easy, as Ethan shared stories of his own culinary failures, but beneath it all, I felt the shadow of what had just slipped away. The warmth that had enveloped the room moments before now felt frigid, the air thickening with the unspoken words I wished I had said. I watched Kayla laugh at Ethan's stories, her eyes sparkling with amusement, and the longing within me twisted painfully.

As the evening wore on, I realized the universe had a way of throwing curveballs when you least expected it. Here we were, the three of us, caught in a web of laughter and stories, and yet all I could think about was the moment that had almost been ours. The cooking adventure had turned into an impromptu gathering, the space between Kayla and me widening with every word exchanged, every glance diverted.

I leaned back against the couch, a quiet storm brewing within me, the complications of my heart tangled further in the web of friendship and something unnamable. Would I ever find the courage to take that leap, to unravel the tension that held us captive? Or would I let the chance slip away, allowing the fear of losing what we had to dictate my choices?

The evening unfolded like a well-rehearsed play, with Ethan weaving in and out of conversation as if he were a character designed to distract from the burgeoning tension between Kayla and me. His laughter was bright, almost buoyant, filling the room with an easy charm that contrasted sharply with the swirling emotions trapped within me. I watched them converse, a casual ease blossoming between them, and felt like a mere observer in my own life, stuck in the periphery of something that was rapidly slipping away.

"I thought we were having a cooking showdown," Kayla teased, leaning against the counter, her arms crossed, radiating a playfulness that felt almost flirtatious. "Ethan, you're just lucky you showed up when you did. We were about to burn the kitchen down."

Ethan laughed, a sound that filled the space with warmth, and I felt a twinge of jealousy twist in my stomach. "I mean, if you need a fire marshal, I'm your guy," he quipped, winking at me as if we shared an unspoken understanding.

"Fire marshal, huh? Good to know you're versatile," I shot back, forcing a lightness into my tone that didn't quite reach my heart. I tried to shake off the disquiet creeping in, but it lingered, heavy and unyielding.

"So what's next for you two culinary masterminds?" he asked, plopping down onto the couch, clearly settling in for a long evening of banter.

"We were just discussing the merits of fictional dinner guests," I replied, shooting a glance at Kayla, who seemed to be enjoying the spotlight Ethan had unintentionally cast upon her. "You know, the kind of ridiculous fantasies that reveal way too much about our personalities."

"Do I want to know who you picked?" Ethan asked, arching an eyebrow, clearly intrigued.

Kayla, never one to shy away from sharing, grinned. "Well, I went with Mr. Darcy because who wouldn't want to have a brooding gentleman at the dinner table?"

"Classic choice," he nodded, his expression shifting into one of mock seriousness. "But can he cook? Because if I'm having him over, I'm not doing all the work."

"Please! That's the whole point!" she laughed, her voice light. "I want the romantic tension, not a kitchen disaster!"

"Speaking of tension," I interjected, trying to steer the conversation back, feeling the heat rising in my cheeks as the words slipped out. "Let's not forget the sheer thrill of unplanned culinary chaos."

Kayla caught my eye, and for a moment, I thought I saw a flicker of something there—an acknowledgment, a challenge, a spark—but it vanished as quickly as it came. She turned back to Ethan, the moment dissipating like smoke in the wind, leaving me stranded in a sea of longing and frustration.

"Chaos is one way to put it," Ethan said, glancing at me with an almost conspiratorial grin. "You should see Kayla's kitchen after her 'culinary adventures.' It's like a tornado swept through."

"Hey! At least I try," she shot back, a playful pout on her lips. "Some people are perfectly content to order takeout every night."

"Takeout's not such a bad thing," I countered, wishing I could steer the conversation away from the simmering tension. "At least it comes with no risk of a kitchen disaster—unless you count the time I accidentally ordered Thai food three nights in a row."

The trio of laughter that followed felt both familiar and distant, as if I were watching from behind a glass wall. I couldn't shake the feeling that the night was slipping away from me, each moment thickening the fog of unspoken feelings between Kayla and me.

As the clock ticked, the evening transitioned from playful banter to an oddly charged silence, punctuated only by the faint sounds of jazz spilling from the speakers. Kayla leaned back against the couch, her fingers brushing against mine as she reached for the remote. I could feel the warmth radiating from her, a comfort and a torment all wrapped into one.

"Okay, okay," she said, breaking the silence that had settled around us. "Let's pick a movie to lighten the mood. We need something with at least a 90% chance of ridiculousness."

"Can I suggest anything but a rom-com?" Ethan asked, raising his hands in mock surrender. "I'm really not ready for emotional turmoil tonight."

"Oh come on, where's your sense of adventure?" Kayla teased, her laughter twinkling like the stars outside. "How about we go full cheese with a classic? Something that guarantees a few cringe-worthy moments?"

"Fine, but I'm holding you responsible for my psychological well-being afterward," he grinned, and I couldn't help but admire the easy camaraderie between them.

Kayla started scrolling through the streaming options, her brows furrowing in concentration. I was lost in my thoughts, staring blankly at the screen, trying to shake off the nagging uncertainty that had settled into the pit of my stomach.

"Got it! 'The Proposal' it is!" Kayla declared triumphantly, her excitement palpable. "Sandra Bullock and Ryan Reynolds? You can't go wrong!"

Ethan groaned playfully. "Great, now I'm going to have to endure a bunch of 'I love yous' and 'I hate yous.' Just what I need tonight."

As the opening credits rolled, I sank deeper into the couch, the weight of everything pressing in around me. The movie unfolded, lighthearted and filled with comedic moments, but I found myself distracted. My thoughts drifted toward Kayla, her laughter mingling with the dialogue, her enthusiasm wrapping around me like a blanket of comfort. Yet, within that comfort lay the tension that had been growing, and my heart raced at the thought of breaking the delicate silence that had been carefully woven around us.

Halfway through the film, there was a particularly funny scene, and Kayla burst into laughter, her eyes sparkling. I looked at her, captivated by the way her joy illuminated her features. My heart swelled, and before I could second-guess myself, I leaned closer.

"Isn't this where they start to realize they have feelings for each other?" I murmured, my voice low, trying to gauge her reaction.

She turned to me, a teasing smile on her lips, but there was something deeper in her gaze, a flicker of acknowledgment that sent a thrill through me. "Are you implying we're at that point? Because if so, we might need a Ferris wheel for that kind of confession."

"Or a rainstorm for a dramatic kiss?" I shot back, unable to suppress the grin spreading across my face.

"Now you're just asking for a romantic cliché," she laughed, but the lightness didn't mask the intensity that had built up between us.

The movie played on, but the plot blurred into the background as the tension thickened. I could feel the moment shifting, a palpable crackle in the air, and I wondered if she felt it, too. My heart pounded in my chest, urging me to speak, to bridge the chasm that had widened between us, but fear clamped down on my throat, a vice I couldn't escape.

Then, in a moment that felt both surreal and electrifying, Kayla leaned closer, her shoulder brushing against mine. "Do you think they'll actually end up together?" she whispered, her breath warm against my ear.

In that split second, the world around us faded away. All I could see was her, the way her lips curled into a soft smile, the light in her eyes igniting the longing that had been simmering within me. "I think they're meant to," I replied softly, daring to meet her gaze, feeling as if I were standing at the edge of a precipice, the leap both terrifying and exhilarating.

Before I could gather the courage to say more, the doorbell rang again, breaking the fragile moment that had unfurled between us. The sudden noise sliced through the charged atmosphere, dragging me back to reality with a jarring thud. Kayla's expression shifted, disappointment flashing across her face before she masked it with a quick smile.

"I'll get it," she said, standing up, but the moment felt irrevocably changed.

I watched as she walked to the door, the heaviness of unspoken words hanging between us like a thread pulled taut. As she opened the door, my heart raced in a mix of anticipation and dread. What if it was someone unexpected, someone who would pull her attention away from me for good?

When she opened the door, I could only see the outline of a figure standing there. My breath hitched in my throat as the silhouette stepped into the light, and the weight of uncertainty settled heavily once more, leaving me perched on the precipice of what could have been.

"Hey!" Kayla exclaimed, her voice brightening. "I didn't expect to see you tonight!"

As the figure stepped fully into the light, my heart sank. There stood Mark, her ex-boyfriend, the ghost from her past I had never wanted to confront, and in that moment, everything shifted again. I was no longer just a friend caught in a tangled web of feelings; I was a spectator in a drama I hadn't anticipated, teetering on the edge of a cliff I never wanted to approach.

"Mind if I crash?" he asked, a smile playing on his lips, and the tension in the room snapped tighter than ever. I could feel the air shift, the possibility of what had almost blossomed slipping further from reach.

# Chapter 18: The Fall of the Mask

In the warm glow of early autumn, the air felt electric with tension and the promise of change. As I trudged onto the practice field, the familiar scent of damp grass mingled with the crispness of fallen leaves, creating an olfactory tapestry that should have brought comfort but instead filled me with dread. The laughter and camaraderie that had once echoed off the bleachers seemed like a distant echo, replaced by hushed whispers and sidelong glances that pierced me more deeply than a defender's tackle.

"Hey, are you going to stand there all day, or are you actually going to join us?" Kayla's voice broke through the murky haze of my thoughts, pulling me back to the present. Her easy smile held a warmth that was hard to resist, but even her support felt strained. The team had shifted beneath my feet like quicksand, and each passing moment felt like an inescapable trap closing tighter around my chest.

"Yeah, I'll join in a minute," I replied, forcing a smile that felt too brittle. With a quick flick of my hair, I tried to shake off the heaviness clinging to me like a second skin. But as I walked toward the group, the stares intensified, and I could almost hear the invisible strings of Ryan's machinations weaving through the air, tightening around me.

Practice began, but it was different—my teammates moved like shadows, flickering in and out of focus. Passes that once zipped effortlessly between us now stumbled, the rhythm of the game disrupted by the invisible weight of suspicion. Each throw felt like an accusation, and I half expected the football to ricochet back at me, a physical manifestation of Ryan's sabotage. The whispers I had overheard only days before replayed in my mind, each one a dagger aimed at my heart.

"Did you hear she's not as dedicated? Skipping training for her classes..."

"Must be nice to think you can juggle it all, but I guess some people just can't commit."

"Think she's really cut out for this team? Not everyone gets to wear that jersey."

With each passing moment, my frustration grew, simmering just beneath the surface, ready to boil over. Ryan was orchestrating a campaign against me with all the precision of a conductor leading a symphony, and I was the unwitting soloist floundering on stage. I could feel the weight of their doubts pressing down, threatening to crush me under its force. But what hurt the most was the realization that the laughter we had shared felt like a relic of the past, a faint whisper of what we had once been.

"Focus, Sam!" Coach Miller's bark cut through my spiral of thoughts, pulling me back into the present. I squared my shoulders, determination mingling with rising anger. No longer would I let Ryan's insidious campaign snuff out the flame of my passion. I needed to confront him, but I had to be smart about it.

After practice, as the sun dipped below the horizon, casting long shadows over the field, I found Kayla leaning against the bleachers, arms crossed, her eyes flickering with concern. "You okay? You've been quieter than usual," she remarked, a hint of worry edging her voice.

"I'm fine," I said, my tone sharper than intended. "No, I'm not. I'm not fine, Kayla. Ryan's turned the team against me. I can't just let this slide."

Her gaze softened, and she stepped closer, lowering her voice as if sharing a secret. "You need to talk to him. Call him out. Don't let him get away with this."

"You think I can just walk up and have a heart-to-heart with a guy who's clearly trying to sabotage me?" I huffed, frustration seeping into my words.

Kayla chuckled lightly, shaking her head. "You've always been too nice, Sam. Sometimes you've got to fight fire with fire. This is football, not a tea party."

The truth hung between us like an unspooled thread, and I felt my resolve harden. Maybe it was time to unleash the more feral side of me, the one that had fought tooth and nail to be seen as an equal on the team. "You're right. I can't keep dancing around it. I'm going to confront him tomorrow."

Kayla nodded, her smile returning, though it was tinged with apprehension. "Just be careful. He's not going to take it lying down."

I brushed off her concern, a smile breaking through my facade. "What's the worst that could happen? He spreads more rumors?"

She raised an eyebrow, skepticism dancing in her expression. "Oh, you know, only the end of your entire football career. No biggie."

The banter lightened my mood, but the weight of what lay ahead still loomed large. That night, sleep eluded me, thoughts whirling like autumn leaves caught in a tempest. Each scenario played out in my mind, varying shades of confrontation and fallout. The thought of facing Ryan twisted my stomach into knots, but I reminded myself of the resolve sparking within.

The next morning, I arrived at the field earlier than usual, the dawn casting a gentle light over the dew-kissed grass. It felt like a cleansing moment, a reminder of the fresh beginnings that came with every sunrise. As my teammates began to trickle in, I spotted Ryan lounging near the goalposts, a smirk plastered across his face, as if he were the king of an empire built on lies.

"Hey, Ryan," I called, striding toward him with purpose, my heart pounding in my chest. His gaze flickered to me, and for a brief second, surprise registered before the smirk returned, masking any hint of vulnerability.

"Sam, I didn't expect to see you here so early. Wasn't sure if you'd be skipping again," he quipped, the taunt dripping from his lips like venom.

"Cut the crap, Ryan," I snapped, taking another step closer, my hands balling into fists at my sides. "I know what you've been saying about me. This ends now."

His laughter rang out, harsh and mocking, sending a ripple of discomfort through my spine. "You think I have that much power? Please, you're doing this to yourself. Maybe if you dedicated more time to practice instead of your 'other commitments,' you wouldn't feel so insecure."

Each word felt like a knife, and I could feel my resolve wavering, but I stood firm. "I'm not going to let you undermine my hard work. You may think you're clever, but the truth has a way of coming out. People will see you for who you really are."

His expression shifted, a flicker of annoyance breaking through the bravado. "You're not in my league, Sam. You're just playing dress-up in those pads."

"Funny, I was just thinking the same about you," I shot back, a smirk creeping onto my lips. "But at least I'm not afraid to play the game."

As the tension crackled in the air between us, I felt a swell of confidence rise within me, a flicker of hope igniting the darkness that Ryan had cast over the team. Perhaps this was the moment I needed to reclaim my voice, to remind everyone, including myself, who I was and what I stood for.

The sun hung low in the sky, casting golden beams that filtered through the leaves and created a dappled pattern on the grass. The light felt almost magical, a stark contrast to the tension that had settled among the team like a heavy fog. I stood on the sidelines, watching as my teammates milled about, their laughter carrying over the field like a distant melody. Yet, it felt hollow, like an echo of a world I once belonged to but now seemed worlds away.

"Hey, why do you look like you just walked into a haunted house?" Kayla's voice cut through my reverie as she approached, a playful grin lighting up her face despite the heaviness that lingered in the air. "You know the practice doesn't start for another fifteen minutes, right?"

I forced a smile, but it felt more like a mask than anything genuine. "Just mentally preparing for the circus act that has become my life," I replied, glancing toward the goalposts where Ryan stood, still exuding that smug confidence that infuriated me.

"Don't let him get under your skin," she said, her tone turning serious. "You've worked too hard to let him chip away at your confidence."

"Right, because nothing says 'confidence' like dodging verbal bullets all day," I shot back, folding my arms as if that would shield me from the onslaught of negativity.

Her expression softened. "You're tougher than you think. Just remember, the truth has a way of unraveling lies. It's just a matter of time."

As if on cue, Ryan strutted toward us, his swagger a deliberate display. "What's up, ladies? Planning a strategy to keep Sam in the game, or just wasting your breath?" His smirk was maddening, a reminder of all the ways he sought to undermine me.

"Actually, we were just discussing how you might want to prepare for your next career as a stand-up comedian," Kayla retorted, her eyes narrowing defiantly.

"Oh, Kayla, sweetie, you're adorable when you try to be tough," Ryan replied, dismissive. "But honestly, what's the point? Sam here has already resigned herself to being a benchwarmer."

I felt the heat rise in my cheeks, a mixture of anger and embarrassment swirling within me. "Funny, coming from someone whose only talent is running his mouth," I shot back, summoning the courage I'd felt earlier.

"Careful, Sam," Ryan said, his voice dripping with condescension. "That kind of attitude will get you nowhere, fast."

Before I could respond, Coach Miller's whistle pierced the air, calling us to gather for the day's practice. As the team assembled, I couldn't shake the weight of Ryan's words. Each insult was a thorn, digging deeper into my psyche, making me question my place on the team and my commitment to the sport I loved.

Practice began, and I threw myself into drills with a fervor that surprised even me. Every pass, every sprint, every drill felt like a lifeline, a momentary escape from the murky waters of doubt that threatened to pull me under. Yet, even as I pushed myself, I could sense the eyes of my teammates watching, weighing, assessing.

"Good job, Sam!" shouted Chris, a defensive back who had always been a solid ally. The praise felt like a balm to my wounded pride, but it was fleeting. Ryan's laughter echoed in the distance, a sharp reminder that not everyone shared Chris's view.

During a water break, I overheard snippets of conversation from nearby teammates, their voices low, but the words cut through the air like a knife. "She doesn't belong here," one muttered. "It's embarrassing to watch her try."

I clenched my jaw, anger boiling just beneath the surface, threatening to erupt. Kayla shot me a concerned glance, and I gave her a tight smile, but inside, I felt the simmering rage and frustration begin to coalesce into something sharper, more focused.

"Let's do a scrimmage," Coach Miller announced, breaking into my spiraling thoughts. "I want to see everyone's commitment out there."

"Just what I need," I muttered under my breath, eyeing Ryan as he cracked his knuckles, a sinister grin playing on his lips. The thought of him on the opposite team filled me with a mixture of dread and determination.

As the whistle blew, we split into teams, the air charged with competition. I positioned myself on the field, heart racing, ready to reclaim my ground. The scrimmage unfolded with an intensity that sent adrenaline surging through my veins. Each tackle, each run felt like a battle, and I was determined not to lose.

Ryan, predictably, played dirty, his attempts to rattle me becoming more blatant as the game progressed. A hard shove here, a low jab there—he clearly relished the chance to push my buttons. But I was ready. Each time he tried to get into my head, I countered with a fierce determination that surprised even me.

When it was my turn to receive the ball, everything narrowed into focus. I took off, dodging tackles, and the world around me faded into a blur. The cheers from my teammates faded in and out, a rhythm that pulsed with every stride I took. I felt powerful, unstoppable, as I sprinted down the field, dodging Ryan's reach with ease.

But in a split second, everything changed. As I moved to evade, I caught a glimpse of Ryan rushing toward me with an intensity that sent a chill down my spine. It felt like time stretched, a moment suspended in the air as he barreled into me, a predatory gleam in his eye.

The impact knocked me off my feet, and for a moment, the world spun. I hit the ground hard, the breath whooshing out of my lungs, a sharp pain blooming in my side. Distant shouts and laughter melded into a cacophony, the field now a chaotic whirlwind of sound and sensation.

"Sam!" Kayla's voice broke through the fog, urgent and panicked. I blinked, trying to focus, but the world tilted precariously around me. Ryan stood over me, an expression of triumph etched on his face, as if he had just claimed victory in a battle.

"Didn't see you there," he said, feigning innocence. "Careful next time. You don't want to get hurt, do you?"

The disdain in his tone ignited a fire within me, but before I could respond, Coach Miller was at my side, concern etched across his features. "Sam, are you alright?"

I pushed myself up, pain radiating through my side, but I refused to let him see me falter. "I'm fine," I grunted, though the tremor in my voice betrayed me.

"Let's take a break," he said, his voice firm. "I need to check on you."

I shook my head, steeling my resolve. "No, I can keep going. I'm fine, really." The words came out in a rush, desperate to prove I wouldn't back down, that I wouldn't let Ryan's cheap shot define me.

"Alright," he relented, though skepticism lingered in his eyes. "Just don't push yourself too hard."

As the game resumed, I felt the lingering stares of my teammates, a mixture of concern and uncertainty clouding their expressions. But amidst it all, I could hear Kayla's unwavering voice. "You've got this, Sam. Show him what you're made of."

With renewed determination, I stepped back onto the field, ready to reclaim my place in this game and prove that Ryan's lies would not define me. The challenge had become not just about the game, but about standing tall against the very shadows that sought to pull me down.

The game resumed, but my world felt strangely muted, each sound distorted as if I were trapped in an underwater bubble. With every step I took, the pain in my side throbbed like a persistent reminder of Ryan's brutal tackle. Yet, the adrenaline coursing through me transformed that pain into fuel, igniting a fierce determination I hadn't known I possessed. I would show him that I was not someone to be trifled with, that I wouldn't back down without a fight.

As the play unfolded around me, my eyes remained fixed on the field, searching for openings, evaluating strategies. A quick pass found its way to me, and I caught it cleanly, my heart racing as I pivoted to make my move. The exhilaration of the game surged through me, a wave of energy that drowned out the doubts. I pushed forward, dodging defenders with newfound agility, weaving through bodies like a thread through a needle.

But Ryan was relentless. I could feel his eyes on me, watching, waiting for a moment of weakness. "Nice catch, Sam! You should really work on that run, though. Wouldn't want to trip over your own feet!" he yelled, laughter lacing his words, but it only spurred me on.

"Thanks for the tip, Ryan! I'll send you my next training schedule," I shot back, my voice dripping with sarcasm as I sprinted past him, determined not to let his words penetrate the armor I was building around myself.

The ball found its way back to me again, and with a fierce thrust, I launched it toward the end zone. I could see Chris rushing to catch it, the light catching the determination etched on his face. He dove, arms outstretched, and I held my breath as time seemed to slow.

He landed with a thud, cradling the ball triumphantly against his chest. The team erupted into cheers, and for a moment, it felt like the cloud of doubt that had hung over me began to dissipate. In that moment, we were a unit, a team bound by sweat and ambition, and I felt a flicker of hope igniting deep within me.

But Ryan was not finished. As the cheers subsided, he huddled with a few of the other players, whispering conspiratorially, casting sidelong glances in my direction. I tried to shake off the sensation of being an outsider in my own team, but it was like a chill in the air that refused to dissipate.

With the scrimmage nearing its end, I could sense the shift in energy. The camaraderie I had fought to reclaim felt fragile, like a spiderweb glistening with dew but easily torn. I was determined not to let Ryan's darkness snuff out this brief glimmer of light.

The final whistle blew, signaling the end of practice, and as the team gathered for a cooldown, I found myself pulled back into reality. I watched as Ryan sauntered away from the group, a triumphant smirk still plastered across his face.

"Sam!" Chris called, breaking my focus. "You played great today! I've never seen you run like that!" His enthusiasm was infectious, and it brought a genuine smile to my face.

"Thanks, Chris! I guess a little pressure can be a good motivator," I replied, shaking off the remnants of doubt clinging to me.

"Don't let Ryan get to you," he added, his expression turning serious. "He's just jealous. You're good, and you know it."

"Yeah, well, I'm tired of his games," I said, glancing back toward the edge of the field where Ryan stood with a few of his minions. "Maybe it's time I turn the tables."

"Just be careful," Kayla chimed in, her brow furrowed with concern. "You don't want to give him any more fuel."

"Trust me, I'm ready to take this head-on. I'm done playing defense."

As the team broke up to head home, I felt a rush of adrenaline mixed with a newfound resolve. I couldn't allow Ryan's toxicity to fester any longer. I needed to confront him, not just for myself but for the sake of the team I loved.

Later that night, my phone buzzed on the kitchen counter, the light flickering in the dim room. It was a message from Kayla: You sure about this?

Yes, I typed back. He needs to know I'm not afraid.

The evening air was crisp as I stepped outside, the stars twinkling overhead like distant promises. I made my way toward Ryan's house, a creeping sense of anxiety tangling with the determination surging through me. With each step, I felt the weight of the confrontation looming, but it was necessary.

I reached his place, a small house at the end of a cul-de-sac, the porch light casting an eerie glow that illuminated the shadows dancing around me. I took a deep breath, summoning my courage, and rang the doorbell.

A moment later, Ryan appeared, leaning casually against the doorframe, an expression of mock surprise on his face. "Well, if it isn't my favorite benchwarmer. What's the matter? Can't handle a little competition?"

I crossed my arms, forcing myself to maintain eye contact, refusing to back down. "I'm not here to discuss football. I'm here to talk about the rumors you've been spreading."

His expression shifted, a flicker of annoyance crossing his features. "Oh, come on. It's just a bit of fun. You're too sensitive."

"Fun? You think it's fun to undermine someone's hard work and commitment? You're trying to tear down everything I've built. That's not just fun, Ryan. That's malicious."

He straightened, the playfulness draining from his demeanor. "And what do you plan to do about it? Whine to Coach? Cry on your little friend's shoulder?"

"I plan to stand my ground. I'm not going to let you bully me or anyone else on this team."

"Is that so?" He stepped closer, his smirk returning, but this time it held a darker edge. "You really think you can take me on? You're just a girl playing a boy's game. You'll never fit in."

The taunt struck a nerve, igniting a blaze of fury within me. "You're wrong, Ryan. I'm here to stay, and you can either accept that or be prepared for a fight. But make no mistake—I will not back down."

His eyes narrowed, the tension between us crackling like static electricity. "You think you're tough? I'll show you tough."

Suddenly, the ground beneath us seemed to shift, and before I could react, he lunged forward, shoving me hard against the side of the house. I gasped, the impact knocking the breath from my lungs.

But as I struggled to regain my footing, a voice sliced through the air—a voice I never expected to hear in this moment. "What the hell is going on here?"

I turned to see Coach Miller standing there, a mix of confusion and anger flashing across his face. The world froze around us, the air thick with tension as both Ryan and I stared at him, caught in a dangerous moment of revelation.

"What are you doing?" Coach's voice was low, dangerous, as he stepped closer, ready to intervene.

I could feel my heart racing, the weight of the confrontation hanging heavy in the air, knowing that everything could change in an instant. Would this be the moment I finally exposed Ryan for the bully he was? Or would I become just another victim in a game that had spiraled beyond my control?

# Chapter 19: Confrontation

The gym hummed with the rhythmic thud of sneakers against polished wood, each echo a testament to countless hours spent chasing dreams or escaping reality. I stepped inside, the smell of rubber mats and the faint whiff of sweat filling the air, a concoction both invigorating and oppressive. My heart raced, thudding in time with the bass of music pumping from the speakers. It was a strange mix of nerves and exhilaration; after all, I was about to face Ryan.

I spotted him in the corner, bathed in fluorescent light that accentuated the sharp lines of his jaw and the confident tilt of his head. He was in his element, pushing through a set of weights with a focus that felt almost intoxicating. For a moment, I hesitated, the weight of our history pressing down on my chest like an anchor. Memories of laughter, late-night confessions, and heated arguments flooded my mind. But those moments had become ghosts, shadows of what we once were—now eclipsed by his betrayal.

With determination flooding my veins, I crossed the room, each step a march toward reclaiming my narrative. "We need to talk," I stated, my voice cutting through the air, steady despite the whirlwind of emotions whirling within. The room felt suddenly quieter, the chatter and music fading into the background as his gaze met mine, an amused spark dancing in his eyes.

"Oh? And here I thought you'd be too busy sulking to confront me," he replied, a smirk playing at the corners of his mouth. I clenched my fists at my sides, resisting the urge to punch that smug look off his face. His casual demeanor only fueled the fire inside me.

"It's not sulking. It's called processing," I shot back, my tone sharper than I intended, but I didn't care. The air between us crackled, charged with unspoken words and unresolved tension. "We can't keep pretending like nothing happened."

Ryan leaned back against the wall, crossing his arms over his chest in a way that exuded confidence, but I could see the flicker of something else—uncertainty? Guilt? "You're right. We can't. But what do you want me to say? That I'm sorry?" He laughed, but it didn't reach his eyes, and for a moment, I thought perhaps he was genuinely unaware of the depth of his actions.

"Sorry isn't enough," I replied, stepping closer, the distance between us shrinking with each word. "You took my trust and stomped all over it. You don't get to decide how I feel or who I am because of your choices."

He straightened, the smirk vanishing, replaced by an intensity that made my pulse quicken. "You think I wanted this? You think I set out to hurt you?" His voice rose slightly, frustration spilling over as he pushed off the wall and closed the space between us. "You've turned this into a tragedy, but it was just a mistake!"

"A mistake?" I echoed incredulously. "You had a choice, Ryan. You chose to play with my heart, to drag my name through the mud while pretending everything was fine." My words cut like a blade, but I had to speak my truth, no matter how much it hurt. The anger bubbled to the surface, a hot tide that threatened to engulf me.

For a moment, silence hung between us, heavy and suffocating. I could feel the weight of his gaze, piercing and calculating, as if he was trying to dissect my soul. I inhaled deeply, willing myself to stand my ground, to show him that I wasn't the same girl who had been too willing to forgive, too eager to forget.

"You don't get to define me, Ryan," I continued, my voice softer but no less fierce. "I'm not the girl you can manipulate into feeling guilty or ashamed. I'm reclaiming my narrative, and I won't let you steal it away from me."

His expression shifted, the mask of confidence slipping just enough for me to see the boy beneath. "You're acting like I did this on purpose," he said, a hint of desperation creeping into his tone. "You think I wanted to hurt you? I was trying to protect you!"

"Protect me?" The laugh that escaped my lips was bitter, an ugly sound that echoed off the gym walls. "By betraying me? By lying to me? If that's your version of protection, I'd rather be on my own."

I watched as the color drained from his face, the realization of his actions dawning on him like a cruel sunrise. The gym, once a cacophony of life and energy, now felt like a void, filled only with the remnants of our shattered connection. I could see the fight leaving him, the smug façade cracking as the truth of my words sank in.

"I never wanted it to end like this," he murmured, his voice low, almost a whisper. The cocky bravado was gone, replaced by a raw vulnerability that made my heart ache. "You mean more to me than I can say."

"Then why didn't you act like it?" I shot back, but the edge in my voice faltered slightly, a crack in my armor. "I deserve more than your half-hearted attempts at care."

The silence stretched, a palpable tension that pulled at the air around us. My heart raced, torn between the anger I felt and the flicker of longing that still danced in my chest. Did I want to fight for this? Did I even want him in my life after everything?

"Maybe it's too late for us," I said, my voice barely above a whisper, the words tasting bitter on my tongue. The weight of the moment settled heavily on my shoulders, the truth of it both liberating and crushing. I turned to leave, my heart thundering with each step, but Ryan's voice stopped me.

"Wait," he called, the desperation in his tone compelling me to pause. I turned back, half-anticipating his next words, half-dreading them. "I don't want this to be the end."

"Wait," he called out, and the urgency in his voice pricked my curiosity. The gym, once a haven of noise and activity, faded into the background, leaving just the two of us suspended in a bubble of raw emotion. I turned slowly, my heart a fluttering bird caught in a cage of my own making.

"What do you want me to say?" I shot back, my tone sharp, but underneath it all, a hint of vulnerability threatened to crack my composure. "You can't just throw those words around and expect everything to magically fix itself."

He pushed off the wall, the moment stretching taut as he closed the distance between us. "I want to say that I'm not the person you think I am," he said, his voice dropping to a near whisper. "You're right; I messed up. But it's not just about what I did; it's about who I am when I'm with you. You make me better."

The weight of his admission hung heavy in the air, and I could feel the walls I had meticulously built around my heart quiver at the edges. "Make you better?" I echoed, incredulous. "That's rich coming from the guy who treated me like a passing interest instead of someone worth fighting for."

His eyes flashed with something I couldn't quite decipher—was it regret? Anger? "And what about you? You've built this image of me that fits your narrative but forget that I'm a real person, too. I have my own struggles, my own demons. You think it's easy to keep everything together? To juggle expectations and still show up as the guy you want me to be?"

I crossed my arms, trying to mask the way his words pierced through my defenses. "I don't expect you to be perfect, Ryan. I just want you to be real. To be honest."

"Honest?" He scoffed, running a hand through his hair, the frustration bubbling back to the surface. "That's rich, coming from you. You've been hiding, too—hiding behind your studies, your friends, pretending like this whole thing with us didn't mean anything."

I opened my mouth to protest, but the truth stung more than I anticipated. I had been retreating into the comfort of my routines, avoiding the messy emotions that clung to our connection like ivy to a brick wall. Perhaps he was right. "This isn't about me," I insisted, trying to regain control. "This is about you taking my trust and tossing it aside like it was nothing."

His expression softened, the sharp edges of his demeanor dulling into something almost vulnerable. "I didn't mean to hurt you. I never wanted that. I was scared, okay? Scared of losing you."

I hesitated, uncertainty flooding my mind like a tide pulling me under. "Scared of what? That I would see you for who you really are?"

He stepped closer, the scent of his cologne wrapping around me like a familiar embrace, one that I had missed more than I cared to admit. "Scared of what you would think if you knew the truth—that I'm not the golden boy you imagine me to be. I have my flaws, my fears, and the way I handled things was... cowardly."

The raw honesty in his eyes stirred something deep within me, an unexpected spark of empathy that made my heart ache. "You think you're the only one scared? I've been terrified, Ryan. Terrified that I invested so much of myself into someone who didn't see me. And now I have to ask myself if I can trust you again."

"I don't want to lose you," he murmured, the urgency in his voice betraying the calm exterior he often maintained. "You're the best part of my life, and I let my fear cloud that. I messed up, but I want a chance to make it right. Let me prove it to you."

The silence between us hung heavy, the tension a taut wire, both thrilling and terrifying. I looked into his eyes, searching for the sincerity I desperately needed to see. Was he being genuine, or was this just another act of desperation?

"Prove it," I replied, the challenge slipping out before I could rein it in. "Show me that you're worth the risk, that you can be the person I believed you were before this all happened."

He nodded slowly, determination flickering in his gaze. "What do you need from me? I'll do whatever it takes."

"Start by being present. No more half-truths or distractions. If you're in this, then be in it completely. I'm tired of the games," I stated, my voice steady as I laid down the gauntlet. "And if you mess up again, I'm out. No second chances."

"Deal," he agreed, and I couldn't help but notice the way relief washed over him, the tension in his shoulders easing. But even as I said the words, a small part of me quivered with uncertainty. Could he really change? Could I trust him again?

"Okay," I said, feeling the weight of my decision settle like a lead blanket on my chest. "Let's start small. You can help me with my training for that 5K I've been avoiding."

His brows lifted in surprise, a playful glimmer returning to his eyes. "Training? I thought you'd want me to plan a grand gesture or something."

"Grand gestures are overrated," I replied, crossing my arms defiantly. "Besides, I need to know you can handle the basics before we tackle anything bigger."

He chuckled, the sound warm and familiar. "Well, if you think running around the track with me is enough to prove I'm worth your time, I'm all in. Just don't blame me if I outrun you."

"Oh please, cocky much?" I teased, feeling a sense of camaraderie creep back into our exchange. "I'll be the one leaving you in the dust."

The playful banter felt like a balm, a reminder of the easy connection we once shared. But as I stepped away, my heart still a battleground, I knew this was only the beginning. Would we truly find our way back to each other, or was this just a temporary reprieve before the inevitable fallout?

The tension still crackled in the air, heavy with unspoken words and lingering doubts, yet as I left the gym, I felt a flicker of hope ignite within me. Maybe—just maybe—we could navigate the storm together.

The air crackled with unfiltered energy as I stepped away from the gym, my heart still racing from the confrontation. With every stride, I could feel the lingering tension between Ryan and me, a frayed thread tethering us together, but the question remained: could it withstand the weight of our history? I pushed open the glass doors, stepping into the crisp evening air, the cool breeze a sharp contrast to the heat simmering within me.

I wasn't ready to embrace what lay ahead. As much as I wanted to believe Ryan's words, the scars of betrayal were fresh, and trust was not something easily regained. My thoughts spiraled as I wandered aimlessly, the campus bustling around me, students hurrying to late-night study sessions, laughter ringing out from groups sprawled on the grass. But I felt like a ghost, floating through a world that no longer seemed familiar.

"Hey! Earth to Ava!" a voice called out, breaking through my reverie. I turned to see Lily waving her arms, her short curls bouncing with each step as she approached. Her bright smile lit up her face like a beacon, but I felt a shadow cast over my mood.

"Sorry, just... lost in thought," I said, forcing a smile as I tried to shake off the weight of my conversation with Ryan.

Lily arched an eyebrow, her expression shifting from cheerful to concerned. "You sure? Because you look like someone just stole your last cookie."

I let out a laugh, though it felt strained. "No cookies were harmed, I promise. Just had a... talk with Ryan."

"Ah, the infamous Ryan," she said, crossing her arms in a dramatic flair. "What's the latest scandal? Did he dazzle you with his charm while simultaneously stepping on your heart?"

"Something like that," I replied, my voice dropping to a whisper as we started to walk. "He's trying to make amends, but I don't know if I can trust him again."

"Trust is a tricky little thing," she mused, her eyes thoughtful. "You can't just hand it over like a slice of pizza. It's earned, and it takes time. What does your gut say?"

I paused, feeling the weight of her question. My gut was a stormy sea, tossing and turning with uncertainty. "It's telling me to be cautious," I admitted. "But there's this part of me that wants to believe he can change."

"Believe in yourself first, Ava. He's not the only one who has to earn back trust; you have to trust your instincts too," she said, giving me a reassuring smile.

Her words lingered in my mind as we parted ways. I continued my walk, contemplating everything that had transpired. I loved how Lily could strip away the layers of doubt, but I still felt like I was walking a tightrope, balancing my feelings for Ryan and the desire to protect my heart.

As I rounded the corner toward my dorm, I caught sight of Ryan sitting on the steps, his silhouette framed against the soft glow of the campus lights. My stomach flipped, a mix of anticipation and apprehension. He looked up as I approached, and I could see the tension in his posture—shoulders rigid, jaw clenched.

"Hey," he said, his voice low. "I didn't know if you'd come back."

"Thought I might be a ghost for the rest of the semester," I replied, trying to keep things light, but the air between us was thick with unresolved emotions.

"I'm glad you're here," he said, shifting to make room for me on the steps. I hesitated, the space between us almost tangible. "Can we talk? Just... you and me? No distractions?"

I settled beside him, the night air wrapping around us like a soft blanket. The stars twinkled overhead, indifferent witnesses to our conversation, and for a moment, the world outside faded.

"I'm listening," I said, my voice steady, trying to shield myself from the vulnerability swirling around us.

"I've thought a lot about what you said," he began, his gaze fixed on the ground. "I want to show you that I'm not just some jerk who takes your trust and stomps on it. I want to be someone who deserves to be in your life."

"Words are easy, Ryan. You've proven that," I replied, my heart pounding as I braced myself for whatever came next. "You've got to show me you mean it."

"I know," he said, his voice a low rumble. "What if I start with this? No games, no lies. Just the truth. Can we make a deal? I tell you everything—my mistakes, my fears—no secrets."

My breath caught in my throat, the weight of his offer washing over me. "Everything? That's a tall order," I replied, skepticism lacing my tone. "What if it only makes things worse?"

"Then we'll face that together," he said, his eyes locking onto mine, the sincerity palpable. "But I'd rather be honest with you now than risk losing you completely."

The silence that followed felt charged, like the moment before a storm. I wanted to push back, to demand he prove himself in smaller ways before spilling everything. But the longing for connection tugged at me, urging me to take the plunge.

"Okay," I said finally, my voice barely above a whisper. "But you start. No holding back."

He took a deep breath, the tension in his shoulders easing just slightly. "Alright. The first thing you need to know is that I'm not just some charming guy who can sweet-talk his way out of anything. I've been scared of letting anyone in, scared of how much it would hurt to lose them."

"Sounds pretty relatable," I said, trying to lighten the mood, though my heart raced at his admission.

"Yeah, but here's where it gets messy," he continued, running a hand through his hair. "I thought I could keep you at arm's length, but when I saw you connecting with someone else, it terrified me. I realized I was losing something precious without even trying."

"So, you thought betraying me was the solution?" I challenged, feeling the familiar anger flare.

"No! God, no," he exclaimed, frustration spilling over. "I thought I could protect you from what I am. From my mistakes. But instead, I just created a bigger mess."

The vulnerability in his eyes tugged at my heartstrings, but the anger still simmered just beneath the surface. "Ryan, you can't just decide what's best for me. I'm not a damsel in distress waiting for you to swoop in."

"Believe me, I know that now," he said, his tone earnest. "But there's something else you need to know. Something I've never told anyone."

The gravity of his statement hung in the air, the tension morphing into something more profound. "What is it?" I asked, my heart pounding, caught between dread and anticipation.

He opened his mouth to speak, but suddenly the distant sound of footsteps interrupted us. A figure approached, cloaked in shadows, their voice carrying through the night, chilling me to the bone. "There you are, Ryan. We need to talk."

I turned to see a woman emerging from the darkness, her expression unreadable, but the way she looked at Ryan sent a shiver down my spine. The unease in the air intensified, and my heart raced with a mix of confusion and fear. Who was she, and why did it feel like our moment was slipping away, replaced by a new and unpredictable storm?

"Who is she?" I demanded, my voice steady despite the turmoil within. Ryan's eyes widened, the tension unmistakable.

# Chapter 20: The Reckoning

The air crackled with tension, electric and sharp as I strode away from Ryan, each step a rebellious echo of defiance against the storm brewing in his eyes. I could feel the weight of his words pressing against my back, a heavy shroud of dread that threatened to pull me under. But I was done being intimidated, done playing the role of the frightened victim who cowered in the corners of life. I was ready to reclaim my narrative, to script my own destiny even if it meant walking through a battlefield strewn with the remnants of my past.

The café on the corner, a tiny refuge of warmth and the rich scent of coffee, beckoned me. Inside, the chatter of familiar voices created a cocoon of safety, the clinking of cups and laughter a soothing balm against the harsh reality I had just faced. I squeezed past a few tables, the wooden floors creaking beneath my sneakers, a welcome reminder of the ordinary, the mundane. In this space, my worries could dissolve into the froth of a latte, and the sun-drenched windows served as a barrier between me and the brewing storm outside.

"Hey, you look like you just saw a ghost," Sophie chirped, her vibrant red hair swinging as she leaned across the counter, eyes sparkling with mischief. She had a knack for pulling me back into the present with just a flicker of her playful spirit. "Or worse—ran into Ryan?"

"Is it that obvious?" I replied, forcing a laugh as I sank onto one of the plush stools at the counter. "I just had a little chat with him."

Her brow furrowed, the easy playfulness shifting into concern. "You know you don't have to engage with him. He thrives on this—whatever sick game he's playing."

"I know, but I can't just ignore him." My fingers wrapped around the ceramic mug, the warmth seeping into my palms. "He thinks he can intimidate me. I won't let him."

Sophie sighed, her expression a blend of admiration and worry. "You're braver than I could ever be. But, please, be careful. He's unpredictable."

A shiver ran down my spine, a vivid reminder of the venomous glint in Ryan's eyes, a stark contrast to the warmth radiating from the café's atmosphere. I took a sip of my drink, the smooth taste of caramel and espresso swirling comfortingly in my mouth. Just as I was about to respond, the door swung open with a jangling bell, and in walked Ethan, my unexpected lifeline. His presence filled the room, the very air shifting with his easy confidence.

"Did someone order a hero?" he called out, a smirk dancing on his lips as he navigated through the tables. He slid onto the stool next to me, the scent of his cologne—a mix of cedar and something earthy—drifting over like a soft embrace. I had always loved how effortlessly he carried himself, as if the world was merely a playground meant for his enjoyment.

"More like a comic relief," I retorted, nudging him playfully. "Sophie was just reminding me of the dangers of engaging with a certain someone."

Ethan leaned closer, his voice low and conspiratorial. "You mean Ryan? I swear, if I had a dollar for every time I wanted to throttle that guy..."

"Careful, or you'll end up in a cage match," I teased, but the laughter felt hollow. There was something about the way Ryan had looked at me, a predator sizing up its prey, that gnawed at my insides. I shook my head, trying to clear the thoughts swirling like a storm cloud. "But seriously, I don't know what he wants. It's like he's playing some twisted game, and I'm just the unsuspecting pawn."

Ethan's brow furrowed, a flicker of concern crossing his features. "You're more than a pawn, you know that, right? You're a queen, ready to take the throne." His words wrapped around me like a comforting quilt, infusing me with warmth and courage.

"Thanks, I needed that," I said, my voice quieter now, the truth of his statement sinking in. Maybe I was starting to discover my own power, the strength buried beneath layers of self-doubt and fear. "But I'm not sure what my next move should be. How do I fight back against someone like him?"

Ethan pondered for a moment, the corners of his mouth twitching into a thoughtful frown. "How about we gather some intel? You know, uncover his weaknesses? If he thinks he can intimidate you, we'll turn the tables. It's time to make him understand he picked the wrong target."

The idea resonated deep within me, igniting a flicker of determination I hadn't realized I possessed. "You really think we can?"

"Absolutely. But first, we need to establish a game plan. We'll outsmart him." His eyes sparkled with a mix of mischief and confidence, like a boy about to pull off the best prank of his life.

As I listened to Ethan lay out his ideas, I found myself leaning in closer, a surge of adrenaline filling me with excitement. This wasn't just about Ryan anymore; it was about reclaiming my life and defining my own terms. The café around us faded into the background, the chatter and clinks blending into a symphony of hope and resilience. The sun poured in through the windows, illuminating the path ahead, urging me to step into the light and embrace the fight that lay before me.

Just then, the door swung open again, and my stomach dropped as I caught sight of Ryan's familiar silhouette. He stood there, framed by the entrance like a dark storm cloud, his presence instantly sucking the warmth from the room. The playful banter faded, replaced by an unsettling silence, all eyes darting toward him, a wary hush descending over the café.

I felt Ethan tense beside me, a protective aura radiating from him like an invisible shield. The atmosphere shifted, the air thickening with unspoken tension as Ryan's gaze locked onto mine. My heart raced, a wild drumbeat echoing in my ears, but this time, I wouldn't back down. I squared my shoulders, forcing a smile that didn't quite reach my eyes. I was done running. Let the games begin.

The moment hung suspended, a tightrope walk between anticipation and dread, as Ryan stood there, a dark figure against the sun-drenched café. I could practically feel the room holding its breath, the chatter stifled, eyes darting nervously between us as if awaiting a match to ignite a powder keg. But I wasn't about to be a timid mouse in his predatory gaze. No, I was done being intimidated. I met his stare, unflinching, my resolve crystallizing like ice around a fire.

"Don't you have somewhere else to be?" I shot back, the sharpness of my voice slicing through the tension. It was a weak retort, perhaps, but it felt good to put him on the defensive, even for a moment. The corners of Ryan's mouth twisted into a sardonic smile, the kind that didn't quite reach his eyes.

"Maybe I'm just here to see how long you can keep up this charade," he replied, his tone dripping with disdain.

A flicker of anger ignited within me, but I clamped down on it, choosing instead to summon my own brand of humor. "Oh, trust me, I've got a PhD in charades. What's your specialty? Blustering and blathering?"

This caught him off guard, his smug expression faltering for a split second. I seized the moment, feeling a surge of victory. This wasn't just about me standing my ground; it was a clever dance of words, a psychological duel that brought a thrill like no other.

But that thrill was quickly doused by the realization that Ryan was not just some blustery bully; he was a storm brewing on the horizon, and I was standing too close to the edge. As I turned to retreat back to the safety of my friends, a cold, commanding voice pierced through the tension.

"Don't walk away from me, Alana."

I paused, my heart plummeting. His words hung in the air like a threat, and I could feel the chill creeping up my spine. I steadied myself, inhaling deeply, the aroma of freshly brewed coffee mixing with the scent of fear, a reminder that I needed to regain my footing.

Ethan shifted beside me, muscles coiled like a spring ready to pounce. "We're done here, Ryan. You need to back off." His voice was a low growl, protective and fierce.

Ryan turned to him, dismissive. "And you are? Her knight in shining armor?" He scoffed, the contempt palpable in his tone. "Let her speak for herself."

I could feel the heat of embarrassment creeping into my cheeks, but I pushed it down. "I can handle myself, thank you very much," I asserted, forcing my voice to remain steady, even as my heart raced. "But maybe you should take a good, hard look in the mirror. That reflection is the only thing you should be worried about."

Ryan's eyes narrowed, an unsettling flicker of anger crossing his features before he chuckled darkly. "You're feisty. I can respect that." He leaned in closer, a predatory glint shining in his eyes. "But don't forget, feistiness can also land you in trouble. I hope you're prepared for what's coming."

With that, he turned on his heel and strode out of the café, leaving a trail of confusion and tension in his wake. The door swung shut behind him, but the weight of his threat lingered like smoke in the air. I blinked, trying to regain my composure as the chatter of the café resumed its lively rhythm.

"What just happened?" Sophie whispered, her eyes wide with a mix of disbelief and concern.

"Just a little showdown," I replied, attempting to keep my tone light, even as the unease churned in my stomach. "No big deal."

Ethan was scanning the room, his protective instincts kicking into overdrive. "That guy is a ticking time bomb. We need a plan, and we need it fast."

His resolve was comforting, a steady anchor amidst the turmoil. I could feel the camaraderie building, the unspoken bond between us strengthening with each passing second. "You're right," I said, nodding. "But what can we actually do? I can't just ignore him, but I also don't want to escalate things."

"We can't let him think he's won," Ethan replied, his voice steady. "We need to be smarter. He may have the intimidation factor, but we have something he doesn't: support."

The thought of the café, the laughter of friends, and the safety it provided filled me with warmth. "You're right. I have my friends, and we're not going to let him scare us."

Just as I felt a flicker of courage igniting within me, my phone buzzed with a text. I glanced down, and my heart sank as I read the message from Ryan. Don't think this is over, Alana. I'll be watching.

"Great," I muttered, tossing the phone onto the counter as if it were a venomous snake.

"What did he say?" Sophie asked, her brow knitting together in worry.

"Just a little reminder that he's not going anywhere." I couldn't keep the bitterness from my voice.

Ethan leaned closer, his tone serious. "We have to turn this around. We can't let him have the upper hand."

"Agreed," I replied, feeling a surge of determination course through me. "What if we get some dirt on him? Find out what makes him tick?"

Sophie's eyes sparkled with mischief. "Ooh, I like this plan. What if we play the social media angle? I bet he has a few skeletons lurking in his closet."

"I can be your undercover detective," Ethan said, his expression transforming into that of a playful rogue. "I'll infiltrate his inner circle, charm the pants off his friends—figuratively, of course."

I couldn't help but laugh, the tension easing slightly. "You'd make a terrible spy, you know that? You'd charm everyone into spilling their secrets, then accidentally expose yourself as the hero."

"I prefer to think of it as a hero-in-training," he shot back, grinning.

"More like a hero-in-denial," I teased, the warmth of camaraderie wrapping around me like a cozy blanket.

But beneath the lighthearted banter lay a current of urgency. As we shared ideas and rallied around one another, the stakes felt higher than ever. Ryan was not just a passing annoyance; he was a shadow looming over my life, and I needed to shine a light on the darkness he threatened to cast.

With a determined glint in my eye, I said, "Alright, let's gather our intel and turn this game around. It's time for Ryan to realize he's picked the wrong opponent."

The words hung in the air, a declaration, a promise. We were entering a new phase, a chapter where we would reclaim control and disrupt Ryan's twisted game. And for the first time in a long while, I felt an exhilarating rush of hope.

A storm brewed inside me as I sat across from Ethan and Sophie in the café, our laughter hanging in the air like a sweet melody punctuated by the sharp notes of uncertainty. It felt surreal, a delicate balance of camaraderie and conflict. The momentary reprieve of joy would soon fade, like mist dissipating in the sunlight, leaving behind the stark reality of the battle that loomed ahead.

Sophie was scrolling through her phone, her brows furrowing in concentration. "Alright, so how do we get this operation rolling?" she asked, her voice a mix of eagerness and determination. "What dirt can we dig up on Ryan?"

"Let's start with his social media," I suggested, my mind racing with possibilities. "He's the kind of guy who probably posts every mundane detail of his life, thinking it makes him look interesting."

Ethan chuckled, shaking his head. "Insecurity and showmanship wrapped in one package. Classic. It's like he wants everyone to know he's important, even if he has to force it."

Sophie nodded, her eyes sparkling with the thrill of a plan. "I can sift through his posts. Who knows? Maybe he's shared something that reveals a weakness. Or, even better, something that could embarrass him. If we can catch him off guard in public, that'll rattle his confidence."

"Let's dig deeper," I said, my own excitement bubbling up. "We need to understand who he hangs out with, what makes him tick. The more we know, the better our chances of turning this around."

Ethan leaned forward, his expression earnest. "Alright, I'll handle the friends angle. If Ryan has any weaknesses, I'll find them." The look in his eyes told me he was fully committed to this mission, and I felt a sense of camaraderie that surged through the air between us.

With our plan set, we spent the next hour researching, combing through Ryan's online presence and piecing together fragments of his life like detectives in a mystery novel. As Sophie whispered updates about his recent posts, I could feel the tension shifting, morphing into something more empowering. Each shared laugh and excited whisper transformed our anxiety into a tangible weapon we could wield against Ryan.

"Hey, I found something!" Sophie exclaimed suddenly, her eyes wide as she pointed at the screen. "Look at this. A picture from his birthday party. He tagged a bunch of friends here, and wait—who's this?" She zoomed in on a girl with striking blue hair and an enigmatic smile.

"Jenna. I know her," I said, squinting at the photo. "She used to work with Ryan. I didn't think they were still close."

"Well, she might have some intel we can use," Ethan chimed in. "If we can get her talking, who knows what we might uncover about him?"

Sophie grinned. "Operation: Make Friends with Jenna is a go! I'll reach out to her."

Just then, my phone buzzed again, and I picked it up, heart thudding in my chest. The screen lit up with another message from Ryan, and a knot formed in my stomach. You really think you can gather your little crew and take me down? I admire your spirit, but you're playing a dangerous game. Be careful.

"Damn it," I muttered, trying to keep my voice steady. "He's onto us."

Ethan's jaw tightened. "We can't let him intimidate us. He thrives on fear."

"Fear or not, we need to stay vigilant," I replied, determination washing over me. "Let's focus on our plan and keep our heads down. The more we can learn without him knowing, the better."

As the sun dipped below the horizon, casting long shadows across the café, a renewed sense of purpose enveloped us. We spent the next few days unraveling the threads of Ryan's world, gathering intel and piecing together the puzzle that was his life. I texted Jenna, cautiously inviting her out for coffee, and to my surprise, she accepted, eager to catch up.

Meeting Jenna felt like stepping into the unknown, the air thick with potential. When we sat across from each other, she greeted me with an enthusiastic smile, her blue hair framing her face like an avant-garde painting. "It's so good to see you!" she said, her voice bright and friendly. "I've missed our chats!"

I smiled back, my mind racing as I tried to navigate this conversation with care. "You too! How's everything been with you?"

"Busy, but good! I've got a new job at the art gallery downtown, which is fantastic," she said, her eyes sparkling with passion. "But enough about me. How's life treating you?"

"Oh, you know, just navigating some interesting waters," I replied, trying to sound casual, though I could feel my heart pounding. "Actually, I wanted to ask you about Ryan."

The moment I mentioned his name, Jenna's expression shifted, a flicker of wariness crossing her features. "Ryan? Uh, well... he's a complicated person. We had some good times, but he can be... intense."

I leaned in, my curiosity piqued. "Intense how?"

"He just has this way of needing control," she said slowly, choosing her words carefully. "It's like he has to be the center of attention at all times. And when things don't go his way, he can be... well, unpredictable."

The way she said "unpredictable" sent a shiver down my spine. It was one thing to know Ryan's history, but hearing it confirmed by someone who had been close to him added weight to my growing unease. "Have you noticed any changes in him lately? Anything that might suggest he's... desperate?"

Jenna frowned, her gaze darting around the café as if searching for the right words. "I've heard whispers—things about him getting involved with some unsavory characters. I don't know much, but I wouldn't underestimate him if I were you."

The warning hung in the air like a distant thundercloud, ominous and heavy. "Thank you for telling me," I said, my voice steady even as my heart raced. "I just want to be careful."

The conversation continued, but in the back of my mind, the pieces were shifting. Ryan wasn't just a bully; he was a threat wrapped in charisma and danger. The tension was mounting, the stakes higher than I had imagined.

As we wrapped up our conversation, Jenna leaned in closer, her voice dropping to a whisper. "Just be careful. If he feels cornered, he might lash out in ways you can't predict."

I nodded, the weight of her words pressing against my chest as I stood to leave. "Thanks for the heads-up. I appreciate it."

Stepping back into the street, I felt the cool evening air wrap around me, a stark contrast to the heat of our conversation. The world outside felt vibrant, alive with the pulse of life, yet it was tainted by the shadow of Ryan's looming presence.

That night, as I settled into bed, my phone buzzed again. Another message from Ryan. You think you've got the upper hand? You really have no idea what you're up against.

The hairs on the back of my neck stood on end, a sense of foreboding curling like smoke in the corners of my mind. Just as I set my phone down, the power in my apartment flickered, and a moment later, the lights went out, plunging me into darkness. My heart raced as I fumbled for my phone again, the dim light revealing a shadowy figure just outside my window.

Panic surged, adrenaline racing through my veins as the figure stepped closer, their features obscured by the darkness. In that chilling moment, I realized the game was escalating, and I was caught right in the middle of it.

"Ryan," I breathed, a chill creeping through me as I backed away from the window, knowing this was no longer just a battle of wits. This was a fight for survival.

# Chapter 21: Allies Unite

The air in the locker room crackled with a newfound energy, a lively hum that seemed to wrap around us like a cozy blanket. I leaned against the cool metal lockers, taking in the animated chatter of my teammates, their faces bright with excitement. Kayla, with her flaming red hair and infectious laugh, was spinning tales of what the community event could look like. "Imagine a fair, but instead of cotton candy and ferris wheels, we have art, music, poetry! A real showcase of what makes each of us unique."

Her enthusiasm was contagious, igniting sparks of creativity in my mind. I pictured vibrant banners splashed with colors, each bearing the name of someone in our circle, a shout-out to our individual talents and quirks. I could already see the food stalls—probably run by Kira, whose cinnamon rolls were legendary—and a stage where those with the courage to perform could share their hearts with an audience. A sweet mixture of nervousness and thrill coursed through me at the thought.

"What if we turned this into a fundraiser?" I suggested, my voice barely above the clamor. "We could donate to a local charity, maybe one that supports mental health initiatives. It'd show we care, not just about ourselves but about our community." The room fell momentarily silent, all eyes turning to me, and for a moment, my heart thudded in my chest.

"Brilliant idea!" chimed in Jake, our ever-enthusiastic quarterback, flashing a grin that could light up the darkest day. "We can charge a small entry fee, and maybe have a donation box set up? We can even auction off some of Kayla's artwork!"

Kayla pretended to swoon, placing her hand dramatically on her forehead. "My artwork? Oh, what an honor! But I must warn you, it comes with an emotional price—every piece has a story, and I'm not sure the world is ready for that."

Laughter erupted in the room, the weight of my earlier confrontation with Ryan lifting like fog under a warm sun. Each chuckle felt like a stitch pulling our frayed fabric closer together, weaving our bond into something stronger. I had spent too long feeling isolated, the pressure of expectations suffocating my voice. But here, among my teammates, I was reminded of the magic that happens when allies unite.

"Let's make a list," I said, springing into action. "What talents can we showcase? I mean, this is our chance to strut our stuff!"

With Kayla leading the charge, we began to bounce ideas off each other, a flurry of dreams and aspirations erupting in the otherwise mundane locker room. Emily, who had a penchant for poetry, suggested an open mic for spoken word, while Tara proposed dance performances. "What about a fashion show?" she added, her eyes sparkling. "We could wear outfits that represent who we are. I can see it now—like a runway but with heart and soul."

Each suggestion layered on top of the last, transforming our simple gathering into a vivid tapestry of creativity and camaraderie. We found ourselves delving deeper into our shared passions, revealing hidden talents we had kept tucked away like secret treasures. As I listened to the ideas flow, I realized that this event was more than just a celebration; it was a declaration of who we were as individuals, a defiant shout against the whispers of judgment and conformity.

But it was not just my teammates who rallied around this vision. As word spread across the campus, we received messages of support from students I had barely interacted with before. There was something undeniably electrifying about the collective excitement that surged through the air. When I saw Leah, the quiet girl from my chemistry class, posting on social media about our event, it felt like a small victory. "Can't wait to share my photography! It's time to show the world my perspective," she wrote, her words bursting with newfound confidence.

As the days passed, the plans for our community event blossomed like wildflowers breaking through concrete. We met in the evenings, our brainstorming sessions turning into laughter-filled gatherings, where ideas flowed as freely as the snacks we brought along. I marveled at the transformation around me—each of us shedding our labels, stepping out of the shadows into a vibrant spotlight.

Yet, as the date approached, an undercurrent of tension began to weave its way through our plans. I caught wind of whispers in the halls, casual conversations that hinted at discontent. Not everyone was thrilled about our little revolution. Some still clung to the old ways, the stereotypes we had fought against. I overheard a couple of upperclassmen snickering about our "little fair" during lunch. "They think they're going to change the world with a few performances and some art?" one scoffed, the disdain dripping from their words like poison.

But with every sneer, my resolve hardened. Our event wasn't just a fair—it was a platform for every misfit, every dreamer who felt out of place in this rigid world. If they couldn't see that, then we had to shine brighter, be louder, and stand firmer.

Determined, I reached out to our school's administration for support, hoping they would see the merit in our mission. To my surprise, the principal's face brightened at my pitch. "We need more of this, more creativity and individuality celebrated," she said, her voice booming with encouragement. "I'll even help promote it."

As the school's backing solidified, I felt a surge of excitement mixed with fear. It was one thing to plan a gathering in the safety of our locker room, but putting it out into the world felt like setting a ship to sail in stormy seas. Would we find safe harbor or be tossed about by waves of criticism? I glanced around the locker room at my teammates, their faces set with determination, and knew we were ready to brave whatever came our way. The storm might roar, but we would be the lightning that cut through the darkness, illuminating our path to freedom and expression.

The days leading up to our community event felt like a whirlwind, each hour crammed with planning and brainstorming that left little room for doubt. I could hardly keep up with the influx of ideas—each more colorful than the last, a kaleidoscope of creativity spilling forth from my teammates. We transformed our locker room into a makeshift headquarters, walls adorned with sketches and lists, our chatter rising and falling like the tide.

One afternoon, while we huddled around a table strewn with pizza boxes and notebooks, Kayla launched into a passionate rant about the design for our promotional posters. "It has to be bold! Like, think graffiti meets an art gallery explosion!" She waved her arms animatedly, her enthusiasm infectious. "And the tagline... what about 'Unleash Your Color'? No one gets left out in a rainbow!"

"Not a bad idea," Jake interjected, munching on a slice and leaning back with a contemplative look. "But what if we went darker? 'Dare to Stand Out' could give it some edge. Like, we're serious about this!"

"Oh please, who wants to stand out in the dark?" Kayla shot back with a smirk, her green eyes dancing with mischief. "This is about light, not shadows. We're here to shine!"

I chuckled, reveling in their banter, the kind of playful jabs that made our friendship feel effortless. I wanted to bottle up this moment—the laughter, the camaraderie—and carry it with me through the inevitable storms ahead. The initial exhilaration of our project mingled with a whisper of anxiety, a subtle reminder of the naysayers lurking just beyond our vibrant bubble.

As the week unfolded, we pooled our resources and reached out to local artists and musicians, inviting them to showcase their talents. The response was overwhelming. Each message that trickled in felt like a stitch weaving us closer to our goal, a sign that our small revolution was gaining momentum. Leah agreed to exhibit her stunning photography, her usual shyness dissolving under the spotlight of our collective ambition.

The evening before the event, we convened at the park where it would take place, the sun dipping below the horizon, casting everything in a warm, golden hue. I stood among my friends, the crisp air filled with the scent of freshly mown grass and blooming wildflowers. It was a serene contrast to the chaos of our planning sessions, and I felt a sense of calm settle in.

"Look at this place," I murmured, glancing around at the wide open space where laughter and music would soon fill the air. "It's perfect."

Tara leaned against a tree, her arms crossed, surveying the area with a critical eye. "It could use a little more... pizzazz. What about a fairy light canopy? Imagine it—twinkling above, illuminating our masterpieces!"

"Fairy lights?" Kayla's eyes lit up. "Count me in! I'll get my hands on as many as I can. They'll make the whole thing feel magical."

"Because nothing says 'artistic revolution' like fairy lights," I teased, and Kayla shot me a mock glare, her laughter spilling over.

Just then, our jubilant planning was interrupted by the sound of approaching footsteps. A group of students, their expressions unreadable, strolled into the park, clearly not there to admire the scenery. Ryan was at the forefront, flanked by a couple of his friends, the very same ones who had been quick to dismiss our efforts.

"Nice little gathering you've got here," Ryan called out, his tone dripping with sarcasm. "What is this? A talent show for the misfits?"

A cold wave of dread washed over me. My stomach knotted as I watched my friends tense, their expressions shifting from joy to uncertainty. It was a moment of sheer vulnerability, a stark reminder that we were still standing on shaky ground.

"Just a little something to celebrate individuality," I shot back, summoning my courage, the words tasting bitter on my tongue. "Not that you'd understand, Ryan."

"Oh, I understand perfectly," he retorted, stepping closer, his friends snickering at his side. "You think throwing a party is going to change anything? You're still the same people, still the same labels."

The air thickened with tension, and I felt my heart race. But before I could respond, Kayla stepped forward, her chin raised defiantly. "Labels? We're showing everyone that we're more than that! And if you can't handle it, then maybe it's time you look in the mirror."

Ryan faltered, clearly taken aback by her boldness. His friends shifted uncomfortably, glancing at each other, the bravado dimming. It was a moment of reckoning, a subtle shift in power that felt like the first rays of dawn breaking through a stormy sky.

"Let's just see how this little party goes, shall we?" he sneered, but I could sense the crack in his facade. With that, he and his friends turned away, their laughter trailing off like smoke, leaving us enveloped in a stunned silence.

"Wow," I breathed, looking at Kayla, admiration bubbling within me. "You were amazing."

She shrugged, a hint of a blush coloring her cheeks. "Someone had to put him in his place. We're not backing down, are we?"

"No way," I said, the warmth of her conviction rekindling my own resolve.

The encounter hung in the air like a storm cloud, but instead of dampening our spirits, it steeled our determination. The next morning, the sun rose bright and clear, casting an optimistic glow over the park. As we arrived to set up, the gentle breeze danced through the trees, and I could almost hear the whispers of support from those who believed in us.

We unfurled our banners, arranged tables for artwork, and plugged in sound equipment for the performers. With every detail, I felt the collective heartbeat of our group, a rhythm that thrummed with the promise of something beautiful.

As the event began, students trickled in, curiosity etched on their faces. I watched as Leah nervously adjusted her camera, a shy smile tugging at her lips. Across the way, Jake was chatting up a group of classmates, his laughter infectious as he shared snippets of our plan. It was an odd blend of nerves and excitement, and I couldn't help but marvel at how far we had come.

With every passing moment, I sensed a shift—not just in our spirits, but in the atmosphere around us. People began to mingle, share stories, and discover common ground. I realized that we were building something far more significant than a community event; we were creating a sanctuary, a space where every voice could be heard.

Just as the first notes of music floated through the air, I spotted Ryan and his friends lingering at the edge of the park, their expressions unreadable. An unfamiliar blend of dread and exhilaration rippled through me. The stage was set, and the spotlight was not just on us—it was on everyone who had ever felt invisible. The moment was now, and I was determined to seize it, come what may.

The morning of the event dawned with an electric buzz that danced in the air, a palpable excitement coursing through the campus. I arrived early, the sun spilling golden light across the park, igniting the flowers and casting playful shadows beneath the trees. The world felt alive, vibrating with potential, and I reveled in it. As I stepped onto the grass, my sneakers squished into the damp earth, grounding me in the moment.

I found my teammates already setting up, their energy infectious. Kayla had arrived with an armful of fairy lights, her eyes gleaming with mischief. "These babies are going to make everything look magical!" she proclaimed, pulling out a tangled mass and promptly starting to string them through the branches of a nearby tree.

"Careful, we don't want a fairy light catastrophe," I quipped, recalling a previous event where Kayla had nearly blinded an entire audience with an ambitious lighting scheme.

"Oh, please! That was one time!" she protested, though her laughter betrayed her. "And besides, if a few lights go out, we can always blame it on 'atmosphere.'"

As I helped her, I noticed the sound of music beginning to filter in from the stage area. Jake was coordinating with the local band we had managed to snag, his enthusiasm lighting up the atmosphere like Kayla's fairy lights. He turned to me, a grin stretching from ear to ear. "This is going to be epic! I can feel it in my bones!"

"Let's just hope those bones hold up through the whole event," I teased, knowing his penchant for overzealous planning. "We want everyone to make it home in one piece."

With every set-up detail, I felt the weight of anticipation mingling with anxiety. My friends buzzed with excitement, but a flicker of worry danced at the edges of my mind. Would our efforts truly resonate? Would the crowd embrace our vision or scoff at our ambition?

As the sun climbed higher, the first guests began to trickle in, drawn by curiosity and the promise of something different. Leah stood near her photography display, her nerves palpable as she adjusted the frames for the third time. I walked over, offering her a reassuring smile. "You're going to knock their socks off," I said, my voice steady. "Your work is incredible."

She glanced up, the gratitude in her eyes sparkling brighter than the sunshine. "Thanks, but what if they don't like it?"

"Who cares? This is your art, your perspective. Just enjoy it." I offered her a smile, hoping to infuse her with a little of my own confidence.

As the crowd grew, I spotted a few familiar faces—friends from classes, kids from the soccer team, even a couple of seniors who I'd never thought would step foot at our gathering. Each smile ignited a sense of belonging that warmed my heart. It was a patchwork of people, stitched together by the simple act of showing up.

When the band started their first set, the energy in the park shifted dramatically. The music swelled, lifting spirits and beckoning even the shyest attendees to let loose. I watched in awe as people began to sway, drawn together by the rhythm that filled the air. I felt a wave of exhilaration wash over me, filling the gaps where doubt had lingered.

As the afternoon wore on, Kayla and Tara ran a mini fashion show, showcasing outfits that told stories—clothes that reflected the vibrant individuality of our peers. One girl strutted down the makeshift runway wearing a dress made of pages from old books, while another donned a vibrant patchwork ensemble, each patch representing a different part of her identity. Their confidence was infectious, rippling through the crowd, igniting a sense of pride in our differences.

Just as I began to relax, enjoying the flow of the event, I spotted Ryan lurking at the edge of the crowd. He was standing with his usual crew, his posture radiating the kind of disdain that could curdle milk. I felt my heart rate quicken, a knot of tension tightening in my stomach.

"What are they doing here?" I whispered to Kayla, who was currently wrangling a group of excited students.

"Let them watch," she replied with a shrug, but her eyes flickered with concern. "We're not giving them any power. This is our moment."

But Ryan didn't just watch. He began to weave through the crowd, a predatory glint in his eye, and I could see his intentions forming like storm clouds overhead. The music continued to play, but my focus narrowed, the vibrant colors of the event blurring into a background of anxiety.

Suddenly, he stepped onto the stage, grabbing the microphone with a swagger that radiated arrogance. The music faded into a low murmur, and a hush fell over the crowd. "Hey, everyone!" he shouted, his voice dripping with mock enthusiasm. "What a fantastic little circus you've got here! Celebrating individuality? More like showcasing your weirdness!"

A murmur of discontent rippled through the audience, and I could feel the collective tension rise. Kayla and I exchanged glances, our hearts racing. "This is not happening," I whispered, urgency lacing my tone.

Jake rushed to the front, attempting to reclaim the mic, but Ryan pushed him aside, leaning in closer to the crowd. "Look around you! This is a gathering of misfits, parading their quirks like they're trophies. Newsflash: Nobody cares!"

Gasps echoed around us, shock mingling with outrage. I could see people's faces falling, the vibrancy of our event dimming under the weight of his words. Panic clawed at my insides.

"Ryan, get off the stage!" I shouted, my voice slicing through the murmurs, but he simply laughed, a cruel sound that made my skin crawl.

"You all want to celebrate individuality? Fine! But let's be real for a second. This is just a distraction from the fact that you're all still trying to fit into a world that doesn't care about you."

Fury ignited within me, hot and consuming. "You're wrong!" I shouted back, my voice shaking but resolute. "We care! We're here for each other, for our passions! You don't get to define us!"

Ryan smirked, the crowd hanging on his every word. "And what happens when this fairy tale ends? You're just going to go back to being the same people you always were. Maybe the world isn't ready for your little rebellion."

My heart pounded in my chest, and I glanced at my friends, who looked as stunned as I felt. This wasn't how it was supposed to go. But as I stood there, a fire ignited within me, fueled by the support surrounding us.

"Maybe it's time for a new world," I countered, feeling the resolve in my voice deepen. "One where we decide who we are, regardless of what anyone else thinks!"

The crowd began to stir, murmurs turning into cheers, a swell of voices rising to meet Ryan's. The air crackled with renewed energy, and I could feel a shift, a tidal wave of defiance building behind me.

But before I could fully grasp the shift in momentum, Ryan's expression morphed from smug to furious. He thrust the microphone toward the ground, shattering the momentary peace. "Fine, then. Let's see how far this rebellion goes!"

And with that, he turned sharply, his friends falling in line behind him, the threat of something darker hanging in the air like a storm cloud on the horizon.

Just as I thought the tension might ebb, a loud crack sounded from the crowd. Someone in the back screamed, and all heads turned toward the source of the chaos. My heart dropped as I spotted a group of students pushing through, their faces flushed with anger, faces I recognized from the football team.

"What's going on?" I whispered to Kayla, the panic evident in my voice.

"They're not here to celebrate," she muttered, her brows knitting in concern. "They look ready to cause trouble."

As the crowd began to part, tension thickening like fog around us, I braced myself, a chill running down my spine. The laughter, the music, the joy we had woven together teetered on the edge of chaos, and I realized we were no longer just standing together. We were now at the center of a storm, and the outcome hung in the balance, unpredictable and terrifying.

# Chapter 22: The Community Event

The morning sun poured through the wide glass windows of the community center, spilling golden light onto the polished wooden floors. The air buzzed with excitement, a tangible energy that felt almost electric as people trickled in. My heart raced with a blend of anticipation and trepidation. Today was not just any day; it was a canvas painted with the hues of hope and connection, a testament to what we could achieve when we came together as a community.

Kayla and I had worked tirelessly to prepare for this event, and I couldn't help but smile as I caught sight of her, a whirlwind of enthusiasm dressed in her favorite apron adorned with cheeky food-related puns. "You think we have enough snacks?" she joked, brandishing a platter of vibrant vegetable skewers that looked almost too pretty to eat.

"Only if you're planning to feed the entire population of this town," I quipped back, taking a moment to appreciate the way her face lit up with laughter, her eyes sparkling like sunlit waves. "But let's be real; the way you cook, they'll be begging for more."

As we set up our booths, I marveled at the transformation of the center. Bright banners fluttered overhead, each one representing a different culture and tradition, fluttering like flags in a gentle breeze. The scent of spices mingled in the air, teasing my senses and stirring memories of family dinners and celebrations. Our cooking demonstration booth, adorned with fresh herbs and colorful ingredients, stood ready to share recipes from around the world. Meanwhile, the boxing workshop area was alive with energy, the rhythmic thud of gloves against bags echoing as participants tried their hand at this empowering sport.

With a final flourish, I placed a bowl of homemade salsa at the front of our booth, the vibrant red tomatoes and green cilantro gleaming like jewels. I stepped back, taking in our small corner of the bustling center. "It's perfect," I said, more to myself than to Kayla, a sense of pride swelling within me.

"Let's get this party started!" she exclaimed, clapping her hands together as if to summon the crowd. The first wave of guests arrived, and I felt the flutter of excitement in my stomach. As they approached, I could see the diverse tapestry of our community—families, couples, and friends from all walks of life, their expressions ranging from curious to eager.

I caught a glimpse of Mr. Thompson, the elderly gentleman who lived down the street, his gait slow but determined. He approached with a twinkle in his eye. "Is that your salsa? Smells like heaven!" he declared, as Kayla beamed at the compliment.

"It's made with love and a bit of chaos," I responded, leaning in conspiratorially. "If you don't love it, I might just have to bribe you with cookies."

His laughter boomed through the air, breaking any remaining ice. As the event progressed, I watched with satisfaction as our small booth became a hub of activity. We shared stories behind each dish we prepared, weaving the history of flavors into the fabric of the gathering. It was a feast for the senses—laughter mixed with the clattering of utensils, the enticing aromas mingling with the warmth of conversation.

I marveled at how walls could come down when the right ingredients were mixed together. A group of teenagers, initially hesitant, gathered around our table, their curiosity piqued. They exchanged shy glances before diving into a discussion about their favorite foods. "I dare you to try this spicy salsa!" one of them exclaimed, handing a chip to his friend, who grimaced comically before taking a bite. The collective gasp turned into raucous laughter as the friend fanned his mouth, feigning dramatic distress.

The boxing workshop area, a little farther off, began to draw a crowd of its own. Kayla, with her characteristic flair, was demonstrating basic punches and footwork, her voice carrying over the growing chatter. I glanced over, her infectious enthusiasm radiating warmth, as she encouraged an older woman to try a few jabs. "Just imagine you're swinging at your ex's face!" she joked, and the room erupted in laughter, tension dissolving in the light of shared humor.

The atmosphere shifted as the day unfolded, barriers crumbling one laugh at a time. Families who had lived side by side for years began to connect in new ways, and old grudges melted in the heat of the shared experience. I could see it in the way a mother introduced her shy daughter to the man who ran the local bakery, or how the teenage boys, once just faces in a crowd, now animatedly debated their favorite boxing techniques with Kayla. Each conversation, each shared bite, was like adding another thread to the tapestry of our community.

But just as I began to relax into the warmth of the day, the faint sound of raised voices pierced through the laughter and music. My heart sank as I turned to see a small group of people at the edge of the event, their expressions clouded with tension. The sight of them made me uneasy; they didn't seem to belong to the celebration that was unfolding.

"Do you think we should—" I started, but Kayla, catching my glance, waved me off with a look of determination. "Let me handle it," she said, her tone leaving no room for doubt.

She approached the group with the confidence of someone who had faced down far worse than mere hostility. I watched as she engaged them, her gestures animated and her voice steady. It was then that I realized the power of this moment—the way she radiated strength, like a beacon drawing others in.

As I continued to prepare our booth, I felt a mix of hope and apprehension. Today was about unity, but would that fragile harmony hold when faced with adversity? I took a deep breath, steeling myself for whatever might come next, ready to embrace both the joy and the challenges this vibrant community would present.

The laughter and chatter filled the air like a lively symphony, a testament to the sense of belonging we had created. I watched as Kayla deftly navigated her way through the group, her bright energy wrapping around everyone like a warm hug. Her voice rose above the crowd, urging them to participate, to step out of their comfort zones. I felt a swell of admiration for her as she threw herself wholeheartedly into this mission of bringing people together.

Just as the tension around the newcomers began to dissipate, an unexpected commotion erupted from the back of the hall. I turned just in time to see a table of display pastries wobble ominously before a stout man, clearly overwhelmed, inadvertently bumped into it. The fragile tower of cupcakes began to sway like a ship in a storm, and I could almost hear a collective gasp as frosting and cake spiraled through the air in slow motion. I reached out instinctively, but it was too late; the sweet confectionery cascade erupted, showering nearby guests in a flurry of sugary chaos.

"Perfect! Just what we needed," I murmured under my breath, watching a chocolate cupcake land precariously in Mr. Thompson's lap. The old gentleman looked utterly bewildered, like a man who had just stepped into a dream where cakes were falling from the sky.

"Looks like it's your lucky day!" I called over to him, a teasing smile tugging at my lips. "You could start a new trend—cupcake couture!"

He chuckled heartily, the surprise of the incident melting away into the warmth of laughter. Kayla, never one to miss a chance for a quick fix, dashed over with napkins as if they were magical wands ready to undo this sugary mishap. "Don't worry, Mr. Thompson! I hear chocolate is great for the skin," she joked, patting him on the shoulder while handing him a few napkins.

The laughter rippled through the crowd, a reminder that sometimes the best moments came from unexpected mishaps. I felt a sense of camaraderie, a connection among all of us as we navigated this playful disaster.

"Okay, I think it's time for a food fight!" shouted one of the teenagers, his eyes sparkling with mischief. The room erupted in a mix of laughter and playful protests, but I could feel the energy shift. What had begun as a moment of chaos had morphed into a shared experience, a story that would be told and retold in the years to come.

As the jovial atmosphere wrapped around us, I spotted the small group that had initially seemed confrontational, still lingering at the edge of the festivities. Their expressions had softened somewhat, intrigued by the laughter. I recognized their hesitation, a mix of curiosity and uncertainty. I took a deep breath, feeling the urge to bridge that gap between them and the warmth radiating from the heart of our gathering.

"Hey, Kayla, I'm going to see if I can bring them in," I said, nodding toward the group.

"Good luck! They look like they just stepped off the set of a soap opera," she replied, her eyes sparkling with mischief. "But who knows? You might just find out they're the best improv actors in town."

I approached them, heart racing with every step, hoping my smile was welcoming enough to dissolve whatever walls they had built. "Hi there!" I called out, my voice carrying over the vibrant sounds of the event. "Care to join us? There's plenty of delicious food, and I promise, we've got more cupcakes than we know what to do with."

The group looked at each other, and for a moment, I feared I had miscalculated. Then one of the women, a tall figure with striking green hair and a fierce gaze, stepped forward. "What kind of food are we talking about?" she asked, her tone skeptical but not unfriendly.

"International cuisine! We're sharing recipes and cooking demos from around the world," I replied, my enthusiasm bubbling over. "And if you like boxing, Kayla is leading some workshops too. You could unleash your inner champ."

"Boxing? Now you've got my interest," she said, a hint of a smile breaking through her guarded expression. The others leaned in closer, curiosity piqued.

"Come on! I'll even introduce you to Kayla; she's got a great way of making everyone feel like a champion," I encouraged, gesturing for them to follow. As they stepped into the heart of the event, I felt a sense of triumph wash over me. It was a small victory, but every connection mattered.

Kayla caught my eye, her face lighting up as I led the newcomers toward her. "Look who's joining us! Meet some potential future boxers," I announced, and she greeted them with her signature blend of humor and warmth.

"Welcome! Just a fair warning—if you hit me, I might just hit back," she quipped, and laughter erupted once more, dissolving any lingering tension.

We spent the next hour immersed in laughter and spirited exchanges, culinary secrets flying alongside playful jabs about boxing techniques. It was magical, watching the barriers dissolve as stories flowed freely. The newcomers shared their experiences, their hopes for the community, while we taught them the art of folding dumplings and perfecting the jab.

As I rolled a piece of dough between my hands, I caught a glimpse of Mr. Thompson, now fully recovered from his earlier pastry encounter, chatting animatedly with a family he had never spoken to before. It struck me then—this was what we had hoped to create: a space where connections were forged, where people could find common ground amidst their differences.

Yet, amid the joy and laughter, a familiar knot tightened in my stomach. The atmosphere, once buoyant, felt subtly tinged with uncertainty. What would happen when the event ended, when we returned to our individual lives? I pushed the thought away, choosing to focus on the now, on the vibrant energy around me.

But just as I was beginning to lose myself in the warmth of the moment, I heard the unmistakable sound of a microphone crackling to life on the stage at the front of the room. I turned, my heart racing again, as a figure I recognized stepped into the spotlight. It was the town mayor, his demeanor all business even amidst the vibrant celebration.

"Excuse me, everyone! If I could have your attention," he called, his voice cutting through the laughter like a knife. The room quieted, the sudden shift in energy palpable. I exchanged glances with Kayla, concern flickering in her eyes. What could he possibly want to announce now, in the middle of such a joyful gathering?

The mayor's voice echoed through the hall, the cheerfulness that had enveloped the event suddenly dampened by the air of authority that accompanied him. "I hope everyone is having a fantastic time," he began, his eyes scanning the room like a hawk. "However, I need to address some concerns that have been brought to my attention regarding the ongoing community projects."

My heart sank. Concerned murmurs rippled through the crowd, a wave of uncertainty settling in. I caught Kayla's eye, and we exchanged a knowing glance. We had worked so hard to build something beautiful, and now it felt as if the mayor might be preparing to rain on our parade.

"Due to budget constraints and other pressing issues, we may need to reconsider funding for certain programs," he continued, his tone serious, yet somehow devoid of warmth. The words hung in the air like a dark cloud, suffocating the joy we had cultivated all day.

As he droned on, detailing fiscal responsibilities and the need for community input, I noticed Mr. Thompson shifting restlessly in his seat. The older man's earlier cheer had faded, replaced by a deep furrow in his brow. I felt a surge of protectiveness for our community, for all the connections we had fostered. This gathering was more than just an event; it was a lifeline for many, a testament to our resilience.

Just as I was about to leap up and implore the mayor to focus on the positivity of the day, Kayla stood up. "Excuse me, Mayor Jenkins!" she called out, her voice ringing with that fearless spirit I admired so much. "I think it's important to remember that today is about unity. We've created an incredible atmosphere here—why would we want to undermine it?"

A murmur of agreement rippled through the crowd, and I could feel the energy shifting again. The mayor looked momentarily taken aback, his lips pressed into a thin line. "I appreciate your enthusiasm, Kayla, but we must prioritize the town's budget. Not every initiative can be funded indefinitely."

"Sure, but maybe instead of slashing funds, we could explore creative solutions? We've all come together today, and that alone is worth investing in," she replied, her voice steady, though I could sense the simmering tension in the air.

"Creativity won't pay the bills," he retorted, his patience wearing thin. The crowd began to murmur again, a blend of discontent and curiosity building. I held my breath, sensing the thin thread of tension ready to snap.

Then Mr. Thompson rose, his frail frame appearing smaller but somehow more formidable in that moment. "With all due respect, Mayor, perhaps if you engaged with us more, you'd see how valuable these community programs are. We're not just numbers; we're neighbors, friends, families," he said, his voice wavering but filled with earnest passion.

Kayla's eyes lit up with gratitude. "Exactly! We're stronger together. Look at how far we've come just today." Her gesture encompassed the room, and people began to stand, their voices rising in support of one another.

The atmosphere shifted from passive acceptance to active rebellion. "We need to make our voices heard!" shouted one of the teenagers, and others chimed in, each voice melding into a chorus of determination. I felt a surge of adrenaline coursing through me. It was no longer just about the event; it was about our community's future.

The mayor's composure cracked slightly, and for a moment, I thought I saw a flicker of uncertainty in his eyes. "We can discuss this later," he said, trying to regain control, but the tide was turning. I glanced at Kayla, who was practically vibrating with energy, urging me silently to join her cause.

"Let's take a stand!" I called out, my voice rising over the din. "We can organize, come up with ideas, and make this community even better together! We have strength in our numbers!"

The room erupted into applause, people rallying together in a way I had never witnessed before. Laughter and determination filled the space, but there was also an undercurrent of worry. I felt it like a weight pressing against my chest.

But just as the energy swelled, the mayor raised a hand, signaling for silence again. "I can appreciate your passion," he said, trying to salvage the situation. "However, I must remind you that any changes to the budget require a thorough review and council approval. We cannot simply decide on a whim."

"Then let's give you something to think about," Kayla said boldly, stepping forward. "Let's create a petition right here, right now! We'll gather signatures, we'll show you that this community cares, and we won't let it fall apart without a fight!"

The crowd erupted again, and I could feel my heart racing. This was turning into something far bigger than I had anticipated. The spirit of defiance, of camaraderie, surged through the room, electrifying the air. I could almost see the barriers we had once felt so acutely crumbling around us.

As the crowd surged forward, eager to add their names to Kayla's burgeoning petition, I pulled her aside. "Are we ready for this?" I asked, my voice low but urgent. "What if it backfires? What if the mayor doesn't listen?"

Her eyes sparkled with determination. "We have to try. We can't just sit back and let them decide for us. Today is proof that we can come together. This is our moment."

I nodded, my own heart swelling with a mix of fear and exhilaration. But just as we turned back to the crowd, a loud crash resonated from the other side of the hall, followed by startled gasps.

I spun around to see a large banner, hung with pride, had suddenly torn free from the wall, cascading down and sending decorations flying in all directions. The room froze for a heartbeat, a collective intake of breath shared among us all.

Then, from the midst of the chaos, I saw the mayor's expression shift. His eyes widened, not with concern for the event but with something darker—something that hinted at secrets buried beneath the surface. As the crowd began to murmur in confusion, I caught a glimpse of the mayor's clenched jaw and the flicker of something unspoken passing between him and one of his aides.

"Something's not right," I whispered to Kayla, unease creeping into my voice. "This isn't just about the budget. There's something more here."

Before I could say more, the mayor took a step back, eyes darting around the room as if calculating his next move. I could feel the tension crackling in the air again, a storm brewing just beneath the surface. And then, as if to confirm my worst fears, he raised his voice over the crowd, his expression darkening.

"Ladies and gentlemen, I'm afraid there's been a misunderstanding—"

The moment was thick with anticipation, and just as I thought I might understand the direction this was headed, a flash of movement caught my eye near the exit. A figure slipped out, shrouded in shadow, leaving behind a sense of foreboding that settled over the crowd like a shroud.

"What was that?" I gasped, and Kayla's eyes narrowed as we exchanged a glance filled with uncertainty.

But the mayor continued, "I need to make it clear that certain decisions have already been made."

The room held its breath, and I felt a chill run down my spine, knowing this was just the beginning of something much bigger than any of us had anticipated.

# Chapter 23: Cracks in the Surface

The air hung thick with anticipation as the sun dipped below the horizon, casting long shadows across the outdoor venue where laughter and music intertwined like old friends. Colorful string lights twinkled overhead, illuminating the gathered crowd, their faces alight with excitement and a hint of mischief. I stood amidst them, my heart a cacophony of hope and apprehension. This event was supposed to be our moment—a celebration of resilience, a chance to step forward into the light. But then Ryan appeared, his presence darkening the festivities like an unwelcome storm cloud rolling in.

Dressed in a fitted leather jacket that clung to his athletic frame, Ryan sauntered in with the swagger of someone who believed the world revolved around him. The laughter dwindled, replaced by an uncomfortable hush, as if the universe itself held its breath, waiting for the inevitable clash. I felt a shiver ripple down my spine. "What a joke, Calderon," he sneered, his voice dripping with disdain, cutting through the air like a knife. The crowd shifted, a living entity that sensed the tension brewing, their gazes flickering between us as if we were performers in an uninvited drama.

I squared my shoulders, fighting the impulse to retreat. It was a familiar dance, this confrontation, but I was tired of being the one forced to sidestep his barbs. Just when I thought the event would be a turning point, here he was, an echo of past struggles and insecurities. "And yet, here I am, still standing," I replied, my voice steadier than I felt. My heart raced as I soaked in the murmurs of support rising from the crowd. Their presence bolstered my resolve, lifting me like an unyielding tide.

Kayla, my steadfast friend, stood beside me, her grip tightening around my hand. The warmth of her fingers curled around mine was a lifeline, steadying me amidst the storm. Her confidence radiated like a beacon, an unspoken reminder that I wasn't in this battle alone. "We all know who the real joke is here," she shot back, her tone laced with a blend of defiance and charm that could turn any argument on its head. The crowd responded with a chorus of nods and murmurs, their support swirling around us like an invisible shield.

But Ryan's eyes, dark and calculating, narrowed as he leaned in closer, the distance between us shrinking. "You think you're clever, don't you? Playing the underdog while you rally your little fan club. How quaint." There was a thin layer of mockery beneath his words, an attempt to strip away the sense of unity building around me. "This isn't about cleverness; it's about integrity, something you wouldn't understand," I shot back, feeling a flicker of power ignite within me.

The crowd began to pulse with energy, emboldened by our exchange, whispers rippling through them like waves crashing against a rocky shore. They were leaning in, eager to witness the clash, and in that moment, I knew I had to give them a show. But I also had to tread carefully, knowing that a single misstep could bring the whole façade crashing down.

Ryan grinned, the kind of smile that never reached his eyes. "Integrity? Is that what you call it? Hiding behind your little friends?" His words dripped with condescension, but I could see the uncertainty flickering beneath his bravado. The more he pushed, the more his facade began to crack. "If you think this is going to intimidate me, you're sorely mistaken. I've faced far worse than you," I retorted, my voice ringing clear and strong.

The crowd erupted, a wave of cheers and shouts echoing off the walls of the venue, washing over me in a rush of adrenaline. There was something intoxicating about the support, a surge of strength that lifted me higher than I'd ever imagined. For a moment, I could almost forget the dread swirling inside me, the echoes of self-doubt that had plagued me for far too long.

But Ryan, his expression shifting from amusement to irritation, stepped closer, invading my space. I could smell the faint hint of his cologne, a mixture of musk and something altogether too confident for my liking. "You're making a fool of yourself. Just walk away, Calderon. This isn't worth it," he taunted, his voice low and dangerous, attempting to pry me from my newfound strength.

"Not a chance," I declared, feeling the heat of defiance rising in my chest. I realized in that moment how much I craved this confrontation, how desperately I needed to reclaim my narrative. "I'm done being pushed around by you or anyone else."

The words hung in the air, a bold declaration that demanded attention. Around us, faces lit up with excitement, a shared acknowledgment that something pivotal was unfolding. Kayla squeezed my hand again, her support radiating warmth that contrasted sharply with the tension brewing between Ryan and me.

For the first time, I saw a flicker of doubt pass over Ryan's face, the armor he wore so confidently beginning to chip away. Perhaps he hadn't anticipated this level of resistance, and the thought filled me with a strange sense of triumph. But just as quickly as the realization bloomed, I saw the anger flaring in his eyes. This was more than a confrontation for him; it was a battle for supremacy, a desperate attempt to assert his dominance in a world he had always taken for granted.

"Fine," he hissed, his lips curling into a sneer. "But this isn't over. You've just put a target on your back." The threat hung in the air like a storm cloud ready to burst, but I refused to flinch.

"Let it come," I shot back, my voice steady and unwavering. As he turned on his heel, flanked by his entourage, I could feel the crowd's energy swell around me, buoying my spirits. In that moment, I knew I had forged a small victory, a crack in the surface of Ryan's carefully crafted persona, revealing the truth lurking beneath.

And as the evening wore on, laughter and music resumed, wrapping around me like a comforting embrace. The weight of the confrontation lingered, but it was a reminder of the strength I'd found within myself, a flicker of hope illuminating a path forward, one step at a time.

The vibrant hum of the gathering resumed, but the air still crackled with the remnants of tension. Laughter and conversation flitted around us like colorful butterflies, but I could still feel Ryan's disdain like a shadow creeping back into view. It was both disconcerting and liberating to have drawn a line in the sand. As the crowd began to settle into the rhythm of the event once more, I caught Kayla's eye, and the unspoken bond between us flickered with newfound strength.

"Let's get some drinks," she suggested, her voice a low murmur meant only for me, her eyes sparkling with mischief. It was a welcome distraction, a way to navigate the aftershocks of our confrontation without letting Ryan's words linger too long in my mind. We wove through the crowd, the thrumming energy of the event carrying us along like a current. As we approached the refreshment table, laden with an assortment of brightly colored drinks, my heart began to settle.

"Do you want something fruity or... something more adult?" Kayla asked, her smile teasing. I eyed the options, from vibrant punch to the deep red of sangria. "You know me too well; I'm feeling adventurous," I replied, a playful grin stretching across my face. We filled our cups, the sweet scent of berries and citrus wafting up, making my spirits lift a little more.

As we made our way back into the throng of party-goers, I took a moment to breathe, the crisp evening air mingling with the intoxicating aromas of food and laughter. The twinkling lights overhead seemed to dance in celebration, a gentle reminder that the world continued to spin, irrespective of the storm brewing just moments ago. But that sense of calm was short-lived.

A loud crash echoed from across the yard, and the laughter screeched to a halt. I turned to see a table tipped over, cups and plates scattering like fallen leaves. My heart sank. Ryan's voice boomed above the crowd, punctuated by a harsh laugh. "Watch where you're going, idiot!" he yelled, his tone drenching the atmosphere in a mix of aggression and mockery.

Before I could process the chaos, a tall figure emerged from the crowd, fists clenched and jaw set. Alex, a quiet, brooding type with a knack for drawing attention only when necessary, had seen the incident unfold. He took a step forward, a wave of protective energy radiating from him. "Ryan, what's your problem?" he called out, his voice steady but edged with steel.

I felt a rush of gratitude wash over me. Alex was one of those friends who often stood in the background, but tonight, he stepped into the fray like a knight ready to defend his castle. Ryan turned, momentarily thrown off guard, and for a heartbeat, the tension shifted.

"Mind your business, Sanchez," Ryan spat back, but the way his words stumbled indicated that the tables had turned just a bit. The crowd began to murmur again, a swell of support edging closer, emboldening Alex and me.

Kayla leaned in, her voice just above a whisper. "We can't let him get away with this," she said, determination knitting her brows together. "Let's back Alex up." I nodded, feeling a rush of adrenaline pulse through my veins. It was time to stand together, a united front against the bully who thought he could dictate our night.

With a quick glance, we joined Alex's side. "You heard him, Ryan. Back off," I said, my voice firm and laced with confidence. "What are you trying to prove, anyway? Picking fights isn't a good look, especially when you're outnumbered."

Ryan's eyes darkened, and for a fleeting moment, uncertainty flashed across his face. It was almost satisfying, watching him wrestle with the sudden realization that he wasn't invincible. "You think you're so clever, don't you? This is just a joke," he replied, his bravado faltering, though the crowd didn't seem to buy it.

"Not a joke, just a bad show," Kayla chimed in, crossing her arms defiantly. The crowd erupted in laughter, the tension deflating like a punctured balloon. Ryan's friends shifted uncomfortably, glancing at one another as if waiting for someone to take charge.

Just then, a petite woman with curly hair and an infectious laugh approached, her eyes gleaming with mischief. "Is there a party I wasn't invited to?" she said, her smile contagious as she cut through the heaviness. "Because if this is all about your little temper tantrum, Ryan, count me out." The crowd exploded into cheers, her light-heartedness breaking the ice.

"Go home, Ryan," she continued, leaning in slightly, as if sharing a secret. "I'm sure your ego can use the rest." The crowd howled with laughter, and Ryan's expression twisted into a scowl that did little to mask the humiliation he was experiencing.

I felt the tide shift decisively in our favor, the energy of the group wrapping around us like a protective blanket. It was as if the universe had finally decided we were worthy of a little reprieve from Ryan's relentless bullying. But just when I thought we might finally send him packing, he stepped closer, his demeanor shifting from brash to dangerously calm.

"Enjoy your little moment, Calderon. I'll be waiting," he said, the threat woven into his tone heavy enough to suffocate. He turned on his heel and strode away, his friends trailing behind him like shadows retreating from the light.

The crowd erupted into applause and laughter, their cheers washing over us like a soothing balm. I turned to Kayla, my heart still racing from the confrontation. "We did it!" I exclaimed, barely able to contain my excitement.

"Of course we did! You were brilliant!" she replied, her enthusiasm infectious. Alex chuckled, shaking his head as if in disbelief. "I'm still amazed you stood up to him like that. You've got guts, Calderon."

As we raised our drinks in a celebratory toast, the evening took on a new life. Conversations bubbled around us, laughter mixing with the music that began to play again, carrying us away from the remnants of the confrontation.

But beneath the surface of my excitement lurked a nagging doubt, an unsettling feeling that Ryan's threat wasn't merely bluster. Even as I laughed with my friends, a shadow stretched behind me, a reminder that not all battles are won in the moment. I glanced around, searching for any sign of his return, a heartbeat of anxiety flickering in the back of my mind.

Kayla nudged my side playfully, pulling me from my reverie. "Come on, let's dance!" she said, her eyes sparkling with mischief. I hesitated for a heartbeat, caught between the urge to join in the revelry and the worry that loomed. But as she tugged me toward the dance floor, I felt the weight of the evening's victory surge within me, reminding me that I was stronger than I ever thought possible.

With each step, I shook off the remnants of fear, surrendering to the rhythm of the music and the warmth of friendship that surrounded me. For now, I would dance; I would laugh and be present in this moment, knowing that whatever shadows lay ahead, I wouldn't face them alone.

The music pulsed like a heartbeat, wrapping around me as I surrendered to the rhythm. I twirled, letting the moment consume me, the laughter of friends and the smell of warm, spiced cider mingling in the air. Each note lifted the remnants of anxiety that clung to my thoughts, allowing me to lose myself in the moment.

Kayla danced beside me, her laughter like a melody that harmonized perfectly with the beat.

"Look at you, all brave and fierce!" she exclaimed, spinning in a circle, her dress flaring out like a burst of color. "Who knew you had it in you to take down a bully? Maybe I should start taking notes!"

"Please, I can barely keep my balance half the time," I replied, grinning as I adjusted to the beat. The tension that had once threatened to suffocate us had transformed into exhilaration. The evening was ours, and I savored every second of it. I could almost convince myself that Ryan was nothing more than a fleeting shadow, a brief storm that had already passed.

But then, a chilling sensation crept along my spine, a sense of being watched. I glanced around the crowd, laughter and joy mingling with shadows, but there he was—Ryan, lurking at the edge, his gaze boring into me like a laser beam. I faltered mid-dance, my heart sinking. He had returned, and the confident façade I had worn moments ago felt suddenly fragile, like glass poised to shatter.

Kayla noticed my change in demeanor, her playful expression faltering. "What's wrong?" she asked, her voice laced with concern. I nodded toward Ryan, who leaned against a tree, arms crossed, an unsettling smirk dancing across his lips. The crowd buzzed around us, but in that moment, it felt like a bubble that could burst at any second.

"Looks like the bad penny has turned up again," Kayla muttered, her playful tone replaced with the steel of determination. "We should ignore him. Let's keep dancing."

"Easier said than done," I replied, trying to shake off the weight of his stare. But as the music faded, the cheers of the crowd turned into a murmur, the partygoers caught in the tension that seemed to radiate from Ryan like a heatwave. "What does he want?"

"Probably to ruin our fun," she sighed, scanning the room as if searching for allies. "Let's not give him the satisfaction."

I wanted to take her advice, to ignore him completely, but every laugh felt muted under his scrutiny, every twirl lost its joy. My heart thudded louder, drowning out the music, reminding me of the threat he represented. "Maybe we should just—"

Before I could finish, Ryan pushed off the tree and sauntered toward us, his swagger full of practiced ease. "Didn't think you could keep the party going without me, did you, Calderon?" he drawled, a mockery evident in his voice that sent a chill racing down my spine.

"I think we were doing just fine," I replied, forcing a smile that didn't quite reach my eyes.

"Fine?" he scoffed, stepping closer. "Is that what you call this? A pathetic attempt to pretend you're something you're not? A queen in a court of jesters?"

"Ryan, it's over," Kayla interjected, stepping forward. "You've made your point. We're not scared of you anymore."

His laughter cut through the air like a sharp blade. "Oh, but that's where you're wrong. This isn't just about you and me. It's about all of us. You're in over your head, sweetheart." He leaned closer, the sickly sweet smell of his cologne suffocating me. "And trust me, I'm just getting started."

"Back off," I said, my voice steady despite the whirlwind of emotions. "You don't get to dictate what happens here."

His eyes flickered with something that resembled amusement. "So brave. But bravery without wisdom is just reckless, don't you think?" He gestured to the crowd, many of whom had turned to witness our standoff, anticipation crackling in the air like static. "I wonder how long they'll stand by you when they see the real you."

At that moment, I felt a sharp pang of uncertainty. What did he know? My thoughts raced as I tried to ground myself, to find the confidence that had surged through me earlier. Kayla squeezed my hand, her warmth a reminder that I was not alone.

"Let's not keep the crowd waiting," she said, her voice a calm amidst the storm. "If you think you can scare us away, you're sorely mistaken."

Ryan's expression shifted slightly, a flicker of annoyance breaking through the veneer of his arrogance. "You're all talk, but let's see how long that lasts when the fun stops." With that, he turned on his heel, a cloud of friends following him like devoted disciples, but his laughter trailed behind, wrapping around us like an insidious fog.

The tension broke, laughter and music returning to fill the void left in Ryan's wake, but I couldn't shake the unease that churned within me. The crowd resumed its revelry, yet a heavy pall clung to my heart. The fear that had threatened to consume me earlier had merely retreated, lying in wait like a predator stalking its prey.

"Are you okay?" Kayla asked softly, her concern cutting through the noise. I managed a smile, but the weight of doubt lingered. "I think so. Just... unsure about what happens next."

"Next?" she replied, her brow furrowing slightly. "What do you mean?"

"I mean, if he's serious about coming after us, we can't just pretend he'll vanish," I said, my voice dropping to a whisper. "What if he's plotting something? We can't just ignore that."

Her eyes narrowed, determination rising like a phoenix from the ashes. "Then we'll be ready for him. I'm not letting him ruin this for us, and neither should you."

"I know," I replied, feeling the fire of her resolve ignite a flicker within me. "But it's not just about us anymore. What if he turns this into something bigger?"

Before she could respond, a loud bang echoed across the yard, drawing every eye toward the makeshift stage at the far end. Fireworks erupted in a burst of colors—red, blue, and gold—lighting the night sky and drowning out our conversation. Gasps of wonder replaced the tension, and for a brief moment, I was swept away by the beauty of it all, the shimmering bursts painting hope across the darkness.

But as I watched, a figure emerged from the shadows, a dark silhouette standing just beyond the glow of the fireworks. My heart plummeted as I recognized the shape, the familiar outline that seemed to loom larger than life. Ryan.

He stood there, a sinister smile spreading across his face, and with a flourish, he raised his arm, a small device glowing ominously in his hand.

And then, without warning, the sky erupted again—not with the joy of fireworks but with chaos. A loud crack echoed through the night, followed by a series of explosions that sent the crowd into a panic. People screamed and stumbled, confusion erupting as chaos spread like wildfire.

The world shifted, a rush of bodies and voices swirling around me as the reality of the situation slammed into me. There was no more laughter, no more music—only fear.

In that moment, my heart raced, pounding against my chest like a drum signaling impending doom. I turned to Kayla, adrenaline coursing through me. "We have to get out of here!"

But as I reached for her, I realized she was staring, her eyes wide, locked onto Ryan, who stood at the edge of the chaos, the device still glowing in his grasp.

I opened my mouth to call out to her, but the noise drowned my voice, and the crowd surged around us like a tidal wave, separating us in the chaos.

"Kayla!" I shouted, panic clawing at my throat as I searched for her in the fray. But she was lost to me, swallowed by the crowd and the chaos.

And as I turned back toward Ryan, my heart sank at the realization that this wasn't over. Not by a long shot.

# Chapter 24: Strength in Vulnerability

Standing behind the microphone, I felt as if the entire world had narrowed to the small, circular stage beneath my feet, the glossy wood reflecting the soft glow of the overhead lights. Each beam illuminated a sea of faces, some familiar, many not, but all drawn together by the shared intent of this gathering. I could hear the rustle of clothes, the low hum of whispered conversations, and the faint clinking of glasses nearby, each sound blending into a soft symphony of anticipation. The scent of fresh coffee mingled with the crispness of autumn air that had slipped in through the slightly ajar windows, wrapping the room in a warm embrace.

"Today is about embracing who we are," I began, my voice steadier than I felt. My heart pounded against my ribs, a rhythmic reminder of the vulnerability I was about to lay bare. I glanced out into the audience and locked eyes with Kayla. Her expression, a mix of encouragement and something deeper, gave me the strength I needed. With every word, I poured my soul into the air between us, weaving my narrative into a tapestry of shared experiences.

As I spoke, I could see the flicker of recognition spark in some of the listeners' eyes. "We are more than the labels placed upon us," I continued, allowing the words to resonate in the room. "We are artists, athletes, dreamers, lovers, and, yes, sometimes even fools." A gentle laughter rippled through the crowd, an acknowledgment that cut through the tension like a warm knife through butter. It felt good to share that. Each person was a mosaic of stories, each fragment equally vital, and I hoped to show them that today.

I recounted my journey through fear and self-discovery, how each stumble and fall had led me to this moment. The silence in the room thickened as I recalled the nights spent questioning my worth, the loneliness that gnawed at my confidence. "I've stood in front of countless mirrors, searching for something to love, and it took me a long time to realize that the only validation I needed was my own," I admitted, my voice barely above a whisper, yet carrying the weight of years.

I could see some people leaning forward, their expressions shifting from casual interest to genuine engagement. I pressed on, inviting others to reflect on their stories. "What if we all took a moment to shed our masks? What if we shared the fears that keep us up at night?" The vulnerability of the moment wrapped around us, creating an invisible thread that connected each individual in the audience.

Then, like a stone thrown into a still pond, the atmosphere shifted. A woman in the back stood up, her eyes glistening with unshed tears. "I lost my job last year," she said, her voice trembling. "I felt so lost, so broken. I didn't know who I was without that title." Her honesty pierced through the haze of uncertainty that hung in the air, prompting a ripple of sympathy and understanding from the crowd.

As she spoke, I felt an unexpected pang in my chest, a reminder of the fragility of our identities. I nodded, urging her to continue, and felt the warmth of solidarity fill the room. The audience shifted, murmurs of agreement echoing softly like a chorus of shared struggles. "I used to think that my worth was tied to my success," she continued, her voice gaining strength. "But now I realize it's more about the connections I make with others."

The room swelled with stories, each voice layering onto the last, creating a vibrant mural of human experience. A teenager, vibrant and full of energy, shared her struggle with self-acceptance, and soon, she was met with laughter and nods of understanding from those around her. "I never thought I could be an artist, but now I paint every day. It's my way of saying I'm here," she declared, her confidence blooming with every word she spoke.

I stood there, spellbound, as one by one, people offered their truths like precious gifts, wrapped in the delicate paper of vulnerability. It was a powerful exchange, a shared moment of raw honesty that bound us closer together. Each story added a brushstroke to the portrait of who we were becoming, and I realized then that this gathering was more than just an event; it was a movement, a safe haven for every soul yearning to be heard.

Suddenly, a familiar face caught my eye, standing at the back—a friend from high school, Ethan, who had always been the class clown. His presence was unexpected, like a surprise twist in a well-worn plot. I hadn't seen him in years, yet here he was, his disheveled hair and easy grin sparking memories of laughter shared in hallways filled with insecurities.

"Hey, I've got a story too!" he called out, his tone light yet earnest. The crowd quieted, eager to hear what he had to share. "I spent years hiding behind jokes, using humor as a shield. But inside, I was terrified. Terrified of being ordinary, of not being seen." His admission resonated, drawing nods of recognition from those around him. "It took me losing a loved one to realize that laughter doesn't erase pain; it merely distracts from it. Now, I'm learning to embrace the silence that follows laughter, to face my fears head-on."

With his words, a wave of understanding washed over me. Here we were, an eclectic mix of stories and struggles, each revealing our scars and triumphs. And in that moment, the air crackled with the promise of transformation. We were shedding our layers, allowing our vulnerabilities to shine, and forging a bond that transcended our individual journeys.

As the stories flowed, I couldn't help but feel a shift in myself, a lightness that began to wash away the weight of my fears. With each shared truth, the connection among us grew stronger, weaving an intricate web of empathy and hope. It became clear that while we may walk different paths, the journey toward acceptance and love was one we all shared.

The room pulsed with energy, each heartbeat resonating in the space as more stories flowed, intertwining like strands of a tapestry. I felt as if we were standing on the precipice of something monumental, the kind of moment that clings to you long after the lights dim and the applause fades. The air was thick with emotion, a heady mix of laughter, tears, and the sweet scent of vulnerability that hung in the air like the lingering aroma of vanilla candles.

Ethan, still basking in the glow of shared laughter and camaraderie, leaned into the microphone again, his face illuminated by the soft glow of the overhead lights. "You know," he began, the mischief in his eyes flickering to life, "I used to think that the best way to connect was through making jokes. But if you want the truth, the real comedy happens when you drop the facade and let people see the real you." His words elicited a ripple of laughter, but it was layered with understanding.

"You're right, Ethan," I chimed in, eager to keep the momentum alive. "There's nothing funnier than realizing how ridiculous we all are. I mean, have you ever tripped over your own feet while trying to impress someone?" The audience erupted into laughter, the kind that comes from the belly and feels like a hug for the soul. It was cathartic, this exchange, a moment where we all embraced our shared awkwardness.

As the laughter subsided, a quiet fell over the room, allowing a deeper introspection to settle in. Kayla caught my eye again, her gaze unwavering. It was as if she was drawing strength from my vulnerability, and in turn, I felt emboldened by her silent support. "This isn't just about sharing our fears," I continued, feeling a surge of determination. "It's about recognizing our strengths, too. Let's talk about what makes us proud."

A young man at the front stood up, his hands trembling slightly as he ran them through his hair. "I was a D student in school," he confessed, the admission drawing sympathetic murmurs from the crowd. "But instead of wallowing in it, I started a podcast about how to navigate education without the pressure to conform. Now, I have listeners from all over the world who share their own stories of overcoming obstacles."

A cheer erupted, and I felt a swell of pride for him. "See? That's what I'm talking about! Turning what you thought was a weakness into a strength!" I exclaimed, feeling the thrill of connection that surged through the crowd. The man's face lit up, and I saw a glimpse of the joy that comes from finding one's purpose.

The conversation rolled like waves, each voice adding to the chorus. A woman shared how she had turned her battle with anxiety into a successful career as a mental health advocate. "I learned that it's okay to not be okay, and my vulnerability became my greatest asset," she said, her voice steady, each word dripping with newfound confidence.

It was remarkable how this space had morphed from a simple gathering into a sanctuary for healing and understanding. But just as the moment felt solid and safe, a tension began to weave itself into the fabric of our gathering. A figure emerged from the back, a man in a tailored suit whose presence felt more like an intrusion than an addition. The room's warmth shifted as whispers filled the air, the atmosphere suddenly charged with uncertainty.

"Excuse me," he interrupted, his tone cool and authoritative. "Is this a support group or a comedy show? Because I came here expecting to hear about real challenges, not stories that are merely heartwarming." His words fell heavy, like a sudden downpour on a sunny day, catching us off guard.

I felt the air thicken, and a wave of disbelief washed over me. Who was this man to belittle our moments of bravery? I glanced at

Kayla, who looked equally taken aback, and then at Ethan, whose expression had transformed from light-hearted amusement to steely resolve. "What's your deal, man?" he shot back, his voice gaining volume. "We're here sharing our stories. Maybe you should try it sometime."

The tension thickened like fog, wrapping around us and obscuring the warmth we had just built. I took a deep breath, channeling the courage I had discovered in this gathering. "You might not understand," I said, my voice steady, "but every story shared here is a piece of someone's truth. It takes immense strength to be vulnerable. If you think that's merely heartwarming, perhaps you haven't experienced the power of connection."

A murmur of agreement rippled through the crowd, emboldening me further. The stranger's demeanor shifted slightly, though he seemed to struggle against the tide of camaraderie that had swept the room. "Fine," he said, his voice tinged with defensiveness. "But I still think you're all avoiding the real issues."

"Real issues?" Kayla stepped forward, a fire igniting in her eyes. "This is real. We're talking about mental health, self-acceptance, and community. Isn't that worth something? Maybe you could learn a thing or two instead of criticizing."

The room buzzed with energy, people leaning forward, drawn into the electric back-and-forth. It felt like a dance, the energy surging as everyone engaged, defending not just their stories but the collective experience we had forged together.

The man shifted uncomfortably, his bravado cracking under the weight of so many voices. "I just thought it would be different," he mumbled, and I could see the slightest hint of vulnerability peek through the tough exterior he had tried to maintain.

"Well, maybe different isn't what you need," I replied, a slight smile playing on my lips. "Sometimes the unexpected is where the magic happens."

And just like that, the energy in the room shifted again, a shared understanding washing over us like sunlight breaking through clouds. The man took a step back, and in that moment, it was clear that he was no longer the focus of our gathering. Instead, we were reigniting the flame of connection, forging ahead with our stories, laughter, and truth.

As the conversations resumed, I felt a renewed sense of purpose. This gathering was a reminder that vulnerability was not a weakness but a profound strength, binding us together in our shared humanity. I glanced at Kayla, her eyes sparkling with unspoken pride, and knew we had turned a corner. Today was about embracing our true selves, and I could feel the threads of resilience weaving tighter with every shared moment.

The laughter and heartfelt conversations washed over the room like a tide, but the earlier confrontation with the man in the suit left a lingering tension that seemed to hang in the air. It was as if we had inadvertently cracked open a door to deeper truths, revealing not just our strengths but also the vulnerabilities of others. I could sense a shift, the atmosphere thickening with a cocktail of bravado and insecurity. We had shared so much, yet beneath the surface lay untold stories waiting to be unearthed.

I took a deep breath, the scent of vanilla and sandalwood mingling with the crisp air, steadying myself as I scanned the audience. Many faces still shone with hope, a few looked contemplative, and one or two bore the faint traces of anger. I wondered what had drawn them here and what burdens they carried. It felt like a puzzle—each piece important, yet obscured from view.

A gentle murmur spread across the crowd as a woman with fiery red hair and striking green eyes stood up. "Can I share?" Her voice rang out, confident yet tinged with an undercurrent of vulnerability. I nodded, inviting her to the forefront.

"I'm Tara," she introduced herself, her hands fidgeting nervously at her sides. "A year ago, I was in a car accident that left me with a permanent limp. I spent months feeling like a shadow of my former self." Her voice quavered slightly, but she pushed through. "It took me a while to realize that the world didn't define me by my physical abilities. I'm still the same person, just with a new story to tell."

A hush fell over the room as her words resonated with a painful truth. I could see tears glistening in the corners of her eyes, but there was also a fierce light igniting within her. "So, I picked up painting again, a hobby I abandoned years ago. It became my therapy. I pour my soul onto the canvas, and with every stroke, I reclaim my identity."

The crowd erupted in applause, and I felt my own heart swell with admiration for her courage. This gathering was transforming into something so much more than I had anticipated. It was a kaleidoscope of emotions, each story adding a vibrant hue to the collective experience.

As Tara stepped down, a woman in the front row caught my eye. Her brows knitted together, and she seemed to wrestle with a decision. Finally, she stood, her voice steady but quiet. "I'm Sarah," she said, her tone laced with determination. "I've struggled with an eating disorder for over a decade. I was always praised for my discipline, but nobody saw the war I was waging inside my head. This is my first time sharing this part of my life, and honestly, it terrifies me."

The weight of her admission hung in the air, and my heart ached for her. "But I'm tired of hiding," she continued, her eyes blazing with a newfound strength. "I'm learning to embrace my body as it is, scars and all. Today, I take my power back."

Another wave of applause erupted, punctuated by cheers. I realized that each person who stepped forward was not only sharing their story but was also inviting us all to bear witness to their healing.

It was an act of bravery, and together, we were building something profound—an invisible fortress of shared experience and support.

But the momentum was quickly interrupted when the man in the suit, still lurking at the edge of the crowd, interjected again. "Isn't it a little self-indulgent to dwell on personal struggles? What about the bigger picture? What about the issues that actually affect us as a society?" His words struck like a stone dropped in still water, sending ripples of discomfort through the audience.

Ethan stepped forward, fists clenched at his sides. "If you think personal struggles don't matter, you're missing the point! This is how we change society—from the ground up. By addressing our issues, we're actually engaging with the world around us."

The man scoffed, a derisive smile playing at the corners of his lips. "Good luck with that. You think sharing stories will solve anything?"

I stepped in, my voice firm. "It's not just about solving problems. It's about human connection. Sharing our vulnerabilities makes us stronger, and maybe, just maybe, it inspires others to find their own voices." I could feel the tension rise again, thick and unyielding, and my heart raced at the thought of this escalating.

With the mood shifting, I could see Kayla's face turning pale, and I knew I had to steer this gathering back on course. "What if we turn the question around? Let's focus on solutions instead of criticisms. Each of us has the power to make a change, no matter how small."

As if on cue, the crowd began to nod in agreement, the atmosphere morphing back into one of solidarity. "Let's brainstorm how we can support each other in our journeys. What can we do to uplift one another and drive real change?"

A chorus of voices filled the room, people pitching in ideas about community projects, support groups, and outreach programs. It was exhilarating, the way the energy shifted, transforming frustration into purpose. It felt like we were on the brink of something significant, ready to take this conversation beyond these walls.

Yet, just as the ideas began to flow, an unexpected sound cut through the laughter and chatter—a loud crash followed by a frightened gasp. A moment of silence enveloped the room, a collective intake of breath as we all turned to the source of the noise.

At the back of the room, a table had toppled over, scattering papers and a projector crashing to the ground. A figure darted from the scene, an unfamiliar silhouette moving swiftly toward the exit.

"Hey! Wait!" I shouted, instinctively stepping forward, my pulse quickening as curiosity ignited. The laughter faded, replaced by a tension that crackled in the air.

I caught a glimpse of a face hidden beneath a hood, the expression a mix of fear and desperation. My heart raced as I thought about the impact of this sudden disruption—was this person connected to our gathering, or had they stumbled in from outside, their intrusion a consequence of something far more sinister?

Ethan took a step toward me, his brow furrowed. "Should we follow? What was that all about?"

"I have no idea," I admitted, the adrenaline coursing through my veins, but I could feel the pull of the unknown. The gathering had transformed into a sanctuary, but it also had the potential to unravel in a single moment.

As the last remnants of the room's laughter faded, a sense of unease settled in, an invisible shroud enveloping us all. "Let's check it out," I said, already moving toward the exit, my heart pounding with anticipation and uncertainty. "Something tells me this is only the beginning."

And as I stepped through the doorway, the air thickened with an unsettling foreboding, leaving us all teetering on the edge of an unknown precipice, waiting to see what lay on the other side.

# Chapter 25: The Fallout

I woke to the distant rumble of thunder, the kind that hangs heavy in the air, promising storms both inside and out. My phone buzzed incessantly on the nightstand, a cacophony of notifications that drew me from a restless sleep. As I rubbed the remnants of dreams from my eyes, I was met with a virtual tempest. Ryan had unleashed a barrage of vitriol on social media, twisting my words like a pretzel and packaging lies in shiny, clickable memes. The comments section felt like a digital battlefield, where each post was a tiny grenade, exploding in my chest.

Scrolling through the outrage, my heart sank deeper with each swipe. Some had taken to calling me a fraud, while others made crude jokes about my supposed incompetence. The outrage felt like a suffocating blanket, wrapping tightly around me, making it difficult to breathe. But there, in the midst of the negativity, was a spark. Kayla stood beside me, her eyes narrowed in determination, fists clenched at her sides as if she were ready to charge into battle.

"We'll fight this together," she assured me, her voice firm yet laced with warmth. The solidarity in her words struck me like a lifeline. I had been so caught up in my own despair that I had almost forgotten I wasn't alone. The support I had garnered over the past few weeks was no fleeting moment; it felt like the beginnings of a movement, a community ready to rise up against the tide of slander.

With Kayla at my side, we began to strategize. I spread out the fabric of my thoughts like a patchwork quilt, each piece representing the plans I'd formed over countless sleepless nights. "We need to reclaim my narrative," I said, feeling the embers of resolve spark to life within me. "We can't just react; we have to set the tone."

"Right. But we also need to make it personal," she replied, already flipping through her phone to gather potential allies. "People connect with stories. Let's show them who you really are."

Her words resonated deeply. I had always believed in the power of stories, how they can bridge gaps and soften hearts. As we crafted our counter-campaign, we decided to share my journey—the challenges I had faced, the triumphs I had celebrated, and the community I had built. Each post would be a thread woven into a larger tapestry, creating an image of resilience and authenticity.

The plan began to take shape as we plotted our course with a mixture of excitement and trepidation. "We'll start with a video," Kayla suggested, her brow furrowing in concentration. "Something raw and real. We'll show them the truth behind the headlines."

I nodded, the thought invigorating me. "And let's invite others to share their stories too. Make it a movement, not just about me but about everyone who has ever felt silenced or attacked."

As the hours passed, the air crackled with energy. We gathered a small group of friends, each more spirited than the last. We transformed my living room into a makeshift studio, surrounded by bright lights and cameras, the scent of coffee and determination mingling in the air.

"Okay, action!" Kayla called, and suddenly, all eyes were on me. The camera was daunting, its lens like an unblinking eye. I took a deep breath, remembering why I had fought so hard for my voice to be heard in the first place. I began to speak, my voice trembling at first but growing stronger with each word.

"I'm here today not just for myself, but for every person who has ever felt unjustly attacked or misrepresented," I declared, the passion in my voice igniting a fire within me. "We all have stories worth telling, and I refuse to let anyone take that away from us."

With every line, I poured my heart into the camera, sharing my fears, my hopes, and the beautiful community that had rallied around me. The more I spoke, the more the tension in my shoulders eased, as if shedding a heavy coat I had worn for too long.

Once the video wrapped, a collective cheer erupted. It was a cathartic release, a powerful reminder of our shared purpose. "Now, we get it out there," Kayla said, her eyes gleaming with excitement. "Let's make some noise!"

The next few days were a blur of activity. We launched our campaign, flooding social media with stories and posts that highlighted not just my journey, but those of others who had faced their own struggles. The response was overwhelming. Messages poured in from people I had never met, sharing their own tales of resilience, support, and solidarity. Each story added another layer of depth to our campaign, transforming it into a vibrant tapestry of human experience.

In the midst of this whirlwind, I found myself leaning on my friends, their support like an anchor grounding me amidst the chaos. We held late-night meetings filled with laughter and brainstorming sessions that sparked new ideas. I discovered an unexpected joy in our collective creativity, a camaraderie that felt like a warm embrace.

Then came the moment of reckoning. Ryan's followers began to notice our movement, and with each passing day, their comments grew more desperate. It was as if I could see the fraying edges of his narrative, unraveling as my truth seeped through the cracks. I reveled in the thought that I might be gaining ground, that the tide was shifting in my favor.

But there was a lingering tension, a reminder that the battle was far from over. I could feel Ryan's presence lurking in the shadows, waiting for an opportunity to strike back. He was nothing if not cunning, and I knew he wouldn't go down without a fight. Yet, with Kayla and our friends rallying behind me, I felt a fierce determination burning brighter than ever. We were poised to reclaim my narrative, and this time, we wouldn't be silenced.

The energy in my living room crackled like static electricity, the kind that promises something big is about to happen. As we sat around my coffee table—now littered with empty mugs and hastily jotted notes—our collective determination solidified into something tangible. Kayla stood at the helm, her natural leadership emerging as she rallied our small band of supporters. "Alright, team," she declared, her voice booming with a playful bravado that made me grin despite the storm raging outside. "It's time to turn the tide. Let's show them what we're made of."

We divided ourselves into task forces, each armed with smartphones and an unyielding desire to rewrite the narrative. I took charge of crafting the core message of our campaign, heart pounding with excitement as I typed furiously on my laptop. It felt exhilarating, like I was wielding a sword instead of a keyboard. Each word was carefully chosen, meant to pierce through the haze of misinformation Ryan had spread.

"Just remember," Kayla said as she typed out our social media strategy, "this isn't just about you. It's about everyone who feels unheard." Her words hit me like a gentle reminder wrapped in a hug, affirming the larger mission we had taken on. We were not simply countering falsehoods; we were creating a space for voices that had been muffled or ignored.

With every meme we crafted, every story we shared, I felt myself leaning into vulnerability. I revealed the raw moments—the fears I had faced, the sleepless nights spent worrying about my future. There was something oddly liberating about peeling back the layers of my life for the world to see, exposing the messy bits that made me human.

"Wow, I knew you had a way with words, but this?" Kayla read my latest draft aloud, and her brows shot up. "This is poetry, not a post!"

I couldn't help but laugh, a lightness blooming in my chest. "Maybe I should just drop the campaign and start a blog about my feelings."

"Or you could write a novel titled How to Ruin a Reputation in Ten Easy Steps," she shot back, her eyes twinkling with mischief.

The laughter was a balm, soothing the tension that had built up in my chest. We needed these moments to remind ourselves that our mission was driven by more than just the chaos around us; it was fueled by our friendship and the desire to uplift others.

As the days passed, our campaign gathered momentum. Each story we shared garnered more support, our hashtags began trending, and the tide felt like it was finally shifting. I received messages from strangers, people who had faced their own battles, thanking me for speaking out. It was like finding a constellation of kindred spirits in a dark sky, each one illuminating the path ahead.

But beneath the surface, I could sense Ryan's frustration bubbling. He wasn't one to fade quietly into the background. The way he had orchestrated the initial smear campaign made it clear he thrived on attention, even the negative kind. The thought of him strategizing in the shadows sent a shiver down my spine.

I tried to push those thoughts aside, focusing instead on our growing community. We organized live chats and workshops where people could share their experiences, creating a platform for others to find their voices. The support we received was overwhelming, pouring in from unexpected corners of the internet.

Then one evening, as I was preparing for a live Q&A, I received a direct message that made my stomach drop. It was from an anonymous account, the kind that always seems to pop up during a controversy. The message was simple yet chilling: "You don't know who you're messing with. Back off while you can."

My heart raced as I stared at the screen, the room around me suddenly feeling too small, too confining. I showed the message to Kayla, who was engrossed in her own preparations. "We need to take this seriously," she said, her voice dropping to a more somber tone. "This could escalate."

The words hung between us like the heavy air before a storm, and I couldn't shake the feeling that I was standing on the precipice of something dangerous. But just as quickly as the fear surfaced, my resolve reasserted itself. "We can't back down," I replied, gripping her arm tightly. "We've come too far to let intimidation win."

Our live event began, and I was acutely aware of the eyes watching, the anticipation humming in the air. I took a deep breath, reminding myself of all the reasons I was here, all the people who believed in me. The questions rolled in, and I felt the power of my voice steadying my nerves.

In the midst of answering questions and sharing experiences, I noticed a familiar name popping up in the chat. It was one of Ryan's closest allies, someone I had never expected to see among my supporters. "You're doing great," the message read, accompanied by a heart emoji.

I couldn't help but raise an eyebrow. Was this genuine support or a ploy to gather information? My instincts screamed caution, but the warmth of community ignited a spark of hope. I decided to respond, carefully crafting my reply. "Thank you! It means a lot to have support, even from unexpected places."

The chat exploded with activity, my followers rallying around the unexpected ally. But in the back of my mind, I kept an eye on the other messages flowing in. The anonymous threats, the laughter from Ryan's camp—it all mixed together in a potent cocktail of uncertainty.

As the live event wound down, a rush of adrenaline coursed through me. I had done it; I had stood tall despite the pressure. But as I ended the stream, a new notification blinked on my screen, and my heart dropped again.

It was a video, shared widely, featuring Ryan sitting in front of a camera with that smug look of his. He was grinning, the kind of grin that could freeze ice on the hottest summer day. The title blared in bold letters: "Exposing the Truth About [My Name]."

I exchanged a panicked glance with Kayla, who was already typing furiously to counter his claims. "We'll take him on," she vowed, her expression fierce. But deep down, I knew we were stepping into the lion's den, and this time, it felt different. The stakes were higher, and the stakes were now personal.

The moment I clicked on Ryan's video, a wave of unease washed over me, cold and unrelenting. His image filled the screen, and he leaned forward, that trademark smugness etched across his face. "Let's talk about the truth," he began, his tone dripping with feigned sincerity. I could feel my heart racing, each beat echoing in my ears like the pounding of a drum, urging me to brace myself for the inevitable barrage of lies.

"Who is this victim really?" he asked, the words designed to sting like a wasp. "What's her story? Is it even true?" He proceeded to dissect my past, recounting moments of vulnerability with a glee that made my skin crawl. The clips he used, the carefully chosen snippets, painted me as a fraud—a mere puppet master manipulating the narrative to gain sympathy and attention.

"Can you believe this guy?" Kayla scoffed beside me, her fingers drumming against the table as she watched me watch him, her expression a mixture of disbelief and anger. "He's really pulling out all the stops, isn't he?"

"Seems like it," I muttered, anger simmering just beneath the surface. "But he's not going to take this lying down. We can't just sit here and let him twist everything."

I quickly opened a new window on my laptop, determined to counter his claims. "We need facts. Let's gather everything we can—support from those who know the truth, testimonials, and receipts."

Kayla nodded, already reaching for her phone to organize our next steps. "I'll start digging through the comments. I saw a lot of supportive messages during our last livestream; maybe we can compile those into something impactful."

As I worked, my thoughts churned with anxiety and adrenaline. Ryan's video was a calculated attack, and I had no doubt he'd come armed with more than just words. It felt like I was in a boxing ring, gloves on but nowhere near ready for the first punch.

Within a few hours, the internet exploded with reactions. Our counter-campaign gained traction as people rallied to support me, sharing their own stories and countering Ryan's narrative. It felt exhilarating, like riding a roller coaster with the wind whipping through my hair. But just as quickly as the excitement rose, dread settled in my stomach.

That evening, after another exhausting day of battling comments and rallying support, I plopped onto my couch, my fingers trembling from overuse. "I don't think I can do this," I confessed to Kayla, who was sprawled on the opposite end, scrolling through Twitter updates.

"Hey," she said, her voice steady and reassuring, "you're not alone in this. We're in it together, remember?"

I let out a shaky breath, the warmth of her reassurance cutting through the fatigue. "It's just...he's relentless. And I can't shake the feeling that he's planning something bigger."

"Then let's find out what that is," she replied, her eyes narrowing with determination. "We'll uncover whatever he's scheming and hit back harder."

Fueled by her words, I turned my attention back to my laptop, determined to search for whatever incriminating evidence I could find against Ryan. As I sifted through articles, I stumbled upon something unexpected: a connection between Ryan and a small group of influencers notorious for their shady practices and online bullying. My heart raced as I read, the pieces of the puzzle starting to fit together.

"Kayla!" I shouted, startling her from her phone. "Look at this. It's like a hidden web of deceit, and he's right in the middle of it."

She rushed over, peering over my shoulder as I clicked through links, revealing a trail of their activities that led back to Ryan. "This could be huge," she whispered, her eyes wide with excitement. "If we can expose this, it might turn the tide in our favor."

But just as I felt the flicker of hope ignite within me, my phone buzzed insistently. A message from an unknown number flashed on the screen. "Stop digging, or you'll regret it." My heart plummeted, the weight of the threat pressing down on my chest.

"Who is it?" Kayla asked, her voice suddenly tight with concern.

"Don't know," I muttered, my pulse racing as I stared at the screen. "But it doesn't feel good."

I thought about ignoring it, but something gnawed at my insides. "No," I said, resolutely shaking my head. "If they think I'll back down because of some half-hearted threat, they're wrong. We need to dig deeper."

"Are you sure?" Kayla asked, her brows knitting together in concern. "This feels dangerous."

"Maybe," I admitted, glancing between my phone and the screen. "But I won't let fear dictate my actions. Not now. Not after everything we've built."

We spent the next few hours analyzing every scrap of information we could find, and I could feel the heat of adrenaline coursing through me. Each revelation about Ryan's connections only solidified my resolve.

Suddenly, my phone buzzed again, this time with a call from a familiar number. I picked it up without thinking. "Hello?"

"Is this [My Name]?" A deep voice on the other end sent a chill down my spine. "You need to stop what you're doing."

"I'm not afraid of you," I shot back, emboldened by my growing anger.

There was a pause, a tense silence that hung thick in the air. "You should be. You have no idea who you're dealing with."

Before I could respond, the call abruptly ended, leaving a hollow emptiness in its wake.

"What was that?" Kayla asked, her face pale.

"It was someone warning me to back off," I replied, my hands shaking as I dropped the phone onto the table. "But I don't think I can."

The moment hung heavily between us, the air thick with unspoken fears and uncertainty. It felt like a dark cloud was descending, a storm gathering on the horizon, ready to break.

"Whatever happens, we stick together," Kayla said, a fierce light in her eyes. "We'll uncover the truth and expose him for what he really is."

I nodded, swallowing hard. Just as I turned back to my laptop, a notification flashed across the screen—a tweet from Ryan. My breath hitched as I read the words: "Game on, [My Name]. Prepare for the fallout."

The weight of his threat settled heavily on my shoulders, a grim reminder that the battle was far from over.

# Chapter 26: Rising Tensions

The air in the gym buzzed with an energy that crackled like static electricity, a storm brewing just beneath the surface. As I maneuvered through the crowded space, the scent of sweat and the echo of basketballs bouncing filled my senses, wrapping around me like an old, familiar blanket. But today, that blanket felt tighter, suffocating even, as whispers flickered through the air like shadows chasing the light. Each glance exchanged between my teammates carried a weight that gnawed at my insides, a reminder that alliances were shifting, and I was standing in the middle of a battlefield, clutching my resolve like a tattered flag.

Kayla leaned against the bleachers, her blonde ponytail swinging like a pendulum as she threw me an encouraging smile. Her eyes, a shade of green that reminded me of sun-dappled leaves, sparkled with mischief. "Hey, superstar," she called out, her voice cutting through the tension like a knife through butter. "Ready to show them who's boss?"

I couldn't help but grin back at her. "Boss? You make it sound so easy." I tossed my bag over my shoulder, adJuliag my stance. "More like I'm about to step into the lion's den."

As we made our way to the court, I felt her presence beside me, a steadying force in a sea of uncertainty. Practices had transformed from the rhythm of teamwork to a precarious dance of alliances, and Kayla had chosen to be my partner in this twisted waltz. But beneath our playful banter lay an undercurrent of something more complex, a tension that bubbled just below the surface. My heart raced at the thought, a whirlwind of confusion that I desperately tried to ignore.

"Don't forget," Kayla said, her tone shifting slightly as we settled into our routine. "We're in this together. No matter what."

Those words, laced with sincerity, resonated within me. As much as I wanted to believe them, doubts crept in like unwelcome guests.

I could feel the eyes of my teammates, some filled with skepticism, others with open support, and I wondered how long it would be before the fragile web of loyalty frayed.

The whistle blew, signaling the start of practice, and I dove into the familiar rhythm of drills, my body moving instinctively. Yet, even amidst the sweat and exertion, my mind couldn't shake the feeling of being watched. Kayla and I formed an unspoken bond as we navigated the drills together, her presence giving me a surge of strength. We exchanged quick glances, little inside jokes that made the tension seem momentarily manageable.

But as the session wore on, I noticed the shift in the air, the way conversations stuttered when I approached, how laughter dimmed to whispers. Each missed shot echoed louder than the last, each mistake a reminder that I was the target of scrutiny, the girl daring to challenge the status quo. It made my chest tight, a knot of frustration threatening to unravel me.

After practice, the locker room buzzed with a cacophony of voices, but I felt a distinct isolation that hovered around me like a fog. Kayla moved through the group effortlessly, her laughter a beacon of light, but my heart sank as I overheard snippets of conversations swirling around us. The latest gossip was a direct hit aimed at my ambition—how I was stepping over bounds, how I didn't deserve to lead.

I turned to Kayla, who was hanging back, her brow furrowed as she caught my eye. "What do you think?" I asked, my voice barely above a whisper.

"They're just scared," she replied, her gaze steady. "You're a force, and they're feeling the heat."

"Or maybe they just want to throw me off the team," I muttered, bitterness creeping into my tone. "Maybe I should just quit."

Kayla shook her head, her expression fierce. "No way. You're stronger than them, and they know it. You've worked too hard to give up now."

Her belief in me sparked something within, but it was a fleeting flame in a tempest of doubt. "What if I fail?" I blurted out, the vulnerability escaping before I could rein it in. "What if I'm not enough?"

Kayla stepped closer, her voice low and firm. "You are enough. You always have been. And even if you stumble, I'll be right here to help you back up."

In that moment, the world outside faded, and it was just the two of us, suspended in a bubble of understanding and unspoken feelings. My heart thudded against my ribs, caught between the comfort of friendship and the exhilarating terror of something deeper. But before I could process it all, the moment shattered like glass, as a teammate interrupted, her laughter a harsh jarring note in our symphony.

Kayla took a step back, the moment lost to the chaos of our surroundings. I clenched my fists, frustration simmering beneath the surface. Just as I opened my mouth to retort, the coach called us over, her voice cutting through the chatter. The rest of the team gathered, and the air thickened with anticipation.

"Listen up," the coach said, her tone all business. "We've got a big game coming up, and we need to focus. Tensions are high, and it's showing on the court. We can't afford any distractions."

As she laid out our strategy, I could feel the weight of the moment pressing down on me. The game loomed large, a looming specter filled with the potential for triumph or failure. But amidst the planning and the strategy, I caught Kayla's eye across the huddle, and for a heartbeat, everything else faded. In her gaze, I found a flicker of determination—a promise that no matter the outcome, we would face it together.

Yet, as the meeting adjourned and the team dispersed, I couldn't shake the feeling that the rising tensions were only the beginning. Beneath the surface, a storm was brewing, and I was right in the eye of it, caught between the storm of ambition and the undercurrents of emotion that threatened to pull me under.

The gym pulsed with energy, but beneath the surface, it felt more like a pressure cooker, the heat rising with every passing day. Our upcoming game loomed like a dark cloud, and as practices continued, I could feel the atmosphere thickening with unspoken words and unresolved tension. The basketball court, once a sanctuary of teamwork and camaraderie, now echoed with the weight of judgment and uncertainty. Every dribble, every shot seemed to draw the lines deeper, dividing us into factions—those who believed in my vision for the team and those who resented the disruption I represented.

As I stood at the free-throw line during practice, I could sense the gazes of my teammates pressing down on me like an invisible weight. Kayla stood at the perimeter, her eyes a mix of encouragement and concern, and I felt a jolt of determination surge through me. I took a deep breath, focused on the hoop, and shot. The ball arced gracefully before clanging against the rim and bouncing away. I couldn't help but groan in frustration.

"Close, but no cigar," Kayla called out, her voice laced with the kind of teasing that only friends can muster. "Try again. Imagine the hoop is your greatest fear. Show it who's boss!"

I turned to her, eyebrows raised. "Greatest fear? You mean the fear of being benched because I can't hit a free throw?"

"Exactly! You can't let the hoop intimidate you," she laughed, but her laughter faded into a knowing smile. The moment was a brief respite in the growing storm, a flicker of light in a dimming room.

As practice wrapped up, I felt the tension unravel slightly, but a knot still twisted in my stomach. Kayla and I collected our bags, and

I stole a glance at the other players, who were huddled in clusters, their voices low and conspiratorial. "You know they're talking about us," I murmured, trying to sound nonchalant.

"Let them," Kayla said, shrugging off the concern as if it were a pesky fly. "What matters is what we think."

"Right, but what if what they think becomes reality? What if this backfires?" I rubbed the back of my neck, feeling the sweat trickle down. "What if I push too hard, and we lose? It'll be on me."

Kayla's gaze turned serious, her expression softening. "You won't. You're a fighter, and you're not in this alone. Just remember, sometimes the loudest voices are the ones you don't want to listen to." She paused, studying my face. "Besides, you've faced worse. Remember the time you broke your leg trying to impress that guy from the track team?"

I snorted, the memories flooding back. "Oh, he wasn't worth it. Just a few scrapes and a hefty dose of embarrassment. But you were there for that, too."

"Of course, I was," she replied, her voice low. "And I'll be there this time too."

As we stepped outside into the late afternoon sun, the world felt different—brighter, almost. But that warmth was soon shadowed by the lingering unease from the gym. I leaned against the cool metal of my car, stealing glances at the horizon where the sky met the trees, their leaves whispering secrets in the gentle breeze. "How do we fix this?" I asked, my voice barely above a whisper.

"By proving them wrong. We'll come up with a game plan, rally the supportive players, and focus on what really matters—our game," Kayla suggested, her eyes bright with resolve. "Let's meet tonight. We can map out our strategy like it's a secret mission. Just us against the world."

I smiled at her enthusiasm. "It's like a covert operation, then. Spies in the gym, armed with water bottles and energy bars."

"Exactly! Now you're getting it. But remember, we need to keep our cover. No one can know our true intentions," she teased, and for a moment, I felt the weight lift, if only a little.

Later that evening, as twilight draped its velvety cloak over the town, I made my way to Kayla's house. The familiar scent of popcorn greeted me as I walked through the door, and I was immediately reminded of our countless nights spent together, laughing and plotting like a couple of misfit strategists.

Kayla was sprawled on her couch, a sea of notebooks and highlighters surrounding her like a creative tornado had hit. "Welcome to my war room," she announced dramatically, gesturing to the chaos.

I couldn't help but laugh, feeling a sense of ease settle in. "Impressive. Do I need to don a military cap to blend in?"

"Only if you want to look ridiculous," she shot back, her eyes sparkling. "But you might find it boosts morale. Who doesn't love a good hat?"

We dove into brainstorming, the hours melting away as we sketched out plays and strategies, our laughter intertwining with the tension of the past days. As we tossed ideas back and forth, I caught myself stealing glances at her, her brow furrowed in concentration and her lips quirking into a smile at some joke only she understood. It was moments like these that made my heart race, though I dared not dwell on the implications of that feeling.

"Okay, how about we capitalize on our speed? We can run circles around them!" I suggested, adrenaline sparking through me.

"Love it! And we can use that sneaky play we practiced last week. It'll catch them off guard for sure," she replied, her excitement contagious.

Just as the atmosphere shifted, a sudden ping from her phone drew her attention. I watched as her expression changed, the laughter fading and concern creeping in. "It's my mom," she said softly, tapping the screen. "She needs me to come home for a bit. Something about a neighbor's dog? I think it's stuck or something."

"Oh, no. That sounds... urgent?" I said, my teasing laced with genuine concern. "Do you need to go?"

"Yeah, I should," she replied, looking torn. "But I'll be back. We can finish this later, right?"

"Of course! The war room will still be here when you return," I assured her, though I felt a pang of disappointment.

After Kayla dashed off, I lingered in her living room, the remnants of our planning session hanging in the air. I picked up one of the notebooks, flipping through the pages filled with our chicken-scratch writing, each doodle telling a story of our shared dreams and determination.

I felt a sudden urge to capture this moment, to solidify the bond we shared in a way that would linger even when we weren't together. It was then, as I sat in the dim light, that I realized something important: I didn't just want to win the game; I wanted to win for her, for us. And that intention stirred a deeper resolve within me, transforming the quiet tension into something powerful, something that could propel me into the next day.

As I finally stepped outside into the cool night, the stars blinked down at me, each one a reminder of the possibilities that lay ahead. I took a deep breath, the chill in the air invigorating. I was ready. Whatever the outcome, I would embrace it, side by side with Kayla, and face whatever storm awaited us.

The following days slid into a routine that felt more like a precarious balancing act than a series of practices. Mornings began with the echo of sneakers squeaking against polished wood, while evenings were filled with strategizing that danced between exhilaration and doubt. As the big game drew closer, the tension in the gym grew thick enough to slice. Whispers swirled like autumn leaves caught in a gust of wind—each sound a reminder of the divisions forming amongst my teammates. I could see it in their eyes; some were supportive, rallying behind me, while others cast skeptical glances as if I were a walking threat to their status quo.

Kayla remained my steadfast ally, her unwavering support like a lighthouse guiding me through a stormy sea. Each late-night session felt sacred, our laughter filling the gaps left by uncertainty. "What if we just showed up in ninja costumes?" I suggested one night, my voice a mix of seriousness and jest. "Sneak in, distract them with our superior stealth, and win by default."

She laughed, a sound like music breaking through my doubts. "As much as I love the idea, I think that's illegal. Plus, our gym's not ready for that level of chaos. We might get banned for life."

"True," I conceded, leaning back against her couch, a fortress of cushions enveloping me. "But it would be legendary."

"Legendary doesn't win games," she quipped, tossing a crumpled piece of paper at me. "Focus, genius! We need a solid plan."

Her determination ignited something within me, and as we continued to flesh out our strategy, the hours slipped by unnoticed. But as the sun dipped below the horizon and the sky darkened, a wave of unease washed over me. The game was looming like a predator stalking its prey, and I could feel the weight of expectation pressing down. The voices of dissent were growing louder in my mind, mixing with my own insecurities. What if all our planning wasn't enough? What if we lost?

Just as I was about to voice my concerns, Kayla's phone pinged with a message. Her face lit up momentarily before shifting into an expression of frustration. "It's my mom again. Something about another neighbor's dog. This is turning into a full-time job."

I bit my lip, wishing to ease her burden. "You can go. I can hold down the fort here. I'll figure something out."

She shook her head, her brow creased in determination. "No way. This is our mission. We're in this together, remember?"

"Right," I replied, though uncertainty clawed at me. "Still, you might need to check on the canine crisis."

After some back-and-forth, she finally relented. "Okay, fine. I'll be back soon, I promise. Just don't let the strategy crumble without me!"

As she dashed off, I flopped back against the couch, feeling a strange mix of relief and loneliness settle in. The room felt emptier without her infectious energy. I glanced around at our scattered notes, the plans we had meticulously crafted. Could I really carry this weight alone?

Minutes turned into an hour, and my thoughts spiraled as I paced the living room, the quiet gnawing at me. I could feel the shadows creeping in, the doubts multiplying like rabbits. I tried to focus on the game plan, but the words blurred together. Suddenly, my phone buzzed, breaking the stillness like a sudden clap of thunder. It was a text from Kayla.

"Just got to the neighbor's. Apparently, the dog is fine, but my mom thinks I should take him for a walk. Will be a bit longer. Hold tight!"

I chuckled to myself, grateful for her persistence. That was Kayla—always ready to lend a hand, whether to me or a four-legged friend. But a creeping sense of dread gnawed at the corners of my mind. What if the time spent waiting led to doubt? What if I faltered?

I grabbed my basketball and headed out to the driveway, determined to shake off the unease. The cool air hit my face, refreshing and grounding. I started shooting hoops, the rhythmic thump of the ball against the pavement calming my racing thoughts. Each shot was a release, a moment of clarity amidst the chaos.

Just as I was about to walk inside, a car pulled into the driveway. A familiar vehicle that made my heart leap—though I couldn't quite put my finger on why. The door swung open, and out stepped Lila, one of my teammates I had barely spoken to in weeks. The confidence she usually wore like armor was conspicuously absent, replaced by a hesitant air.

"Hey," she called out, her voice uncertain. "Mind if I join you?"

"Sure! I mean, I'm just practicing my—uh, dazzling skills," I replied, trying to mask my surprise. "What brings you here?"

She stepped closer, her gaze flickering nervously. "I just wanted to talk. About everything that's been going on... with the team."

My heart sank slightly, apprehension creeping in. "What about it?"

Lila took a deep breath, her posture shifting from cautious to assertive. "I think we're all feeling the pressure, and I wanted to make sure you knew not everyone is against you. I'm not. We need to stick together."

Relief washed over me, but suspicion tugged at the edges of my thoughts. "Really? Because it feels like a lot of people are choosing sides."

"I know it does, but it's not just about you. We've all been feeling the heat. The coach is cracking down on us, and it's making us act crazy."

"Crazy is one word for it," I muttered, shaking my head. "But I can't change what others think."

"Maybe not, but you can change how you respond. We can't let the noise drown out our goals," she urged, her voice steady. "I came here to say I'm with you, and I think others might be too. We just need to rally them."

A flicker of hope ignited inside me. "That's... really good to hear."

"But," she continued, the tension returning. "You should know that there are still some who believe this isn't the way to go. They think we're risking everything for a fight."

"Then what do you suggest? Just roll over and let them dictate how we play?"

"Not exactly. I'm saying we need to find a balance. Lead with strength, but also listen to what others are feeling. It's a team, after all."

Before I could respond, a sound echoed through the night—distant but unmistakable. A loud bang followed by the unmistakable sound of shouting. My heart raced as I turned towards the source. The commotion came from the direction of the parking lot, where shadows moved erratically under the flickering streetlights.

"What was that?" Lila asked, her eyes wide with alarm.

"I don't know, but we should check it out."

We hurried towards the noise, a mix of adrenaline and apprehension surging through me. As we approached the parking lot, the shouts grew louder, a discordant symphony that set my nerves on edge.

The sight that greeted us froze me in my tracks: several teammates stood in a chaotic huddle, their expressions a mix of anger and fear, while one figure at the center was gesturing wildly, a basketball in hand like a weapon.

"—can't believe you'd even think about it! You're risking everything for what?" the voice rang out, sharp and accusatory, causing the crowd to murmur uneasily.

I exchanged a glance with Lila, a silent agreement that propelled us forward, but the knot in my stomach tightened. The energy was electric, charged with an intensity that felt dangerous, and the confrontation seemed to be escalating. Just as I stepped closer, the figure turned, and I was met with a face I recognized—Chloe, the captain of the team, her eyes blazing with fury.

"Chloe, wait!" I shouted, my heart racing as the air around us thickened.

But before I could reach her, a ball flew through the air, hurtling toward us with unexpected speed. I ducked instinctively, and the moment stretched into a surreal freeze-frame. The chaos felt like it was spiraling out of control, and I was caught in the eye of the storm, uncertainty swirling all around me.

"Get ready, because this is about to get ugly," Lila murmured, her voice barely a whisper, as we braced ourselves for whatever was to come next.

# Chapter 27: A Moment of Truth

The soft hum of the engine was a welcome distraction as I leaned against the cool leather of my car seat, the faint scent of cinnamon lingering from last week's drive-through chai latte. Outside, the sky erupted in a riot of color, streaks of tangerine and rose competing for supremacy as the sun sank lower, casting long shadows that danced across the pavement. My heart beat in tandem with the rhythm of the fading light, a steady reminder that the moment was upon me.

The decision to reach out to Kayla had clawed at my insides like a feral cat demanding attention. It was maddening, this simmering tension, the knowledge that I had waited too long to speak the words that clung to the back of my throat like a stubborn cough. I could feel the weight of everything unsaid pressing down on my chest, squeezing tight enough to make breathing a challenge. Would she even want to hear what I had to say? I wondered.

"Can we talk?" I'd asked, my voice trembling slightly as if the mere act of speaking might shatter the fragile reality I had built around my feelings for her. My thumb hovered over the screen of my phone, the contact photo of Kayla smiling brightly a balm to my anxiety, yet a reminder of the stakes.

When she arrived, the air crackled with anticipation. I could see her before she even stepped out of her car, the familiar silhouette casting its own shadow against the backdrop of twilight. Dressed in a simple denim jacket and her favorite floral sundress that hugged her figure just right, she looked effortlessly enchanting. Kayla had that unique ability to make the mundane seem magnificent. The warmth of her smile, even from a distance, ignited something deep within me—an ember glowing, waiting for a spark to turn it into a blaze.

"Hey, what's up?" she greeted, her voice bright, yet I could detect an undercurrent of curiosity. I forced a smile, though inside I felt like a juggler with too many balls in the air, ready to drop them all at any moment.

"Let's walk," I suggested, hoping the gentle movement would ease the tension that hung between us like an uninvited guest. As we strolled down the familiar path toward the park, the sun's last rays kissed the earth goodbye, painting everything in a warm golden hue. I focused on the sound of gravel crunching beneath our feet, the rustle of leaves swaying in the evening breeze, trying to ground myself in the present moment.

We reached a bench nestled beneath a towering oak, its branches reaching out like a protective canopy. As we sat, the atmosphere shifted; the chirping crickets began their evening serenade, but my thoughts felt like a cacophony of noise, drowning out everything else.

"Is something bothering you?" she asked, concern etched on her delicate features. I noticed how the light caught her hair, giving it a halo effect, and for a fleeting moment, I was mesmerized.

"Yeah, kind of." The admission hung between us, weighted with the gravity of unspoken feelings. My heart thudded painfully, each beat echoing in my ears as I searched for the right words. "Kayla, there's something I need to tell you."

She turned slightly, her gaze piercing yet gentle, urging me to continue. The world around us faded; it was just the two of us, suspended in this intimate bubble, and the reality of what I was about to say loomed larger than the sky above.

"Okay," she said, the word soft but filled with an eagerness that sent butterflies swirling in my stomach.

"I—" I hesitated, the honesty I craved tangling with the fear of vulnerability. What if this changed everything? "I have feelings for you. Like, real feelings. Not just 'we're friends' feelings, but something deeper. Something terrifyingly real."

Silence draped itself over us like a blanket. The night grew still, the crickets halting their symphony as if they too were waiting with bated breath. I dared a glance at her, searching for any hint of her reaction.

Kayla blinked slowly, and for a moment, I feared I had crossed an unseen line. But then, her expression shifted, a flicker of something akin to surprise mingling with delight. "Wow," she breathed, her voice almost a whisper, as if she were afraid to disturb the delicate magic of the moment. "I... didn't see that coming."

I chuckled nervously, the sound breaking the tension that had wrapped itself tightly around us. "Neither did I, honestly. It's like my heart decided to throw a surprise party, and I wasn't invited."

She laughed, a rich sound that rolled off her tongue like honey, sweetening the air. "Okay, so you're telling me you've been hiding this big secret all along? What was the plan? Just drop it on me before the game?"

"Well, it seemed like a bad idea to spring it on you in front of a crowd. I didn't want to risk your game face getting messed up," I teased, grateful for the lightness in her tone.

"Right, because nothing ruins a big match like a confession of love," she replied, rolling her eyes playfully, though her smile revealed she wasn't entirely opposed to the notion.

As we bantered back and forth, the sharpness of my initial anxiety began to dull, replaced by a warmth that spread through me, igniting hope. The conversation flowed effortlessly, punctuated by laughter and the occasional teasing nudge.

Yet, amidst the playful exchanges, I sensed an undercurrent of seriousness that lingered just beneath the surface. The air shifted slightly, and I knew that while we were basking in this moment of newfound honesty, the weight of my confession was just the beginning. The reality of our feelings—and what they meant for our friendship, our futures—loomed like the darkened horizon beyond the last glimmers of sunset.

"Okay, but what if this changes everything?" she said suddenly, her tone turning contemplative. "What if we're not ready for this?"

Her words hung heavy in the air, and I felt a pang of unease. Perhaps this was the twist I hadn't anticipated, the stark reminder that love, while intoxicating, often came with complications. I needed to tread carefully, not wanting to scare her away.

"Maybe it doesn't have to change anything," I suggested, a note of hope threading through my voice. "What if we just see where this goes? We're still us. Just... with a little more honesty."

Kayla met my gaze, her eyes shimmering like stars in the emerging night. "You make a compelling case," she said, the hint of a smile creeping onto her lips. "And I do like a good adventure."

Adventure, indeed. As I sat beside her, the night wrapping around us like a cozy blanket, I realized this was only the beginning of our journey, and I was more than ready to embrace the unknown.

A cool breeze rustled the leaves overhead, as if nature itself was listening in on our conversation, eager to witness the fragile moment unfolding between us. Kayla leaned back on the bench, the light from the streetlamp catching the glint in her eyes, transforming them into twin pools of warm gold. I felt my heart flutter in a mix of excitement and trepidation, the playful banter between us allowing a bit of levity to balance out the weight of my confession.

"So, you're telling me that all this time, you've been secretly pining for me?" she asked, her voice laced with playful incredulity. "And here I thought you were just particularly fond of my questionable fashion choices."

I chuckled, grateful for her lightheartedness. "Hey, your ability to pull off polka dots with that much confidence is nothing short of impressive. But let's focus on the real issue here—my apparent inability to confess my feelings like a normal human being."

"You should've seen me last week at the coffee shop," she continued, an impish grin spreading across her face. "I thought you were about to propose a game of charades or something, with all the gestures and awkward smiles."

"Next time, I'll bring props," I quipped, loving the playful rhythm of our exchange. But beneath the lightness, I felt a knot of anxiety tighten again. What if I had just ruined everything?

"I mean, it's not like I haven't noticed," she said, her tone shifting slightly, a hint of seriousness creeping in. "You've been a bit... distracted lately."

Distracted. I almost laughed at the understatement. "Distracted doesn't quite cover it. More like I've been dodging my own feelings like they're a swarm of bees. And, honestly, they're starting to sting."

Kayla bit her lip, clearly weighing her words. "And now that you've let the bees out of the hive? What are we supposed to do with them?"

I took a breath, ready to dive deeper into the conversation, when the sound of a nearby car backfiring cut through the night. I flinched, my nerves suddenly on high alert. "See? This is what I get for trying to have a heartfelt moment. The universe is clearly against me."

Kayla laughed, and the sound was music to my ears, soothing my frazzled nerves. "Well, if it helps, I'm not exactly against you. I mean, I didn't know we were in the midst of a dramatic confession, but here we are."

"Right. Here we are." My stomach twisted in a way that felt simultaneously exhilarating and terrifying. "So, what now? Should we just sit here and pretend that I didn't just spill my heart out like it was a smoothie on a first date?"

Kayla's expression softened, and for a moment, the world faded away, leaving just the two of us in our cocoon of honesty. "I don't want to pretend. I've felt something too, but I didn't want to overstep. It's like I was waiting for you to make the first move."

"Wait, you've been holding back too?" I leaned closer, captivated by the depth of her gaze. "Why didn't you just say something?"

She shrugged, a wry smile playing on her lips. "You know me—always cautious. Plus, I didn't want to ruin the friendship we have. It's too good to lose."

"Who says we have to lose it?" I replied, a sudden burst of confidence igniting within me. "This could be a chance to make it even better. We can navigate the rocky terrain together."

Her laughter echoed like wind chimes, and I felt my heart lift. "You really think so? That we can just slide into a romance without derailing everything?"

"Absolutely," I insisted, emboldened by the warmth of her laughter and the thrill of possibility. "But, you know, no pressure. We can take it slow, like two turtles in a race. Maybe even slower."

"Ah yes, the classic slow-turtle strategy," she said with mock seriousness, her eyes twinkling. "Very strategic. It'll take us at least a month to decide who gets the last slice of pizza."

"Now you're speaking my language," I replied, feeling buoyed by her playful demeanor. "Pizza and slow-moving romances—it sounds perfect. No high stakes, just us figuring things out one cheesy slice at a time."

As we settled into a comfortable silence, I noticed how the moon cast a silvery glow across the park, illuminating our surroundings like a scene from a movie. It was serene, almost magical, and I couldn't help but wonder if this was a moment I would always remember—this junction between friendship and something more, fragile yet full of potential.

Then, as if sensing my reverie, Kayla's expression shifted. "But what if someone else has feelings for you?" she asked, her voice tinged with a vulnerability I hadn't expected. "I mean, it's a big world, and you're... you."

"Me?" I scoffed, feigning incredulity. "Who in their right mind would have feelings for me? I'm just a dorky friend who's a little too obsessed with trivia and knows way too many useless facts about the history of pizza."

"I think you're selling yourself short," she said, her tone earnest. "But I get it. It's hard to see ourselves as others do."

"Well, if you're right, then I'm a hopeless romantic who's terrible at reading the room," I admitted, my confidence wavering. "Maybe I should start practicing my grand gestures. You know, serenading you with a ukulele or something equally embarrassing."

Her laughter echoed again, filling the air with warmth. "I'd pay good money to see that. Just don't quit your day job."

"Noted. But seriously, if someone else has feelings for me, then that's... complicated. Do I need to have a talk with them, or can we just pretend it's not happening?"

"We can't just pretend," she replied, her gaze steady. "If we're going to do this—whatever 'this' is—we have to be honest with each other and whoever else is involved. No more secrets, remember?"

"Right. Secrets are bad. Unless they're about surprise birthday parties, of course." I leaned back, contemplating her words. "What if it's someone I don't want to hurt? That complicates everything, doesn't it?"

Her brow furrowed, the gravity of the situation settling over us like a thick fog. "Life is messy, and love is messier. But if it means we can be honest with each other, then I think it's worth it."

She spoke with a maturity that caught me off guard, her determination radiating like the moonlight around us. "We're stepping into unknown territory. But we're not doing it alone."

"Okay then," I said, inspired by her confidence. "Let's do this together. One awkward conversation at a time."

As we stood, ready to face whatever challenges lay ahead, I realized that the uncertainty didn't feel quite so daunting. With

Kayla by my side, I felt anchored. Whatever came next, we would face it together, armed with our shared laughter and a newfound courage to embrace the unexpected twists life had in store for us.

As the sun dipped below the horizon, the remnants of daylight seemed to spill onto the street, casting a warm glow around us. Kayla stepped out of her car, her figure silhouetted against the fading light. She moved with a grace that had always captivated me, but tonight, it felt different—charged with an electric tension that thrummed beneath the surface. I wanted to tell her everything, to unravel the web of emotions that tangled my heart, but the weight of my unspoken words hung heavily in the air.

"Hey," she said, her voice tinged with uncertainty. "What's up?"

I gestured toward the empty park bench under the grand oak tree nearby, its leaves whispering secrets in the soft evening breeze. "Let's sit for a minute," I suggested, forcing a casual tone despite the whirlwind inside me.

We settled on the bench, the coolness of the metal seeping through my jeans. I stole glances at her, the way her hair caught the last of the sunlight, framing her face like a halo. I wished I could memorize every detail of her—the playful lift of her eyebrow when she was curious, the way her smile could light up the darkest room. The very thought of admitting my feelings felt like standing at the edge of a cliff, peering into the abyss below.

"I've been thinking about us," I finally said, my voice barely above a whisper.

Her eyes widened, a flicker of hope mixed with apprehension. "Us? Like... as friends?"

"More than that," I replied, the truth spilling out before I could stop it. "I mean, yes, we're friends, but it's more complicated. I've liked you for a long time, Kayla. Longer than I care to admit."

The silence stretched between us, thick enough to cut with a knife. I felt exposed, like I was standing naked in the cold wind.

Would she laugh? Would she turn away, shaking her head at my foolishness?

"I—" she started, her voice catching. "I had no idea. I mean, I thought maybe... but I didn't want to assume."

"Assume what?" I prodded gently, desperate to keep the conversation alive, to dig deeper into this sudden chasm of honesty that had opened up between us.

"Assume that you'd feel the same way," she said, her cheeks flushing as she spoke. "I didn't want to ruin our friendship."

The air shifted, carrying an unspoken promise. I shifted closer, emboldened by her admission. "What if I told you that keeping it a secret feels like a heavy weight on my chest? What if I said I want to take that risk?"

She bit her lip, a familiar nervous gesture, and my heart raced at the sight. "You really mean that? After everything we've been through?"

"Yes. I do." I took her hand, the warmth of her skin grounding me, filling the void of doubt that had been my companion for far too long. "I can't pretend anymore. I don't want to. Not when every time I see you, it feels like something is alive inside me."

Kayla searched my eyes, as if looking for the truth among the swirling emotions. "This is terrifying," she finally admitted, a soft laugh escaping her lips. "What if we mess it up?"

"Then we mess it up together," I replied, my tone lighter, teasing. "But we'd still be us, wouldn't we? Just a little more... complicated?"

A small smile broke across her face, illuminating the dusk around us. "I suppose it's always been complicated, hasn't it?"

The shared laughter eased the tension, but the truth still loomed large between us. Before I could respond, a sudden rustle from the bushes nearby interrupted our moment, a jarring reminder that we weren't alone. We both turned, our gazes locked on the shadows shifting just beyond the tree line.

"Did you hear that?" Kayla asked, her voice laced with a mix of concern and curiosity.

"Yeah," I replied, my instincts sharpening. "Probably just a raccoon or something."

"Raccoons don't rustle like that."

I hesitated, feeling the atmosphere shift from sweetly intimate to something sharper, more urgent. "Maybe we should—"

Before I could finish, a figure emerged from the shadows, stepping into the soft glow of the park lights. It was a man, tall and broad-shouldered, his face obscured by the brim of a cap. My heart raced, and a flicker of unease settled in my stomach.

"Hey! You two!" he called, his voice gruff and demanding. "What are you doing out here?"

Kayla's grip tightened on my hand, her expression shifting from warmth to alarm. "We're just talking," I replied, trying to keep my voice steady. "It's a public park."

The man took a step closer, his eyes narrowing. "I don't like the look of you two. You need to leave. Now."

The playful atmosphere evaporated, replaced by a tension that crackled in the air. "We're not causing any trouble," I said, keeping my voice calm even as my heart raced.

"Trouble has a way of finding people who think they're just chatting," he warned, taking another menacing step forward.

"Let's just go," Kayla whispered, her voice trembling.

But before I could respond, the man lunged forward, his intentions clear. Instinct kicked in, and I jumped up, putting myself between him and Kayla. "Get away from her!" I shouted, adrenaline surging through my veins.

In that moment, everything shifted. The world narrowed to a point of focus, a razor-thin line separating fear from the fierce desire to protect the person who had just laid bare her heart to me. I glanced back at Kayla, her eyes wide with panic, and I knew that this was no longer just about confessing feelings. This was about survival, about facing whatever darkness loomed ahead.

As the man advanced, I prepared to fight, adrenaline thrumming in my veins. Just then, a sharp noise echoed through the night, a sound that both startled and confused us all. The man froze, glancing over his shoulder.

It was then that I realized this was only the beginning.

# Chapter 28: The Game and the Heart

The roar of the crowd surged like a wave, washing over me as I stepped onto the field, my heart thrumming with the rhythm of anticipation. The stadium, a sprawling coliseum of bright lights and bustling fans, pulsed with energy. It was the final game of the season, a moment where dreams and aspirations collided under the bright floodlights. I could hear the chant of my name—an anthem that resonated in my chest, spurring me forward. Yet, amidst the cacophony, it was Kayla who anchored my attention, her figure a vibrant splash of color against the backdrop of bleachers. The way her eyes sparkled, reflecting both excitement and worry, felt like a tether, pulling me deeper into my own swirling thoughts.

With each step toward the center of the field, the familiar scent of freshly cut grass mingled with the sharp tang of sweat and adrenaline. The players around me were in their own zones, focused, strategizing, and whispering playful jabs to ease the tension. I joined their banter, a smile breaking through my pre-game nerves. "Think you can keep up with me today, Carter?" Ryan teased, nudging my shoulder as we took our positions. I laughed, playfully shoving him back, but my thoughts drifted again to Kayla. What if this was our last game together? What if everything changed after this moment?

As the whistle blew, the game commenced with a fervor that ignited my competitive spirit. The ball sailed from player to player, each pass a dance of skill and precision. I could hear the shouts of my teammates, the echoing cheers of our supporters, but all I could see was Kayla, her hands clasped in anticipation, urging me on with her unspoken confidence. Every time I made a play, I could feel her energy, a silent current fueling my determination.

Halfway through the first quarter, I intercepted a pass, and adrenaline surged through my veins as I darted down the field, my cleats digging into the turf, the ball firmly in my grasp. My world narrowed to the singular focus of the end zone ahead. I could see the defenders closing in, but my mind was clear; I had trained for this. The thrill of the game coursed through me, igniting my senses. The cheers of the crowd became a distant hum, replaced by the pounding of my heart. But as I reached the twenty-yard line, I caught Kayla's eyes again, her expression shifting from hope to a quiet plea that seemed to vibrate in the air between us.

It was then that I felt it—an unexpected pull that diverted my attention from the game. Everything around me faded as I allowed myself to be ensnared by her gaze, that soft yet fervent look of encouragement intertwined with something deeper. I could hear the gasps from the crowd, the urgent calls of my teammates fading into a distant echo as the moment elongated, each second stretching into an eternity. The rival defender loomed closer, a hulking figure intent on stopping me, but I didn't care. In that fleeting instant, authenticity eclipsed victory.

I threw the ball—not to the intended receiver, but into the waiting hands of the defender who had anticipated my every move. The collective gasp from the crowd sent a shiver down my spine. Time slowed as I watched the defender break away, the stunned silence punctuated only by the echo of my heart sinking into my stomach.

"What the hell was that?" Ryan's incredulous voice broke through my haze, but I barely registered it. My mind spiraled as I turned toward Kayla, searching her face for understanding, for a sign that I hadn't just thrown away the game, my season, and perhaps my chances with her. The looks around me shifted from confusion to frustration, and I could feel the tension coil tightly in my chest.

But there she was, the very beacon I had sought in that critical moment, her gaze unwavering. To my surprise, a smile crept onto her lips, a mischievous glint lighting her eyes. It was as if she understood me in a way that transcended the game. Maybe it was the wild chaos of the moment, or perhaps it was simply the joy of being true to myself that made her smile all the more radiant. I couldn't help but grin back, though the gravity of my blunder weighed heavily on my shoulders.

The game continued, but my focus had shifted entirely. I became a spectator in my own life, following the rhythms of the game yet acutely aware of Kayla's presence, her laughter bubbling through the chaos like a cherished melody. Even when I missed tackles and fumbled passes, I couldn't shake the buoyant energy that she infused into my spirit. Each mistake became less catastrophic in the face of her unwavering belief.

As the game wore on, the score hung precariously in the balance, but my priorities had realigned. I wasn't just playing for the championship anymore; I was playing for something far more significant—my chance at authenticity, a connection that transcended the confines of the field. The final minutes ticked down, tension rising like the crescendo of a symphony, and every breath felt charged with possibility. The weight of the moment pressed down on me, but my heart raced with a newfound clarity.

Then, with mere seconds remaining, an unexpected twist emerged. Our quarterback, poised and fierce, suddenly faltered, the ball slipping from his grip like a gift from fate. Without a second thought, I sprinted forward, an instinct driving me to reclaim control. It wasn't just about the game; it was about my place in this world, a world where I could either rise to the challenge or continue to let the moment slip away.

I lunged for the ball, feeling the shock of impact as I crashed to the ground, the world around me blurring into a swirl of colors and sounds. But as I grasped the ball, cradling it like a treasure, I knew—this was my moment, and I was ready to face whatever came next.

The rush of the game faded into a haze as I lay sprawled on the turf, the ground beneath me surprisingly cool against my flushed skin. The ball, my treasure, nestled securely against my chest, was a momentary victory in a day already thick with chaos. My heart raced, not from the exertion but from the realization that I had stepped out of the expected path. The crowd erupted around me, a cacophony of cheers and gasps that felt like a distant echo. I could sense the world swirling around me, but my focus was singular—Kayla.

As I rose, shaking off the dust and the bewilderment, I caught her gaze again. She was on her feet now, her hands clasped together in disbelief. I couldn't help but smirk, buoyed by the undeniable connection that crackled between us. "Well, that wasn't the plan," I mouthed, my lips forming the words despite the roar of the stadium. The corners of her mouth lifted in a smile that danced with mischief, a look that spoke volumes more than any words could convey. In that moment, the game transformed into something else entirely; it was a stage set for a larger story, one where I could be the lead in my own narrative rather than merely following the script written for me.

The final minutes of the game passed in a blur, every second thick with anticipation. Each play brought a swell of excitement that cascaded through the stands, with the tension palpable enough to slice through. My teammates rallied around me, their energy infectious as we pushed toward the end zone once more. Ryan, ever the jokester, shot me a sideways glance. "What were you aiming for, the stands? Or were you just showing off your arm strength for Kayla?"

"Hey, I'll have you know that my throwing skills are legendary," I shot back, a teasing smile on my face. "It's just that my judgment got clouded by the glittering beauty in the stands." I didn't mind the playful jabs; they were a necessary balm to ease the burning embarrassment still tinged at the edges of my thoughts.

With less than a minute left on the clock, I could feel the pulse of the crowd synchronizing with my heartbeat. My mind flickered back to the moment I'd thrown that ill-fated pass. It was reckless, perhaps foolish, but wasn't there a certain thrill in embracing that unpredictability? The play resumed, and as I found myself in the huddle, the gravity of my choices sat heavy on my shoulders. This time, I would make the pass, but not just any pass. I'd ensure it would count.

The quarterback called for a play that echoed in my ears, and I nodded, a steely determination seeping through me. I could do this. As the ball snapped, I focused fiercely, moving fluidly down the field, my eyes scanning the chaos for an opening. The game had transformed into a living, breathing entity, each player a vital thread in a tapestry of athleticism and ambition. My body responded instinctively, weaving through defenders like a leaf caught in a gust of wind, all the while seeking that one fleeting opportunity.

And then it came—a glimmer of hope amid the tumult. My teammate broke free, a slender figure darting into the open space, and I didn't hesitate. I released the ball, the leather slick under my fingertips, and it spiraled through the air, a perfect arc gliding toward its target. Time slowed as I watched it travel, the collective intake of breath from the crowd a reverberating silence around me.

When the ball landed safely in my teammate's hands, a cheer erupted, a triumphant explosion that echoed across the stadium. My teammates mobbed him in celebration, but I couldn't help but search for Kayla's reaction, the warmth in her gaze like sunlight breaking through a stormy sky. There it was—her infectious laughter mingling with the cheers, her expression radiant.

The final whistle blew, and as the celebration intensified, I caught her eye once more, weaving through the throng of players and fans. A path opened up for me, and I seized it, determined to reach her amidst the whirlwind of excitement.

"Hey!" I called out, my voice barely cutting through the din. "Did you see that last play?"

Her laughter rang like a bell, clear and sweet. "You mean the one where you almost handed the game to our rivals? Classic!"

I rolled my eyes, but a grin broke across my face. "That was all part of my elaborate plan to keep you on your toes."

She stepped closer, her eyes shimmering with a mix of pride and mischief. "Right, because nothing says 'I'm a great player' like a pass to the opposing team."

"Touché." I couldn't help but laugh, the tension of the day melting away as I reveled in her presence. "But you know I redeemed myself, right? That last pass was pure magic."

"Magic?" she echoed, her brow raised. "More like a lucky shot. But I'll give you credit for the effort."

"I'll take it!" I exclaimed, my heart swelling with gratitude. The adrenaline coursing through my veins felt more potent than the aftermath of the game itself. In that moment, standing close to Kayla, I understood that the thrill of victory paled in comparison to the electric charge of being near her.

Just then, Ryan stumbled into our conversation, clearly still riding the high of our hard-won victory. "So, what's next for you two? A romantic dinner? A celebratory ice cream binge? Maybe something dramatic like a roller coaster?"

I shot him a look, unable to suppress my laughter. "Well, if we survive the roller coaster, I suppose ice cream could be on the agenda."

"Make sure it's double scoops," Ryan winked, and with a theatrical flourish, he waved us off. "Don't keep her waiting. Who knows when you'll get another chance?"

I felt a flicker of anticipation at the thought of spending more time with Kayla. As Ryan rejoined the fray of celebrating players,

I turned back to her, our eyes locking in a moment thick with unspoken possibilities.

"So, about that ice cream?" I ventured, my voice a teasing whisper.

Kayla's smile widened, an invitation wrapped in playful intrigue. "I'm all for it, but only if you promise to keep your eyes on the game next time."

"Deal," I replied, heart racing in a way that had nothing to do with the adrenaline of the field. As we stepped away from the chaos, leaving the echoes of cheers behind, I realized that this was merely the beginning of our story—one that promised to be just as exhilarating as any game I'd ever played.

The sweet scent of victory hung thick in the air, mingling with the fading warmth of the day. Kayla and I strolled away from the stadium, the din of celebration behind us becoming a distant hum. My heart still danced with the adrenaline of the game, but now, it pulsed with the thrill of her presence beside me. The streetlights flickered on, casting a golden hue over everything as the sun dipped low on the horizon, wrapping the world in a gentle embrace.

Kayla laughed, her eyes sparkling like stars emerging in the twilight. "So, the infamous Alex Miller takes the field with all the grace of a gazelle on roller skates," she teased, nudging my side playfully.

"Hey, I'll have you know that gazelles are actually quite nimble," I retorted, feigning indignation. "But if I was like one, then you must be the queen of the savanna, stealing the spotlight and leaving me in the dust."

"Flattery won't save you from the next ribbing," she replied, her laughter a soft melody that wove through the air. The warmth of her teasing felt like sunshine, illuminating the path we walked as the night wrapped around us.

We turned onto Main Street, the familiar buzz of the local cafés and shops beckoning with their inviting lights and laughter. I had suggested ice cream earlier, and now it felt like a perfect moment for that promise. "How about we grab some of that famous peanut butter fudge swirl? I think I've earned a little indulgence after my 'spectacular' performance."

"Peanut butter fudge swirl, huh? So we're going big, then?" she said, raising an eyebrow with mock seriousness. "What happened to that wholesome, health-conscious athlete I thought I knew?"

"Oh, he's still in there, lurking beneath layers of chocolate and sugar," I said, matching her playful tone. "But he might need a little coaxing after today's debacle."

"Let's just say your 'debacle' turned into a riveting story for my Instagram feed," she said, winking. "The caption practically writes itself: 'He threw the game but still won my heart.'"

Her words sent a jolt of warmth through me, igniting a feeling I had yet to fully grasp. There was something magnetic about her, a pull that was almost irresistible. "Maybe I should throw more games then," I replied, half-joking, but there was an undercurrent of sincerity that lingered in the air between us.

As we reached the ice cream shop, the bell above the door jingled, heralding our arrival. The interior was a cozy haven, filled with cheerful colors and the enticing aroma of waffle cones being freshly made. The owner, a jovial man with a bushy mustache, waved from behind the counter, clearly used to the smiling faces that came in for their sweet fixes.

"What can I get for you two lovebirds tonight?" he asked, a twinkle in his eye.

I felt a blush creep up my cheeks at the label. "Just two scoops of peanut butter fudge swirl, please," I said, grinning at Kayla.

"Make that three," she chimed in, nudging me with her elbow. "One for each of us and one for the shy gazelle that needs a little coaxing out of hiding."

I chuckled, the playful banter igniting something deeper within me. As we waited for our cones, I stole glances at her, marveling at the way the overhead lights reflected in her hair, creating a halo effect that made her seem even more radiant. The shop felt warm and intimate, the perfect cocoon to share in the magic of the evening.

When we finally stepped outside with our cones in hand, the air felt electric. I turned to her, my heart racing. "You know, this game was more than just a last-minute throw. I feel like it opened up something in me. Maybe it was all the adrenaline, or maybe it's just you," I said, my voice dipping to a whisper.

Kayla's expression softened, her gaze shifting from my eyes to the sidewalk, where shadows danced in the glow of the streetlights. "You really threw caution to the wind, didn't you?"

"Maybe I did," I replied, emboldened by her vulnerability. "But I think that's the kind of risk worth taking. The thrill of being authentic, of really living in the moment, it's... intoxicating."

We walked slowly, savoring our ice cream, the world around us blurring into a backdrop of laughter and light. But with each passing moment, I could feel a tension rising, the kind that hung in the air just before a storm. "What about you?" I asked, breaking the comfortable silence. "What risks are you willing to take?"

She stopped suddenly, her expression contemplative. "I think... I think I've been playing it safe for too long. I've been so focused on school and the future that I've forgotten what it means to live in the now."

"Why not start with small things? Like trying that new sushi place next week instead of your usual burger joint," I suggested, trying to lighten the mood. "Or maybe spending an evening dancing like no one's watching?"

Kayla chuckled, a hint of excitement flaring in her eyes. "Okay, dancing sounds fun. But what if I really am terrible?"

"Then we'll be terrible together," I said, grinning wide. "It'll be a beautiful disaster."

Just then, as we rounded the corner, a flash of headlights lit up the street, illuminating the figure standing on the sidewalk ahead of us. My heart dropped as I recognized the unmistakable silhouette—Jordan, the rival player I'd thrown the ball to during the game. He leaned against a car, arms crossed, a smug grin plastered on his face that set my nerves on edge.

"What's this? A celebratory ice cream outing?" he called out, his voice dripping with sarcasm. "How romantic. You really think you can steal the spotlight from me just by throwing a game-winning pass? That's cute."

Kayla stepped closer to me, the sudden tension palpable. "What do you want, Jordan?" I shot back, irritation flaring inside me like a live wire.

"I'm just here to remind you that the season isn't over yet," he said, pushing off the car, advancing toward us with a swagger that made my fists clench. "You think one lucky game was enough to secure your spot? Just wait until we meet again."

The confidence in his tone twisted something in my gut, igniting a protective instinct toward Kayla. "What do you mean by that?" I demanded, stepping forward, ready to confront the source of my discomfort.

He smirked, and for a moment, it felt like the world had slowed to a crawl. "Let's just say, I have plans for the next matchup. You might want to keep your eyes on the field next time, Miller. Because I'm not done playing."

Before I could retort, he turned, walking away with the same swagger he'd approached with, leaving behind a silence that hummed with unspoken challenges. My heart raced, a storm of emotions swirling inside me as I turned back to Kayla, who looked both concerned and intrigued.

"Is he serious?" she asked, her voice low and steady, but I could see the uncertainty glimmering in her eyes.

I swallowed hard, feeling the weight of his words settle heavily in my chest. "I don't know, but I have a feeling the next game is going to be about more than just football."

As we stood there, the world around us faded away, leaving just the two of us, poised on the edge of something new and thrilling. The air buzzed with tension, a fragile thread connecting us both as we stepped deeper into the unknown, a chapter waiting to be written. The horizon ahead was uncertain, but as I looked into Kayla's eyes, I knew we were ready to face whatever came next—together.

# Chapter 29: Embracing the Future

The sun hung low in the sky, casting a warm golden glow over the field, where the remnants of the game lingered like the sweet scent of freshly cut grass. I stood there, heart racing, the roar of the crowd still echoing in my ears, but it was Kayla's presence that anchored me. She glowed with an effervescent energy that made everything around her seem a little brighter, a little more alive. As she rushed toward me, her eyes sparkled with a mix of triumph and joy that left me breathless. I hadn't just played; I had unveiled parts of myself I'd long hidden away.

"Julia! You were incredible!" she shouted, and I could see the excitement radiating from her, almost palpable like a warm breeze. She wrapped her arms around me, squeezing tightly, and in that embrace, I felt a rush of gratitude and exhilaration. It was as if the world outside had faded, and only we existed in that moment, suspended in our own universe. I could hardly believe that the quiet boy who had once feared rejection could now stand in the spotlight, bathed in love and acceptance.

"It was just a game," I replied, brushing off her enthusiasm with a lighthearted chuckle, though I could feel the blush creeping up my cheeks. She pulled back slightly, her gaze searching mine, and I saw that she understood. This was so much more than a game. I had shared my truth with the world, and the freedom that came with it was intoxicating. I could almost hear the soft thrum of my heartbeat syncing with the rhythm of the crowd, a jubilant celebration of my newfound authenticity.

"Just a game? You went out there and played your heart out! You showed everyone who you are!" she insisted, her voice rising with fervor. "That's what matters." The conviction in her words settled deep within me, igniting a flicker of defiance against the insecurities that had once loomed like storm clouds overhead.

As we made our way off the field, hands clasped tightly, I couldn't help but steal glances at her. Her hair danced in the wind like strands of sunlight, and her laughter rang clear and bright, weaving through the air like a melody. The way her eyes sparkled was almost ethereal, and I thought for a fleeting moment that she was somehow more than just a person; she was a force of nature, fierce and unwavering. It was impossible not to feel drawn to her.

We slipped away from the throng of cheering fans, into a quieter part of the park where the trees whispered ancient secrets. "I didn't know you had it in you," she teased, nudging my side playfully. "I mean, you're full of surprises, aren't you?"

"Careful, or I might just start thinking I'm interesting," I retorted with a smirk, enjoying the banter that felt so effortless between us.

"Interesting? Please, you're practically a legend now. The crowd won't stop talking about that last play!" She gestured animatedly, her enthusiasm infectious.

"Okay, okay, let's not get carried away. I just did what I had to do," I said, trying to sound modest, but the corner of my mouth twitched upwards in a grin. "Besides, I think they were just excited to see me trip and fall on my face."

She laughed, her eyes lighting up with mischief. "You've got to admit, it was a spectacular fall. I'm surprised they didn't give you a medal for it!"

I feigned horror, placing a hand dramatically on my chest. "A medal? What about the honor of being known as the guy who tripped over his own shoelaces in front of the entire school?"

"You know what? I think we need to throw a party just to celebrate that moment," she declared, her eyes gleaming with mischief.

"Only if you promise to make those amazing cupcakes," I replied, thinking of her infamous vanilla cupcakes, each one frosted with a mountain of fluffy icing.

"Deal," she shot back, raising an eyebrow playfully. "But only if you promise to wear that ridiculous jersey of yours. The one that's two sizes too big and has more patches than fabric."

"Not a chance," I laughed, shaking my head. "You'll have to pry it off me while I'm asleep."

The banter flowed like water between us, a blend of teasing and warmth that made me feel alive in a way I hadn't in ages. Yet, beneath the laughter lingered a tension, a silent acknowledgment that something had shifted. My heart raced not just from the thrill of the game but from the realization that our connection had deepened.

"Hey, can I ask you something?" she said, her tone shifting, becoming softer, more serious. We paused under the sprawling branches of an oak tree, its leaves rustling gently above us, the sunlight filtering through like a soft golden veil.

"Of course. Anything," I replied, my stomach knotting slightly.

"What's next for you, Julia? I mean, after all this?" Her eyes held a mix of concern and curiosity, as if she were looking for a glimpse of my future.

I hesitated, the weight of her question settling over me like a heavy cloak. "I guess I'm just figuring it all out. I mean, I've spent so long hiding who I am that it's a little overwhelming to think about what comes next. I want to embrace this part of myself, but... I also don't want to lose who I've been."

"Hey," she said, stepping closer, her voice steady. "You won't lose anything. You're just adding layers. Think of it like a cake."

"A cake?" I echoed, bemused.

"Yeah! You're like a cake with so many flavors. Each layer is part of you. The past is still there, and now you're just frosting it with who you really are."

I couldn't help but smile at her comparison. "So, I'm a cake? That's surprisingly fitting."

She grinned, that mischievous sparkle dancing in her eyes again. "Exactly! A delicious, multi-layered cake that's ready to be devoured!"

I chuckled, feeling lighter, the tension easing as we shared that moment of laughter. I looked at her, really looked, and saw not just a friend but a partner, someone who encouraged me to explore this new journey without fear. I wanted to embrace it all—the laughter, the joy, and yes, even the chaos that would come with discovering my true self.

As the sun dipped lower, casting long shadows and painting the world in shades of pink and orange, I felt the promise of tomorrow unfurling before me like a vast horizon. Whatever lay ahead, I knew I wouldn't be facing it alone. With Kayla by my side, I was ready to embrace the future.

As the sun surrendered its brilliance to the encroaching twilight, we made our way toward the park exit, the air filled with the scent of damp earth and blooming wildflowers. Laughter and chatter from the after-game celebration echoed behind us, but we seemed cocooned in a world that belonged solely to us. Kayla walked beside me, her fingers entwined with mine, creating a warmth that chased away the evening chill.

"You know, it's kind of funny," she said, breaking the comfortable silence. "You spent so long trying to fit in, and now you're this whole new person, strutting around like you own the place."

I chuckled, picturing myself as some sort of peacock, feathers on full display. "Strutting? More like a confused chicken trying to figure out where to roost."

"Confused chickens can still be quite entertaining," she teased, shooting me a sidelong glance that made my heart skip.

Our playful banter continued, a delightful rhythm that felt as natural as breathing. But even amidst the laughter, a part of me couldn't shake the lingering anxiety about what lay ahead. Sure, I had found the courage to step into the spotlight, but it was a different matter entirely to live in it.

"Seriously though," Kayla's voice turned more serious, the lightness slipping away. "You're really okay with all this? I mean, the attention, the change... everything?"

"Yeah, I think so," I replied, my voice barely above a whisper. "But it's scary, too. What if I mess up? What if they don't like this version of me?"

Her gaze softened, and I could see the flicker of understanding in her eyes. "You're going to mess up. We all do. But that doesn't mean you're not worthy of love or respect. Besides, anyone who doesn't appreciate the real you isn't worth your time."

I nodded, her words wrapping around me like a comforting blanket. "You make it sound so easy, like there's a magic formula."

"If only," she sighed dramatically. "But really, it's just about finding your people. The ones who love you for you, who won't flinch when you spill coffee on yourself or trip over your own feet."

"Great, so I'll just start a club for awkward people," I joked. "The official motto: 'We may trip, but we do it with style!'"

Kayla laughed, and the sound was like music, lifting my spirits. "And I'll be your president. Together, we'll rule the land of misfits."

We reached the edge of the park, where the soft glow of streetlights began to flicker on. Kayla paused, turning to face me, her expression serious once more. "Just promise me one thing."

"What's that?" I asked, my heart beating a little faster.

"Don't let anyone else's opinion define you. You're so much more than a game or a role or a label. You're... you."

I felt a lump rise in my throat. "I promise," I said, meaning it with every fiber of my being.

We lingered there, the weight of our shared moment hanging in the air, until the vibrant colors of the sunset faded into dusky twilight. Just as I thought we'd lost ourselves in that gaze forever, a raucous cheer erupted from behind us.

"Julia! Kayla!"

We turned to see a group of friends barreling toward us, faces flushed with excitement and exhilaration. It was as if they were charging out of the very heart of the celebration, and in an instant, the intimate bubble we'd formed burst like a soap bubble on a hot summer day.

"Did you see that play?" one of them shouted, his eyes wide. "You were like a gladiator out there!"

"More like a chicken with a sword," I muttered, causing Kayla to snort.

As the group surrounded us, each voice clamoring to share their own highlight from the game, I felt the initial pang of discomfort return. I was the center of attention again, but this time, something was different. I had friends who were genuinely excited for me, not just people who wanted to gossip or dissect my every move.

"Julia, you should totally give a speech!" another friend called out, grinning ear to ear. "You can regale us with tales of your epic victory!"

"Oh sure," I replied with a wry grin, "and while I'm at it, I'll also share my most embarrassing moments. Like when I tried to do a backflip and ended up in the bushes."

Laughter erupted, and for the first time, I felt less like an imposter and more like someone who belonged. I was still me, just... a more vibrant, self-assured version.

"Come on, let's celebrate!" Kayla pulled me closer, her enthusiasm radiating like sunshine. "We need to find the biggest slice of cake they have and eat it like there's no tomorrow!"

The group cheered in agreement, and as we walked together toward the makeshift refreshment area, the atmosphere buzzed with a sense of camaraderie. Friends clapped my back and exchanged stories, their voices mingling with the soft notes of music drifting through the air.

Yet, amid the revelry, I caught sight of someone standing slightly apart, a shadow among the vibrant chaos. It was Max, his arms crossed, his expression unreadable. Our eyes met, and for a heartbeat, the world around us faded.

I remembered the weight of our past interactions, the unspoken words that hung between us like a dense fog. In a flash, I was back in the locker room, before the game, feeling that familiar twinge of uncertainty.

Kayla noticed my distraction and squeezed my hand gently, grounding me. "Hey, you okay?"

"Yeah, just... I think I need to talk to him," I replied, my voice steady despite the tremors of anxiety threading through me.

"Are you sure?" she asked, concern flashing in her eyes.

"Yeah. It's time I face whatever this is."

She nodded, her encouragement like a steady flame. "Just remember, you've got this."

With a deep breath, I disentangled my hand from hers and made my way toward Max, the crowd parting like waves as I approached. His posture was rigid, the lines of tension on his face sharper than I remembered.

"Max," I called out, my voice steady even as my heart raced.

He turned to me, his expression inscrutable. "Julia."

The silence stretched between us, heavy and thick, filled with the unsaid. "Can we talk?"

"About what?" he replied, arms crossing tighter, a defensive posture that sent a wave of apprehension through me.

"About everything," I said, striving for clarity in the muddled air of unspoken grievances. "I want to understand where we stand."

"Isn't it obvious?" he shot back, irritation flaring in his voice.

"Maybe it is," I admitted, "but I'm tired of hiding from it. I want to know if you can accept me for who I am now, or if you're stuck in the past."

For a moment, the world around us blurred into a soft hum, and it felt as if we were the only two people in existence. His expression softened, just a fraction, as though he were weighing the words carefully.

"I don't know if I can, Julia. You changed. And I—"

"You didn't give me a chance to show you who I am now," I interrupted, a surge of frustration bubbling to the surface. "I was so scared of being rejected that I didn't give you the chance to be part of my life."

The vulnerability of that admission hung in the air, and I could see the flicker of surprise in his eyes. "I didn't realize you felt that way."

"Then maybe it's time we talk it through."

With that simple statement, the tension shifted, and we stood on the precipice of something new. It was a chance, a risk, and I could feel the weight of every choice pressing down upon us. But for the first time, I believed it was a risk worth taking.

The air between Max and me felt electric, charged with the weight of unspoken words and unresolved feelings. I searched his face, desperate for a glimpse of the boy I had once known. The one who had shared laughter with me over late-night homework sessions and whispered dreams in the shadows of our youth. But now, there was a wall between us, built brick by brick from misunderstandings and fears.

"Let's just start fresh," I suggested, my voice steady, even as my heart hammered in my chest. "We can't change the past, but we can decide how we want to move forward. I'm not the same person I was, and I want you to know that."

Max's brow furrowed as he processed my words. "It's hard, Julia. I mean, you're out there being celebrated, and I'm—" He hesitated, as if unsure how to voice the turmoil brewing within him. "I'm just... still figuring things out. You have this new life, and I feel like I'm still stuck in the old one."

"Then let's figure it out together," I replied, trying to infuse my words with warmth. "You don't have to go through this alone. I'm still here."

His gaze flicked away, a shadow crossing his features. "You don't know what that means to me. But I don't want to hold you back, either."

"Max, you won't." I stepped closer, the distance between us feeling like a chasm. "I want to build something new. I want you in my life, whatever that looks like."

He inhaled sharply, as if my words had pierced through the fog of uncertainty clouding his mind. "It's just... hard for me to let go of who we were."

"Maybe we don't have to let go entirely," I countered, my voice softer now. "We can take what was good and build on it. It's not about forgetting the past; it's about embracing it as part of our journey."

Max's expression softened, and I saw a flicker of hope ignite in his eyes. "You make it sound so simple, but it's anything but."

"Life is complicated. But isn't that what makes it worth living?" I smiled, and the warmth of our shared history began to thaw the tension.

Just then, the crowd behind us erupted into another cheer, laughter ringing through the night air like a sweet melody. It pulled our attention momentarily, the sound of celebration underscoring our fragile truce.

"Do you want to join them?" Max asked, a tentative smile breaking through his earlier seriousness. "You are the hero of the hour, after all."

"I don't know about that," I replied, a hint of self-deprecation coloring my tone. "I think I'm still just that awkward guy who stumbled his way into the spotlight."

"Hey, if it works, it works," he said with a chuckle, and just like that, the atmosphere shifted again.

Before I could respond, Kayla burst through the crowd, her face alight with excitement. "There you are! I was starting to think you two were plotting to take over the world or something."

"We were just having a deep and meaningful conversation," I said, trying to keep a straight face. "You know, world peace and all that."

She rolled her eyes dramatically. "Well, while you were busy solving the universe's problems, we found cake. Massive, beautiful cake! Are you in, or do you want to keep discussing existential crises?"

"Cake sounds excellent," I declared, relief washing over me. Max's presence beside me felt like a warm ember, flickering but steadfast.

We followed Kayla through the crowd, the vibrant sounds of celebration enveloping us. The evening was alive with music, laughter, and the sweet smell of baked goods wafting through the air, making my stomach rumble in eager anticipation.

As we reached the refreshment table, my friends cheered again, hoisting plates filled with oversized slices of cake. "Julia, you have to try this!" someone called, presenting me with a slice that looked more like a small mountain than dessert.

"Don't get too cocky now," I joked, my eyes wide as I glanced at the towering confection. "If I eat this entire thing, I'll need a nap and a new wardrobe."

"Just think of it as fuel for your continued stardom," Kayla quipped, smirking as she bit into her slice. "And besides, you deserve a little indulgence after today."

As I took my first bite, a wave of sweetness exploded on my palate, rich and satisfying. I closed my eyes for a moment, savoring the flavors, the laughter of my friends, and the comforting presence of Max nearby. It was a moment that felt almost surreal, a mixture of happiness and relief that I had been craving.

We spent the next few minutes exchanging playful jabs and anecdotes about the game, the atmosphere electric with camaraderie. Yet, through the laughter, I couldn't shake the lingering thread of tension woven between me and Max. It was like an unplayed note in a symphony, waiting for resolution.

Just when I thought the evening couldn't get any better, a voice rang out, cutting through the jovial atmosphere. "Hey, look who finally decided to show up!"

My stomach sank as I turned to see Riley, a familiar figure who had always had a knack for turning moments sour. He stood at the edge of the gathering, flanked by a few friends, a smug grin plastered across his face.

"Well, if it isn't the team's new golden boy," he said, his tone dripping with sarcasm. "What's next? A reality show? Maybe you could document your transformation from nobody to somebody?"

Laughter erupted from his friends, and the air around us shifted. It was a stark reminder that not everyone was ready to accept my change, and Riley was determined to make sure I felt every ounce of that discomfort.

"Riley, why don't you do us all a favor and go back to whatever rock you crawled out from under?" Kayla shot back, her eyes narrowing with righteous indignation.

He shrugged, unbothered. "I'm just saying it's a little rich to see you flaunting your success when you've been hiding in the shadows for so long. It's not exactly an inspiring comeback story."

I felt my cheeks flush with anger and embarrassment, a heat rising in my chest. But before I could formulate a response, Max stepped forward, a protective glint in his eye. "Why don't you take your negativity elsewhere, Riley? This is a celebration, not a platform for your petty jealousy."

Surprised, I glanced at Max, his bravery igniting a flicker of admiration within me. This was the Max I had missed, the one who didn't shy away from standing up for what was right.

Riley looked taken aback for a moment, but then his smirk returned, even more smug. "Oh, so you've chosen sides, huh? Interesting. Just remember, things can change fast, Max. One moment you're in, and the next—"

"Stop it," I interjected, my voice stronger than I felt. "This isn't about sides or drama. I'm just trying to be me, and I'd appreciate it if you could respect that."

Riley laughed, but it was a hollow sound that only added to the tension. "Respect? That's rich coming from you, Julia. You're still the same guy underneath all that bravado. It won't last."

"Is this what you call support?" Kayla retorted, stepping in front of me as if to shield me from his words. "Because it sounds more like a desperate attempt to bring someone down."

"Look, I'm just saying the truth hurts sometimes," he shot back, crossing his arms defiantly. "But good luck. You'll need it."

With that, he turned to leave, his laughter trailing behind him like a bad aftertaste. I could feel the remnants of his words hanging in the air, heavy and oppressive, a reminder that not everyone was ready to embrace my journey.

As the crowd resumed their celebrations, I stood there, trying to shake off the unease that settled in my stomach. Max's presence beside me felt like a tether, grounding me amidst the chaos.

"Don't let him get to you," he said quietly, his voice steady. "You've come so far."

"Yeah, I just wish I could shake this feeling that it's not over yet," I admitted, glancing back at the retreating figure of Riley.

Max nodded, his expression serious. "Just remember, it's about who you choose to surround yourself with. You have people here who care about you, and that's what matters."

I appreciated his reassurance, but as I watched the party unfold around us, a chilling thought crept into my mind. Was Riley right? Would I truly be able to hold on to this new version of myself, or was it destined to unravel at the first sign of conflict?

Just as I was about to voice my concerns, a loud crash echoed through the night, drawing everyone's attention. I turned to see a table of refreshments toppled over, drinks spilling everywhere, and a group of students scrambling to clean up the mess.

"Great. Just what we needed," I muttered, but then something in the chaos caught my eye. A flash of movement. Someone darting through the crowd, their expression unreadable, weaving in and out of the laughter and excitement.

Before I could process it, that person was gone,

Milton Keynes UK
Ingram Content Group UK Ltd.
UKHW042004281024
450365UK00003B/157